THE RULE OF MIRRORS

ALSO BY CARAGH M. O'BRIEN

The Vault of Dreamers
The Keep of Ages

The Birthmarked Trilogy
Birthmarked
Prized
Promised

THE RULE OF MIRRORS

· CARAGH M. O'BRIEN ·

BOOK 2: THE VAULT OF DREAMERS TRILOGY

SQUARE
FISH

ROARING BROOK PRESS
NEW YORK

An imprint of Macmillan Publishing Group, LLC
175 Fifth Avenue, New York, NY 10010
fiercereads.com

Square Fish and the Square Fish logo are trademarks of Macmillan and are
used by Roaring Brook Press under license from Macmillan.

Our books may be purchased in bulk for promotional, educational, or
business use. Please contact your local bookseller or the Macmillan Corporate
and Premium Sales Department at (800) 221-7945 ext. 5442 or by
e-mail at MacmillanSpecialMarkets@macmillan.com.

Library of Congress Cataloging in Publication Control Number: 2015035535

ISBN 978-1-250-11535-5 (paperback)   ISBN 978-1-59643-941-2 (ebook)

Originally published in the United States by Roaring Brook Press
First Square Fish edition, 2017
Book designed by Elizabeth H. Clark
Square Fish logo designed by Filomena Tuosto

1 3 5 7 9 10 8 6 4 2

AR: 4.3 / LEXILE: HL620L

For my sister,
Alvina K. Hart

CONTENTS

THE RULE OF MIRRORS

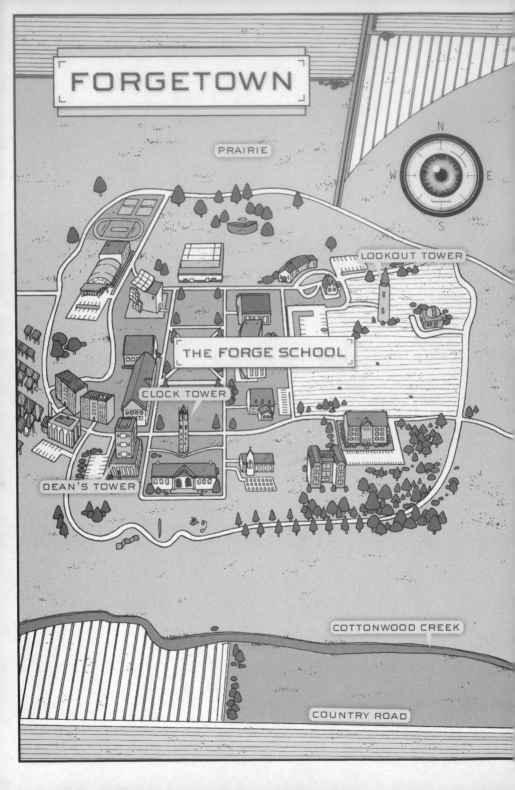

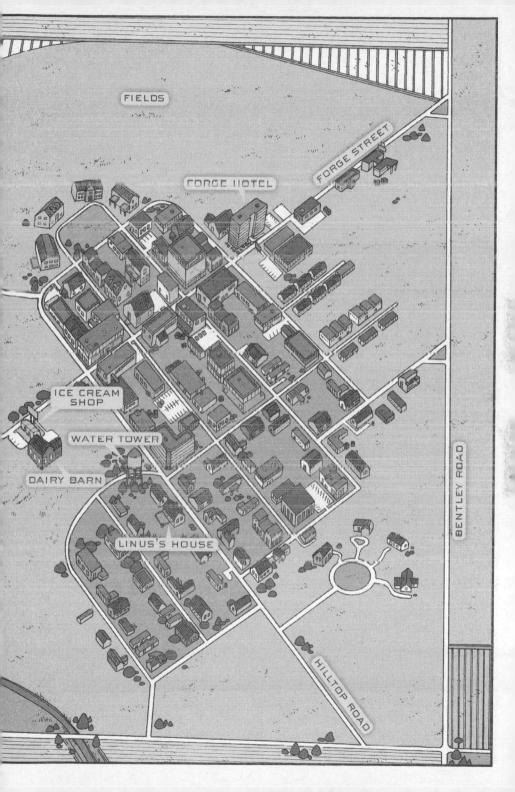

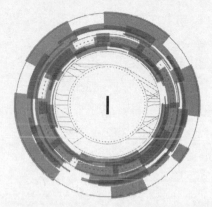

— ROSIE —

THE VOICE THAT STAYED BEHIND

WHEN I FEEL SOFT, breathy pressure on my lips, I open my eyes and grab the guy's throat.

"Stop," I say. It's my first word out loud ever, and the power of it thrills me.

The guy jerks free from my grasp and rubs his throat. He's ugly and young. Mousy hair. Wispy, loathsome mustache. He's in scrubs, like he's a hospital attendant, but I'm not deceived. This is no hospital. It's a vault of dreamers.

"You can't be awake," he whispers. He looks rapidly over his shoulder and then back to me. "Whoever screwed up your meds, it wasn't me." He reaches for the drip that will infuse a new dose of narcotics into my veins.

"No, wait," I say. "Just wait, please. I need to talk to you."

"This is impossible," he whispers furiously. "You must be talking in your sleep."

"Do I look like I'm sleep talking?" I stretch my eyelids super wide and reach up for his face.

"Don't do that," he says, with hushed urgency, and he pushes my arm back to my side.

"I know you like me," I say. "You were this close to kissing me."

"No, I wasn't!"

"No one else has to know," I say. "Is your name Ian? Is that what I heard? Please, Ian. Please talk to me for a second. I'm so lonely."

From my inert position in my sleep shell, lying on my back and dressed in a thin gown, I doubt I could look more helpless if I tried, but I put every bit of pleading into my eyes, and before I can stop myself, real tears brim over. I hate appealing to him like this. I hate that my loneliness is so true.

He frowns above me, this ugly boy-man with droopy, soft lips. Big ears. Bulbous eyes. Soft everywhere. He might be man height, but I swear his voice never changed.

"Don't cry," he says. "I don't believe this is happening." He touches his sleeve to the corner of my eye, and then he smiles shyly. "All right. I'll talk, but just for a second. I'm a big fan of yours."

"Really?"

He nods. "I used to watch you on *The Forge Show*. I couldn't believe my luck when you came here."

"Where's here?"

2

His brows lift in surprise. "This is the Onar Clinic, out of Denver. We do sleep therapy and research. You're here to recover. Now hold still. This shouldn't hurt. I just have to check your port." He leans over the place in my chest where an IV goes into my skin and peels off some tape.

I try to make sense of this information.

The last thing I knew for certain was that Dean Berg had me trapped in the vault of dreamers under the Forge School. Linus was there, too, and a pang accompanies my memory of his limp body lying on the operating table. Dean Berg mined me that night, and the pain was excruciating.

Or wait. I recall a span of time after that, too. I was trapped in another vault, maybe this one. I glance up at the supply lines that run along the ceiling. Yes. I'm as certain as I can be that this is the same place. Ian was in that memory, too. I was here a couple of weeks or more, and I still had my other voice with me then. We tried to comfort each other. We tried for hope, but then—it comes to me fully now, the last thing I remember, when Dr. Ash was mining me. Us.

The gilded, honeyed lights surrounded our memory-dream of our sister Dubbs on the train tracks, ripping it away, mining it savagely out of us, and when my other voice couldn't bear to lose our sister, she wrapped herself around Dubbs and held on so tightly that they both were torn away from me. A shattering of star bits swirled around me in the aftermath and broke the night into slivers of gold while I, in disbelief, in agony, screamed and tried to follow.

It was useless. The schism was complete, and my other

voice was gone. I was left behind in our body. Me. The other, lesser voice who spoke only in our head, never aloud. Until now.

Ian slides a new IV into my chest, and the prick hurts. "Sorry," he mumbles. He peels off a new piece of tape to secure it.

This is what I've struggled to wake up to. This hideousness. I've come close to surfacing before, enough to be certain that Ian has lingered over me previously, but this is the first time I've actually broken through.

It's so hard to know what's real.

I always depended on my other voice for reason and logic. She made our decisions while I mocked and doubted, loitered and craved. Of course, I have my own quicksilver, instinctive way of drawing conclusions, and I fall back on that now. Keep him talking.

"How old are you?" I ask.

"What would you guess?" he says.

I have no idea. "Twenty-five?"

He laughs and then modestly adjusts my gown once more. "I'm nineteen," he says. "Three years older than you."

"Four years," I say. "I'm fifteen."

"No. You had your birthday in December. You're sixteen now."

Alarm slams me. "How long have I been here?" I ask.

"Let me think," he says. "You came right before Halloween, I remember. It was wild. Four truckloads of dreamers showed up at the same time, and Berg told us we had to keep a special eye on you. I was like, that's her, Rosie from *The Forge Show*.

4

I was so psyched. I loved watching your blip rank go up. The show wasn't the same at all after you left."

"But how long ago did I come here?" I insist. "What's the date today?"

A mumbling of voices carries from the distance, and Ian looks over his shoulder until the noise passes. I can't see much from my angle, but from the way Ian keeps turning, I assume a doorway opens in the direction of my feet. He faces me again.

"Today's February eleventh," he says.

My mind balks. I've been here in this vault for more than three months! *Three months!* This is worse than a prison. It's stealing my life! I thrash my hand up in desperation.

"Please, Ian!" I say. "You have to help me. I can't stay here like this!"

"Careful." Ian catches my hand and holds it down.

"Are they mining me? Do *you* mine me?" I ask.

He smiles. "No. Not me."

"Dr. Ash, then? Does she mine me?"

"Look, it's all for your own good," he says. "You have to calm down. It's not right for your heart rate to go up like that. It'll change your metabolism and everything else." He reaches for the narcotics dial again.

"No, please!" I say. "I'm calm. See? I'm fine." I try to smile.

"I mean it," he says. "If you destabilize, they might decide to move you."

"To where?"

"The main research lab," he says. "To be honest, Onar is more of a sorting station than anything else. It's strange for a

5

dreamer to be here this long, but that's what Mr. Berg ordered for you. I think it has to do with confidentiality. He trusts us here."

"I don't want to go anywhere," I say, willing myself to be calm. I know, at some level, he's my only chance. He's the one who lingers over me. I must manipulate him right. "I want to stay here with you."

"You're lucky it wasn't one of the others who noticed you were awake," he says. "I really ought to report this. The doc will want to adjust your meds."

"Don't tell them," I say. "It wasn't luck. I waited to wake up just with you."

"Is that right?" he asks, looking pleased.

"I have an idea," I say. "Why don't you lighten up on my meds so you and I can talk sometimes? I'll keep it a secret if you will."

He rubs his nose and smiles again. "That's funny," he says. "You're asleep all the time. You have nobody to tell."

Duh. Exactly, I think. "I like to see you smile," I say.

He glances over his shoulder again and leans near so I can smell the potato chips on his breath. "I like your smile, too. This is the most exciting thing that's ever happened to me."

"Don't tell anybody," I say.

He whispers confidentially. "Okay."

"Can I ask you something? Do you have a girlfriend?"

Straightening again, he shakes his head, but a touch of color rises in his cheeks. "I never know how to talk to girls."

"You're talking to me," I say.

"I guess. This is different, though."

"No, we are definitely having a conversation, and I am definitely a girl."

He breaks into a quick, private smile and then frowns again. "I really need to put you back to sleep."

"Will you do me a favor?" I ask.

He looks a bit wary. "What?"

"You smell like the outdoors," I say. "Like the forest." This is patently untrue. He reeks of tobacco. "Could you bring me something green to smell?"

"You want something alive, from outside?" He sounds surprised.

I nod. "It would mean so much to me."

He is grotesque to me, this evil troll, but when he pauses to consider, his eyes take on a liquid, dreamy quality, and he looks younger. He pushes back his mousy hair and rubs behind one ear.

"It might help your dreams," he says pensively.

"Is something wrong with my dreams?" I ask.

He hesitates, then shakes his head. "No. They're fine."

He's lying, obviously. Panic tingles at my throat. Dean Berg hasn't killed me in a brief, merciful way. He's been mining me for over three months. He's kept me wasting. Tethered. This is exactly the hell my other voice foresaw when she escaped.

"Ian, please. You have to help me! You can't let them keep me here!"

He reaches for the dial on my IV again. "Don't get excited," he says. "It's your job to sleep."

"Just bring me something green," I say. "That's all I want. Promise me!"

He shakes his head. His lips go straight and firm.

I want to scream at him.

"When can we talk again?" I ask. "Ian?"

His eyes go sad. "That's enough, now. Just close your eyes."

I hate obeying him. He infuriates me. But I do what he says.

It's an exquisite kind of horrible, lying there blind, hearing him breathing and knowing he's turning the dial on my IV. We have a fragile new pact that's built on us both knowing that I'm awake. He could do anything to me, and I'm helpless to stop him, but I have to hope he enjoys the power he has. The control. The mercy. I want him to sense how grateful I am for his decency and gentleness.

Not that he's decent at all. He's a pawn. A Berg tool.

The brown, warm heaviness seeps into my blood. I hold out as long as I can, resisting the meds with will power. If only I knew how to be smart like my other voice was.

Where are you? I call to her.

I listen to the hollow of my mind, waiting while the delicate emptiness plays in my ears, but only my own echo answers back, mocking me. She's gone. I miss her. I hate her, too, and bleating for her won't bring her back. A swirl of bitterness fills me. If she's extinguished, it's no less than she deserves for abandoning me.

I never asked to be in charge, but I'm all I have left now.

"I'm sorry," Ian says softly. "That was a mistake, talking to you. I didn't mean to get you upset."

He smears a touch of gel on my eyelids. In a moment, he'll close the lid of my sleep shell and walk away. He'll never let me wake again.

"Kiss me goodnight, Ian," I whisper.

"What?" he asks.

It's my last trick to play, and I can't bear to say it again.

Gentle pressure lands not on my lips, but on my forehead—a kind kiss from a monster. It tears at me. I can't tell which of us has won this round, him or me.

Then my lungs fill with pure loneliness, and I'm back to the airless agony at the bottom of my pond.

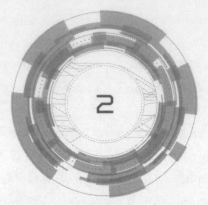

— THEA —

THE VOICE THAT LEFT

MY BELLY DIPPED, returning to gravity. I could breathe again, too. The weighty fullness of my body swelled into being around me, and each warm, corporeal cell of flesh dazzled. My second breath brought the raspberry scent of roses, cloying and near.

An indifferent twilight lingered inside my eyelids. The strands of honeyed light that I last recalled spinning around my sister and me were gone, and so was the euphoria of release. My hands felt small and empty.

Are you there? I asked silently.

I lay waiting for the familiar shift of my inner voice to stir at the back of my mind, but my mental corners remained as clean and still as a swept pine floor. I felt odd. Not just awake, but new. Inhaling deeply, I filled each tiny pocket of my lungs. My muscles came painfully alert, like they might respond if I tried to move, but I didn't dare to test them or open my eyes until I had my bearings. If I was still in the vault, someone could be watching.

Approaching wheels gathered volume until they squeaked to a stop.

"Good morning, Mr. Flores," a woman said. "Coffee?"

A man spoke up in a deep, weary voice, as American as a cowboy's. "Thanks. Black will do. What time is it?"

As liquid poured audibly into a cup, the aroma of fresh coffee cut through the redolence of the flowers, and the clues of normalcy thrilled me. Let this be real, I thought, and not some dream.

"Five eleven," she said. She had an unfamiliar accent and a lilting voice. "Looks like a beautiful day out there. How's your daughter? Any change?"

"Her heartbeat's up slightly," he said. "I don't know if that means anything."

Me. They had to mean me.

"There it goes again. See that jump?" he said.

"Right. This will be the day," she said. "I have a good feeling about it. You said black, right?"

"Yes, perfect. Thank you," he said.

The coffee lady wished him a good day, and the rolling noise receded into the distance. No way could I still be in a vault of dreamers. Whoever these people were, wherever I was, I must have escaped, which set me teetering on the possibility of joy. For a last moment, I primed myself, readying for anything and guarding myself against disappointment.

Then I opened my eyes on a painfully bright world.

I blinked, squinting at a hospital room, and my gaze shot to the window. Just outside, a pine stood under heavy snow, bulging and clean against a fresh blue sky. Each minute, crystalline surface of the flakes glittered, and my heart ached at the pure beauty of it.

Beside the window, a man turned a paper cup idly in his hand and aimed his attention outward, toward the view. He was a regular, middle-aged guy, not some attendant in a lab coat. That alone was reassuring, but he also had a fit, big-boned frame, and rugged, dark-skinned features that appealed to me as unaffected and down home.

It hit me, with growing pleasure, that I had surfaced in a safe, normal place among everyday people instead of TV stars or the victims of a maniac. A black-and-silver rosary rested beside a vase of yellow roses. A TV was mounted near the ceiling, and a white board was covered with scribbles. I didn't see a single camera anywhere. My happiness soared.

The man turned to look my way, and when his eyes met mine, he lowered his cup to the window ledge so rapidly that a few drops spilled. He touched a hand to his heart. He shook his head, as if overcome, and then he seemed to both melt and levitate at the same time.

"Hello, *m'ija*," he said. "*¿De veras estás despierta?*"

I recognized Spanish, but I couldn't understand him.

He came over to set a kiss on my forehead, and then he beamed his warm eyes directly into mine. "Are you back with us again?"

Yes, I'm here, I thought, but trying to transmit the words to my lips brought only a thickness to my tongue. I felt my first flicker of fear.

"It's all right," he continued. He laughed and straightened and wiped at his eye. "I can hardly believe this. You're actually awake, aren't you?"

He went off in another stream of Spanish, but I hardly heard him.

I couldn't speak. What else couldn't I do? I moved my head slightly and twitched my fingertips, but I wasn't getting any signals from my toes. When I tried to shift my legs, they were too heavy, as if instead of the sheet I could see, a lead apron pinned down my lower limbs.

I wasn't going to panic yet.

"She moved her head, Madeline," the man said, now speaking into a phone. "I swear. She's looking at me right now, clear as can be. Get yourself down here." He smiled at me, a stiff pinch of lips. "You're hearing every word I say, aren't you? Unbelievable." He set down his phone and reached forward to lift my hand into his.

Except it wasn't my hand. The hand at the end of my arm was all wrong: too knuckly and stubby. Too dark. *What on earth?* My heart pounded, and a simultaneous beep startled me from behind. *Wait!* I checked the other hand and it was wrong, too.

13

"Forgive me if we've done wrong," the man added. "We've only wanted what's best for you, and if this was a mistake coming here, I beg you to forgive us."

Just explain what's happened to me, I thought. *Cut the apologies and spell out the facts.* I needed my inner voice now. *Where are you?* I asked her insistently.

A nurse strode in, and I turned to her eagerly.

"Will you look who is awake? Welcome back!" she said. Her voice had a lilting, unfamiliar accent. "Are you not a sight. Tracking is dead on already, I see. Very nice. I'll inform the doctor. You're probably a little confused, are you not?"

What is this body? What am I doing here?

She smiled. "It's perfectly natural. We will fill you in, I promise. For now, you just relax, okay? You're doing very well. Beautifully, in fact."

She flipped back her brown braid and reached for a computer screen at the side of my bed. Tapping followed. I tried to see her screen, but the angle was wrong. I tried to read her nametag, but it was written in some foreign script.

"Can she talk?" the man asked.

"Those eyes are certainly expressive," she said. "We will have to see where her language is. The doctor will be able to tell you more, but her tracking is a very good sign. Does she seem to know you?"

"I couldn't say. *Ha pasado mucho tiempo, mi niña. ¿Conoces a tu papito todavía?*"

I had no idea what he meant.

14

The nurse leaned near me. "Where is your father, *dúlla*? Can you look at your father?"

There was only one man in the room, and he wasn't my father, but I felt his need pulling like a vortex. I flicked my gaze in his direction, and a dawn rose in his features.

"This is unbelievable. You have no idea," he said, choking and then clearing his throat. "If you'd seen what they scraped up after her motorcycle accident, you'd have sworn this day would never come."

"It's no less than you deserve," the nurse said kindly. "Careful, here." She set a straw to my lips. "See if you can sip. Go on."

I didn't want to sip. I wanted answers. But I complied. It took concentrated effort to open my lips and set them tightly around the straw. When I sucked up my first taste of water, my eyes closed in pure pleasure. *More*, I thought.

"They are always thirsty," the nurse said. "To be honest, your daughter was the worst case I have ever seen Dr. Fallon attempt. She won't normally take on anyone who is so far gone."

Fallon. I felt an instinctive spike of fear as I tried to place the name.

"My wife can be very persuasive," the man said. "And my daughter's a survivor."

The nurse laughed. "Indeed she is."

It hit me. Dr. Fallon had been Dean Berg's contact in Iceland, the woman he had sent dream seeds to. My pulse jumped and

15

set off the beeper again. The nurse reached behind me to make the noise stop.

"Is her heart okay like that?" the man asked.

"She is a little agitated, understandably," the nurse said. "We can give her something to keep her calm."

I didn't want anything to keep me calm. I needed to stay awake. With Dr. Fallon involved, whatever they'd done to me could only be bad. She could have hooked me into some sick experiment. This all seemed real, but it might still turn out to be some illusion. My parents weren't here, either—another bad sign. I needed to get out of here and go home to Doli.

Quick footsteps approached, and then a small, angular woman stopped in the doorway. She clasped her hands together against her chest. Around her pale, strained face, a shock of short, silvery hair stuck out in all directions.

"Good Lord," she whispered. "Diego, is it true?"

He rose out of his chair to a lanky height. "I tell you, Madeline, she's following every word we say. She just had a sip of water from a straw, our very own girl."

Madeline moved closer to me, slowly, disbelief visibly warring with her hope. "Hello, my little Althea," she said. "I am so happy to see you. Praise God. I have lived for this day, honey. I have prayed for it, as the Lord is my witness."

Althea.

Althea was not my name. The intensity of this woman rolled over me in a pounding wave of claim, but she was not my mother.

I'm Rosie, I thought. *I'm not your daughter.*

No matter how hard I tried to summon the words, I couldn't get them past my lips.

Madeline gave me a tender kiss on the cheek and set her hand on my belly. She smiled at me with brimming eyes. "Have they told you? You're baby's just fine," she said. "All this time you've been in a coma, your little baby has been growing along just perfectly inside you."

My ears stopped working. Her mouth kept going but my mind froze.

No.

No baby.

I could not be pregnant. I could not be in some other girl's body. This whole thing with the snow outside and the hospital and the strange hands attached to my arms had to be a nightmare. It had to be some new torture from Dean Berg, some dream seed or mining gone wrong.

Just then, my belly dipped again, only now I recognized that it wasn't just gravity pulling at me. I had a creature in there. Nudging. Horror should have woken me from a nightmare, but it didn't. It couldn't.

This was real. This body was real, and it was mine.

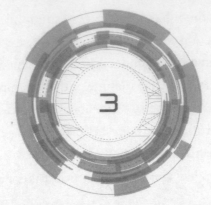

3

— THEA —

BLINK TWICE

WHERE ARE YOU? I screamed silently.

But still there was no answer. My inner voice had vanished, and I'd jumped into my new hell alone.

I flailed my hand against the bedrail, desperate to jolt awake or jar myself back to my old body, but the sharp pain did nothing except start the heart monitor beeping again.

"Althea, stop. You'll hurt yourself," Diego said.

I didn't care if I hurt myself. I had to get out and away from all of this. I struggled to move, but my scrawny arms had hardly any strength, and my body responded only by bumping awkwardly under my coverlet. Panic made me wild, and I reached frantically for the nurse. She caught me firmly.

"Calm down, now," she said. "I'm sure you have a lot of questions, but thrashing about will not help anybody."

You don't understand, I thought. *These are not your normal questions. What happened to me? Where's my real body?*

My tongue was as stupid as clay.

"Let me, Ida," said Madeline, and she slipped forward to take my hands. "You're all right, Althea. Look at me. You're going to be just fine. We're all here to help you."

I looked back and forth between Madeline and Diego, who clearly thought they were my parents. But they were not.

"Are you in pain anywhere? Does anything hurt? Your head? Your joints?" Madeline asked.

I paused to take stock. My belly was a compact knoll in the landscape of my bed, and that turning I'd felt seemed ready to happen again. I pulled free from Madeline and pressed my hands to my belly, astounded by the dense curve. My normal waist was utterly gone. I touched my face. To my fingertips, my cheeks and jaw felt too wide and boney. On my head, I found a fine softness that was nothing like my old thick waves of hair. I needed to see myself.

I looked Madeline straight in the eye and willed her to understand me. Then I patted my cheek deliberately and held my hand up before my face, mimicking that I was gazing into a mirror.

"She wants to see herself," Diego said. "Madeline, she's asking for a mirror." He laughed again in disbelief.

"One sec," Madeline said. She rustled through her purse, opened up a compact, and handed it to me.

The sight in the little circle was bizarre. My hazel eyes, curly dark hair, and gap-toothed mouth were all gone. Instead, a girl with wide-set, sunken, gray eyes gazed back at me. Her tan-skinned cheeks were unnaturally wilted, and patches of acne marred her chin, nose, and forehead. Her lips were full, but dry and tender looking. When I turned my head slightly, I found a scar along her right temple that disappeared up into her hairline, and when I smoothed back my new soft hair, brown and silky limp, I saw the tip of her ear was missing, as if the road had taken a bite out of it. I touched it tenderly, hearing the faint tracing sound of my finger along the ridge. I peered at her eyes again, trying to see if any hint of Rosie would shine back out at me, but the mask was complete. My physical exterior was entirely new.

Whoa, I thought. It didn't seem possible, but somehow my consciousness had arrived in another girl's body. When I'd made my leap with my love for Dubbs, I'd never imagined that this could happen. I tilted the mirror slowly, trying different angles. I tugged at my skin, trying to absorb the truth. This sad-eyed, wasted girl in the mirror was me. I'd ended up in a Halloween mask I couldn't take off.

What had happened to my old body?

"Don't you worry," Madeline said gently. "You might not look like your regular lovely self at the moment, but we know she's in there. That's all that matters."

The irony was laughable. I didn't look anything like myself, but at least Althea didn't look like herself, either. I took a more critical look at Madeline, and the girl in the mirror, noting the resemblance of the wide-spaced eyes. Under the sickliness, my new face had a mix of features from both parents, with my chin and darker coloring closer to Diego's. The way he spoke Spanish clicked. Althea had some Latina heritage, I thought.

"She seems so alert," Diego said. "I can't get over it. After all this time."

"Remember the doctor who told us to unplug her?" Madeline said.

"Which one?"

"That first one," she said. "That genius back in Houston. I wish he could see this now. Have you called your father yet?"

"I will. He'll be over the moon. The whole family will."

A tap came at the door, and a woman in a white coat walked in. "I hear someone's awake," she said, smiling.

At the sight of her, a shock of jangled memories ignited in me like a whole grid of power surging on at once: overheard calls between this doctor and Dean Berg, nights of sneaking around the Forge School, and the vault of dreamers I'd uncovered deep under the school. I'd endured the torture of being mined when I was still impossibly awake.

Linus! Panic hit me again. They had taken Linus, too!

The alarm sounded behind me once more, and the nurse reached for it again. The beeping changed to a regular, soft blip noise that matched the tempo of my heartbeat.

"She has been very excited," the nurse said, shifting to make room for the doctor.

"I'm not at all surprised. This is a big day," Dr. Fallon said. "We can mark down February twenty-fifth as her second birthday. Hello, Althea. I'm Dr. Fallon, your surgeon. How are you feeling? A little confused, maybe. Any pain?"

Try anger.

They raised the head of my bed more. Dr. Fallon shone a

21

penlight to blind me in one of my eyes, and then the other. "Can you follow the tip of my finger?" She lifted a digit before my eyes and began to move it slowly left and right, up and down.

Try explaining how you stole months of my life and stuffed me in a different body.

I ignored her finger and studied her face instead, searching past the afterglow of the penlight for a hint of the monster inside her. Her pale skin, black hair, and red lipstick were as vivid as a model's, and her eyes were frost blue. This was the doctor who had bought dream seeds from Dean Berg after he mined them from unwitting students at Forge. She'd collaborated with him. As far as I was concerned, she was as vile and evil as he was. My heart monitor audibly kicked into a faster rhythm.

The doctor lowered her finger. "Interesting," she said.

"She was just looking at us and following our voices fine," Diego said.

"I believe you," the doctor said. She straightened, crossing her arms in her white coat. "She's choosing not to cooperate with me."

My heart monitor went silent an instant, betraying me, and then blipped onward.

"Althea?" Madeline said. She looked mortified. "What is this? We need you to do what the doctor tells you."

The doctor smiled. "There's no need to scold. It's actually a very promising sign of autonomous intelligence." She swiveled closer to me once more. "Let me introduce myself again. I'm Dr. Huma Fallon, and you're staying with us here at the Chimera Centre just south of Reykjavik, Iceland. You had an accident six months ago and fell into a coma. Your parents brought you here to me three weeks ago, and we were able to perform a surgery to help revive and restore your memories." She reached to clasp my hand. "Can you squeeze my hand twice if you understand me?"

I glanced at Diego and Madeline, who both had their gazes locked on my hand. Behind them, the nurse was also watching gravely.

I squeezed twice.

Madeline let out a startled gasp.

The doctor patted my hand. "Perfect! Very good," she said. "Over the next few weeks, you're going to go through a series of changes. You'll relearn to use your body and your voice. Most important, you'll have to relearn to use your own mind." She clicked her pen a couple of times. "There's no other way to say this. You've suffered massive brain damage. Your memory is going to have gaps in it. You might not remember people you once knew and loved dearly. You might not even recognize yourself at times, and this, understandably, could be highly disorienting. But you're in good hands here. You've come to the premier facility in the world for this kind of recovery, and we'll do everything we can to see you through," she said. "I promise."

You are a scheming liar, I thought. *How fast can I get out of here?*

"Please squeeze twice if you understand," Dr. Fallon said.

I did and then tugged free of her as quickly as I could.

Diego reached an arm around Madeline's shoulder and gripped her tight. "How long will it be before we can take our girl home?" Diego asked, his voice rough.

"I'll have a better idea of that after we run a few tests," Dr. Fallon said. "We had one young man who was ready to go home in a month, almost fully recovered. Another one of our patients took six months to go home, and he's still slowly improving there."

"That's not counting your patients who never revived," Diego said.

"That's right," Dr. Fallon said. "Obviously, Althea doesn't fall into that category."

"Or the ones that relapsed," Diego said.

"That's always a possibility, as we've discussed," Dr. Fallon said. "These next few days are especially critical. We'll be watching her very, very carefully for the slightest regression."

"I just can't get over the way she's watching us," Madeline said. "It's a miracle. Do you think she really understands us?"

"Blink twice, Althea," Diego said.

The three of them turned to me again, like I was a puppy who would perform for a treat. *Fine. I'll play. For now.* I blinked twice.

Madeline laughed, pressing her hands together before her mouth.

With an effort, I pointed to my water cup, and then I touched the fingertips of my two hands together, asking for more.

Madeline nodded. "What's she doing?"

"It's sign language. It means 'more.' She's thirsty," the doctor said. She passed Madeline my cup, and with trembling hands, Madeline held the straw to my lips again.

I sucked up the ice water and drank deeply, until the cool fluid slaked my thirst.

"But how did she know that 'more' signal?" Diego asked. "Did you seed that into her?"

"No. She must have known it before," Dr. Fallon said. "Old things from deep in her memory can be coming back to her. Did you use sign language with her as a toddler?"

"No," Madeline said, glancing at Diego. "We never did."

"Maybe some caretaker did, or a friend," Dr. Fallon said.

I knew all the sign language to "The More We Get Together." Dubbs had taught me the song after she learned it in preschool, and we had practiced it for hours, singing it with shadow hands on the wall above her bunk.

I missed her, my smelly kid sister, and a twist of sorrow spun through me. I couldn't help thinking that my love for Dubbs was what had landed me here, in this new body. The last thing I remembered from my old body was the time Dr. Ash was mining me. I'd had a memory of Dubbs on the train tracks near our home, with the flowers and the sunlight, and it had snared inextricably into a dream Dr. Ash was mining from me. I would never forget the swirling, euphoric release when I leapt free from my trapped body. I'd had to escape to survive.

My inner voice had been furious, though. She'd begged me not to go. She'd warned me. I had no idea now what had happened to the part of me that was left behind. Had she survived in my old body without me? Was my old body dead? I had to find out.

"Has ido de un misterio a otro, ¿no?" Diego said. *"Dime que mi pequeña todavía está ahí adentro."*

I looked to Madeline, half expecting her to translate.

"She doesn't understand me," he said quietly. His eyes were dark with dismay. "She's lost her Spanish."

"Be grateful she's alive, Diego," Madeline said. "Look how alert she is."

"Be honest with us, doc," Diego said. "Althea was going places. She was ready to start college last fall. She had plans to be a psychiatrist. Is there any point dreaming that big anymore?"

"These are early days yet," Dr. Fallon said. "I think your daughter will have options, but for now, you'll have to be patient and see."

"I don't want her to suffer anymore," Madeline said. "That's all I want."

The doctor kindly put a hand on Madeline's arm. "We're doing all we can," she said.

"Yes, I know," Madeline said quickly. "And we're beyond grateful. I mean, look at her. Look at my baby girl."

They looked. I looked back, absorbing the weight of their hopes. I couldn't help liking Althea's parents, but I was destined to disappoint them when they realized who I wasn't. I signaled "more" again, and Madeline helped hold my cup and straw. These people needed the girl they'd lost, not me.

Me. That was pathetic. I hardly knew who I was anymore. I wished I had a clue where my body was. My original self. I hoped, wherever she was, that she wasn't still captive in Dean Berg's vault.

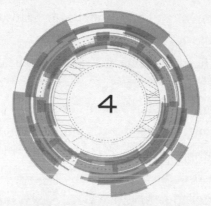

— ROSIE —

THE SMELL OF GREEN

WHEN IAN APPROACHES my sleep shell, I'm ready for him.

Once, a couple years back, Dubbs put a coil of fresh fly-paper inside our freezer to see if the temperature would affect its stickiness. When she hung the frozen helix from a lamp on the back stoop that night, flies and moths came to it by the dozens, sticking and struggling until their wings disintegrated, until Dubbs cried and I doused the writhing flypaper in a bucket of water.

Now I'm as cold as that flypaper. I lift my hand in a flimsy wave and compose my sweetest smile.

"You shouldn't do that," he says as he opens my lid. "What if it wasn't me?"

"It has to be you," I say, and beam gratitude. "Nobody else lets me wake up."

"If Dr. Ash figured out what I'm doing, she'd kill me," Ian says.

Every now and then, Ian lightens up on my meds. When the narcotics wear off, I can come around, and usually he's beside me already, waiting for me.

"So why do you, then?" I ask.

"You know why," he says. He glances over his shoulder and then back at me with a shy smile. "I've been thinking of you."

He hovers awkwardly closer, and I close my eyes. His lips are light on my cheek, with a tickle of mustache, and I know he wants me to turn to him, but I just can't. He's too repulsive. I'm grossed out by the possibility he might actually press his lips to mine. So far, since he knows I'm conscious, he has refrained, but I don't know how long that will last.

"I brought you something," he says.

I open my eyes as he passes me a sprig of fresh mint.

"It's from my grandmother's greenhouse," he says. "It's fresh. You have to crush it a little. Hold on. I'd better do it for you or you'll get it on your fingers."

He pinches a few of the green leaves, and when I brush the soft foliage against my nose, a burst of ripe scent fills my nostrils.

"Wow," I say, and inhale again. The tangy mint is the essence of green.

"Like it?" He drums his fingers on the side of my sleep shell and smiles.

28

"It's amazing," I say. This much is true. I lick a corner of one leaf.

"Don't eat it. We can't mess with your digestion. But go ahead and smell it again. Todd's out on break, and Harvey called in sick. Or his kid's sick, in any case."

"So it's just you today? You have a lot of responsibility."

We should have more time to talk, I think. More time for me to work on him.

"It's not that hard. We're down to only seven dreamers right now," he says. "We should get more next week, though."

"Then it'll be busy?"

He nods. "In a good way. Excuse me. I have to clean your port." He undoes the shoulder snaps of my gown and folds it down carefully to reveal the port in my chest, inches above my left breast. It's a lump under my skin, shaped like a mini donut and as big as a quarter. As we talk, he takes the old IV needle out of me and cleans the surrounding skin. "You know what I like most about this job?" he asks.

"What?"

"The dreams," he says. "Seeing them. Dr. Ash lets me watch while she's mining, and you wouldn't believe the things you all come up with. Flying's my favorite, but I like the twisted dreams, too, the ones that make no sense. You can never guess where they'll go. Oh, and the flashing color ones, those are good, too," he said. "You have very nice dreams," he adds politely.

"Do I?"

"Yes. Very colorful and unpredictable. Even the awful ones are interesting."

"What awful ones?"

He puts in a new IV. "You dream about the black guy who falls off the tower," Ian says. "Sometimes he turns into your little sister. She falls backward and screams and then you, like, scramble."

I fixate on a vivid image of little Dubbs with her arms out. She's a silhouette against a blue sky, falling and pinwheeling with panic. Her fall stretches out and rips into me because I can't save her, and then I slam down the door in my mind to block it out.

"I don't want to talk about my sister," I say.

"Sorry."

Instead, I recall the real episode of falling off the observatory ladder, hitting into Burnham on my way down, and plummeting with him to the ground. There's an awful crunch, a sound I don't consciously remember hearing at the time, and then a suspended silence before a bird chirps in the distance.

"You're making me remember things," I say.

"Is that bad?"

"I don't know." It's better than being asleep forever.

"That black guy wasn't your boyfriend, was he?" Ian asks.

"No," I say.

"Would you date someone black?"

"If I liked him," I answer.

Ian sniffs and wipes at his nose. "You also dream about the other guy," he says. "I forget his name. The kitchen guy. I never liked him."

Linus lay unconscious on Berg's operating table the last

30

time I saw him. Guilt taints my memory, as harsh as the lights on the stainless steel. Linus was there in the vault because of me, and if Berg hurt him, if he scraped through Linus's dreams, it's my fault.

"Maybe you miss him," Ian says. "I understand. That's okay."

I shake my head. I can't bear to think of Linus, either. "We broke up," I say.

Ian pats my shoulder. He sets aside the suction cleaner.

"You don't need to be sad," Ian says. "You have me, now."

"I know. I'm so glad," I say. I force myself to meet his gaze again. "You're so nice and understanding. How did I get so lucky?"

He blushes again and hooks up my IV. "Dr. Ash says you're doing a little better. I was worried you were kind of getting mined out, you know? But I think maybe the stimulation has helped, don't you?"

"I'm sure it has," I say, and smell the mint again. What's *mined out* mean?

"I had one bad moment, though," he says. "I showed up in one of your dreams."

"You did? When?"

"The other day," he says. "I was worried Dr. Ash would guess what we're doing, but you dreamed that I was hunting in a forest with a gun. In camo and boots, with a pistol, which doesn't make much sense from a hunting perspective. How did you know I have a pistol?"

"I didn't," I say.

"I thought it was a close call, but it was also kind of cool," he says. "She didn't ask me anything about it, fortunately. I don't know what I would have said."

"When did she last mine me?" I ask.

Ian flips a tablet at the foot of my sleep shell. "Six days ago."

"I don't remember that," I say.

He smiles wisely, the way he does, with his lips stretched so a line of wet shows at the crease. "Of course not. You were asleep, silly. I for sure don't mess with your meds the day of a mining."

"When will she mine me again? Is that on that chart?"

Ian inspects the tablet again, squinting for a moment. "Tomorrow. I'll give you your full dose when we're done. Don't worry."

My pulse picks up. I have to focus on getting Ian to help me out of here.

"Ian, will you do something for me? Will you call my parents for me and tell them where I am?"

Ian adjusts a shoulder snap on my gown and tucks my blanket softly around my waist. The IV is ready for a final twist of the upper clamp. "They aren't in charge of you anymore," Ian says. "Berg is your guardian."

"But do they know where I am?" I ask.

"Not from me," he says lightly. "They're still offering huge rewards for you, you know. Every time they up the amount, I just have to show it to Dr. Ash, and she gives me a bonus worth twice that much. It's a good deal, to my way of thinking. It may not show, but I'm quite a wealthy guy."

32

Like a faltering stone, my heart slips off the edge of a cliff and plummets. I'll never get out of here. Ian will never help me escape.

"I want to go home," I say. It slips out before I can even think.

"You don't mean that," he says. "This is where you get the treatment you need. Remember? You're getting better."

"Am I?"

"Of course. You shouldn't worry. Look at your mint here," he says running a finger through the sprig. "It's just what you wanted."

"From your grandmother's greenhouse, you said."

Ian smiles. "Yes. Funny thing. She's always telling me to find a girlfriend, but she has no idea. I live with her and look out for her now that my dad's gone to California. He got me this job. Sometimes I wish I could bring you home for Sunday dinner, but of course, I can't."

"Would she like me?" I ask.

"Are you kidding? She'd love you," he says. "I've been watching old episodes of *The Forge Show* with her so she can see what you're like, but I never tell her you're here. It's an amazing secret. She thinks I'm just your fan."

I touch the mint lightly to my lips, and his gaze drops to the gesture. A slow blush comes up his cheeks, and his eyes grow warm again.

"You're so sweet," he says. "Sweet as honey."

He is not the most original guy, but I smile as if I'm flattered.

"What's your middle name?" I ask.

33

"Give me the mint."

I breathe it in. "Not yet, please. Come on. Tell me your middle name."

"Try to guess."

It must be something creepy. "Roderick?"

He laughs. "It's John. Ian John Cowles. It's kind of repetitive because 'Ian' is Scottish for 'John.' Now give me the mint. Be good."

I hand him the mint slowly. "And what's the date today?"

His smile fades. "You don't need to know that."

"Yes, I do," I say, smiling again. "Please? Tell me what the date is. Is it still February?"

"The last time I told you the date, you got upset."

"I won't be upset," I say. "I just need to know. I can't tell how much time is passing unless you tell me."

"It isn't too much time," he says. "Close your eyes."

"Don't put me out again! We have to talk!"

"We did talk. That's enough for now."

"Did we have Valentine's Day yet?" I ask.

He hesitates, looks guilty.

We did. I can tell. Time is vanishing without me.

"You have to let me out of here!" I say. "Please, Ian. You can't let them keep me here. It's not right!"

His expression shuts down, and he reaches for the clamp on my drip. "We can't have these little breakdowns, Rosie."

I struggle against my panic. I've made a mistake. "I take it back," I say, and I reach for his hand. "I'm fine. I know you can't let me out. That wasn't fair to ask. I want to stay here with you, anyway. I love being here with you. You're taking such good care of me."

He sighs and pulls his hand free. "Just close your eyes, Rosie. Don't make this hard."

"Why? What does it matter if I close my eyes?"

"I don't like seeing the whites."

"Are there others here who don't close their eyes?" I ask.

He shifts uncomfortably. "No."

"Ian, is there another dreamer like me? One you talk to?"

"There was only one who opened her eyes sometimes," he says. "She never talked to me. I'm not sure she even saw me. She's not here anymore."

Alarm shatters through me. "Where is she?"

He doesn't answer.

"Did she get mined out?" I ask. "Is that what happened? Did they move her to the main research center?"

"Close your eyes," he says more loudly. "Don't make me be mean."

With a sense of horror, I obey him. I squeeze them tight, and I struggle to make my tone light again. "Thank you for bringing me the mint. It was such a perfect surprise."

"I try to be nice," he mumbles. "It's never enough."

"Of course it's enough," I say. "You're amazing. I'm sorry I lost it there a few minutes ago. I just started hoping we could be together for real."

"We can't. We only have this."

Sightless, I wait to feel his kiss on my cheek again, and I fight a new wave of despair. It's so hard to make any progress with him, and now I fear I'm not the first to try.

"You're pretty when you relax," Ian says quietly.

A soft, bumbling touch along my hair sends my scalp tingling.

I loathe him more than ever. "Thank you," I say.

"Let's never fight."

The meds are already making it hard for my words to come. "Okay," I whisper.

He strokes my hair a second time, and a third, like I'm some big pet doll. I catch another whiff of the mint, very near. This time, I don't fight the narcotics, but it still takes a full, awful count of five before I'm out.

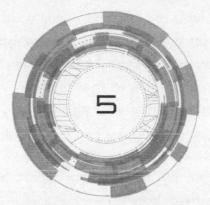

5

— THEA —

THE POINT OF A FORTUNE

MY BODY WASN'T A VIRGIN ANYMORE. Clearly.

But *I* hadn't had sex. The most I'd done with Linus was kiss him. The kissing had been very nice, actually, but we could never go too far on *The Forge Show*, and honestly, that was okay with me. In a way, the cameras made it more exciting because I felt the buzz of taboo at the edge of my consciousness. I could sense the viewers coming on board and my blip rank rising. But the cameras also set a safe boundary, a precise edge of frustration. I could give in to the wild pull I felt with Linus because we both knew, at a certain point, we would have to stop.

It was strange to think of how much I'd shared with Linus, and how messed up things had gotten with him. Now I was pregnant without even a memory of the sex that had gotten me here. It seemed totally unfair. I didn't even know what Althea's boyfriend looked like. I had no way to imagine kissing him, let alone anything more advanced.

"I can't help wondering what she's thinking," Diego said.

I'm thinking about the sex I haven't had, I thought.

Diego was back in his chair by the window, and Madeline was sitting beside me, reading some report. She glanced up and flipped the page closed.

"Does her face look a little fuller to you?" Madeline asked.

"Maybe," he said. "Yes."

Behind him, the sky was overcast today. The roses had been replaced by a vase of red tulips with loose, arching stems.

In the four days since I'd woken up at the Chimera Centre, I'd been prodded by more people than I cared to think of. Dr. Fallon came regularly to examine me, and a nurse midwife came every morning to listen to my fetus's heartbeat and check my urine. When I wasn't getting another MRI, I was in physical or speech therapy.

The first time I'd had a proper look at my body happened when the nurse, Ida, came to change my catheter. She'd rearranged my sheets and gently pulled up my gown. My new legs were skinny and puffy, like ecru-colored nylons stuffed with mush. Far at the other end, my feet sported a waxy, violet tinge between the toes, and when I ordered them to wiggle, they responded in the most casual, disinterested way. *Who, us? Hello.* My belly resembled a spreading, giant jellyfish that had swallowed a basketball. My boobs were tender and way bigger than before. Compared to my old body, which had been tight and strong, this one felt like bread pudding.

My physical therapist was jubilant in his torture of me. I learned to roll from my back to my side, and then to push upward with my arms, protecting my belly during the effort. I felt like a monstrous baby training my weak, clumsy body to obey me, and it hurt, too. My muscles burned from the unaccustomed exercise, and my sessions left me exhausted and irritable.

My garbled efforts with the speech therapist were a joke. But I had quirky, nice surprises, too. Just that morning, I had discovered that I could read nametags, which apparently weren't written in a strange script after all. Letters formed magically into English words that had not been there the day before. It gave me hope that my mind was healing, along with my body.

Madeline leaned near and traced her finger over my cheek. "You've always had the prettiest skin," she said.

It was such a mom thing to say. Madeline made me miss my ma, and I was hungry for news about my old life. I pointed at Diego's breast pocket where I could see his phone and focused my mouth as best as I could: "FFoe."

He touched a hand to his pocket. "You want my phone?"

I nodded. Yes.

"Sure." He arranged my swivel table above my lap and positioned his phone before me. "What do you want to see?" he asked.

I couldn't speak to tell him, but he opened an Internet

search window and let me type. Alien and klutzy, my thumbs worked the letters: ROSIE SINCLAIR.

The browser produced a scroll of posts, all in tiny letters. I had to enlarge them to read them, but I fumbled with the open-tweezers move and the print wouldn't expand.

"Diego. She's using her right hand," Madeline said.

I glanced up at her.

"You're left-handed," she said to me.

I flexed my stubby fingers experimentally, and then I tried my left hand on the screen instead. Instantly, my fingers moved with the smoothness of a familiar tool, astonishing me. Madeline laughed, but I hardly heard her. I manipulated the screen to bring a headline into focus: *Where's Rosie? Still No Sign of the Forge School Star*. The next read, *Rosie Sinclair Sighting: Latest Forge Hoax*.

"What do you have there?" Diego asked. He angled the screen so he could see, and his curious smile faded to a puzzled expression.

"What is it, Diego?" Madeline asked. When he passed the phone to her, she became engrossed. "Who's Rosie Sinclair?" she asked, flipping through the phone. She frowned. "She was a star on *The Forge Show*," she said. "She was expelled last semester. There's some story here about the dean becoming her guardian. Very strange. Have you ever watched the show, Diego?" she asked.

"It's that nonstop one about the art kids," he said. "I never did, but Althea could have. Maybe this is that celebrity quirk Dr. Fallon talked about."

40

Madeline looked thoughtful and passed the phone back to Diego. "I suppose." She turned to me and smiled. "Don't worry, darling. They told us that certain patients develop a fascination for some celebrity or random stranger. It can be a kind of identity escape. It's just a phase. It doesn't last."

I flicked my gaze to Diego. He was staring down at his phone, thumbing slowly through the posts. I reached to indicate I wanted it back. Instead, he slipped the phone into his shirt pocket.

I vocalized again, more urgently. "FFOE."

"Don't be difficult, Diego," Madeline said. "Give it to her. She can type to us."

"I think it'd be better to let her get reacquainted with her real life before bringing the Internet into it," Diego said.

"For heaven's sake. She just wants information. Who wouldn't?" Madeline leaned over my table and held her own phone in front of me. "Maybe you'd like to see some friends. I have some pictures." Her fingers got busy. "See? These are your cousins, and here you are for prom, with Tom. You have more on your own phone. We'll have to get that for you."

The picture showed an arresting girl with sharp features and vibrant eyes. Her slender arm encircled the neck of a muscly white guy in a tux as she mock-choked him. I liked the soft, deep blue of her dress and his bowtie of the same hue. A headband of pearls and glitter was threaded through her hair. The two looked enviably relaxed and happy together. Stylish, too. I slid the photo sideways, and the next pic showed them together again, only this time, the girl was goof-facing the camera, and the big guy, very chill, was smiling at her with open adoration.

Cute, I thought. And then, *that's the guy she slept with. Has to be.*

"You know what'll kill me?" Madeline said. "If she knows Tom but she doesn't know us."

"But she does know us," Diego said. "Don't you, sweetheart?"

I hesitated, uncertain what to say. I couldn't look at Diego. I needed these people, and I was likely to get more of their support if they believed I was their daughter. But I couldn't lie. "No," I said. "Mm sorry."

Madeline bit inward on her lips. She patted my hand. "Not to worry," she said softly. "Give it time."

"But the other day," Diego said. "I swear she knew I was her father."

"Let's give it time," Madeline repeated. "She's coming around. That's the main thing. Every day she's better."

Her tender optimism killed me. When I glanced at Althea's dad, he had a lost, gut-punched expression, and then he turned to the window with the stoic silence of an eagle. The baby kicked inside me again.

"Mm sorry," I said again, and I was.

The snow on the pine had come loose in a couple of places and dropped off to reveal the darkness of the tree underneath.

"I don't suppose you've called Tom," Madeline said.

"No," Diego said. "He signed off on the baby. You know where I am on this."

"But we have to think of her wishes, now," Madeline said. "Althea," she said to me, and I turned. "Would you like us to tell Tom you're awake again? Just say yes or no."

I was curious about the guy in the pictures, but I had no idea what Althea would want, and I couldn't guess how her awakening might affect Tom now. As I wavered, Althea's parents went on.

"Think for a second, Madeline," Diego said. "She was *leaving* him. She was *riding away from him* when she crashed."

"She'd left us, too," Madeline reminded him. "None of that matters now. I'm thinking about his intrinsic rights as a father, regardless of what he signed. The situation has changed."

"But she's still our daughter," he said. "She might not know us, but we have to protect her. He'd only rile her up. You know he would. That's what the bonehead does."

"You just don't want him involved at all."

"Correct."

I watched, intrigued. I'd never seen an argument like this between parents. It seemed so calm, with no one throwing anything or yelling. I kept expecting Madeline to give in like Ma would, but she didn't. She just waited, firm and civil, like a blade.

Diego looked at me. "Do you have an opinion?" he asked.

I balked. *Yes?*

Diego gestured impatiently. "Fine, Madeline. Do what you want."

"Thank you," she said. "I think the news would be best coming from you."

"I don't want him under my roof."

"He's not coming under your roof," Madeline said. "He's just getting some information. I'll feel better when he knows. You can text him. Do you have his number?"

"Of course," Diego said, and poked at his phone for a minute. Then, "There. Done. Happy?"

"Yes. Thank you."

I reached again for Madeline's phone and switched to a notepad app. It took ages with my slow thumbs, but I typed: *What happened to me?*

Madeline sat up straight. "Look what she's typed, Diego. She doesn't remember."

Diego glanced at the phone and then peered thoughtfully at me. "Where to start," he said slowly. "You were in a motorcycle accident. This was last August, August twenty-second, the night before you were supposed to leave for college. You had a fight with your boyfriend Tom, and you borrowed his motorcycle. It was raining, and you hit a wet curve and flew thirty feet into a gully. You had a helmet on, but still. That was six months ago. Your doctors kept on saying we had to wait and see. You've been in a coma ever since."

Six months. From September, that put us into February. I'd lost more than three months since I was at Forge, but Althea's coma had lasted even longer.

"You broke your shoulder and your arm and three ribs," Madeline said. "They're healed now. We thought you might miscarry at first, but you didn't. We flew in different experts. We consulted with the top neurologists."

44

"None of it made a difference. They tried to be optimistic, but when pressed, not one of the doctors could say you'd get any better," Diego said. "We finally decided in December to hire a team of nurses and bring you home, where you could be comfortable."

"Where you could have your horse and your dog nearby," Madeline said.

"That was hard," Diego said.

"Yes," Madeline agreed softly. "That was hard."

A rolling cart went by outside in the hall. All this time, they'd watched their daughter day after day, overseeing her care, waiting while her bones healed and her fetus grew, and wondering when or if she would ever wake up. My heart ached for them.

"Remember Christmas?" Diego said. "The cherry cobbler?"

"Yes," Madeline said, with a misty smile. "And the crèche camels Javier put on her bed?"

Enough of this. I looked down to type some more.

I want to go home.

I spun the phone on the table so it faced them. Madeline and Diego both leaned near enough to read it.

Diego cleared his throat. "I'll call the pilot and tell him to fire up the jet," he said.

"Diego, please," Madeline said.

"You saw what she wrote, Madeline," he said. "Let's get her out of this place. We've got plenty of good doctors back in Texas now that she's out of the woods."

"She's not out of the woods," Madeline said. "Dr. Fallon's

the expert. We're not leaving here until she says it's safe for Althea to go."

Diego lifted both hands. "If Dr. Fallon's so smart, why didn't she tell us Althea could type?"

My laugh came out as a weird, hiccuppy sound that startled me. Madeline and Diego both looked shocked, and then they laughed, too.

"Was there ever a sweeter sound?" Diego asked.

Madeline nodded. "But we're not leaving, Diego. It's too soon."

Go home, I typed again.

Madeline hitched her chair nearer, swiveled my table out of the way, and took my hand.

"Try to understand," she said. "Every expert we talked to said, in so many words, that your case was hopeless. You had no reasoning or thinking ability left. But you could breathe on your own. You had your baby growing. I couldn't get past the idea that some of you still existed inside somewhere. Some tiny spark. Some memory. And then we heard about Dr. Fallon."

I frowned, remembering. I'd looked up Dr. Fallon myself. She donated money to Forge, and I'd read about her clinic, never guessing that I might end up here myself. Madeline looked over to Diego, who rose to lean back against the windowsill and cross his arms.

Then Madeline patted my hand and continued. "We owe her everything. She took a chance on you when no one else would. I trust her implicitly."

"Tell her what Fallon does," Diego said.

"Dr. Fallon specializes in an experimental form of brain surgery," Madeline said. "She takes brain cells from people who have died in accidents. Donors. It's the same principle as when they harvest healthy hearts and livers for people, but Dr. Fallon rescues brain tissue. Dream seeds, she calls them. Her team here grows the cells into a kind of patch, and she injects that into an injured brain, like yours. Your old connections regrow through the patch, recreating your memories and thought processes until you wake up. That's why we're here."

I got it now. They took my dream seed out of my body, grew it for however long, and put it here, in Althea's brain. But Althea hadn't recovered. My dream seed had taken over instead.

"What's the point of having a fortune if you can't spend it on the ones you love?" Diego said dryly.

"We took a chance," Madeline said. "We brought you here and took a chance on Dr. Fallon's technique, and she took a chance on you, even though she warned us it might not work. You're a miracle in so many ways."

Except the procedure hadn't worked right. I wasn't Althea. I didn't have one tiny hint of Althea's memories. She was as lost as ever. I still wanted to leave this place.

Madeline turned to Diego. "We can't take her home yet," she said. "It's too soon, Diego. What if something goes wrong? We have to keep her here."

"Okay, Madeline," he said.

"Please understand," Madeline said to me. "We'll take you

47

home as soon as it's safe, but we can't go yet. Can you put up with all of this a little longer?"

I typed again. *I'm scared.*

Madeline glanced at the screen, and her eyes welled up. "Oh, honey," she said, and she strengthened her grip on my hand. "I know you're scared, but the worst is over. Believe me. You have so much to live for. We'll get you through this if it takes every penny we have."

That brought up a question that had occurred to me. *How rich are we?* I typed.

Madeline gave her attention to my words and let out a bright laugh. "Oh, Althea. You are too much," she said. She held the phone toward Diego.

He smiled and shook his head in amusement. "Your mother invented a nuclear process to synthesize helium," he said. "We're rich as thieves."

"I wouldn't put it that way," she said, smiling. "But I do tend to get what I want. You're rich yourself, too. We gave you eighteen million on your last birthday."

Wait. Eighteen million *dollars?* I grew up in the boxcars of Doli, Arizona, which had the poorest zip code in the United States. I'd never had any money except what I'd earned babysitting and running errands for the McLellens. Eighteen million was enough to buy every home in Doli, or feed a smallish country of hungry children. Eighteen million was madness.

I stared, puzzled that Althea's parents could look like normal people when they were so rich. Madeline didn't wear any expensive jewelry. Her outfits were so understated that I'd barely noticed the muted greens and blues. Diego wore white or blue button-down shirts and conservative jackets. Yet here we were, in an elite, experimental clinic in Iceland, where they'd just bought a miracle for their daughter.

Me, they'd bought. Sure they'd aimed to resurrect Althea, but if I looked past all the research and medical advances and techniques that had gone into Dr. Fallon's surgery, it all boiled down to one basic thing: they'd bought my mind for their daughter.

That was not okay with me.

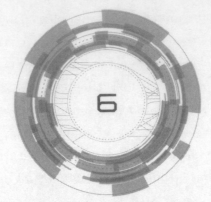

— THEA —

NOT CURIOSITY

I COULD BARELY WAIT until night when I could use the phone Madeline left me. Finally the nurse wished me good night and dimmed my lights. As her footsteps receded, I pulled out the phone and lowered the brightness of the screen. Finally, I could find out what was going on in my real life. I hated to think Berg might have the old me still imprisoned in a vault, sedated and helpless. The chances of getting back into my old body were small, of course, but she might need me.

My first instinct was to call home. No matter how mad I was at Ma, it made sense to start with her and find out what she knew about me. I was going to need her help to get home, too, and restart my life in this new body. I had no real voice yet, though, so a call wouldn't work, and when I tried to log on to my Forge email account, some security wall blocked me and said it didn't recognize my device.

Great. Next I found that my profiles on social media had been deactivated. No doubt I had Berg to thank for that. Reaching out to anybody was going to require me to open a new email account, but I was too impatient for news.

I ran a search of my name again, and this time, I had a chance to peruse the headlines.

Forge Disappearance: Rosie's Guardian Says Girl Is Perfectly Safe, Healing

"Missing" Forge Student Spotted Vacationing in Maui

Where's Rosie? Noncustodial Parents Search for Missing Forge Girl

The Rosie Hoax: The Scheme That Maxed the Ratings

10 Top-Rated Psychiatric Facilities for Teen Celebs

Did Linus Kill Rosie?

Troubled, Creative Teens Crave Attention: A Profile of Rosie Sinclair

Raking It In: "Missing" Forge Girl More Valuable Unseen than Seen

The speculation was rabid. Fascinated, I cobbled together the public story of what had happened to me. The last official footage of me on *The Forge Show* pegged me resting in my sleep shell like all the other girls at six o'clock on the evening of October 29, 2066. By the next day, I was off the show, and Dean Berg announced that I had violated the rules of my freshly signed contract by getting out of my sleep shell during the night. As my new legal guardian, he removed me from the school and admitted me to a private psychiatric hospital for observation and treatment. Case closed.

Except not.

I was gratified to see that tons of people did not believe the dean. The ratings for *The Forge Show* went wild, and reporters flocked to the school. My parents objected violently to my removal. They demanded to know where I was and insisted that Dean Berg release me to them. He declined politely, firmly, and publicly. Within hours, my parents were repped by a pro bono lawyer who filed a lawsuit against Berg and the school. The police interviewed Dean Berg and investigated the grounds. When they confirmed that no crime had been committed, it galled me to think that Berg had gotten away both with stealing me and with his dream mining.

Fans of *The Forge Show* deluged social media with questions and speculation about where I'd gone. A site collected info on sightings and contributions to fund the search for me. Irate donors petitioned for the dean to be fired.

Dean Berg countered with a clip of me on the deck of some mountain cabin, cradling a cup of cocoa and conversing calmly with him. He accused my parents of medical neglect, saying that I had manifested psychiatric symptoms before attending Forge. He claimed that my parents had exacerbated my mental illness with poor nutrition, lack of oversight, and a violent, unstable home life. He said they concealed my troubled school record and heedlessly, knowingly pushed me into the spotlight when they knew the pressure could harm me. He insinuated that my sister, Dubbs, would be better off in foster care.

My parents sued him for libel.

"What Rosie needs most at this time is privacy," Berg said, when cornered by a reporter. "Putting her on a show with a million cameras was arguably the worst thing we could have done to this fragile, brilliant girl. I deeply regret we didn't realize sooner how harmful it was for her, but she's now getting the care she needs. I'm sure you'll all be hearing from her soon. She appreciates your concern. The board is reviewing its health screening process for future students."

I bet it was.

I examined the footage of me on the cabin deck, trying to see how it could have been faked. Berg did, after all, know a thing or two about cameras and CGI, but he also knew that experts could tell when something was rigged. Everything in the clip looked authentic: the lighting, the shadows, even the moving shadow of a plane that passed over the pines in the background. The girl in the clip was dressed in a parka and sunglasses. She didn't move much, but she was unmistakably me, down to the gap in my teeth.

It was a good sign, and I was relieved. At least the original me was alive somewhere, or had been as of the date of this video. Best case scenario, he'd actually moved me to some psychiatric facility like he said. I would hate that, but at least I could be conscious and reason with people there. On the other hand, Berg might still have my body locked up in some vault. He could have hauled me out for show while he filmed that clip and dumped me right back to sleep afterward.

I wouldn't put it past Mr. Evil Incarnate.

What had he done to Linus? I tilted the phone nearer, held my breath, and typed in a search for Linus Pitts.

Top 10 Hottest Guys on *Forge*

The Bare Facts: Linus Pitts Uncensored

Did Linus Kill Rosie?

Found Missing Taps Linus Pitts as New Host

Forge Dishwasher Reunites with Aunt

Forge Staffer Linus Pitts Hosts New Docu-Show

Police Question Forge Staffers, Teachers Re Missing Girl

He was alive. Relief and happiness whooshed through me, and I smiled. I wasn't surprised that Linus's hotness was making headlines. I had picked up on that as soon as I'd met him. Others had become interested in Linus since the half-naked, black-and-white photos of him at age thirteen had come to light. But his looks were only a fraction of what drew me to him, and my smile dimmed. What I didn't understand was how Linus could get from the vault in the basement of the dean's tower to hosting a TV show.

I clicked on an ad of him walking through a paint-chipped playground. "Missing children live among us every day," Linus said. "I know. I was one of them." He moved past the chain of a deserted swing set, and the camera closed in on his face. His dark hair, straight brows, and intense eyes were achingly familiar. "I was orphaned at thirteen," he continued. "When I began working in the kitchen at *The Forge Show*, I had no idea that my Aunt Trudi in Wales was trying to find me." In the next shot, he set his arm around a short, dour-faced old woman who stared distrustfully at the camera. Her shoulders sloped in a gray, formless cardigan, and she bore only the faintest resemblance to Linus. "We're reunited now, thanks to state-of-the-art technology and a new, international clearing-house for missing and exploited children. Now, with a simple phone app, anyone can help with the search. At the playground, in the grocery store, anywhere you go, you can help anxious parents find their missing children. And kids find their folks. Click a picture, and the app will automatically scan for a match and alert local police. We're making a difference and reuniting families. Watch *Found Missing* to learn more about our most vulnerable kids and what you can do to help."

I blinked at the screen. Reuniting families was a beautiful idea, but Linus was asking people to spy on each other. He must realize that. Who would control all that data on the kids? I didn't trust it, and this slick version of Linus made me uneasy.

A soft noise from the hallway made me look over expectantly. I waited for someone to come in my doorway and tell me I ought to be sleeping, but no one entered.

I couldn't stop browsing.

It was easy to find clips of Linus and me together on *The Forge Show*. He'd stepped on stage to be with me often enough. The clips lured me irresistibly, but it was strange, so strange to see a scene reframed by multiple camera angles. They doubled a kind of postcard quality on top of my own memories.

One popular clip showed the time Linus and I ate ice cream together on a bench in the quad while a dozen other students performed spontaneously in the background. I glowed with a teasing happiness, which was impressive considering that my mind had been racing with things I had to hide. Linus ducked his head and looked at me sideways. The shaded light caught in his honey-brown eyes. He relaxed into his shoulders, and when he reached to touch my leg above the knee, I felt the tingle again vicariously.

I set a finger to the screen, pausing it and cropping close on Linus. I'd had no idea back then how bad things were going to get at Forge. My quiet, dim bedroom at Chimera felt a light-year away from that ice cream afternoon. Wistful, I studied the way his dark hair touched his eyebrows, and the color where his red bib apron lay against his neck. This was the Linus I cared for, not the cool guy who hosted *Found Missing*.

My baby gave me a couple nudges, the little insomniac. I closed my eyes a moment, uncertain, and then I set up a new email account for myself. I located an email contact for Linus through his new show. Possibly it would be screened by staff, but I had to try.

Dear Linus,
I've missed you.

Wrong. Way too honest. The last time I'd actually talked to Linus, we'd broken up. If I had to explain that I knew he'd come looking for me on my last night at Forge, it would all get tangled. I deleted and tried again.

Hey, Linus. This is Rosie. I'm in some hospital in Iceland and I've been

I stopped again. "... in a coma" was what I'd been about to say. But Althea had been in the coma, not me. Today was March 1, more than four months since my last day at Forge. I couldn't exactly say that during that time I'd been sleeping and, what, growing in a petri dish?

Hi, Linus. This is Rosie. Sorry I haven't written sooner, but I'm in a hospital. I've had some problems, needless

to say. Please write me back. I need to talk to you. I miss
you.
Rosie Sinclair

I read it over, deleted the *I miss you*, and read it once more.
My heart gave out three heavy, doubting pulses, and then I hit
SEND.

Now I had to wait. Waiting was the worst. Twenty seconds of it killed me.

Guiltily, I realized I probably should have tried to email my
mother before Linus. I looked up her work email and began
typing.

Dear Ma,

I couldn't go on.

Loss, longing, and anger pulled my fingers from the phone.
Ma stood at the bathroom mirror as she tried with her pinky
to get the last dab of color out of a used-up lipstick. Another
time she leaned over Dubbs at the kitchen sink, dribbling her
hair with a lemon rinse. Still later she passed me an ice pack for
my sore face, and a bowl with the last smears of cookie batter.
I longed to hide in her hug. I also wanted to punish her. She'd
hurt me unforgivably in our last phone call, when she agreed
to the dean's ridiculous contract for guardianship. No pro bono
lawsuit could cancel the hurt I felt.

The phone automatically dimmed from disuse.

Then again, I wasn't a child. I'd signed that contract, too, for reasons of my own. Slowly I deleted my email draft. I couldn't contact Ma yet. I felt too much. Better to wait until I could call and actually talk to her.

A faint noise drew my attention to the doorway again, and I was sure that someone was just beyond my view.

"Hello?" I said. "Who's there?"

Puzzled, I kept watching. A nurse checking on me would simply come in. I hadn't imagined the sound, but the silence lingered and no one answered.

I did not believe in ghosts, but they reminded me of my ghost project at Forge, and my cameras, and then Burnham. A mix of guilt and confusion surrounded my memories of him. The night was growing late and I was tired, but I typed in Burnham's name for one last search.

Burnham Fister, Son of Pharmaceutical Moguls, Returns Home to Atlanta

Fisters Thank Doctors, Nurses; Donate New Wing to Sterling Memorial

Top 10 Hottest Guys on *Forge*

Forge Concert for Burnham Raises $30K

Fisters on Sinclair Disappearance: No Comment

Forge Fans Ship Rosie and Burnham

What? Me and Burnham? "I don't know about that," I muttered. Sure I had figured out that Burnham more than liked me, and he certainly was attractive in his own way. But I'd tried to be clear about how I was seeing Linus. I focused on the news that Burnham was better and was grateful for that. Tomorrow I would send him an email through his parents and hope it reached him.

My baby rolled again, and I touched a hand to my belly where a little lump was jabbing out. "You're okay in there," I said, and rolled to my other side, facing away from the door. The baby shifted again to a more comfortable position.

I was getting sleepy, but it was so hard to stop browsing. I needed to feel connected to my old friends and my old life, but nothing was satisfying me yet. Restless, I searched until I found *The Forge Show* streaming. Back in Kansas, the time was early evening, which meant the show was running footage from that morning, twelve hours earlier, on the repeat cycle.

The bare, winter trees around the quad had a light coating of fresh snow, and the grass was covered in white. I pulled up Janice's feed. She'd changed her hair to a silky red color, and her pixie cut had grown out. Down in our old classroom under the library, she was constructing a tiny stage set out of foam core while the noise of a Ping-Pong match bounced in the background. On a hunch, I pulled up Paige's and Henrik's feeds, too, and they were the ones playing Ping-Pong.

Nostalgic, I watched them having fun. My old friends, engrossed in their regular lives, were continuing on as if I'd never existed and no danger of dream mining had ever touched them. I didn't exactly begrudge them their normal lives, but they brought home how much I'd missed. My life could have been golden, like theirs. I didn't see why I was the only one who had been ruined by the dream mining, while their lives sped blithely along, like a train on a parallel track while I was stuck in a pit.

Finally, deliberately, I set the phone away from me.

I lifted a hand in the darkness and pivoted my wrist so my fingers made a silhouette before the window. My hand. I didn't choose to be Althea. The truth finally came to me: it was loneliness, not curiosity, that kept me awake tonight. I trailed my hand softly along my eyebrow, then over my cheekbone, and paused to learn the feel of the bridge of my nose.

When I closed my eyes and went quiet inside, I was still here. If I could dig gently past the old, familiar ache of longing, I found that the reaches and dips of my thinking still felt right. The deepest core of me was still Rosie, and I could hold on to that. The night expanded indefinitely, and home was far away, but I softly filled up with my own blue light.

7

— ROSIE —

CHERRY LIP GLOSS

THE NEXT TIME, Ian brings me cherry lip gloss.

"Do you want me to put it on for you?" he asks.

I'm filled with rage. This stupid, meaningless token is nothing but a tease from the real life I'm missing. I can barely force myself to smile.

"I can do it myself," I say. "Do you have a mirror?"

"I forgot." And then, "Is something wrong?"

I bring my voice light. "No, not at all," I say.

I unscrew the plastic lid and press my pinkie into the waxy color. I'm like his doll now, and he likes to watch my tricks, so I don't hurry. I dab the balm on my dry lower lip first, then my upper. I press my lips together to feel the slight smear, and the taste of cherry pops along my tongue.

He shakes the bangs out of his eyes and slides a hand along the rim of my sleep shell. I can see his nubby fingernails.

"You look nice like this," he says. "It's a good color on you. You didn't smudge at all."

"Thanks."

He presses against my sleep shell. "Say my name," he says.

"Thanks, Ian John Cowles."

He nods. He likes that. He's gross.

"You seem different today," I say. "More confident."

"Really? Funny you should say that. My grandmother said the same thing. She said I'm not mumbling as much. I think you're good for me."

"Maybe because you're good for me," I say. No brainer there. "Are you going to clean my port?"

"Lindsay did earlier. We can't talk long today," he says.

"Why not?"

"Dr. Ash will be here tonight. We're supposed to clean all the dreamers before she comes."

"Won't she see my lip balm?" I ask.

"She won't mind," he says. "She lets me put a little color on the females. Nothing too much. It was my own idea."

I'm surprised that he puts makeup on dreamers who are all but dead. I get the sense that he thinks he's doing us a favor.

"That's nice," I say. "How many dreamers are here right now?"

He turns, and I watch him scan the room, counting. "Eighteen."

"How often does Dr. Ash come?" I ask.

"Every week or so. It's hard for her to get away from Forge during the semester. She has to make the round trip in twelve hours."

"She still works there?" I ask, surprised.

He frowns. "Sure. Why wouldn't she?"

"Does Dean Berg still work at Forge, too?" I ask.

"Of course," Ian says. "That's his job. He's here more in the summer when school's not in session."

This boggles my mind. I guess I've assumed there was an investigation into Berg after I disappeared. Then again, if someone found enough dream mining evidence to arrest him, they would have come to rescue me, too, and I'm still here.

"Who actually mines me, then?" I ask.

"It's Dr. Ash, with Mr. Berg consulting long distance," Ian says. "Nobody else is allowed to touch your mind. You've got warnings all over your chart."

A trickling noise comes from one of the lines above, and Ian glances up. Then he looks over his shoulder.

"You'd better give me the lip gloss," he says. "I'll keep it for you."

I hand it over, but slowly. "The taste makes me hungry."

"You shouldn't be hungry," he says. "Your weight's stabilizing. That's a good sign."

"It is? I feel pretty skinny." My wrists are bonier than before, and I'm definitely weaker. When I shift to look at my knees, they're narrow wedges under the blanket.

"No, you're good," he says. "Dreamers usually lose a lot at

the beginning. We expect that, but then they stabilize when they hit the right nutrient balance." He taps my IV. "One of the reasons I was worried about you before was the way you kept losing all along. I didn't want to tell you until I was sure, but for the last two weeks, you've been steady at one-oh-eight. That's really good."

No wonder my hand looks so frail. I haven't been this thin since I was twelve. I smooth a hand over my hip bone. "That's crazy skinny," I say.

"No, for a dreamer of your height, it's good," he says. "It means you're settling in like." He smiles modestly. "You haven't had a breakdown this time, either, did you notice? That's very good."

A distant clank sounds from the hallway, and Ian glances over his shoulder again.

"Sorry," he says, and reaches for my IV. "I have to put you out. Lindsay's back from her break. This was kind of risky today, but I didn't want you to miss the lip balm."

My heart beats quickly. For an instant, I consider calling out to the other attendant to see if she would help me more than Ian, but already the meds are trickling into my veins, bringing the cool heaviness.

"When can I see you again, Ian John Cowles?" I ask.

"You'll just have to wait and see, Miss Sinclair Fifteen," he says.

It's downright saucy, for him. He settles my hands at my sides and smoothes my nightie and blanket. He doesn't kiss me, but he strokes a finger gently down my cheek.

"Let it be soon," I say.

He closes my lid, and I see his palm pressed on the glass for a moment before he steps away.

I'm dying here. I feel like I'd make more progress begging a slug to throw me a life preserver, but I need Ian's help to get free. I bite my lower lip, tasting cherry misery, and I can barely stop from crying in despair.

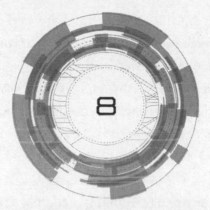

— THEA —

FACE LESSONS

"HOW ARE WE FEELING?" Dr. Fallon asked. "How's your voice?"

She stopped by just as I was finishing breakfast. A mirror in her hand slashed an angle of light around the room before she placed it on my desk. Then she stepped to the window to adjust the shades, reaching in her white coat to expand my view of the trees and mountain. Another cloudy morning beckoned, and over the past week, the snow on the nearby pine had evaporated to a thinner layer.

"About the same," I said. But my voice came out clearly, without the painful crackle I was used to. I touched my throat, amazed. "It doesn't hurt."

"And you sound very nice," she said. "Your parents will be thrilled. Say your Pledge of Allegiance for me, slowly."

I didn't care much for Dr. Fallon, but it did me no good to be openly belligerent. I worked my mouth around the familiar words of the Pledge, surprised by the breathy, melodious sound of the new voice between my ears. I could hear the Texas in my vowels, and a cultured mellowness that struck me as classy. I liked it. It wasn't me, of course, and Althea's voice was higher than my old one, but it was nice. At last I could have an actual conversation.

I glanced at my phone, thinking I could call Ma, but then I realized she wouldn't recognize my new voice. This was going to complicate things.

"Where are my parents?" I asked.

"I met them on my way up and suggested they step outside for a walk," she said. "You'll be out there soon yourself at this rate. How do you like your P.T.?"

"It hurts."

"Because it's working," she said, smiling. "Marcus is very good at what he does. Sit up a bit more."

Even with the heaviness of my belly, it was getting easier to sit up. My muscles had a new, restless eagerness, and my appetite had improved, too.

"What's the mirror for?" I asked.

"I want to get your face going. In a way, it's another form of P.T."

"My face feels fine," I said.

"It's about to feel better."

Dr. Fallon cleared my breakfast tray off my desk and propped up the mirror. The sunkenness around my eyes was noticeably less, and my acne was clearing up, leaving my tan skin smoother. My hair fell in dark, limp strands around my face, clean but dull. My face now belonged more to an acquaintance than a stranger, and I turned to see the little, familiar notch in the top of my ear.

Dr. Fallon pulled over a chair as she spoke. "The truth is, Althea, your features hardly move. They're out of practice. We'll have to teach your facial muscles how to express your feelings again, and once we do, you'll appreciate the way it feels. When your cheeks and eyes feel a smile, for instance, they'll codify backward to your emotions, and you'll feel happier. To start, close your eyes. Now try a natural smile."

I did as she said, curious.

"Is that completely comfortable and natural?" she asked.

"Yes."

I heard a camera click.

"Good. Now open your eyes," the doctor said.

I did. My reflection was basically deadpan, with only the slightest quirk to my lips. By concerted effort, I widened my lips more and achieved a freakish duck face.

"That's frightening," I said.

She laughed. Then she guided me through a series of uncomfortable grimaces. Inside, they felt extreme, but on the mirror, they hardly showed at all. She told me to feel the pull around my ears. I used my fingers to prod my new features—eyebrows, nose, and cheeks. I broke out in a sweat.

"It's like trying to shape a mask," I said and shook my head. "I don't look anything like I did before." As spoke, I realized I meant the way Althea had looked before, in her photos.

"Nobody really looks like they do in the mirror, or in pictures, for that matter," Dr. Fallon said. "We think we know our faces because we put on our makeup in front of a mirror, but scrutinizing each pore doesn't show us how we really look. A mirror never captures the way we laugh unselfconsciously with our friends."

"Film comes closer," I said.

She regarded me curiously. "You have point. The truth is, you're a naturally beautiful girl, but without your normal animation, it won't show."

"I don't care about being beautiful," I said.

"Then you're very unusual," she said. "Most women appear to be ruled by their mirrors. As your doctor, I want you to have every advantage, including your natural expressions. I'll have Marcus add a facial component to your P.T. sessions." She smiled. "You've made tremendous strides these past ten days. You're breaking all our records for recovery."

I lowered the mirror. "That sounds like something you say to all your patients."

Dr. Fallon leaned back. "In your case, it happens to be true, but it also brings me to another point I wish to discuss with you."

"What?"

She slid her manicured hand along the edge of the table. "Your rapid recovery itself is some cause for concern. I don't mean to alarm you. All the MRIs we've been taking are very reassuring. But the seeding operation is a very delicate procedure, and I need you to let me know if you experience any headaches or vision problems."

"Why?" I asked. "What could happen?"

"Sometimes the host brain decides to team up against the new cells and kill them off," she said. "Other times the new cells keep expanding, like tumors. They don't so much kill off the old brain as crowd it, and then they starve off the blood supply. Either way, we need to step in quickly."

"What's that feel like, that crowding or whatever?"

"Headaches, at first," the doctor said. "Double vision that can progress to blindness. If patients lose their speech again, then the overall prognosis is very poor. But please don't worry. So far, we have no indication of anything like that happening to you. I just want you to be on the alert for any symptoms and be sure to tell us promptly."

I hardly knew what to say. She had me pretty scared. "What would you do then?"

"It involves some micro surgery. Some tweaking," she said. "That's why we can't let you go home just yet. We have to watch how everything knits together."

"Do my parents know about this?" I asked.

"I've explained it to them," she said. "We don't want any surprises here, and that's why I want you informed, too. You're your most important advocate."

I studied Dr. Fallon with her perfect pale face and red lipstick. She never had a hair out of place, and it seemed like nothing ever ruffled her, but she might have trained her face to conceal her feelings. I somehow doubted my facial P.T. would include such advanced techniques.

"You said a host brain could fight back, but I thought Althea was brain dead when she came here in a coma," I said.

The doctor regarded me with new attention and tapped a finger on the desk. "Althea didn't have any consciousness in the traditional sense, but she wasn't strictly brain dead. She could still breathe. It's an important distinction."

"But she hadn't recovered for months. I don't get how her brain could have anything left to fight me off now," I said.

The doctor's finger went still. "You're calling Althea 'she,' " Dr. Fallon said slowly. "Do you see yourself and Althea as two separate entities?"

My heart chugged with alarm, and I tried to recall if she'd tricked me into talking about Althea in the third person. "No," I lied. "I just want to know how likely it is that my old cells will fight off my new ones, like you said."

"Small," she said. "The chances are small."

"How small? One percent?"

"Maybe five percent," she said. "I'd give it five to ten percent."

Ten percent sounded big to me. This was not good. "When will I know I'm out of danger?"

"The more days that pass without symptoms, the better," she said. "Listen, I'm sorry. I can see I've troubled you. Let me remind you that you are a very special case. One of a kind. You've already come so much farther than we had any reason to expect."

"What makes me so special?" I asked.

"It's a combination of factors. Your youth, your stability after your injury, your brain's innate elasticity. Your baby matters, too, of course," she said.

I had momentarily forgotten about the baby. "I don't see why," I said. "You have other patients here who aren't pregnant."

"True," she said. "But their brain injuries weren't as severe as yours, either. Your pregnancy was vital to your case. It's a key reason why I took you on. We often think of fetuses as helpless little beings, nurtured in their mothers' wombs, but pregnancy is a complex symbiosis, a give and take," she said. "The hormones and nutrients that have helped your fetus develop have been circulating in your system, too."

"Are you suggesting my baby kept me alive?"

"It was certainly a factor in why we're both sitting here today." She clicked the end of her pen. "Althea, your parents wouldn't have brought you here if they didn't trust me. I wish you could, too."

I eyed her suspiciously. "You've just told me I have a ten percent chance of being attacked by my own brain."

"Only if you don't report any early symptoms," she said. "That's why we need to keep you here a little longer. Will you tell me if you have any sign of a headache, no matter how small?"

I didn't trust her, but my only choice was to play along. "Yes," I said.

A sound at the door made me glance over. Madeline,

dressed in bright blue, gave the door a light tap. Her staticky hair was fluffier than usual, as if it had been ruffled by the wind. She reminded me of a dandelion gone to seed.

"I don't want to intrude," she said, looking at me curiously.

"You're not. We're just finishing up," Dr. Fallon said, reaching for the mirror once more. "I want you to close your eyes again," she said to me. "Think of something happy. Someone who makes you laugh."

Laughing was a gift I'd had far too little of lately. I cast my memory back a couple of years, to Dubbs. We sat in the shadow of our boxcar, drawing in the smooth, cool dirt with sticks. I was teaching her to read by writing words like "poop" and "fart." She was careful sounding out the letters, concentrating and serious, but the instant she grasped a new word, she'd shriek and collapse laughing. I'd laugh, too. I felt so powerful. So proud.

"Hold that," the doctor said. She clicked another photo. "Now open your eyes."

In the mirror, Althea was smiling at me. It wasn't a big smile, but it was a genuine one, and her eyebrows arched up in delicate surprise.

Madeline sighed from the doorway and shook her head. "There she is," she said.

"I'll leave you the mirror," the doctor said to me. "Remember what I said. Communication is important. Use that new voice of yours."

"Okay," I said.

Madeline looked at me uncertainly. "Your voice. I wasn't sure. Is it better?"

"Yep," I said. I pondered what to say next. "What's for lunch?"

She pressed her lips together in a tight, happy grin. Then she nodded and let out a laugh. "I think it's chicken. Oh, won't your dad be thrilled?"

Diego might be thrilled, but he still wasn't my dad. Having a voice gave me new ways I'd have to lie.

9

— THEA —
THE RETURN OF CYRANO

LATER THAT DAY, a technician rolled in an ultrasound machine to check up on the baby. The baby's heartbeat came loud over the speaker, chugging insistently like the wash cycle on the McLellens' washing machine. My own heart lurched in response, and I peered over my shoulder at the screen while the technician tapped measurements into her keyboard with one hand.

Afterward, my midwife, Freyja, sat down with me for a long, cozy talk. While I was in a daze, holding a little black-and-white photo of the baby, she talked about vitamins and diet, Kegel exercises, and the importance of regaining my strength as soon as possible, for the baby's sake.

"This is real, isn't it?" I said.

Freyja smiled and pressed her warm hand to mine. "Yes, it is. You're due in seven weeks, Althea. April twenty-fourth, plus or minus two weeks. That's in no time. We need to keep you and the baby healthy until then, and after. Dr. Fallon's concerned about how the childbirth might impact your blood pressure and stress your brain. You're high risk. It will probably be safest for you if we schedule a C-section when we get closer to the time."

That sounded scary, too. I ran a hand over my abdomen. Freyja had kind eyes and big, steady hands. With her fresh-scrubbed complexion, funky, super-short blond hair, and blue-rimmed glasses, she seemed a little out of place in the antiseptic Chimera Centre. It turned out she'd been hired to come to the island just for me.

"I wish you could come to the U.S. with us," I said. "I don't want to still be here in seven weeks."

She smiled. "Your parents already offered me a fortune to come with you," she said. "I'm thinking about it, but my family's in Reykjavik, and I'm not licensed to practice in the States. You'd need a local midwife or doctor to oversee your case."

"My parents could arrange that."

She smiled. "I'm aware."

When I didn't smile back, she gave my shoulder a light squeeze.

"What's going on with you?" she asked.

At her kindness, I blinked back sudden tears. "I don't know what I'm doing," I said. "How am I going to be a mom?"

"Take a deep breath," Freyja said. "You're just going to live it. You're going to keep it real, day by day. Your baby's fine right now, and so are you, right? That's enough, right?"

I nodded. I felt miserable.

Freyja smiled gently and came around to give me a hug. "You're so young," she said. "Have you talked to the dad yet?"

"No."

"Maybe that'll help, *elskan*," she said.

I doubted it would. I didn't know him from a doorknob.

"Have you thought about names?" she asked. "Maybe a nice Icelandic name?"

She made me laugh and gulp at the same time.

Later, when I mentioned this to Diego and Madeline, they had plenty of name suggestions, especially family names, and Madeline happily jotted down lists for a boy or a girl. Since they had declined to know the gender of the baby, preferring to speculate, I decided not to find out, either. They seemed delighted to talk about the baby as long as nobody brought up Tom. It was also increasingly difficult not to blurt out to them that I wasn't their daughter, especially when Diego would give me a quiet, curious look.

When Madeline eventually led a prayer and they said good night, I was worn out. She straightened the rosary next to the flowers.

"Are we Catholic?" I asked.

Madeline touched her thumb to my forehead, drawing a cross for a blessing. "Yes, of course," she said. "Now rest easy."

My need to talk to my own mother was stronger than ever. Something about hearing the baby's heartbeat and seeing the ghostly figure on the ultrasound had thrust my pregnancy into reality, and turning into a mother made me miss my own. So much had happened to me, and she didn't know any of it.

After the nurse turned my lights low, I huddled down in my bed and calculated seven hours earlier to Arizona. It was Saturday around two in the afternoon there. Ma might be home. I tapped my home number into my phone. I knew Ma wouldn't recognize my new voice, but I'd find a way, somehow, to explain who I was. Ma would believe me. I stared absently out to the hallway as I waited through the rings.

"Hello? Who's calling?" Ma said.

Her mumbly, sleepy voice made my heart soar. I could picture her taking a nap on the couch.

"Ma? It's me. Rosie." My voice choked off. "Did I wake you?"

"Rosie?" she said slowly. "You sound different."

"It's really me! My voice has changed, but it's me," I said. I sat up, keeping the phone close to my ear, and I tried to pitch my voice lower, like mine had been. "How are you? Are you good? How's Dubbs? Does she miss me?"

A rolling noise came from her end of the line. "Tell me where you are," she said. "Are you all right? Is Berg hurting you?"

"I'm okay. I'm in Iceland at a clinic," I said. "Berg isn't even here."

Her voice became doubtful. "Iceland?"

"It's complicated to explain," I said. Suddenly I didn't care at all anymore that she'd messed up my guardianship. I missed her so badly it hurt to breathe. "I want to come home."

"What happened to your voice?" Then, through a muffling, "She says it's Rosie."

"I had a surgery," I said. I struggled to think how to begin. "A lot about me is different."

A bumbling noise came from the other end, and then my stepfather's voice came on. "Who is this?"

"Larry, it's me," I said. "It's me, Rosie. Let me talk to Ma again."

"You think I don't know Rosie's voice? You've got some nerve, harassing us in our own home. We can trace your call. We'll prosecute the crap out of you."

"It's *me*," I said loudly. "You punched me in the face when I told you to get a job. Remember? Last spring? You told Ma to pawn your gun that same night, remember? So we'd have enough to eat? Dubbs was starving."

His end went silent. I could picture him frowning by the couch. A faint pounding noise came, like someone was working outside. I heard Ma's voice in the background, and then she abruptly stopped talking, as if he'd raised a hand to warn her into silence.

"You never got that out of Rosie," he said.

"We own an orange plaid couch," I continued, searching my way. "You read a lot of mysteries, and the antlers over the TV came from your brother's place after he died."

"Who is this?" Larry asked.

I clenched the phone anxiously. "I *said*. I'm Rosie. Your daughter. Let me talk to Ma again, please."

"You mean 'stepdaughter,'" he said with a bark of a laugh. "You blew it, kid. Rosie always threw that 'step' in my face. Now leave us alone." The line cut off with a slam.

"Wait!" I said, but it was too late. The dead connection shocked my ear. Despair clamped my heart. I had so much proof!

80

I'd thought for sure they would know me, despite my voice. Ma did. Larry was the problem. He was always the problem. I immediately called back again, but they didn't pick up. Our landline had no voicemail, no answering machine. I was blocked.

I sat in my shadowy hospital room, stunned. A machine made a soft hissing noise behind me, and I stared bleakly at the bumps of my feet under the blanket. What if no one from my old life ever believed who I was inside? The possibility horrified me. How could I prove I was me without my own voice and body? My parents wouldn't even let me *try*.

I lay down again and rolled over heavily. I couldn't bear another night of being lonely, with no one to talk to. I was afraid I'd vanish if I didn't find someone who knew me as Rosie.

I chewed the inside of my cheek for a minute, remembering how cool it had been talking to Linus at night when I was at Forge. I'd loved trying to guess his expression from the sound of his voice. The rest of the school would be asleep, but I had my walkie-ham in my sleep shell with me, like a lifeline to the outside world. What I wouldn't give to have that now. I still hadn't heard from Linus despite repeated tries over the last few days. I hadn't heard from Burnham, either. In fact, the only person who had tried to contact me was Tom, Althea's old boyfriend, but I had no idea what to say to him. His messages were piled up on my new phone, unlistened to, like too many valentines from the wrong guy.

What I really needed was Linus's phone number so I could text him directly. I did a search for Otis, Linus's friend and landlord, the old guy who worked the camera in the lookout tower at Forge, and found he had a listed number. I tapped it in and listened to the rings.

"Hello?" a man answered.

My heart jumped, and I sat up straight in my bed again.

"Is Linus there?" I asked.

"Thomas Kent runs like a girl," the man said.

The non sequitur threw me. Then I remembered Parker, Otis's partner, the guy with Alzheimer's. I had seen him one night when he was walking in the quad at Forge. He'd paused in front of the dean's tower to pee on the steps, and Linus had run over to take care of him.

"Is this Parker?" I asked.

"Parker here," he said. "I'm busy. I'm on the telephone."

"Hi, Parker. This is Althea. I'm a friend of Rosie Sinclair's. Is Linus there?"

"*I'm* on the phone," Parker said.

A man spoke in the background, and when a new voice came on, I recognized Otis. "Hello? Can I help you?"

I introduced myself as Althea once again. "I'm trying to reach Linus."

"You want the hotline for *Found Missing*," Otis said. "Try this." He rattled off a number. "Good luck to you."

"Wait!" I said. "Please don't hang up. Rosie's been trying to email Linus at *Found Missing*, but he doesn't answer her. She asked me to call him. Does he even see that email?"

"That's the one. They'll route you where you need to go."

"Otis, I really know Rosie. I know about Molly, your dog,

and the way Linus used to carry her up the lookout tower for you every day. Don't hang up on me. I really need a way to reach him."

His voice came slowly. "You've just watched the show."

I scanned my brain for anything I could have seen that was off camera. "You have a toilet behind a curtain up there in the lookout tower. And a begonia. You have a picture of you and Parker tacked to the beam with the hammock. You're never on screen yourself, but I know you like to wear a gray hat with a visor."

I held my breath, listening to the silence of his uncertainty.

"Okay, if you know Rosie, where is she now?" Otis asked. "What's her phone number?"

A distinct click came from his end, like another line picking up, and then a third voice said, "Hello? Who is this?"

It was Linus. My breath caught and my lungs squeezed tight. I didn't know how to speak to him now, when my voice wasn't my own.

"This is Linus Pitts," he said. "Who's calling?"

Miles vanished. His words were in my ear again, just like before, with his distinctive Welsh accent. I could picture his gaze deepening with a frown, and the suspicion hovering just behind his polite curiosity.

"I'm Althea," I said thickly. "A friend of Rosie's. She asked me to call you."

Distance hummed between us, and I heard him weighing whether to believe me.

"I'll take this one, Otis," Linus said.

"Your funeral," Otis said. A click sounded as he hung up, and the connection became slightly clearer.

"Is Rosie with you?" Linus asked.

"Yes," I said, nodding.

"Put her on."

"I can't. She has trouble with her voice. She asked me to talk to you for her."

A shifting came from his end of the line. "Okay, so here's the thing. We get a ton of calls here, and I keep telling the guys to let the machine take them, but Parker has this misguided sense of gallantry that makes him pick up the ruddy phone, and then he gets worked up, and Otis has to step in, and now you've worked up Otis, too, and I'm going to have to ask you to please leave us alone and go through the normal channels to reach the show. All clear now?"

"You paid Otis in blood for your rent," I said quickly. "You did it every six weeks."

I held my phone tightly, fearing that the next sound would be a disconnection.

"I told her that in confidence," he said finally.

"I know, and she's sorry she had to tell me, but she wants you to know she's really here, listening in."

"But she won't talk to me."

"Right. She can't. I'm talking for her. Ask me anything. I'll prove it."

"Okay," he said slowly. "What does Cyrano have to do with anything?"

My heart thumped, and I paused before answering again, as

84

if I were interpreting something from a companion in the room. "You and Rosie could talk for real at night on the walkie-hams, and touch each other during the day, but you could never do both at the same time. You said it made you think of the Cyrano de Bergerac story, but twisted, as if both guys were combined into one person." I gave a brief laugh. "Here I am talking for Rosie. It's sort of another Cyrano thing. Right Rosie?" I paused. "She's agreeing."

A moment later, his voice came again, more softly. "Is she writing answers for you? Is that it?"

I could go with that.

"Yes," I said.

"Then she should just email me."

"She tried. Many times. You didn't reply."

"Maybe because I get dozens of emails every day from people pretending to be her."

"But I can prove she's right here. I'm not pretending."

"Okay. Ask her why she broke up with me. Ask her that."

His question was ridiculously layered and complicated.

"I don't know why," I said softly. "She shouldn't have. She says she's sorry."

His next pause was longer.

"Who is this?" he asked.

For the first time, he sounded like he might believe me. A strangling loneliness lodged in my voice box. "I'm Althea. Rosie's friend."

"Althea who? Where's Rosie?"

"We're out of the country," I said.

"Both of you?" The doubt was back in his voice. "Tell me where and I'll come get you."

I turned toward the dark window. "You can't come for us."

"Then why did you call me? I can get anywhere. I have resources for the show," he said.

I felt a twinge of caution. "You'd come to shoot a segment for your show?" I asked.

"Althea," he said. "Why do you think I have the show? The point of it is to locate missing children. I've been trying to find Rosie since she disappeared in October."

He wanted to locate me for his show, not for us. The truth stung. "She's not interested in being featured on some show," I said. "She's had enough of that."

"Then what do you want? Why'd you call?"

"I just wanted—" I stopped. What *had* I thought? That we'd be friends again? I wasn't even in my own body. "Rosie thought you'd want to know she's alive."

"Of course I want to know that," he said. "But you haven't proven anything. You know some private facts about us, but she could have told them to you weeks ago. You could have forced them out of her."

I clutched my fingers into a fist. "I haven't forced anything out of her. I'm her friend," I said. "Look. I thought when you went down the pit to look for Rosie it meant that you still cared about her. You at least owe it to her to listen to me now."

"Down the pit. What are you talking about?"

"You know!" I said. "You went down the clock tower pit. You went looking for Rosie that last night at Forge."

86

"Put Rosie on," he said. "Put her on now. Rosie? Are you hearing this? If we're on speaker, say something."

I closed my eyes and kept the phone pressed tight against my ear. "She can't talk to you."

"Then listen closely, *Althea*," Linus said, turning the name into something ugly. "If Rosie's really there with you, which I seriously doubt, then let her know this. She has a lot of fans who care about her. They want to know if she's okay, and they want an explanation for where she's been all this time. If she's not okay, they want justice for her sake. That goes for me, too. If you're working for Sandy Berg and you've got her locked up somewhere, I swear we'll get you."

"I'm not working with Berg," I said. "That's ridiculous."

"And one other thing," he said. "If I find out you're using me or my voice to tease her or test her in any way, I'll come for you, personally. Get that?"

"That's just sick," I said. "You're starting to sound like Berg yourself."

"Then where are you? Tell me."

I stared, unseeing, at my dark window. This call had gone nothing like I'd expected. I pressed my fist under my chin. I was lonelier than ever.

"She's changed so much," I said. My voice squeaked closed again. It wasn't a proper answer to his question, but it was the best I had.

"We've all changed," Linus said, and his voice was hard. "Tell her that doesn't matter. Tell her I want to see her again. I want to cover her story for my show. Go on."

I pinched a fold of the blanket. "She heard you," I said.

"What does she say?" Linus asked.

I closed my eyes. "She says she won't be on your show."

"Then tell me why you really called."

I wished I had a good lie, but what came out was painfully true. "Rosie just wanted to hear your voice," I said.

The long distance spun for a moment, and when he spoke again, it was in a calm, quiet voice. "I am not doing this."

I didn't know how to answer. "Please, Linus."

"No. Not happening," he said, still too calm. "If Rosie ever wants to talk to me herself, directly, have her call me. Otherwise, leave me alone."

"But she needs you!" I said.

He gave a sharp laugh. "Did it occur to you how mean this would be? Making me believe you know her. Never mind. I'm hanging up now."

"Linus!"

But he was gone.

I'd done nothing to convince him. If anything, I'd gone backward. I slammed my phone against the table. I had to get out of this crazy place. I had to get back to some version of my own life because if I couldn't, if I couldn't—

The yawning possibility stopped my heart cold. I buried my head in my pillow and squeezed away all the light and sound, but the dread still followed me.

I would have to become Althea.

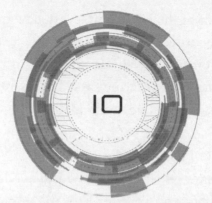

10

— ROSIE —

DESPERATE PEOPLE

AFTER THE LIP GLOSS, Ian brings me a stick of cinnamon bark—dry, brown, and fragrant.

The next time, he brings me a chocolate chip, just one. The silky, melting taste of the chocolate is so sweet and rich that I nearly swoon with pleasure. I look to his hand for more, but he tosses the remaining chocolate chips back in his own mouth and masticates. Bastard. Otherworldly ripples of light emanate around his face like a halo.

"I could only give you one," he says. "More than that might mess up your digestion. Like it?"

I'm salivating. "It's heaven."

Next he holds up my old video camera, the one my teacher from Doli High gave me, the one I used at the Forge School. I know the width of the wristband, every dial and scuff mark. My palm knows its cool weight even before he passes it over.

"Where'd you get this?" I ask.

"I summoned it for you," he says. "The battery's dead, but I thought you might like to hold it for a while. Happy birthday."

I startle. "But I missed my birthday."

"Yes," he says, extending the word into a hiss. "But I bought you three extra years of age. You're nineteen like me now, and I have another present for you. A surprise. I couldn't bring you to see my grandmother, so I brought my grandmother to see you. Let me help you sit up."

The ceiling drifts silently higher until the room is unnaturally tall. Through the door comes an old, bent woman with a cane. She teeters into a cone of light from a spotlight high above, so that her white veil gleams over her gray hair. Bizarrely, she's carrying a dusty wedding gown over one arm and a bouquet of dead flowers in her other hand.

"I thought you could borrow my wedding dress," she says.

A jolt of panic hits me. "This is wrong," I say, looking to Ian. "Is this a dream?" I try to smell him for his tobacco, but the air tastes empty.

"If it is a dream, that doesn't make it untrue," he says.

"I know what's real," I whisper.

"Do you? What about me?"

My heart leaps in terror.

Ian's face shimmers for a second and comes back into focus, nearer and harshly clear. "Desperate people invent desperate solutions. It's not my fault if they do," he says, in the voice of Dean Berg.

"No!" I scream. I bolt up, banging into the lid of my sleep shell.

I wipe madly at the gel on my eyelids and scramble frantically at the curved glass to push it open. I suck in a gulp of air and barely bite back another scream.

The room is dim. I'm alone and fully awake. Shivers of the nightmare fall away from me like black sand, seeping into the floor with a trickling, mocking sound. Rubbing more gel from my eyelids, I find pads and wires stuck to my temples. I rip them off and blink hard. I can't have imagined Ian. I can't have dreamed him all those other times. Our conversations have been too real, and he's brought me things that I know I've touched and smelled.

But he's not here now. I don't have my video camera. There's no granny with a veil.

I'm trembling beneath my gown. In the dark, windowless room, two dozen other sleep shells are parked around me with their lids glowing faintly. The open doorway lets in light from the hall. I check instinctively for cameras, but the upper corners of the ceiling are in shadow, and considering the times when Ian lingered to talk to me, we must have been unobserved. This is my first time fully awake with no one hovering, and I can't waste my chance.

With shaky fingers, I pull down the neckline of my gown to inspect the place where the IV goes into me. A piece of tape holds the IV line in place, and a needle goes directly into the skin over my left breast. The small, foreign lump that serves as a port is fixed under my skin. It feels like a mini jelly donut in there. With a pinch, I loosen the tape and take out the IV needle. A second line leads out of me from a spot several inches below my belly button, and I'm able to disconnect its coupling from the longer tube. I can only hope my plumbing is going to work normally. I swing my legs around and reach my toes down. The floor is cool and smooth underfoot. All I need is a little strength, a little balance, and I lurch across to the next sleep shell.

I brace myself on the lid.

Inside, a pale, blond girl lies with her eyelids covered in translucent gel. She's five or six. I stare, transfixed. I've seen her before, back in the vault under Forge. She had a teddy bear and a fresh wound on her forehead then. Now the wound is healed over. Gracie. That's what Berg called her. Her lips and skin have turned a chalky gray. She doesn't seem to be breathing, and then, just barely, her chest moves.

I jolt back as if she's accusing me of a crime. I can't take her with me. I can't! I tried to save her once before at Forge, and now I can barely save myself. I stagger to the tablet at the foot of her sleep shell to find her name: Huron 6. Like the Great Lake, and the six is likely her age. I'll try to remember. That's the best I can do. I have to get *out*!

My muscles have atrophied so badly that each step is a painful jolt, but I make the doorway. Far down the hall to my right, a door is marked EXIT, and a window shows a square of night. To my left, several open doorways are brightly lit. The nearest gives a glimpse of a metal operating table. Holding my breath, I listen for voices, but the hall yields only a vacant hum.

With one hand skimming along the wall for balance, I head toward the exit. I pass one closed door, and then another. The next door is open, revealing a large closet with a dozen wigs in tidy rows, and a large makeup kit. From a hook, an odd, skeletal frame of plastic hangs. It looks like the supports could be hooked behind a person's back and arms and neck to hold someone in a posed position, like a puppet. It could move a person, too. A layer of sweat breaks out over my entire body.

"What is this place?" I whisper.

A buzzer sounds behind me. I bolt into the closet and close the door. Flipping off the light, I crouch down and wait, my heart charging. The buzzing stops. Nobody comes. I practically taste the fusty smell of wigs in the dark beside me, and then I crack the door open to peer anxiously out. Still nobody comes.

I can't stay here. I have to take a chance.

I lurch back into the hallway and hurry the last few steps to the exit door, where I lean hard against the release bar. The door doesn't budge. I try again, using all my puny strength to push the heavy door open a crack, and a couple of snowflakes drift in.

I gape. They're so fragile and white, and in an instant they melt. I've seen snow in person only once before, and it seems magical now, as if this door opens into a completely new world. When another buzz startles me from behind, I slip out into the night and bolt for the nearest shadow.

Cold knifes through me. I'm backed against the building. A trace of cigarette smoke laces the black air. A single lamp illuminates a small parking lot edged by dark trees, and a thin layer of unshoveled snow rests inches before my feet. Slow, isolated snowflakes drop silently into the sole cone of light above the cars. Already I'm shivering in my thin gown. A narrow porch runs around the side of the building, and I scan frantically along it for the red glow of a cigarette. I know someone's out here. Ian probably, but I see no one.

Below, a smatter of distant lights hints at a valley with civilization, but there's nothing closer. I was expecting a bigger facility, a hospital maybe, but the cinderblock building has the grudging, municipal air of a dog pound after hours.

A sedan, a Jeep, and a pickup truck are parked a dozen yards away. I'm weighing my next move when approaching headlights crown over the ridge. I hurry barefoot down the cold steps, scramble over the snowy gravel, and hunch down behind the far side of the pickup.

Footsteps sound on the porch, and the scent of cigarette smoke grows stronger. The arriving car noses in by the steps, and the engine cuts dead. Then the car door opens with a rush of radio music that's quickly terminated.

"Look who's out smoking. What would your dad think?" says the driver.

I know his voice. He's another attendant.

"Where'd you go?" Ian says.

"None of your business, Gertrude."

"Don't call me that," Ian snaps. "You were gone more than two hours. What if something had happened here?"

"You'd have handled it." He sounds dismissive, despite his words.

I stay low, barely breathing, cupping a hand around my mouth in fear that my fog will lift up and catch the light.

"A man shouldn't be paid for a job he doesn't do," Ian says.

"I'll be sure to remember that, seeing as you're such a man yourself," says the other guy. "Did you get in some good time with your little girlfriend?"

"Have you been drinking?" Ian says.

"Give it a rest."

A jingling noise comes from the car. Then a door slams.

"You should at least take your keys," Ian said.

I grasp onto this information, hopeful that the guy chucked them in his car. The man's boots are loud on the steps.

"Doesn't it ever get to you, what we do here?" the man says.

"It's a good job. A man's job," Ian says. "That's what my dad says."

"Your dad's a regular genius. Where's he now? Miehana? Snaking for those California babes?"

"None of your business," Ian says. "I should report you for shirking."

The guy laughs. "Go ahead, you piece of weasel crap. Then

95

I'll report how you fraternize with the dreamers. How'd you like that?"

The door to the clinic swings open with a squeak. Next, it closes with a heavy click.

I hold motionless, listening, trying to learn if Ian has gone in, too, or if he's still on the porch. Silent snow drops into the cone of light. My teeth chatter once, so I open my mouth and jut my jaw out to stop the noise. The trees whisper with a breeze, and the wintry air skims my back through my gown. I lean forward an inch, and then another, scanning the porch where I heard Ian's voice.

I'm smelling cigarette smoke ever so faintly. I can't see any movement, though, and finally I can't wait a moment longer. Any second now, the man inside will discover my empty sleep shell. He'll ask Ian where I am. They'll start their search.

I touch my way around the truck, bracing myself for balance and wincing at the snowy gravel beneath my feet. A second more I pause, listening, and then I sprint to the car that has just arrived and yank on the handle. The interior light comes on as I jump inside and close the door. I scramble my hands along the dashboard, over the seat, and down by the pedals until finally I connect with the keys.

Shaking, I locate the biggest one and jab it in the ignition.

The door to the clinic bursts open, and a big man hurtles out to the porch. Ian charges out right behind him. I get one clear flash of Ian's stunned expression, his mouth the open O of a gasping fish.

"Hey!" the big guy says.

I turn the ignition with a roar and the headlights shine on. I slam the car into reverse and floor it backward in a wide arc.

"You can't take my car!" the man yells. He's running toward me.

I rip the gear into drive and aim right at the guy. He rushes for the car door, but I hit the accelerator hard, and he gets jolted into the blackness beside me. I jerk the wheel to steer onto the road, barely missing a post that appears out of nowhere. I jab my bare foot harder on the gas and hold myself up by the steering wheel so I can see over the dashboard.

Night trees flash past in a wild kaleidoscope of high beams and black. A void of eager emptiness opens on my left, signaling the edge of a cliff. Bumps jolt me wildly in my seat, but I don't slow for anything—not my seatbelt or ice or stop signs—until I make it out to the flatland and a straight, two-lane highway. Some bottle clinks on the floor, toasting my acceleration, and I roar the car as fast as it will go.

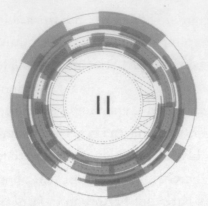

— ROSIE —

THE PICKUP

FREE! I'M FINALLY FREE.

The snow has picked up, and the flakes aim into my head-lights with mad surprise. My windshield wipers thwack away. I manage to pull my seat forward, but I have to sit tall to see be-cause the car was designed, apparently, for a giant. Plus, despite the blasting heat, I can't get warm, so my scrawny muscles are tight with shivering. I'd give anything for a coat. Or shoes.

I sniff and wipe my drippy nose with the back of my hand. I need everything: clothes, food, and a place to hide. I have to get as far away from the Onar Clinic as I can, but I also need to ditch this car, which is easy to track. Every mile feels like a risk either way.

That's why I fly like wild. My wheels catch a patch of black ice, and I swerve in a nasty spin that lands me backward in a full stop. Only then, with the heat ticking in the silence, do I realize how stupid I am. I didn't get out of the vault just to kill myself on the road. I'm not the best driver to begin with. Never got my license. From then on, I'm more cautious. I straighten out and drive for a couple hours through worsening weather. The road meets a clutch of small, dark buildings and a brace of streetlamps, all haloed with falling snow. I turn into the parking lot of an all-night diner and skid slow-mo into a spot. Exhaustion hits me as I turn off the engine.

The slats of the blinds are open in the diner, spilling striped rectangles of yellow light out onto the snow. It's like a Hopper painting, but grainy, and I squint to see inside. Behind the counter, a tall, thin man with a gray complexion is filling sugar shakers. Another man sits on a stool at the counter, methodically eating ham and eggs. The only other customers are two young black women in a booth. They're sharing French fries from the same dish, and the sight of one smearing a long fry in ketchup sets my mouth salivating.

Think, I tell myself. I can't, obviously, go into the diner in my hospital gown, but I can't stay here in this stolen car, either. I check around me once more for anything I might wear or use, but the only article of interest is a bag of weed in the glove compartment. I dump the weed on the floor and slip the bag over my foot. I wrap the bag at my ankle as best as I can, for one sad sock.

As soon as I climb out of the car, the cold swirls viciously around me and steals my breath. I run as fast as I can and try the doors of the Honda Fit, hoping to hide in the back, but they're all locked. I glance toward the diner where the French fry eaters are now rising out of their booth, and then I sprint to the pickup. These doors are locked, too. Crap!

I'm out of options.

In the bed of the truck, a couple of over-sized bags of cat food are collecting snow. The cold is unbelievable, and I instinctively huddle low, balancing on one foot. The diner door opens with a tinkling bell.

"Hang on. I forgot my purse," says one of the women.

"I'll get the car," says the other. "Man, it's cold. Isn't the snow pretty, though?"

At the same time, a Jeep turns into the lot. It pulls up in front of the car I stole and blocks it in. Not good. I try to see into the cab to identify the driver, but the angle is wrong.

The French fry eater crosses through the car's low beams, and before she can come any nearer, I climb into the back of the truck and huddle down. The night is stupidly, brutally cold, and I'm shivering on top of my shivering. How fast can I die in this cold? The truck's door opens audibly, then closes, and a second later, the engine starts.

Peeking over the edge, I see the driver from the Jeep climbing the steps, and as he enters the diner's light, he's clearly Ian, bundled up in a big white coat with fake fur around the hood. I could kill him for his coat alone. He holds the door for the second woman as she exits, and soon after, she gets in the pickup. I lurch onto the nearest bag of cat food as we head down the lip of the driveway, and then the truck turns onto the road.

The truck picks up speed, whipping my hair around me. I keep low and drag the bags of cat food into the corner behind the cab. As I climb onto one, its paper cover breaks open beneath me. The pellets are dry, and they give a bit under my weight. I can actually burrow into them somewhat, and I brace the other bag against me as a windbreak of sorts. It's hardly any shelter, and I'm shaking from cold, but I curl into a ball and put my head down against my knees. It occurs to me dimly that I should knock on the back window of the cab and try to get the attention of the women inside, but it's already too hard to uncurl.

For a time, the cold is unbearable, a pain beyond madness, but soon I slip into a dream. I'm huddled by a fireplace, with a soft white rug beneath me. As long as I don't move, the firelight flickers on my closed eyelids and warmth eases through my body. I smell hot chocolate, and Linus kneels down beside me. I know he's there, even if I don't open my eyes, simply from the feel of his nearness. He says, "Where've you been? I've been looking for you."

It's hard to speak, but I manage a whisper. "I'm freezing," I say.

"Yes. This was an idiotic mistake. But I've got you now."

I feel another layer of warmth as he covers me with a blanket, and I keep very still.

"Don't tell Dubbs," I say.

It's the wrong thing to say because he'll never see my sister. They aren't even acquainted. But he gives me the right answer anyway.

"I won't."

>>>>>>>>

101

Some time later, a new voice comes from far away.

"Portia, check this out."

I can't move or feel anything.

"Don't tell me she's dead," says another woman. "Where'd she come from?"

A touch on my back sends a crackling through my body, like I'm ice and streaks of white are breaking me into pieces.

"We have to get her to the hospital."

"I doubt she'd last that long," says the other. "Help me get her inside." She adds a curse.

I feel them rolling me, but I'm so clenched and cold, I can't do anything to help.

"Look how skinny she is."

"Just get the door. Watch her head."

I pass out again, and when I resurface next, it's to a painful prickling that burns all over my skin. I'm shivering wildly. They've put me in a bathtub to thaw like a Thanksgiving turkey. My lower tube has a new stopper in it. The port in my chest looks horribly foreign. I don't understand my skinny, wasted body. All I can do is stare at the faucet and the water valves, the old-fashioned, knobby kind that squeak when one of the women turns them. They're asking me questions, but whenever I try to unclench my jaw to answer, I chatter too much.

"It's all right," one of them says. "You're going to be okay. Some frostbite, but you'll survive."

I lift trembling fingers to push my hair out of my eyes and smell a trace of cat food. Perfect, I think, and go off in a weird, sniveling laugh. Eventually they dry me off, put me in clean sweatpants and a sweatshirt, and settle me on a couch under a pile of blankets. One of them wraps my wet hair in a towel, and the other brings me a brown mug of warm cocoa to sip. It takes forever for my shivering to stop and the pinpricks of pain to dull into patchy itchiness, and by then, I'm exhausted.

Hiding practically naked in the back of that freezing truck was probably the stupidest thing I've ever done. Even my hallucination of Linus knew it. But I don't regret it now. I survived and I'm free.

I glance around the quiet living room. On a prominent shelf stands a framed photo of a smiling woman in camouflage with her arms around my rescuers, who are obviously her daughters. A series of moths and butterflies, framed in pairs, hangs behind a rocker. Their bright colors stand out against the dullness of fading wallpaper, sagging upholstery, and a wayward crack in the ceiling. Each surface is meticulously clean. I'm the biggest mess this place has seen in years.

"I'm going to call her in," one of the sisters says.

"Don't, Portia. The police will only screw it up. Ten to one we'll end up accused of something."

"But she's not our problem," Portia says. "I don't like the look of those ports. What if she has something contagious?"

"She's not wearing a hospital band. Doesn't she seem familiar to you?"

"Not really."

"I think she's somebody."

The sisters consider me from the other side of the coffee table. They have similar heart-shaped faces and wide eyes, but the one called Portia is heavier and older I'd guess by a few years. The younger one is close to my age. She has a thin, long-legged build and nicely done nails. She inspects the gown I came in, and then she takes a sniff inside the bag I wore on my foot. She passes it to Portia, who smells it, too.

"Weed," Portia says, glancing to me. "Are you sick?"

"It's not mine," I say. My voice is husky, but I can talk. "Thanks for taking me in. I'm not contagious or anything."

"What's your name?" Portia asks.

I don't want to say, but I can't answer their generosity with rudeness, either. "Rosie," I say.

The younger sister reaches for her tablet. "I knew it," she says. "You're that girl from *The Forge Show*. The one that's missing. Rosie Sinclair."

"Who?" Portia asks.

"You remember. The crazy one. Oh, my gosh!" The young one types quickly and then passes the tablet to Portia, who looks up at me quizzically.

"That's you?" she asks, and turns the tablet toward me to show a shot of me from Forge. It lists a reward that would tempt anybody.

I nod. "Please don't call anybody."

"But your family's looking for you," the younger one says. "Tons of people are. They're worried about you. Where have you been?"

"In hell," I say. And then I laugh because I'm actually not exaggerating. "What's the date today?"

"It's Sunday, March 6, 2067," the young one says.

104

Four months. I curl my hands over my skinny knees. No wonder I'm so thin and weak. For months I've been subsisting on whatever nutrients came in my port. I lift my hand to the lamp, and I swear I can see the light glowing through my flesh.

It makes me angry.

Portia sets down the tablet. "Okay, listen. You've been through something horrendous. We get that," she says. "We'd like to help, but we obviously have to call somebody. You've got problems way out of our league."

"But of course we'll help you," the other interrupts. She smiles at me. "I'm Jenny, and this is Portia. I can't get over this. This is huge. Mom's going to go bonkers when she finds out. And we saved you! We're heroes!"

"Hold on. We need a plan," Portia says. "Where'd you get in our truck? At the diner?"

"Yes," I say. "Please don't call anybody yet. I need to think."

"Where were you before that?" Portia asks.

The Onar Clinic, Ian called it, but I don't know what to say. I'm not sure how much of my story I should tell them. "I don't know exactly," I say.

"Were you, like, kidnapped?" Jenny asks. "I knew it. I always knew that dean from your school was evil. Don't worry. You're not going back. Does anybody else know where you are?"

I shake my head.

"Then you're safe here," Jenny says. "We'll look after you."

"We can't just keep her here," Portia says. "She needs a doctor."

"No, I don't," I say. "No doctors."

"What about your ports? What do they mean? What if they get infected?" Portia says.

"I'll look them up online and figure out what to do with them," I say.

"You're joking," Portia says.

"No, I'm not," I say. "I'm not ready to go public. If you report me, the police will start an investigation. They might take me to a hospital at first, but I won't have any choice about where I end up. Please, I just need to rest for a few days and figure out what to do. Let me stay here. I won't be any trouble. You can call in for the reward then, okay? I'll tell everyone you saved me. Jenny's right. You'll be heroes."

Portia leans back, considering.

"You know what Mom would do," Jenny says.

"She'd call in the police right now," Portia says.

"Exactly."

For some reason, this works on Portia, but not the way I expect.

She nods slowly. "All right," Portia says. "For now, you can stay. But if you get an infection, we're taking you in."

Jenny smiles and pulls her feet up on her chair. "Mom's a stickler for rules. It gets annoying."

"Thanks," I say. I settle deeper into the couch and tuck the blanket closer against my cheek. "I don't suppose you have any ketchup," I say.

Jenny steps out and returns a moment later with a red plastic bottle, a small blue bowl, and a spoon. "How much?" she asks.

"A lot," I say.

She squirts a steady stream into the bowl, and then, after glancing at me, another. When I taste my first spoonful, my taste buds go wild. It's heaven, sweet and salty and redly luscious. I eat it all and then reach for the bottle, which is disappointingly light. I give it a little shake, and then upend it above me to squirt more ketchup directly into my mouth.

A swishing click makes me look over. Jenny has taken a picture with her tablet. I freeze.

"Delete it," I say

"You look awesome," she says.

"Delete it! I don't want any pictures!" I say.

"Okay, calm down. I'm deleting it," Jenny says. "Whatever."

I'm shaking again, and I have to fight an impulse to hurl the ketchup bottle and bowl across the room. As I bundle up in my blankets again, the damp towel slips from my hair. I slide it off the rest of the way and dump it on the floor. Portia comes over to pick it up just as I hide completely under the blankets, curled up in a ball. I'm shivering again, with every muscle clenched.

"She's a wreck, poor kid," Portia says quietly.

"What do you suppose happened to her?" Jenny says.

"I don't know, but it was bad."

You have no idea, I think. But I'm not done, and I'm not pathetic or crazy, either. I'm going to get even.

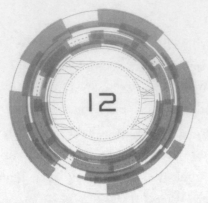

12

— ROSIE —

JENNY

MY LITTLE SISTER searches for a lost puppy in a down-pour of rain, calling plaintively, "Here, doggy!" She pushes her bike through the mud, peering under the boxcars. Her boots sink ankle deep with each step, and I slog along behind her. The rush of water is deafening. When she steps too near the train tracks, a slick river of mud rises from beneath the metal and sucks her under the train. She screams and twists back to grasp at air. Her bike goes down completely, wheels and handlebars slurped into the black muck. Her pale, mud-streaked arms reach out for me to save her, and she gasps for breath. I try to catch her, but I fall in, too, and the muddy water gets us both. I drown with my eyes open, under water, under mud, still reaching blindly for my sister, until suffoca-tion burns my lungs.

I wake panting in a tangled sweat ball. I'm on Portia and Jenny's couch. Bright light streams in the windows, and my heart is pounding with fear. *It's all right,* I tell myself. *I'm alive. I'm out of the vault.* I glance around for Dubbs, but of course, she was never here.

A country station is playing in the other room, accompanied by a sizzling noise. I smell bacon.

Dragging my blanket around me as a robe, I stop at the bathroom. I still have a tube hanging out of me, but I can pee like normal. Yay for small victories. I head for the kitchen. The wooden table by the windows is set for two with chipped blue plates and mismatched cutlery. Jenny, in black leggings and a gray, zippered sweatshirt, is pouring fresh batter in a hot waffle iron. Her ponytail and glowing complexion imply she's been exercising.

"You whimper in your sleep. Just so you know," she says, and passes over a plate of bacon.

"What day is it?" I ask.

"Tuesday, March eighth," she says. "You've been out for two days. We'd have taken you to the hospital, but you freaked out every time we tried to. Plus, blizzard. Again. This is our second snow day in a row, and I'm like yes!"

I don't remember any of it. I take a chair with a view of the road, which is just passably plowed. Two feet of new snow gives the morning a shimmer that's nearly blinding, and I follow the curving lines curiously. I've never seen this much snow before. In the desert, it never piles up like this.

A birdfeeder has a perfect pile of white on top of its pointy little roof, and I frame it up between my fingers for a memory camera. I give it a click.

"That's nice," Jenny says. "Live in the moment, right?"

She passes over a cup of coffee, and I peer gratefully down into the steamy liquid. I lift it an inch off the table and take a sip. It's so good. So real. I guess we'll find out how my digestive tract is working after months of sleep. Jenny peeks into the waffle iron.

"You know what's weird?" she says. "There's been no new news about you. Nobody's looking for you or posting a new reward or anything. We've checked online."

That is interesting. "Maybe Berg doesn't want anyone to know I'm missing," I said.

"That's what we've been thinking, too."

I glance around for her sister. "Where's Portia?"

"At work. She's a poultry processer for Borrds up the road. She normally works the night shift, but they had some problem with the freezer, so they called her in. She wants to be a manager. Here."

She opens the waffle iron and forks a perfectly circular, crusty, fragrant waffle onto my plate. She pushes a dish of butter and a jar of maple syrup close, and starts pouring more batter.

"Don't you want to share?" I ask. "You take half."

"No, that's all right. I'll have the next one," she says.

I eat. The waffle's sweet and good. I want to devour ten of them, but after only a few bites, I have to stop. I lower my fork and poke the tines around in the golden syrup.

"Don't you like waffles?" Jenny says.

"It's fabulous," I say. "I think my stomach shrank."

"What's with that tube of yours?"

I glance down the neckline of my tee shirt to examine the lump in my chest. When I touch it, it doesn't hurt or anything, but I want it out. Same with the hose that comes out of me lower down. I just don't know how to extract them myself. I bundle my blanket around me again so I don't have to see how skinny I am.

"I'll look up how to take them out after breakfast," I say.

"I'm dying to know what's happened to you."

"How much do you know already?" I ask.

Jenny gives me an outsider's version of my disappearance from Forge, and the one thing that's clear to me is that Berg's gotten away with everything. He's still working at the school, like Ian said, and the thought of him going on blithely with his life while he's kept me stuck in a sleep shell all this time infuriates me.

"I went back and watched a bunch of Forge episodes with Portia," Jenny adds. "I can't believe how different you look now. You must have lost twenty pounds. Where've you been?"

"In Berg's custody," I say, and the truth tastes bitter. It's hard for me to trust her, but she and Portia saved my life. I owe her, and I need her sympathy. Haltingly, I tell how I've been kept asleep for months and mined against my will. My emaciation is pretty good proof of my captivity, and honestly, I don't care whether she believes me or not about the dream mining. I'm beyond trying to persuade people of the truth.

"That's horrible," Jenny says. "We have to call the police and tell them. They should arrest Berg."

I shake my head. "I'm not calling the police. I don't trust them. They should have come to find me a long time ago."

"But what about the reward?" she asks.

"I need you to keep quiet a little longer," I say. "I need to get back some strength. I just want to hide for a bit while I figure out my next move."

"That's funny. That's what Portia guessed you'd say," she says. "What are you thinking you'll do?"

I want to kill Berg. That's what I want to do. A strange, warm conviction uncoils inside me, like a hibernating snake has slithered out of a hole. This is what I've wanted for a long time. This is the point of my rage, but until now, I haven't been able to focus on anything except getting out of the vault. I look across at Jenny's wide-eyed eagerness, and I feel a vast separation between her and me, like I've aged or traveled ten thousand miles from any normal life.

"Do you want to go home?" Jenny suggests.

"That's the first place Berg will look for me," I say. "Besides, my parents turned me over to him once before. I'm not sure I can get past that."

"They're offering the reward for you, and they're suing Berg for custody again," Jenny says. "That doesn't sound like they'd turn you over to him."

Doesn't matter. I'm not going home.

"Where are we, exactly?" I ask.

She names a town I've never heard of and adds, "We're a couple hours east of Denver."

Fragrant steam is wafting from the waffle iron, and when the next one's ready, she breaks it in half for us to share, even though I haven't even finished my last waffle and have no intention of eating more. She sits across from me, tidily spreading a napkin on her lap before she digs in. Without prompting, she tells me about her indoor track team and her mom in the National Guard. Under a collection of magnets, the fridge shows pinpricks of rust through the white paint. A pair of binoculars and a butterfly net hang on hooks among jackets and scarfs, and coupons are piled in a tidy basket.

"You have a nice place," I say. "Is it just you and Portia living here?" I ask.

She nods. "Yeah, for now. Mom's serving overseas. She'll be back for good in twelve days. I can't wait."

"You said she's a stickler for rules."

"That's an understatement. She's strict, and she runs everything with precision timing when she's here. Drives me and Portia crazy, actually, but we love her," Jenny says. "We haven't told her you're here. She has enough to worry about over there."

I stir my knife in my melted butter. "How long can I stay with you?" I ask.

"Portia and I have been talking about that. As long as we end up getting the reward for you, you can stay as long as you like."

"That's unbelievably nice," I say.

She sucks syrup off her fork and smiles. "You'd do the same for me. You should know, though, once Mom gets here, she'll call the police."

Fair enough.

A kitten pads softly into the room and dips its head into a bowl of food. The black-and-gray tabby has a dash of white around its mouth and throat, and its softness draws me.

"What's your cat's name?" I ask.

"Gingerbread. Mom doesn't know about her yet, either," Jenny smiles.

"Can I use your computer? I want to see how to get rid of my port and my catheter."

"This sounds fun. Just a sec."

She vanishes into the living room and returns a moment later with a laptop. When she flips it open, the first thing I notice is a piece of black duct tape that covers the camera lens above the screen.

"What's this for?" I ask, setting a finger on the tape.

"That's Mom's precaution," Jenny says. "She doesn't want anyone knowing what her kids look like. Hold on." She gets typing.

"She thinks someone could use your computer camera lens to spy on you?" I ask.

"It's been done," she says, and her gaze narrows at the screen.

We spend the next hour looking up sites about IVs and catheters, and I learn more than I wanted to about total parenteral nutrition and suprapubic catheters. I don't dare to mess with my TPN port, the soft lump under my skin, but apparently my bladder will heal in ten minutes if I snip a stitch and pull out the plastic tube that goes into me.

"You are not seriously going to try that," Jenny says.

"You don't have to look."

"Rosie! You can't learn medicine from a video!"

I turn to meet her worried gaze. "For the last four months, I've been completely helpless," I say. "It's my body. I can do anything I want to it."

I head into the bathroom, and when I come out half an hour later, my catheter is out. The port in my chest is more than I can manage to take out on my own, and I resent it.

Jenny has cleaned the dishes, and she's sitting on the living room couch with her laptop on her knees. "All good?" she asks.

"Ready to pee with the best of them," I say.

She laughs. "Do you want to see my favorite scene from *The Forge Show*?" she asks.

"Sure." I take a seat beside her and hitch my feet up on the coffee table.

"Don't let Mom catch you doing that," she says, but then she puts her feet up next to mine.

She's at the Gorge on Forge site, and without further preamble, she taps a featured video clip of me and Burnham. It's shot from a high angle overlooking the pasture at Forge, and the camera slowly zooms in on us. My memory bursts to life, bringing a mix of emotions: pleasure, guilt, curiosity. From this perspective, I look quirky with my wavy curls, brown sweater, and short skirt. Burnham's tall, square-shouldered, and visibly athletic even when he's still. We stand facing each other along the path in the pasture, where the surrounding grass is darkly soaked from an earlier rain. I recall how Burnham wore no socks with his loafers. That same morning, he showed me the glitches he'd caught in my ghost-seeking footage, and I was ecstatic to have real proof of Berg's evilness, no matter how small the proof was.

"That is one fine-looking brother," Jenny says.

My heart beats oddly. This was our last conversation right before our accident on the observatory ladder, and knowing what's coming gives the video a weird poignancy, like doom hovers over us. The audio catches us clearly, and I'm drawn in by Burnham's warm, resonant voice.

"*I wrote you a letter,*" *Burnham says and passes me an envelope.*

"*When did you write this?*" *I ask.*

"*Last night. After swimming. Wait until you're alone to read it,*" *he says.*

"*Thanks. I'm dying of curiosity,*" *I say.*

"*It's not a love poem or anything,*" *he adds.*

"*Of course not,*" *I say.*

He's standing all quiet and casual, but that only magnifies a shifting tension between us.

"Look at his hand behind his back," Jenny says beside me. "See there?"

He flexes his fingers and then curls them inward.

"Sorry," I say.

"What for?" Burnham asks.

In the clip, I shake my head, and color rises in my cheeks. I recall how awkward I'd felt, but I look almost graceful. My posture is one long curve that mirrors Burnham's.

"Rosie," Burnham says. "I get that you're seeing Linus."

"Yes. I am."

I stop the clip.

Beside me, Jenny objects. "Hey!"

Ignoring her, I back up the clip a couple frames to where I'm leaning toward Burnham, and I scrutinize the image. I distinctly recall spelling out that I was Linus's girlfriend, but my body language says otherwise. I see the hopeful tension in Burnham's shoulders and the attentive way he leans against the wind to hear me better.

"Burnham was seriously into you. You must have known it," Jenny says.

I nod. "I figured that out. But I liked Linus more."

"Uh-huh," she says, and points to the screen.

I tilt my head, studying the image once more. Okay, I liked Burnham, too. I couldn't pinpoint when that started or how much I liked him, but I did. So what did that mean, exactly? I wasn't disloyal to Linus.

"What did his letter say?" Jenny asks.

"He gave me some pills that were an antidote to the sleeping meds," I say. "That's how I was able to stay awake at night."

"I don't get it. Did you use them all the time?" Jenny asks.

"No, at first I just pretended to take my sleeping pill and

secretly spit it out. But then, when the staff checked to see that I swallowed my pill, I used Burnham's antidote," I say. "I was sneaking around the school at night. That's how I found out about the dream mining. Or maybe you don't believe that."

"I know what you said on the show just before you got kicked off," Jenny says. She considers me thoughtfully. "It's too bad you never had any proof. Did Burnham know about the dream mining?"

"I don't know how much he knew," I say. "We never had a chance to talk about it."

"Maybe you will," she says, and nods towards the image of Burnham again. "I mean, you broke up with Linus, right? I'd get on that thing if I were you."

I absolutely do not know what to say. It's clear Jenny admires Burnham, and I can see why, but I can't just switch gears from Linus. My mind doesn't have a language for explaining what Linus means to me. Instead I have this raw, confusing jumble of pain and longing. He made me say publicly, on *The Forge Show*, everything I'd discovered about Berg and the dream mining. He made me look like a fool, and worse, he made me doubt myself. Then, when I least expected it, he showed up and tried to help me, only he got caught by Berg, too. What did that mean for us?

Under all of my doubts is a fear that I'll find out Linus is dead.

Jenny's looking at me strangely. "Okay. Time to check out the ex," she says and types Linus's name into the search window.

I steel myself, and when the first picture comes up and shows him alive, I'm ridiculously relieved. Of course he isn't dead! My emotions orbit madly around my heart for a second, and then I focus hungrily.

Linus gazes deliberately out of his photo, not bothering to smile. He's leaning back against a black, ironwork fence in a dark blazer, a tee shirt, and jeans. Something about the colors and composition tells me the photo was posed for a publicity shot, which puzzles me. My gut tightens as I take the computer from Jenny. I enlarge the photo to study him more closely. His nose is the same straight line. His dark hair is tousled over his eyes, and the last of his earrings is gone. He looks wrong. Bored. Bought. It's like some corporate entity decided Linus would be more attractive with this cool, aloof expression and packaged him like this.

I don't like it.

"He's the host of a new show, looks like," Jenny says. "Did you see?"

I scan the article to learn he's been named the host of a new series called *Found Missing* about missing kids. That explains the new look, but not how he ended up in a high-profile job. I thought he didn't like publicity.

The cat jumps up on the couch beside Jenny, and she absently pats it.

"Could Linus be looking for you?" Jenny asks.

"I don't know," I say. "He never found me, in any case."

He could have tried to reach me. I pull up my Forge email account to log in.

119

"What are you doing?" Jenny asks.

"Checking my email."

"You can't," she says. "You can't contact anybody, especially not the host of a TV show. That reward's a ton of money, Rosie," Jenny says. "We deserve to get paid for helping you. If you're going to go public, our first contact has to be to the reward hotline, not Linus Pitts."

"But, how can—?" I stop. "This is ridiculous."

She gently tugs her computer away from me, and I realize she's serious. I can't contact anybody while I'm with Jenny and Portia. That's what this means. Linus, Burnham, Janice, my family—I can't call any of them.

"I'm sorry," Jenny says. "You understand, right? Portia and I can keep this confidential. It'll be hard, but we can. As soon as it leaks that you're here, though, poof. No reward for us. I'm sorry."

"I get it."

And I do. It's not complicated. This place isn't exactly a prison because I'm choosing to be here, but it comes with strings, like everything else.

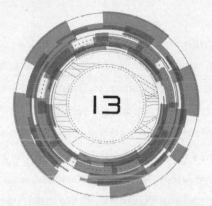

— THEA —

BEHIND THE BLUE DOOR

"YOU NEED TIME TO RECOVER," Ida my nurse said when she caught me trying to walk alone in my room. "Muscles can't mend in a day. Neither can a brain. Besides, if you fall, you could have a serious setback."

"I need to get stronger," I said, tottering but determined. "Can't you give me some steroids or something?"

"Not with your pregnancy. Now sit."

I glanced at the fetus photo I'd propped against the vase and shifted back in my wheelchair. "Do you have kids?" I asked Ida.

"I have four. What was I thinking?" She smiled at me and flipped her braid over her shoulder. "Pregnancy is the easy part, believe me. Once your baby is out and running around, you will never have a minute's peace."

"Great."

"Anytime, *dúlla*."

As the days passed, I was restlessly lonely, and it became difficult to hide my impatience with my slow recovery. I took to exploring the clinic in my wheelchair, propelling myself with my arms as they grew stronger, and it was a relief to be out of my room and away from Althea's solicitous parents.

Chimera was busy with other patients, and though I was curious about their progress and the different languages I overheard, I was not eager to make friends. I prowled from the atrium on the lower level, with its café and concert piano, to the library on the top floor. I stopped by the kitchen, the MRI room, the library, the chapel, and a small, paneled room called the card parlor. In the boutique gift shop, I peered into cases of jewelry and teddy bears, electronics and logoed bottle openers, skeptical that anyone would want a souvenir from this place, as if it were a fancy cruise ship. I intended to forget my stay here as soon as I could.

One sunny day, about a week after my frustrating phone calls with Linus and my parents, I made a solo trip up to the roof of the clinic. It was a flat, Spartan, snow-dusted area with a tile bench and a dreary pot of sand for cigarette butts. Patients, I guessed, didn't normally come here, which made it all the more inviting to me. I wheeled over to the wall and breathed deep. The sky soared above, defying the rugged peaks of the mountains, and the waves crashed in shrunken, petulant bursts on the icy rocks below. Far off, the ocean made a clean line of dark gray where it met the sky, and I followed the horizon north, to the bulky shape of Iceland proper with its hulking volcano.

Snow glittered everywhere except on the puny paths and roads that had been plowed. Shading my eyes, I gazed east, into the valley, where a landing strip lay like an ironed ribbon of silver. A dozen private jets were parked along one side, tiny as pocket toys, and as I watched, another one approached from over the ocean and made a gradual descent.

It was weird to think my family owned one of those jets. *Althea's family. Not mine. Keep that straight.*

A clinking drew my attention. Below, a man in a lab coat hunched his shoulders and cupped his hands to a cigarette, lighting it. He tossed his head back to exhale a blur of smoke. Lean and dark-haired, maybe forty, he stood in a small, sheltered nook beside an outbuilding. It was a hybrid structure, half concrete and half stone cottage, as mismatched as a shoebox glued to a gingerbread house. I watched absently until the smoker stubbed out his cigarette and went inside, and then it occurred to me: in all my roaming around the Chimera Centre, I'd never seen a lab. Where, exactly, did Dr. Fallon do her research? Not her clinical work on patients, but her basic research. That shoebox suddenly looked promising.

The next morning, very early, while the clinic was still quiet, I dressed in my sweats and slippers, climbed in my wheelchair, and headed down the hall toward the elevator.

"You're up early," a nurse said as I passed the desk.

"Couldn't sleep," I said.

"Do you need a hand with anything?" she asked. "Coffee? Breakfast?"

"I'm all set. I'm just going up to the library. I think I left my book there yesterday."

"It should be open. Good luck," she said.

I took the elevator down to the atrium level, where the fountain was off and the café was dead. My wheels made a faint, smooth sound through the hush as I crossed to the doors. I pushed my way out to the terrace, where the early chill touched my face with welcome freshness and fueled my excitement. Then I started around the building.

Frost lines laced the stone walkway, and my breath came out in foggy puffs that vanished into the pre-dawn gloom. I reached the outbuilding and tried the door. It didn't budge. Undeterred, I wheeled myself along, peering in the windows, but it was hard to see more than a few black countertops. Where the building ended, a fenced area contained bins for garbage, recycling, and radioactive waste. Cigarettes butts littered the curb.

I pivoted to start back when my wheel went over a lip of concrete into a crevice and stuck. I stood carefully and tugged at my chair, righting it. As soon as I sat, it rolled and wedged in again.

"Hello," said a girlish voice. "What are you doing back here?"

Behind me, beside a streetlamp, a black-haired teenager straddled an adult tricycle and dangled a helmet from one hand. The shoulder strap of a purse cut diagonally across her gray jacket, and her black-clad legs were as thin as a bird's.

"I came out to smoke and got stuck," I said.

"Patients can't smoke," she said, her accent light but clear. "One sec. I'll give you a hand." She dismounted and chained up her bike. Then she unlocked the nearest door and dumped her helmet and purse inside before she came over to grab my chair.

Wordlessly, she jacked my chair back onto the sidewalk, rocking me side to side in the process.

"Thanks," I said.

"No problem," she said. "What's your name?" she asked.

"Rosie."

To my surprise, she took a little notebook out of her pocket and jotted in it with a nub of pencil.

"What's your name?" I asked.

"Jónína," she said, and headed toward the door.

She was the first regular teenager I'd seen in months, and I was not letting her get away.

"Can I see your lab?" I asked.

She turned back to me, her expression flat. "It's not mine. I just water the plants."

"Let me just warm up again before I head back."

The girl reached for her notepad again, but she didn't try to stop me as I edged my chair past her and muscled over the bump of the threshold. A vinegar-like, chemical smell bit my nose, and my heart gave an involuntary kick. The scent reminded me of the operating room off the vault of dreamers.

"What are you writing down?" I asked.

"Everything," she said.

"How come?"

"That way I know it happened. It's my life experiment. I'm recording it." She pulled off her jacket and put her notebook and pencil in the pocket of her green cardigan. "Touch anything and you die."

She started turning on lights and switches in the shoebox section of the building. A circulation system kicked in, and it became easier to breathe. The lab was a large, open room, sectioned off by counters and cabinets into different bays. Jónína put a watering can into a sink and twisted the faucet, and I noted a dozen different plants tucked on the windowsills. They looked none too healthy.

"How many people work here?" I asked over the rush of water.

"I don't know. Six or seven? We used to have more, but a bunch of people left a couple months ago. We'll never leave. Mom promised. I don't like change. Check this out," she said, and pointed up to a stuffed rodent mounted on a high shelf.

"What is it?" I asked.

"It's a marmoset. I stuffed it myself," she said. "I took it to a taxidermist, Mr. Pall, and he taught me how to do it. The eyes are made of glass. Do they look real to you?"

Real enough to be creepy.

"Yes. They're nice," I said. "How old are you?"

"Me? Seventeen," she said, turning off the water with a squeak.

Older than me. Younger than Althea. When she turned her head, I saw a streak of blue in her black hair.

"Is your mom one of the scientists here?" I asked.

"This is her place," Jónína said. "She's Huma Fallon."

Surprised again, I tried to see a resemblance, but Jónína, with her skinny figure and stilted manner, seemed nothing like the doctor.

"Is your dad here, too?" I asked.

"He's traveling. He's always traveling."

As Jónína tended the plants, I wheeled down the length of the room, curious.

Along one wall stood several large, humming cases with glass doors. The shelves inside were lit with a soft blue light that reminded me of our sleep shells back at Forge, and I peered close. Rows of clear, covered disks filled the interior, each labeled in script too small for me to read. They contained pastel growths of some sort. When I touched the glass door, it was warm.

"Don't do that. Don't touch anything," Jónína called.

"Sorry. I know. I won't," I said, and slid my hand away.

I moved to the next case and the next, which were equally full. A door beckoned at the end of the room. I checked over my shoulder for Jónína, who was carefully tipping the long spout of her watering can into a fern, and then I tried the door. When it opened easily, I wheeled into the next room, which was much smaller.

Instantly, a different hush surrounded me, and my pulse rose a notch. The overhead lights stayed off, leaving me to find

127

my way by the diffused light from more cases. A pungent stench of chemicals and cleanser couldn't mask the putrescence of decay. I moved slowly, careful not to bump anything. Vials, pipettes, and bottles covered the counters in seeming disarray, but two surgical tables, which stood to the side, gleamed clean and cold. I passed a drain in the floor. The far wall was made of stone, and set into it was a strange blue door—an old, arched one with bars over its center window. A dimly lit hallway on the other side led into the old, gingerbread-style section of the building, and the door still had a house number, 6, painted in black at the top.

The blue glow of the nearest case drew me over, and on the outside, a yellow sticky note read: _Do not_ send Sandy any Sinclair 15. Huma's orders. My heart jolted. "Sandy" was Dean Berg's first name. I rose out of my wheelchair to see better. Inside, rows of small, opalescent jars shimmered faintly. Their labels were barely decipherable, but I made out that the jars were arranged in alphabetical order, layers deep, and many of the jars had the same name but a different number: Huron 6: 35/65, Lo 15: 28/119, Minaret 17: 7/10, Richards 18: 25/222, Sinclair 15: 29/300. I stopped, staring at my own name. Then I checked the next shelf: Sinclair 15: 39/300, Sinclair 15: 49/300, Sinclair 15: 59/300. The next five shelves contained jars with my name on them, hundreds of them.

Fear spiked along my nerves.

Silently, I opened the case and picked out the topmost jar with my name on it, Sinclair 15: 29/300. It clung with magnetic resistance to the shelf, but once I slid it free, it was surprisingly light and warm in my palm. The jar had a metal bottom but glass sides and a glass lid, and as I held it up close, I saw a murky, gray substance inside that flashed with electric pinpoints of color, like a miniscule lightning storm. It flowed in a thick, viscous manner when I tilted the jar, and I could have sworn I heard thunder crashing inside: tiny, perfect thunder for a miniature world.

Whatever was in those jars, it was derived from my dreams. A keen, powerful resentment stirred in me.

The door opened behind me, and I quickly shoved the jar down the front of my shirt.

"Rosie? Are you in here?" Jónína asked.

With a shock, I realized I'd given her my real name. I spun to face her.

"You shouldn't be in here," Jónína said. She stood on the threshold of the first laboratory, still holding her watering can.

"I'm coming," I said, plopping back in my wheelchair. "Listen, Jónína. Rosie isn't my real name. I made a mistake saying that."

"But I wrote it down," Jónína said. She tucked the watering can under her elbow, reached for her notepad, and flipped it open. "It says it right here: 'I met Rosie outside the lab.'"

"Can I see?" I asked.

She held the pad tightly. "Nobody sees this."

I wheeled a little closer. "Can you make a correction in your notes?" I asked. "My real name's Althea."

"That makes no sense," she said. "Why'd you lie to me?"

"It was a mistake, not a lie," I said. I smiled and tried for lightheartedness. "Haven't you ever mixed up your own name?"

Jónína stared at me intensely. "No. That's not funny."

The stench of the lab suddenly felt stultifyingly close. Like poison.

"Do you have another name?" I asked softly.

She clutched her notepad and her watering can together, as if they could keep her safe, and her gaze shifted sideways. "My name's Jónína. It's always been Jónína." She frowned at me. "You have to leave. Mom's going to be mad."

"She doesn't have to know I was here. I won't tell anyone," I said.

"She'll know. She always knows everything."

I nodded at her notebook. "Maybe because she reads your journal."

"It's not a journal," she said. "It's an experiment, and I don't let her read it."

A disturbing possibility occurred to me. "Has your mother ever done experiments on you?" I asked.

"No. She *saved* me," Jónína said. She cocked her head in alertness as if listening for something.

I listened, too, and heard nothing. "Saved you from what, Jónína?" I asked.

"I was drowning. I don't quite remember it. I was little. They thought I was dead at the bottom of the lake, but Mom swam down and brought me up."

"Did she operate on you?" I asked.

She gave me an odd look. "Of course. She's a doctor. That's how she saved me."

"Is that when she started all this? Is it all for you?" I asked.

Jónína opened her notebook a crack and gripped her stubby pencil in tight fingers, ready to write. I took the jostling watering can from under her arm, and she stumbled back a pace.

"Are there bodies here, Jónína? Are there dreamers?" I asked.

Her gaze flicked toward the blue door. "You're scaring me now," she said.

"Are they back there? Are they here, in this building?" I asked. I wheeled my chair backward, back toward the blue door, but she shot out a hand and gripped my chair's wheel. The watering can clattered to the floor.

"I don't want bodies here," Jónína said.

Her gaze shifted past my head, and a click behind me made me look over my shoulder.

A thin, motionless man stood on the other side of the blue door, studying us through the glass and bars. His cheeks were sallow and wasted, and soft, brown, boyish hair fell long over his eyes. With his pointy, narrow shoulders and threadbare brown sweater, he seemed both strong and spindly at the same time, as if an unseen wind blew against him and he was only barely managing to stay up.

Then he tilted his head, and a strange, tantalizing flash of familiarity lit up the back of my brain. I'd seen this man before. Not just when he was smoking the day before, but earlier. An old teacher, maybe. I knew him, definitely, from long ago.

My memory shifted. A slim wisp of an idea squeezed past the stony barriers of impossibility and took my breath away.

But it couldn't be.

"Dad?" I whispered.

The man slowly eased backward and then turned to walk away.

I scrambled to spin my wheelchair and barreled toward the blue door. I jerked at the knob. It was locked. "Dad!" I called, rapping at the glass. He retreated in a languid, bow-legged stride and vanished around a corner. I rapped harder. "Dad!"

"He doesn't want to be disturbed," Jónína said.

"But that's my father!" I said. "Dad! Come back!"

"He's not your dad. That's Orson Toomey."

She was wrong. She had to be. He had just been looking at me and watching me. He knew me, too.

"What's he doing here?" I demanded. "How long has he been here?"

"Since forever, I guess," Jónína said. "Mom says Orson's a genius. He doesn't talk much. We leave him alone. He told me he likes my marmoset, though."

I gave the doorknob another frantic tug. "You have to let me in there!" I said.

Jónína shook her head. "I don't have a key. It's private."

"Does he live back there?" I asked.

"Usually, yes, unless he's on a trip like my dad," she said. "Some men like to live by themselves and be left alone. It's just how they are."

132

I spun to look at her, frowning at her maddening superiority. At that moment, a car pulled up audibly outside, and Jónína stepped to the window.

"People are coming," she said, peering out. "Quick. This way. Out the back." She seized my wheelchair and rattled me rapidly through the larger lab to a back exit.

"Take me out of your notebook," I said. "Take me out, or your mom will find out you let me in here. You'll get in trouble."

"I can't take things out. That would be lying to myself."

I gripped her shirt and yanked her close to me. Her eyes bulged in startled fear.

"Then lie," I said fiercely. "Grow up."

I pushed her away and wheeled rapidly outside. I raced my chair along the cliffside path, expecting any second to hear a voice call after me, but none came, and I wheeled up the wooden ramp to the terrace of the main clinic. There I paused, out of breath, and pressed a hand to my face.

My father. Could it really be him? But he was dead. He'd gone missing in action a dozen years before. The military had declared him presumed dead back when I turned six. I couldn't believe what I'd just seen. That man, Orson Toomey, looked exactly like I remembered my father, only older. Hope soared in me, then crashed in confusion. My father couldn't be alive. He certainly wouldn't have any reason to be here.

Yet Orson had looked at me with open deliberation, as if he knew me. But I looked like Althea now. Even if Orson was somehow my father, he couldn't know the girl in this body was his daughter Rosie.

Unless he did know.

Unless he'd been involved with putting me in this new body.

It was too much to take in. Too utterly crazy-making. I suddenly recalled the nights here at the clinic when I'd sensed someone hovering outside my bedroom door. That was Orson, too. I knew it was. He'd been checking on me. My hope careened and dive-bombed again. If Orson truly was my dad, he had years of absence to account for. Any decent man who'd survived the war and turned up alive would have contacted me and my mother long ago. He would have come home to Doli to find us and be with us.

But he hadn't. Like he didn't care.

It didn't fit. My dad used to walk with me on the old train tracks near our home, hand in hand. He helped me balance my bare feet on the rusty, sun-warmed metal of the rail. We would stop to pick blue cornflowers and practice whistling, and when I grew tired, he'd carry me home on his shoulders. I had missed my dad for so long that I didn't believe it was possible to ache for him again in a new way, but the little kid in me broke apart all over again.

"Really, Dad?" I whispered to the gray sky.

Loss spilled out of my heart. It used to be that my sweet, lovable dad was dead—terribly, honorably dead. Now, instead, he was alive, but he'd abandoned Ma and me. Worst of all, he worked with Dr. Fallon, and by extension, with Dean Berg.

Any way I looked at it, my dad was my enemy.

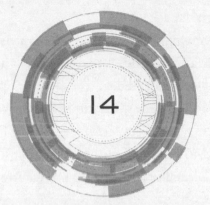

— THEA —

SEEDS

WITHIN A FEW HOURS, the jar I stole went black inside. The tiny lights vanished, and the murky substance congealed into a thick, putrid mess. I'd killed it. Chagrined, I wrapped the jar in a paper towel, concealed it in a box of tissues, and hid the box in the back of my closet. There it festered, the black heart of my anxiety, while I tried to pretend everything was normal.

All that day, I tried to figure out the best way to confront Orson. I had to hear him admit he was my father. Every instinct told me I had to get to him on the sly, but my hours were full, and it was impossible to sneak away in my wheelchair. My parents lingered in my room after dinner, gossiping amiably about whatever while I silently plotted.

"Don't you think, Althea?" Madeline said.

"What's that?" I asked.

"I was just saying we could add an elevator off the library back home," Madeline said. "It would make it easier for you to get around once we go back."

"An elevator?" I asked. What kind of house had an elevator? A big one.

She reached to pat my hand. "You seem a little testy," she said. "Is there something we should know? Are you feeling all right?"

"Of course I am," I snapped. "I'm just ready to get out of this place."

Madeline set her lips in a line, then nodded. "We should probably let you rest."

She led a prayer, and then they kissed me good night. After they left, Chimera settled into its night routine. I was curled in my bed, conserving strength, waiting for the right opportunity to leave my room, when a faint shuffling noise came by my door. I recognized it immediately.

"Come in," I whispered.

The quiet unspooled while I waited, watching for Orson. The door was ajar, but not enough for me to see much of the hallway. I heard a soft footstep and then, just below the upper hinge of the door, in the narrow crack, I saw a shadow and the hint of an eye.

I bolted up. "I see you! Come in!" I called.

The shadow vanished. I pushed off my bed. Bracing myself on the wall, I staggered to the door and threw it fully open. Down the hallway, Orson was striding away in a long brown coat.

"Orson, wait!" I called after him.

He glanced over his shoulder and kept going, faster.

I lurched after him, hanging on to the hallway bannister.

Ida came quickly from the nurse's station. "What's wrong? Where are you going?" she asked.

"I have to talk to that man," I said.

She looked over her shoulder and then back to me. "Althea, please. This isn't safe. You could fall," she said.

I pulled free of her and struggled a few steps farther, but then, with a bing, the elevator door opened, and Dr. Fallon came out.

"Althea!" she said. "Just the person I was coming to see."

I backed against the wall. Not good. This was not good. She didn't normally come around at night, and she never came dressed in scrubs.

"Where are my parents?" I said. "I want to see my parents." I looked behind her for Orson, but he was gone.

"They're in their suite," she said. "Don't be worried. I've just come to check on you. I hear you met my daughter." She knew.

I backed away from her and shot a look at Ida, whose face was drawn with concern. A second nurse came around the nurse's station, ready to assist, cornering me in.

"What are you going to do to me?" I asked.

"You won't feel a thing," Dr. Fallon said kindly. "You'll feel better in the morning. Less confused. I promise."

"I didn't do anything wrong," I said. "I don't want any tweaking. I'm fine. Get my parents."

"They've already approved," she said gently.

I tried to run. I screamed in protest, but they caught me swiftly, and I felt the sharp sting of a syringe in my arm. "No," I whispered, pleading.

Dr. Fallon smoothed the hair out of my eyes. "You'll be fine, Althea," she said. "That is your name, right?"

An instant later, the hallway tipped and went foggy, and I was gone.

>>>>>>>>

When I woke the next morning, molasses had been poured into the clock of my brain to clog the cogs. The sky, an opaque gray outside the window, dropped its cool light on Madeline, whose face was a pucker of worry.

"Thank heavens you're awake," she said, pulling her chair nearer. "How do you feel?"

Like crap.

"I want to go home," I said.

"I know, sweetheart," Madeline said. She reached to hold my hand. "We'll get there. Two steps forward, one step back."

Diego came in, as if he'd been standing just outside, listening. "How is she?" he asked.

"She's awake," Madeline said.

"You let them operate on me again," I said.

"We had to, honey," Madeline said. "You were slipping away from us."

Something was missing. Some key word. My name. I

hovered inside my mind, waiting for the answer, but nothing came. I pushed back my covers and lumbered over to my closet. I pulled open the door, and when I reached up for the tissue box, I could tell from the lightness before I looked into the layers of tissue: my jar was gone.

The jar with my name on it was gone.

"What are you doing?" Madeline asked.

"What's my name?" I asked.

She exchanged a quick glance with Diego. "Althea, of course," she said. "You're Althea Maria Flores."

"No, my *real name*," I said fiercely. It started with an R. Rochelle. No. Rachel. No! I ripped fruitlessly into the tissue. "What is it?" I yelled.

Madeline's eyes went wide with astonishment. "Darling, calm down," she said. "You'll hurt yourself."

I threw the tissue box to the floor and caught myself on the closet.

Diego set a strong, supporting hand my arm. "Is it Rosie Sinclair?" he asked.

I tested the syllables, uncertain. My heart kept pounding. *Rosie Sinclair*. I searched Diego's face. His eyes were sad and full of sympathy.

"You looked her up online, remember?" he said.

I did and I didn't. My memory was spotty. "Rosie Sinclair," I whispered, uncertain.

"Diego," Madeline said warningly. "You'll confuse her."

"It calms her down," he said. "Look at her."

I pressed a hand to my face, still Althea's, and then the

baby rolled to assert its existence in my belly again. I glanced toward the fetus photo that I'd propped against the vase. The pieces settled back in place around a key point of tension: this body was Althea's, but I knew in my heart that the real me was never pregnant, which meant the real me, inside, wasn't Althea. I was still Rosie. *Rosie Sinclair. Yes.* Relief eased through me. Dr. Fallon hadn't erased me, for now.

"Do you want to get back in bed?" Diego asked. "Rest a little more?"

I nodded. Diego helped me back onto my bed, and I sank heavily into the mattress. I'd been punished. Regardless of Dr. Fallon's stated reasons, she had tweaked me because I'd wandered too close to Jónína, Orson, and the Sinclair 15. I was sure of it. She must have read Jónína's notes and discovered I called myself Rosie. She'd discovered the jar I'd stolen.

I wasn't safe here. Not even Diego and Madeline could keep me safe from Dr. Fallon because they trusted the doctor. I was grateful to Diego for helping me remember my real name, but I knew, if I was smart, I had to play Althea as long as I was here.

I gave him a weak smile. "Thanks, Dad. Stay with me?"

"Always, *m'ija*," he said.

>>>>>>>>>

After the tweaking, I was secretly desperate to leave Chimera. I trusted no one, but I needed the therapists and nurses to help me, so I used them like tools and faked my gratitude.

Over the next week, I grew noticeably stronger, and as I finally grasped how pregnancy had shifted my body's center of gravity, I was able to work with it instead of against it. I graduated from my wheelchair to a walker, and then to a cane, celebrating each milestone with my team, but inside, I was as watchful as ever.

Besides that one time with Diego, I never mentioned my real name. I answered to *Althea* like a good girl. I was constantly afraid that Dr. Fallon would tweak me again if she heard I still thought of myself as Rosie. I had no idea what would happen to me if she succeeded in eradicating my consciousness from Althea's mind, but I didn't want to find out.

It tormented me to think my father was one building over, an inexplicable conspirator in the dream mining. Everything about Orson Toomey confused me. Memories of my dad were coming back to me. I had watched, fascinated, as he shaved, tilting his chin before the mirror. I had cuddled in the curve of his arm as he taught me to read, sharing letters and words, back when the paper smelled like magic. He was here, so close, and he didn't care enough to come see me.

Night after night, I checked my phone and tried to reach my old friends, but they never replied. Each time I saw my empty inbox, my loneliness dipped to a new low. I had no one. Sleepless, desolate, I watched my door for Orson until I drifted into nightmares about Dr. Fallon and a thousand savage scalpels.

"When can we go home?" I asked.

Soon, the grownups all said, but never today.

I had to take matters into my own hands.

My chance came late one night when the nurses were called into a different patient's room, and the hallway was unattended. I pulled on my sweats, slipped on my sneakers, grabbed my cane, and tottered down the hall to the elevator. I took it down and headed outside. The smell and sound of the waves below the cliff rose on an up-current of air. A new, light snow had fallen, adding its freshness to the cold night. The clouds had passed, and the stars were brilliant above me. An eerie, blue-green streak shimmered in the sky to the north, and in awe, I took the aurora borealis as a sign for courage.

Outside Orson's lab, I peeked in the dark windows to where the cases glowed with faint blue light. I tried the back door, but it didn't open. I peered in the glass pane of the door, and then leaned back, squinting up toward the gingerbread part of the building where I suspected Orson lived. Those windows were dark, too.

I wound back my cane like a baseball bat and smashed the window in the door. Glass tinkled wildly around me. Reaching in, I opened the handle from inside and let myself in. With the glow of the cases to guide me, I hurried past the stuffed marmoset, into the smaller lab, and over to the shelves that contained the Sinclair 15. In less than a minute, I had a dozen of the little jars piled on the counter before me.

The blue door slammed opened, and Orson charged into the lab. He flipped on the overhead lights.

"What are you doing?" he demanded. "Get back!"

Instead, I picked up one of the jars and hurled it to the floor at his bare feet. The guts of it scattered in a blinking mess.

"Stop!" Orson shrieked.

I took another jar and held it high above my head.

Orson put out a hand in a gesture of caution. Shirtless, with black sweatpants, he inched his toes back from the shards of glass.

"I need some answers, Dad," I said.

"Hold still!" he said. "Don't kill them! You don't realize what you're doing!"

I smashed the second jar and reached for another.

Orson waved his hands. "Stop! Please!"

I held the jar high above my head. "Do you know what my name is?" I asked. "I'll give you one guess."

He hesitated, his eyes wild. I made to throw the jar.

"It's Rosie!" he said. "Rosie Sinclair! I'm sorry. Put that down, please! I'll talk to you, I promise, but only if you don't kill any more seeds."

"You're my father, aren't you?"

"I was, once, yes," he said. "Please, *please* put that down and I'll explain."

I lowered it slightly and tried to ignore the way my heart was reaching for him. He looked like my father and sounded like him, too, which was even more upsetting. Still, he wasn't completely unchanged. His face and body were older, and his bare chest showed dark, jagged scars along his ribcage. He self-consciously hitched at the waistband of his sweatpants.

"I never thought I'd meet you like this," he said.

A laugh caught in my throat. "You didn't expect to meet me at all," I said. "How did this happen?" I wasn't sure which hurt was harder to bear: that he'd never called my family in all these years, or that he'd neglected me even when I was here at Chimera.

A clicking noise came from a speaker over the door. "Everything okay there, Dr. Toomey?" asked a man's voice.

"I'm good," Orson said loudly. "I just dropped a box of recycling."

"You ought to get some sleep."

"Will do."

The speaker went dead. I did a quick scan for camera lenses, but found none.

Orson regarded me intently. "I'm sorry," he said more quietly. "Truly, I am."

"Why didn't you ever call home?" I asked.

"I'm not exactly your father anymore," he said. "This is Robert's body, but I'm not your father. My mind isn't his. I didn't think you'd recognize me. I still can barely credit that you're actually conscious as Rosie. Robert Sinclair died a decade ago. Please put down that seed. We'll talk."

"If he's dead, then who are you?" I asked.

"Orson Toomey. Please," he said gently. "Let me put the jars back in the incubator. They're not safe at room temperature. They'll die."

"They're dreams, aren't they?"

He nodded. "Dream seeds. They start as seeds and grow."

144

"Was I in one of these jars?"

He nodded again. "We nurtured Rosie's seed along before we put it in Althea."

"So these others with my name on them, are they me, too?"

"They're seeds from you, but they aren't conscious," he said. "They aren't aware."

"How do you know that?"

"They need a body to be conscious," he said.

"But they have the potential to be conscious, too, don't they?" I pressed him. "They're alive?"

"The answer to that's more complicated than I can explain in an instant," he said. "Please, Rosie. Let me put them back. They're incredibly fragile."

He sidestepped the broken glass to come nearer, but I raised the jar higher again, and he stopped.

"Tell me about my dad," I said.

He splayed a hand lightly against his chest. "Your father's body was recovered from an ice field in Greenland a few years after the war ended," Orson said. "He was perfectly preserved, and the scavengers who found him sold him to me. That was six, no seven years ago."

When I was nine, I thought, calculating. My mother had remarried by then. "Did you even know who he was?" I asked.

Orson nodded. "I looked him up, of course. The U.S. Army kept records of his DNA, and they'd posted rewards for info about MIAs. Your father was presumed dead by then. I could have turned in his body, I know. No doubt you believe I should

145

have. But I thought, just possibly, if my experiment worked, I could restore him to you alive, not dead. He was physically fit, aside from being dead. In the cold, he was perfectly preserved. He was the ideal subject."

"So you experimented on him?"

He gestured a hand around his lab. "I've been doing medical research for decades. I started in degenerative brain diseases, looking for similarities. Along the way, I developed a method for harvesting dream seeds and preserving them. Then I started implanting them, practicing on cadavers, and I had some startling results. That's when I met your father, so to speak."

"You had no right to experiment on him," I said. "My father was dead. He never consented. He deserved the honor of a military funeral."

"I'm aware of that," he said. "But would he have refused a shot at a second life?"

The idea made me pause. "What did you do to him, exactly?" I asked.

"I put my own dream seed in him," Orson said. "It was supposed to be just a kick-starter for him, but it caught and grew. His brain function reactivated first, starting his heart and breathing. Then gradually his consciousness evolved. Me, again."

"And what about my father? What about his consciousness?"

He shook his head gravely. "I've tried to find any trace of him in me. Any memories. But they're gone."

"So you failed," I said.

"Yes, from your father's perspective. But I also succeeded,

146

from mine." Orson folded his arms across his bare chest. "By the time I woke in this body, it was too late to tell your family what I'd done. I needed your father's body for my own sake. I owed it to him not to make his family suffer more than they already had, so I stayed away and kept silent."

"Where's the original version of you?" I asked.

He gave a pained smile. "I was an old man. I overlapped with this version of me for only a few months, and then the original Orson died. His death ripped me up. It was terribly disturbing. I wasn't sure I deserved to go on after that."

"You didn't," I said coldly.

He shook his head slowly. "But how could I waste this second life? I owed your father. I vowed to use his body wisely."

I backed a step away from him, trying to process it all. I'd never wanted to believe that my father was dead. For years, I had hoped that he somehow survived, but not like this. Never like this.

He nodded toward the jar I was still holding. "Can we please put those away now?"

The little jar in my hand flickered with pinpricks of light. As I thought back to where it had come from and where I'd first been mined, a startling idea hit me.

"You told Dean Berg to mine me, didn't you?" I asked. "You wanted my dream seeds from the Forge School."

"I was curious about you, yes," he said.

"How far back does your plotting go? Did I get into the Forge School on my own, or did they let me in on purpose so the dean could mine me?"

He shook his head. "Getting into Forge was all you," he said. "You applied by your own choice and made it in. I never would have had access to you otherwise, but then you were right there, at Forge, where Berg was already mining seeds from his students. The temptation was irresistible. It felt like fate. I wondered if a seed from you might trigger something old of your father's inside me."

"Did it work?"

He shook his head. "No."

"Then you really don't have any of my dad's feelings or memories left?" I asked. "Not one?"

Orson shook his head. "Do you feel any of Althea in you?"

I didn't, but I was wary about how to answer him. "Sometimes," I lied.

"How much? Memories? Feelings?"

"I'm not here to talk about me."

"But you're all that matters now," he said. "Let me try to explain how important you are. In all of my experiments, only one seeding has resulted in a full-blown consciousness from the seed: mine. But now, you've recognized me as only Rosie could know her father. You identify with your seed, not your host. We need to study you. We need your cooperation. I've been dying to talk to you. I've begged Huma, but she says we're morally obligated to suppress the Rosie side of you in favor of Althea."

"Nobody's getting suppressed anymore," I said. "I can't believe what you've done. You had no right!"

"You weren't supposed to even know about it," he said. "None of the other students ever did. It wasn't supposed to hurt you."

"Not hurt me!" I exclaimed. I held the jar out before me. "Look what's happened! Dean Berg stole my life from me! Look at me now! *Look* at me!" I stood before him in someone else's body. I was so enraged that I could barely speak. I lifted the jar higher again. "I want to go back in my old body. Is she here? Can you put me back?"

Orson lifted his hands like a catcher, ready in case I threw the jar. "You know it's too late for that," he said.

I opened the incubator door again and held it open so I could aim my next throw inside, where it would do the most damage. "Where's my body? Where's Rosie?" I asked. "Tell me or I swear I'll smash every jar."

"You can't," he said quickly. "Those are people's dreams in there. You were once in a jar like that."

I threw a jar into the case where it broke a dozen other jars. Glass and sparks flew.

"No!" Orson cried, leaping forward.

"Stop!" I grabbed another jar and wound up again. I glared defiantly at Orson, who froze three paces away. "Tell me where she is!"

"Sandy Berg keeps her in a storage facility in Colorado," Orson said. "It's called the Onar Clinic. It's outside Denver. For pity's sake, put the jar down."

"Is she still alive?" I asked.

"She's alive, I swear. Sandy's taking very good care of her. She's in a stasis, asleep. He was worried that she would harm herself, but this way she's safe."

"*Safe?*" I said, appalled. I had been in that so-called stasis myself. It killed me to think that the original version of me was still there after all these months. "She's in hell."

The crunching of glass came from behind me, and I whipped around.

Diego stood tall in the doorway, surveying the damage. "What is all this?" he asked calmly.

I kept my jar raised high. "I have to leave here now," I said. "Can you take me home, Dad? Please?"

Diego's gaze flicked from me to Orson while I stood there between my two false fathers.

"She isn't Althea anymore, is she?" Diego asked.

Orson shook his head in a brief negative. "I'd say she's more of a hybrid at this point. We need to study her further."

I let out a bitter laugh. "Your daughter's gone," I said to Diego. The truth felt brutal, but I had to risk that Diego would respect it. "I'm sorry, but I'm all that's left, and I'm not Althea. I'm begging you, get me out of here."

Diego peered at me a long moment, and then nodded. "I'll call up the jet."

I smiled grimly and turned once more to Orson. "You said you tried one of my dream seeds on yourself once, right? But it didn't do you any good?"

"Yes, that's right," hc said warily.

"It didn't work on you because you're death," I said. "All this? It's just death. And you're the king of it."

I slid my last jar onto the counter where it flickered its tiny lights. Done. I was finished.

— ROSIE —

GUARDIAN

JENNY, THE YOUNGER SISTER, is usually friendly, but Portia keeps aloof. She makes a point of taking Gingerbread away if she curls beside me on the couch. They take their phones and computers with them when they leave for work and school, but they're always generous with their food. It takes hardly anything to fill my shrunken belly at first, but I keep at it, and soon I can eat more. By the fourth day, they let me cook, and I take over the kitchen.

Mac 'n' cheese. Cookie dough. French toast. French fries. More ketchup. Grilled cheese with tomato soup. Pasta with ham and alfredo sauce. Fudge. As I start to regain weight, I itch to exercise. My strength is puny, but I find a yoga channel on TV, and every day I try the moves. I add in push-ups and sit-ups and squats, making it up as I go, doing repetitions until my muscles burn. My nights are riddled with horrific nightmares, so I nap during the day instead, as best as I can.

And all the time, without discussing it, the time bomb's ticking. Jenny and Portia are counting down to their mom's return from overseas, and I know that's when they'll call in for the reward. I need a plan before then, but with no car and no money, my choices are limited. I don't want to go public. That much I know. I refuse to surrender my life to adults who think they know what's best for me, and one way or another, whether with Berg or my parents or Family Services, once the world knows where I am, I'm not going to be free anymore.

The port in my chest is a mute, constant reminder of my helpless suffering in the vault. All I really want to do is kill Berg. Distance from the Onar Clinic has crystalized my resentment into a clear goal. I need to leave the sisters before they call for the reward, but not before I'm strong enough to take care of myself. This means that while they're out, I practice jimmying the locks of their bedroom doors, adding oil to the workings and the door hinges, so that I'll be able to get in silently and steal a phone when I need to.

One Friday evening, twelve days after my arrival and two days before their mother is due home, the snowy yard turns the pure, violet color of twilight and beckons me outside. I'm taking a bag of garbage out to the bin at the end of the driveway when a Jeep comes slowly down the road, kicking up felty bits of fresh snow behind its tires. It disappears down the

153

block, but the next time I glance out the window, it's parked a few yards down the road. The lights are off, but a driver is sitting inside and I know, I just know this is bad.

I say nothing to the sisters, but I take the binoculars from the hook by the door and peer out to the Jeep. Zooming in, I spy the soft fur that lines the driver's hood and his hawklike nose. His wispy mustache confirms my suspicions.

It's Ian.

He has found me. He must have been watching for me, but I don't understand how he knew where to look for me. Did Berg send him?

"What are you looking at?" Portia asks, coming into the kitchen.

"Nothing," I say.

I lower the binoculars, and Ian takes that moment to start up the Jeep and drive away.

She glances out the window. "Do you know that Jeep?"

"No," I say.

That night, the Jeep returns to park in the same place, stalking me, and I know it's time to leave. After the sisters go to sleep, I gently pick Jenny's lock, sneak into her room, and find her phone where it's charging next to her bed. I steal it silently, then creep to the downstairs bathroom and close the door to muffle my voice.

I'm paranoid about my Forge email being watched by Berg, but it's also the most likely way Linus and Burnham would have tried to reach me, so I log in. My inbox has 5,662 emails in it. Impressive. I do a search for Linus and focus in on one likely message.

From: Linus Pitts <l.pitts2049@gmail.com>
To: Rosie Sinclair <rsinclair@theforgeschool.com>
Sent: Monday, November 1, 2066, 4:35 PM
Subject: call me

Rosie, if you see this, call me.
314-287-4351
L.

Succinct. Works for me. I jot down the number and his email address on a piece of paper. Next I search for Burnham and find this:

From: Burnham Fister <baf@fister.com>
To: Rosie Sinclair <rsinclair@theforgeschool.com>
Sent: Friday, December 24, 2066, 11:42 PM
Subject: ho ho

Merry Christmas wherever you are.

I stare at the words so long I can hear them in his voice. He sent it shortly before midnight on Christmas Eve, and I feel a wistful sadness as I think of Burnham in some bough-laden house, surrounded by colored lights, thinking of me. I wish I had a number for him. I'm tempted to write him back, but I'm paranoid enough to suspect my Forge email account isn't safe. Berg can doubtless check it for activity. I jot down Burnham's email address and log out.

My heart's doing odd little skips, because I'm back to staring at Linus's phone number. I can't forget that he goaded me into telling all my hard-won secrets to the cameras at Forge, and then he suggested I'd dreamed it all, so that I wavered and doubted myself. It was the absolute worst feeling. Yet later he'd tried to help me, too. He must have believed me, up to a point.

I don't know what to think about him, but I have this urge to reconnect with him and see what he'll say. It feels like a risk just calling him, but I come up with a logical reason: maybe he can tell me something I can use to get to Berg.

I dial his number carefully. I press my thumbnail to the gap in my teeth and listen anxiously through two rings.

"Linus here. What's up?"

I nearly drop the phone. It's his own voice, with his Welsh vowels and a dose of cranky sleepiness. He sounds impossibly near and familiar. My pulse goes haywire, and I squeeze my eyes shut.

"Hi. It's me, Rosie," I say softly.

A shifting noise comes from his end. "Okay, let's hear it," he says.

No surprise. No concern. He sounds almost bored. It hurts. "I was calling to see how you're doing, but if this is a bad time," I say, uncertain.

"How'd you get this number?"

"From your email, remember? You sent it to me."

A creak comes over the line, as if he's switching positions on a noisy bed. "When?"

"Last November." I'm getting irritated. "What's going on?"

"Rosie? Is it really you?" he says.

"Who else would I be?"

"I get a lot of prank callers," he says.

I can tell he doubts me still. Part of me wants to hang up, but instead I try to think of something that will convince him I'm me. "We talked on walkie-hams at night at Forge," I say. "I stole your swipe pass from your pocket that time you loaned me your jacket." I think back. "You used to make spaghetti and watch *Shakespeare in Love* with Otis and Parker when you paid your blood for rent. Do you still?"

"Wow," he says softly. "Where are you?"

"In Colorado. I've been staying with some friends."

"Someone named Althea?" he asks.

"No. Who's that?"

He mutters something I can't hear. Then, "Some girl called me a couple weeks ago. She said she was a friend of Rosie's. She knew everything about us, even the private things we said to each other at night. Are you sure you don't know her? Althea?"

"Never heard of her," I say.

"Then I was right," he says slowly. "All that stuff I thought I was saying to you, you never heard. Why would she do that?"

I lean back against the sink. "I don't know who you're

talking about, but I haven't talked to you since last October, when you were leaving for St. Louis." When we essentially broke up. "What sort of stuff did you think you were telling me?" I ask.

"It was awkward."

"But was it nice stuff?" As soon as it's out, I regret it. "Forget that."

"I've always tried to be nice to you," he says quietly, and somehow that makes it worse.

I've been alone for so long. I thought because he showed up down in the vault that he was on my side after all, but I don't really know anything for sure where Linus is concerned.

"Remember how you thought I was dreaming it all?" I say. "You made me look like a fool on *The Forge Show*. That wasn't particularly nice."

"I know. I'm sorry. I didn't understand yet."

"Did Berg ever mine you?" I ask. "Tell me this. When he had you down in the vault, did he mine your dreams?"

"I don't know," he says. "I didn't feel any different."

"You don't feel different at first. At first, you can't even tell. But then—" I gulp in a big breath. "But after a while, you're not even really sure who you are anymore."

"Where are you, Rosie?" he says, sounding both sad and urgent. "Let me come find you. We need to talk in person."

"I don't want to be on your show."

"Of course not," he says. "I just want to talk."

But talking to Linus is breaking something inside me, and I don't want to feel weak. "If you're so popular and powerful now, why haven't you done anything to shut down Berg?" I ask.

"That's not the simplest thing to do," he says.

I let out a laugh. It shouldn't be any harder than killing him, which I aim to do.

"Where've you been all this time?" Linus asks. "Are you safe now?"

"Berg had me at a place called the Onar Clinic, near Denver," I say. "I escaped a couple weeks ago."

"Why didn't you call me? I've been looking for you. I can help you, Rosie."

"I don't think so," I say. And it's true. That's what hurts. I thought I wanted to hear his voice. I thought reaching out to him might make me feel a little better, but he's been in the real world having a real life while I've been buried alive, and somehow his offer of help feels worse than too late. I don't want help from him. "This was a mistake," I say. "What if your line's bugged?"

"The line's not bugged. Just tell me where you are," he says.

I hold the phone away from my cheek, staring at the numbers. Ian is down the block. He could have some high-tech audio surveillance on the house. He's probably overhearing my every needy word.

"I have to go," I say.

"Rosie!"

I end the call and listen attentively to the house, anxious for quiet. My stupid whim to call my ex might cost me everything.

I have to leave now, before Berg traces my call, and before Jenny and Portia realize what I've done. I delete my call from Jenny's phone. Stealthily, I open the bathroom door, and at that instant, the phone buzzes in my hand.

I jump out of my skin.

I scan the unfamiliar number, and a shiver of foreboding lifts along my arms. I answer and bring the phone to my ear. "Yes?" I whisper.

"This is your guardian, Sandy Berg," he says. His voice is the calm of a poised cobra. "Please tell me you're somewhere safe."

My veins seize up. I have an instant of pure, mindless panic, and then I switch to survival mode and everything goes very clear.

"What do you want?" I ask.

While he's talking, I move swiftly and quietly out of the bathroom and into the dark kitchen. Out the window, the Jeep is still parked in the road with its lights off. I grab the binoculars.

"You're not well," Berg continues. "I know this may not make sense to you, but you've been suffering from delusions. You're liable to feel persecuted. Paranoid. You've left your treatment at a very critical time, and I'm afraid you could suffer a severe setback if we don't get you back home immediately."

At my ankle, Gingerbread gives a soft meow. I gently, firmly shove her aside and keep my binoculars aimed at the Jeep. I can barely make out Ian's figure.

"You never give up, do you?" I say. "I'm not crazy. Quit telling me I am."

"Of course you're not crazy," Berg says. "But you're not at your most stable, either, are you? Please, Rosie. I can find you from this number, but it's time-consuming to search, and we need to minimize the press, for your own sake. Tell me where you are, and I'll come for you myself."

He doesn't know where I am yet, if I can believe him. Ian doesn't seem awake, and he certainly doesn't have a phone next to his ear. He's a piece that doesn't fit in the puzzle.

"What home would you take me to?" I ask Berg. "Doli?"

Berg sighs. "No, my vacation home in Colorado, where you've been recuperating. I've hired a team to take care of you, day and night. Everyone on the staff is very concerned about you. We're all anxious to have you safely back."

"You're lying," I say. "I was in a vault at the Onar Clinic. Dr. Ash has been operating on me. You've been stealing my dreams."

"Dr. Ash has been working at the Forge School, like always," he says. "I see her there every day."

"Don't lie to me!" I say. "I'm not playing your games anymore. I don't believe you!"

"Okay, suppose, just suppose you're right," he says. "I'm not saying you are, but let's suppose you've been in a vault like you say. Suppose you became resistant to your therapy, and I began to fear that your mind was decaying. Suppose I determined that the best antidote for your decay was to allow you to have a little autonomy. A little freedom." A shifting noise comes from his end of the line, and his voice drops softly. "Is it exciting, being out on your own?"

"What do you mean?" I ask, chilled.

"Have you had enough stimulation?" he says.

I punch disconnect and throw the phone away. It skitters across the kitchen table, hits the floor, and bangs against the base of the oven.

He can't make me believe he *let* me escape. I'm not free temporarily for the sake of some stimulation.

Gingerbread meows from behind the fridge. With a shock, I freeze, listening. A thump comes from upstairs. One of the sisters must have heard the bang of the phone. She'll be coming downstairs, and as soon as they realize I've phoned out, they'll want the reward. Portia will call the hotline.

"Rosie?" Jenny calls quietly from above.

I have to go. I retrieve the phone and grab the nearest coat. I shove my feet in mismatched boots. I peer out at Ian in his dark Jeep, and, as I consider the puzzle once more, it hits me: Ian's stalking doesn't fit. The timing's wrong. He was here *before* I talked to Berg, and he hasn't made any move to come into the house. The more I think of it, Ian is the last person Dean Berg would ever send after me, and, finally, a wild idea occurs to me.

Ian isn't here because of Berg. He hasn't been sent. He's here because of us.

Him and me.

Ian has tracked me here by heart.

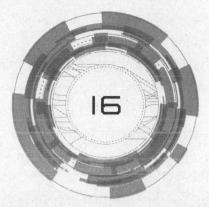

— ROSIE —

SPITFIRE

SILENTLY, SO JENNY WON'T HEAR, I let myself out of the house. The last thing I do before I crunch down the snowy driveway is disconnect the battery from her phone and hurl the pieces into the backyard, where they're swallowed up by the dark and the snow. Wind whips at my cheeks, but I put my head down and aim unwaveringly toward Ian's Jeep.

I knock on the window of the passenger door. "Hey!"

Ian startles, and a second later, the door clicks from within, unlocking. I pull it open to a gust of warm air and the reek of cigarettes. Ian's pale face is ghostly by the dashboard light.

"What are you doing here?" I ask.

He clears his throat, as if he doesn't expect his voice to work properly. "I'm here to help you."

The wind blows a shimmer of snow between us.

"Berg didn't send you?" I ask.

"No," he says. "I came myself. I quit my job."

I glance back toward the house where now half the lights are on.

"Are you going to hurt me if I get in?" I ask.

His beady eyes burn, and he speaks with low, feverish intensity. "I'd rather kill myself."

Good enough for this girl. Like a nightmare, Ian ought to be something I can control if I exert enough will.

"Then drive," I say, and I climb in.

He tosses an oily paper bag off my seat. Then he pulls onto the road. I take a look back and see Portia coming outside just as we turn the first corner. I notice a pet carrier that rests on the backseat of Ian's Jeep. A gun rack with a rifle is mounted above the back window. I check around for visible mics and cameras but find none. A flimsy figurine dangles from the rearview mirror.

"Where to?" he asks.

He blasts the heat.

"We need a place to hide and come up with a plan," I say.

"North, then. I know a place."

I peer over at him. Ian is wearing the kind of gloves where his fingertips come out the ends, like Fagan, and all of his fingernails are bitten down to the quick. His little, wispy mustache is practically the same color as his skin. His coat, a poofy, white number, was probably picked out by his grandmother, but he tracked me here somehow, and I'm not going to underestimate him.

"How'd you find me?" I ask.

"I tailed your car to the diner that first night, but then I lost you," he says. He taps a finger on the wheel. "It took me a few days to remember the black woman who walked out just as I was going in. I asked the waitress who that might be. She didn't know, but I kept watching the diner, and sure enough, a couple nights ago, the same woman came back. I followed her home and watched her house. Then I saw you come out with a bag of garbage yesterday. It was fate."

"You mean stalking."

"Stalking's when you follow the person and won't leave them alone," he says. "Waiting is different. It's a form of tribute, like a vigil, and fate rewards it."

O-kay, I think.

He takes a big, deep breath and keeps his gaze toward the road. "I've had time to think about us," he says. "It isn't always easy, but people need to talk to each other honestly when they're in a relationship."

"That's true," I say cautiously.

"It takes sacrifice and patience," he says. "People make mistakes, but they can be forgiven if they come clean and they're humble enough to ask for forgiveness."

I feel a tingle of foreboding. "Who needs to be forgiven?" I ask.

"You left me."

I glance at his profile to see that he's serious, and I get it. This is a pivotal moment, but if I'm apologetic, then he establishes control. I can't have that. "Not the way I see it," I say. "You let me wake up. You deliberately messed with my meds, and then you went outside on purpose when nobody else was watching so I'd have a chance to escape."

"That's not right," he says.

"You even told me the other guy was leaving his keys in his car."

"I didn't know you were listening. I didn't know you were outside."

"But you *should* have known," I say. "It was your job to watch me, and instead you let me go. That means it's your responsibility that I'm free. And that, Ian, is why I'm grateful to you. I'm not going to turn around and apologize when what I'm feeling is grateful."

He keeps his gaze aimed on the road. "You're grateful," he says.

"Since we're speaking honestly, yes, I am."

He taps the wheel again. "Then that's all right." His lips quirk in a tiny smile.

I am not deceived. Ian is dangerous. He dreamed up our relationship, and he used me as his fantasy girlfriend when I was helpless. Just like before, it's essential for me to play him exactly right, but I have the advantage now because he cares for me, and all I do is despise him.

"What's this," I ask, fingering the statuette that hangs from the mirror. It feels like an air freshener, but it doesn't stand a chance against the cigarette stench.

"That's Gandhi," he says. "For peace."

"Like your rifle?"

"That's for peace, too."

Sure it is. The Jeep is toasty warm now, so I reach to turn the heat down, and the rushing noise drops to a hum. I check the gas level, which is full. We could go many hours before we need to stop, and it's possible he has a spare battery with him. I check the back again and notice a couple of boxes on the floor before the pet carrier. One of them, I swear, says Fister on it, like for Burnham's family's company.

"What are those boxes?" I ask.

"Some drugs, just in case I find an injured animal on the road. They'll work for you, too, if you get a headache or you can't get to sleep."

My heart stops completely, and then I instinctively touch my hand to my shirt. I can feel the lump of my port under my skin.

"Are they the sleep meds from Onar?" I ask.

"Yes, but I didn't steal them. They were expired. I was supposed to throw them out, but they still work just fine."

He has the means to drug me to sleep, right here in the Jeep. I swallow hard.

"Pull over," I say.

"How come?"

"Just pull over!" I say. "We're throwing out those boxes."

"We are not," he says. "They're worth a ton of money, and you don't know what could happen to you. You could need those meds."

"Pull over! I mean it! I want them out!"

"Would you just listen?"

I roll down my window. I take off my seat belt and flip around to reach behind the seat. He brakes and swerves the Jeep until we bump to the edge of the snowy road and come to a stop. I grab the nearest box. He makes no move to interfere as I pull back the lid. A dozen little vials are inside. A handful of syringes are, too, and a half dozen IV drips. I hold up one of the vials, ready to throw it out. These are what have ruled my life. This is the poison that has controlled me. Cold wind swirls in my window.

"I understand that you're sensitive about the meds," Ian says calmly. "But you can trust me. I'll only use them on you if you ask."

"I hate these drugs," I say.

"I know. I'm sure. But they're harmless now. Trust me."

I glance up to find him watching me with patient, rodent eyes. I'm desperate to throw out the drugs, but with the weight of the vial in my hand, I realize it's a weapon, too. It's power. I can use it to let him think I trust him, but that will also mean keeping the drugs in the car.

Ahead of us, our high beams cast whiteness over the dark, snowy road. Dawn is coming, but for now, we're far from anywhere. If I get out to walk, I'll probably freeze to death before I reach shelter. By contrast, Ian and the drugs are known evils.

I take a deep breath, still holding the vial. "Why do you have a pet cage back there?"

"I keep it with me as a memento of my old cat, Peanut," Ian says. "And sometimes I use it for the hurt animals I find on the road. I've got some gloves back there, too."

He is completely serious.

I resist a snide desire to laugh. "Peanut," I say.

"Peanut the cat. Eleven years I had her."

I take a deep breath to calm myself. Then I think of him loving his cat, like it was practice for me. "Promise me you won't use these drugs on me," I say.

"I promise," he says.

I shift the box to the floor by my feet and roll up my window. Ian reminds me about my seat belt and pulls back out on the highway. I watch the sky grow from dark gray to pinker. Ian sniffs occasionally beside me. He asks if I mind if he smokes. I tell him to go ahead, and he cracks the window while he does. He rolls it back up with a sucking noise when he's done.

"You're probably wondering where we're going," Ian says, some time later. "I know a nice motel on a lake where I used to go duck hunting with my dad. The season's wrong, but it's peaceful there. Not a lot of people. The motel rooms all have a coffeemaker and a minifridge. It's a drive, though. We won't make it 'til late tonight. How's that sound?"

"Fine," I say. I intend to ditch him long before then. I stretch my legs a bit. I reach down to take off my boots and manage a stealthy grab from the drug box. "I remember you once told

169

me you had another girl you talked to at Onar," I say. "Who was she?"

"She didn't ever really come around all the way like you," he says. "I just imagined she did. I know the difference."

"What happened to her?"

"I don't know much about it. They moved her out to Miehana."

"Where do the dreamers come from?" I ask.

"I already told you. St. Louis. You were an exception."

"But where in St. Louis? They don't just have a bodies factory there."

He glances over briefly. "They get them from the Annex," he says. "It's an emporium. You can buy whatever you need there. Berg orders them online." He warms to his topic, as if proud to share his expertise. "We have two kinds of dreamers, the ones that are basically soil, for seeding dreams into, and the mineable ones that haven't fully decayed yet. Those are the valuable ones."

"Where does the Annex get the bodies?" I ask.

"I don't know. Pre-morgues, I guess. It's fully legit, if you're worried about that." He glances my way again and smiles. "You think it's gross."

"I may be biased."

Ian laughs. "There's nothing wrong with it," he says. "I mean, I know most people aren't comfortable with the idea of shipping bodies around, but they don't like to think about where their meat comes from, either. Personally, I'd rather have brains recycled than left to rot in graves. This way they can help somebody. How's it any different from recycling eyeballs or hearts?"

"It's completely different if the person isn't dead, like me," I say.

"I know that. You were a special case."

"If you knew that, why did you let them mine me?"

The road hums under our wheels for a stretch while he doesn't answer. I realize I sound too accusatory and lower my voice.

"Ian John," I say. "You knew I was from *The Forge Show*. You knew I wasn't like the other dreamers. You told me so."

"I know."

"So then, why did you let them mine me? Didn't you see it was wrong?"

He shakes his head. "You were sick. Berg said that sleep therapy was the best thing for you. The mining you didn't even notice. It was like trimming your fingernails. It was nothing. A pinch of sand from the seashore."

He sounds suspiciously like he's parroting what he's heard. I'm not going to be able to persuade him otherwise. I think I was too perfect a temptation for him.

I pull one of my feet up under me on the seat. "Berg told me I was staying at his vacation place. He says he hired people to look after me there and I imagined the vault."

"I don't know about that. He visited you at Onar, though. He took you out for air."

"What do you mean?"

He looks at me sideways. "It was part of your therapy. He'd dress you up and prop you up for a visit out on the porch."

I recall the closet of clothes and wigs and gear at Onar, and suddenly it takes on horrifying possibilities.

"And you let him do this?" I ask, shocked.

"Sometimes you have to trust people who know what's best for you," he says.

"That is total crap."

"I don't like this way you're talking to me," he says.

"Berg *destroyed* me. He ruined my life, and you let him!"

"We saved you. You needed treatment. I saw what you were like on *Forge*, Rosie, and you were a mess, no offense."

I fume, glaring out the window. Unbelievable. I hate this person. I hate everything about him, from his cat cage to his mustache. I hate him almost as much as I hate Berg.

"Take me to St. Louis," I say.

"No. Your old boyfriend's there. We're going to the hunting motel. You'll like it. You need some quiet."

He pets my arm, and I jump out of my skin.

"Don't touch me!" I say.

He returns both hands to the wheel and accelerates the Jeep. "I was trying to be nice."

"I don't like being touched," I say.

"I don't like to be yelled at," he says.

"Then you shouldn't have touched me!"

The road flicks by, straight and ever faster. Any wavering of the steering wheel would send us into a ditch. I have to be smart. Now.

"I won't yell anymore," I say in a low voice.

"Say you're sorry."

He's got me. He has brought me back to this. He's still speeding up.

"I'm sorry. I might not be the easiest girlfriend," I say, "but I'm trying."

"Try harder."

I struggle to think like him and guess what he wants. "We were never going to fight," I say. "We promised, remember? I'm so sorry. It's all my fault. Forgive me?"

He slows the car slightly, and I hear him take a big, steady breath.

He taps the steering wheel again with his Fagan fingers. "I guessed you were a spitfire underneath," he says.

I cringe into myself, despising us both. My biggest fear now is that we'll drive all day and get to his duck hunting, minifridge motel before we have to stop for gas. But I have a handful of the sleep med vials and syringes in my pocket. I am not unarmed.

— THEA —

HOME

I WASN'T PRIVY TO THE CONVERSATION between Diego and Madeline, nor the showdown when they talked to Dr. Fallon, but by dawn, Althea's parents and I were flying away from the Chimera Centre in our private jet. I watched the island drop below me and shrink as we rose over the ocean.

"Do you need anything? Feel okay?" Madeline asked me.

"I'm fine," I said, pressing the armrest button to lean my seat back. In fact, I was a mess of emotions, from grim relief at finally leaving Chimera to sick fear for Rosie who was still asleep somewhere in Berg's control.

"I still think this is a mistake," Madeline said. "I don't see how talking to one scientist changes everything. If anything, this hybrid glitch of Althea's is all the more reason why we should stay. Dr. Fallon is still the best person in the world to be treating her."

"We're done here," Diego said.

I sent him a grateful look. Apparently, there were rare times when he called the shots for the family. I gazed out the airplane window at the ripply clouds below and tried to process all I knew. My gut told me Ma needed to know that my father was alive, but even if I was able to communicate with her, the news would rip her up. She was married to Larry and had been now for years, but I knew she still grieved for my dad. I was starting to understand why Orson never told her. In the ways that counted, he wasn't actually my father.

Still, it felt wrong not telling her. I wished I could talk it all over with a close friend. Someone like Rosie. She would empathize.

It was so strange to think that two of us could exist now. As soon as possible, I intended to get to the Onar Clinic and free her, and I couldn't guess what I'd find. I felt inwardly complete, like I'd taken my soul, my inherent me-ness with me when I'd escaped. But that presented a puzzle for what I'd left behind. Did she feel whole, too? Had we split neatly into two? She might be lost in an unthinking stupor.

I needed to find out. Despite what Orson had said, I couldn't help wishing there was some way I could still return to my old body and leave Althea's life behind. At the very least, I needed to discover what had happened to her.

Hours later, as we approached Holdum, Texas, the welcome sight of green rose to meet us. Our jet touched down, and with my first whiff of warm, balmy air, I shook off my last hunch of winter. A driver collected our gear while I took a backseat in a fancy, new-smelling SUV. A big sky arched above the sprawling landscape, and random, solitary trees ruled over plots of green. We passed a barbed wire fence strung with catfish heads and a yard full of birdbaths for sale. I liked Texas.

"Almost home," Diego said.

At the next corner, we turned off the highway onto a private road.

"At last," Madeline said softly. "Would you look at the laurel."

Shrubs of blue flowers edged the road, which went on for another couple of miles before we slowed to pass through a security gate. As we came around a final bend, a wide, sunny valley opened up on my right, like a giant hand had scooped out a perfect bowl of earth and filled it with grasses and wildflowers. On a ledge overlooking the valley stood a huge, rambling house of wood and stone. I counted five chimneys. An enormous beech tree dropped dark shade over the front yard and the porch, where a beagle rose to its feet.

"You didn't tell me we lived in a castle," I said as we pulled up.

"It's just an old farmhouse, really," Madeline said. "We added on."

"Hey, girl. Hey Solana," Diego said, getting out. "Look who's back."

The dog trotted eagerly over to Diego. I smoothed my

sweater over my belly, caught up my cane, and stepped out of the car.

Madeline moved beside me and crouched down. "Solana, come here, girl! It's Althea. Get over here and say hello."

The dog came over to sniff at my knees and sneakers, but she showed no special recognition.

"It's okay," I said. I reached down to pat the dog's soft head.

"I don't understand it," Madeline said. "I thought she'd be ecstatic. She still sleeps at the foot of your bed."

A door slammed, and up on the porch, a dozen people came spilling out. They hurried down the steps, calling and laughing in welcome.

"Althea!"

"*¡Bienvenida a casa!*"

"Really, Diego?" Madeline said.

"*Es nuestra familia,*" Diego said. "What could I say?"

Two dozen aunts, uncles, and cousins surrounded us, all laughing and talking at once. Most of them were Latino, like Diego, but a few were from Madeline's side of the family, and all of them seemed bent on hugging me to death. Madeline tried to introduce people, but the names blurred together. Sunny and sassy, avuncular and intense, the different personalities were overwhelming. Aunts patted my belly and exclaimed over the baby, and a little boy cousin shyly gave me a home-made fuse bead star.

The last person to claim me was a big, hulking man with a strong resemblance to Diego. Althea's grandfather wore a hat

177

and a button-down shirt, as if he'd dressed up to bring some dignity to the occasion, and when he calmly took my hand, his grasp warmed me through.

"*Mi corazoncita,*" he said. "I'm so happy to have you home again! Let me see you." He studied me openly. "Tell me honestly now," he added. "How much do you remember?"

Around us, the others grew quiet. I glanced awkwardly from one face to another.

"I'm sorry," I said. "I've never seen this place before. I don't remember any of you." A flicker of headache pulsed through my brain, and I squinted against the brightness.

In the stillness, the little boy cousin tugged his mother's skirt. "Can I have a popsicle yet?" he asked in a loud whisper.

The others stirred again and smiled.

"It's all right," Grampa said to me, patting my hand. "The heart knows where it belongs."

"Okay, everybody," Madeline said. "Let's give Althea a chance to settle in."

"That's right," added an aunt. "Food's on. Aim for the kitchen."

The circle broke up, and the family began drifting back inside.

Grampa offered me his elbow, and I shifted my cane so I could take his arm.

"Have you talked to Tom?" he asked. We walked slowly up the steps into the soft shade of the porch.

I shook my head.

"I'm surprised the boy hasn't shown up," he said. "Maybe

he's learned some sense. If you need anything, you let me know, hear?"

"Okay," I said.

"'Yes, sir,' you mean," he said gently. "That's how we do it here."

I gave him a quick look, but his expression was kind.

"Okay. Yes, sir," I said.

He gave my hand another pat and released me as we stepped into the darker coolness of the house. He headed toward the kitchen, and I instinctively breathed deep, curious to see if the place might feel familiar in any way and awaken a trace of Althea inside me.

The air was redolent with a mix of furniture polish, a tang of wood smoke, and the sweetness of baking brownies. Laughter and the clink of silverware carried from the back of the house. The driver came in with a couple of suitcases and headed up a wide staircase toward a landing with big, tall windows. On my right, in the living room, a bronze sculpture of a duck sat on a small table by the windows, and books were piled and tucked into every corner. Time-mellowed woodwork laced up to a high ceiling, and a soft, heirloom carpet in indigo and beige beckoned me to take off my shoes. Already I could see glimpses of a library, a solarium, and a music room.

"This is beautiful," I muttered, and stroked my hand along the back of a chair, liking the satiny wood. None of it was familiar.

"It's home," Madeline said from behind me.

I turned to see her taking a desultory pass through the

mail on the hall table. She had a subtle new air about her, still commanding but more relaxed, like she'd arrived where she belonged.

She glanced up at me and smiled. "*Something* here ought to resonate, don't you think? Eventually? Even if it doesn't, you can learn your memories again. That's what Dr. Fallon said. Enough to get by and go forward."

"It wouldn't be learning *again*. It would just be learning, the first time around," I said.

Her smile pinched at the corners. "We're saying the same thing."

We weren't, but I didn't see the point of arguing. "Yes, ma'am."

She gave my arm a motherly squeeze. "Come get a bite to eat."

"I could use a minute to freshen up, actually," I said.

"Of course," she said. "Head on up. Take your time, and I'll see to the family. Your father's right. We couldn't keep them away, but they don't have to stay forever, either. Solana, go with Althea. Go on."

Solana and I looked doubtfully at each other.

"Hi, Solana," I said. "Want to go find my room?"

The dog wagged her tail. I pointed with my cane, and she bounded up the steps ahead of me. I had just reached the top of the stairs when I heard a commotion below and paused to look back.

"Thea!" a guy called. "Thea! Where are you?"

Solana gave a bark, barged past me, and scrambled down the stairs again. I held on to the bannister, peering over.

Down below, a guy sank his hand into Solana's furry neck, looked up my way, and froze. I stared in surprise. I recognized Tom instantly from his photos, but he was utterly different in real life. Whiplash energy coiled in his frame and bright, compelling eyes lit his face. A bolt of alertness shot through me.

"Thea!" he said. "You're actually here. I don't believe this!"

A man charged in from the side and tackled Tom out of sight.

"Outside!" Diego yelled. "I don't want you under my roof!"

I came down the steps as fast as my legs would let me and found Tom backed against a wall, both his arms up, with Diego inches from his face.

"I just want to talk to her," Tom said.

"I want you out!" Diego gave him another shove.

Tom shot his gaze to me. "Thea, come outside with me. I'm not going to fight your father."

Diego packed a jab into Tom's gut, and with an Oof! Tom folded over.

"Thea!" Tom said.

I was shocked by Diego's sudden violence, but even more, I was stunned by my reaction to Tom. A foreign sense of urgency, a deep, reaching awareness syphoned all of my attention toward him. I was riveted by the turn of his neck and the ruddy color in his cheek as he glanced up at me from his pained position.

Diego hauled Tom toward the front door and delivered another punch to his gut. I winced in vicarious pain. A swarm of men rushed in from the kitchen and pulled Tom and Diego apart. The rest of the family flooded in, too, shouting questions.

"For heaven's sake," Madeline said. "Get ahold of yourself, Diego!"

"I don't want him under my roof!" Diego bellowed.

Tom shook off the men who were holding him and strode outside.

I started after him.

Diego caught my arm. My cane clattered to the floor. "You don't have to talk to him," he said. His chest was heaving. "I'll kick his mangy butt off the property. You just got home and already! Already it begins!"

"I want to hear what he has to say," I said. "Let go of me."

Diego only held tighter. He shook his head, back and forth, like a bulldog that refuses to negotiate. "He's going to twist you up. He always does. He's going say things that make you think we're the bad guys, me and your mother, and that's the last thing we need right now. The last stinking thing this family needs."

"Would you let go?" I said fiercely, tugging against his painful grip. "I'm not stupid."

He released me suddenly. He glared at me a long, conflicted moment, and then his lips closed in a hard line. "You might not be stupid, but look at you. What's he doing to you already?"

I didn't know. Some new excitement buzzed in my veins, and I wasn't surprised that it showed. I turned to look toward the doorway, where sunlight gleamed beyond the porch, beckoning. "I'm just going to talk to him," I said.

A dozen worried people surrounded us, but no one spoke. In the silence, Grampa bent over to pick up my cane.

"You said yourself you don't know anyone here," Diego said to me. "But we know you, and we know him, too. Trust me. You don't need to talk to him. Listen to me, please, this once."

"I am listening," I said. "But it's my life now. Mine to make my own mistakes with or not."

"You're killing us," Diego said. "Tell her, Madeline."

But Madeline only shook her head. I'm not sure I would have heard her speak, anyway. The feverish curiosity in me was burning with a life of its own, lighting me up inside and drawing me toward Tom. I had to answer it for my own sake as much as his.

"Unbelievable," Diego said. He turned on his heel and elbowed through the others.

I took my cane from Grampa, passed out the front door to the porch, and paused at the steps, wondering at the churning that charged my pulse. It had nothing to do with logic.

Tom stood in the shade of the big beech in the yard, facing away, toward a breathtaking view of the valley. The leaves were a dark, purply red, and the trunk was a melting gray color that seemed to pour downward rather than grow out of the ground. Together, Tom and the distant horizon and the tree created a striking, eternal picture. A splash of sunlight dropped through the leaves and lit up the shoulder of his shirt, and when he turned to face me, every cell in my body calibrated to a new hum.

My cane made a hollow noise on the wooden steps as I started down. Behind me, I heard the movement of a dozen people, and then the distinctive ratchet noise of a rifle being cocked.

"Upset her in any way, boy, and I'll shoot you dead," Diego said clearly.

"Thanks, Dad," I said. "I'll take it from here."

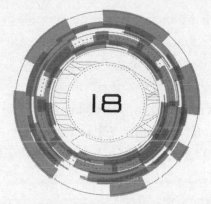

18

— THEA —

MAROON

I STRODE SLOWLY DOWN TO TOM, and I tried with each measured placement of my cane to still the adrenaline in my veins. Behind me, my pseudo-father, who had seemed so sensitive and gentle at Chimera, had just demonstrated a shocking capacity for violence. I wasn't sure what to make of any of it.

"Don't mind my father," I said. "He doesn't mean anything with the gun."

"Except he does," Tom said. "He'd love to shoot my nuts off."

Up close, Althea's boyfriend was nothing like the easy, adoring guy in his photos. In a faded plaid shirt over loose-fitting, dusty jeans, the real Tom was taller and leaner. The dappled shade made each detail of him vivid, from his worn, scuffed boots to a blotchy freckle on his collarbone. His short hair was lighter than I had expected, and softer looking. His blue eyes were harder.

"Did he hurt you?" I asked.

"No." He wiped the corner of his mouth and nodded toward my cane and my belly. "How are you?"

I smoothed a hand down my blue sweatshirt. "Not bad. I'm awake and pregnant."

"I see. And the baby?"

"Healthy."

He peered at me with grim, unnerving directness. "You were essentially dead," he said. "You know that, right? What did your parents do to you?"

"They managed to get me out of a coma," I said. "Is that a problem?"

He closed his eyes for a moment and opened them again with a pained expression. "I'm sorry," he said. "You would not believe how many times I've imagined talking to you again, and now I don't know what to say."

"You're happy to see me?" I suggested.

He winced briefly and then gave a slow, crooked smile. "Yes. Of course. I'm sorry. Do over?"

My heart gave a tiny kick. "Sure."

He pointed toward the road. "Want to walk to the stables? Can you go that far?"

For a moment, I considered the risk of getting to know him at all. I wasn't here to pose as Althea in her old life. I wanted to get well enough to go find Rosie, and Tom could only be a complication. Still, there was something bluntly compelling about him.

I smiled. "Let's find out," I said.

I glanced back toward the house, expecting Diego to still be armed on the porch, but he had gone inside with everyone except Grampa, who was settled in a wicker chair. He tipped his hat and shook out a newspaper. I waved back.

Tom and I soon left the road for a dirt lane that was bordered by laurel, and each tiny bell of blue petals was a perfect witness to our awkwardness. He said politely that he was glad I was back. I thanked him. I felt self-conscious with my cane. Tom's stride, matched to mine, was hardly less stilted. An empty paddock beside the barn was fenced in white. A muted clanking came from inside the barn. Above, a greenish copper vane of a running horse pointed west into the breeze, and I breathed deep. After months of confinement, it was heaven.

"It's so pretty," I said.

"Yes."

In the open door of the barn, I paused at the smell of horseflesh. I held my breath and gazed down a row of horses, huge and dark in their stalls. When I breathed again, the scent magnified into a noxious mix of sweat, hay, and manure. I turned instead for the paddock.

"Are you okay?" Tom asked, following me.

"The smell's too strong in there," I said, unzipping my sweatshirt.

"Can I get you anything?" Tom asked. "Do you want to sit?"

"No," I said. "I'm totally fine. My sense of smell's just sharper than it used to be." I took a few more steps toward the white fence and focused on the pure air. The riding ring inside the fence was carpeted with overturned clods of rich, dark earth.

"I feel like I should do something for you," he said.

I smiled. "You can't, really."

"This is weird," he said. "Isn't it weird to be back here together?"

"It's weird period," I said.

"What's it like to be pregnant?"

I laughed. "It's like having a whole new body. It's like being taken over by an alien who loves to kick your bladder. Sometimes it's actually kind of wonderful, but more often it's terrifying."

He nodded, watching me closely. "I want you to know I plan to be a good father," he said. "That's why I came. To tell you that. And I'll do whatever it takes to support the baby."

"You don't have to do anything."

"Yeah, but I do. And I'm sorry," he said. "I'm sorry for everything. Fighting with you, and then signing off on the baby. I only did it because I thought it would help. You realize that, don't you?"

"Help how?" I asked. "I'm not sure what you're saying."

He braced a hand on the top rail of the fence and frowned toward the valley. When he looked over at me again, his eyes were deeply troubled. "Okay. You have to know what bad shape you were in after the accident. I couldn't stand to see you suffer anymore. I thought signing off as the baby's father was a technicality I had to agree to before the doctors would pull the plug on you. Then your parents claimed guardianship of the baby and used your pregnancy to justify keeping you alive."

"They never told me this," I said. "Is that even legal?"

"They were already calling the shots for you," he said. "The baby just made their position stronger. I wasn't going to fight them at that point."

"Let me get this straight," I said. "You wanted me to *die*?"

"You were *already* dead, Thea," he said. "You were just a body barely breathing. For weeks you were like that, and you weren't getting better. The only sound you ever made was a tiny, guttural whimpering sometimes. It was the most heart-breaking sound. That's when I wanted to let you die. Was I wrong?"

I had to see the irony of him asking me this, except I wasn't Althea who had survived. In the end, her consciousness was gone. "I don't know," I said. "If I had died, the baby would have died, too."

"I know. That ripped me up. Believe me," Tom said. "But it was cruel to keep you alive and suffering for the baby's sake, especially when you'd never even wanted it."

"I didn't want the baby?"

He tilted his head, and then his voice dropped low. "They didn't tell you."

Althea didn't want this baby. The idea blew my mind. I'd thought since she was Catholic, she had wanted her baby.

I was only alive now, standing by this fence, because Althea had been pregnant when she went into a coma. However bizarrely I'd come to exist in Althea's body, I owed this baby my latest life. I didn't know why this news shifted the debt I felt, but it infused it with sadness, and somehow, it gave me a different ownership of this fetus within me. We needed each other more than ever.

Tom was watching me thoughtfully. "You look confused."

"I am. It's a lot to take in," I said. "Are you Catholic, too?"

"Yes," he said. "How much do you remember from your life before?"

"Nothing," I said.

His eyes narrowed. "But you can talk and everything just fine. Your mind's working like normal."

"Not exactly normal," I said. "I don't remember any details from my life before."

"Are you saying you don't remember *me*?"

Nerves swirled in my gut. "I'm sorry," I said slowly. "I don't."

He let out a snort. "You might be mad at me or whatever, but you couldn't forget about us."

"Don't try to tell me what I know," I said.

"Then don't talk crap," he said.

I braced my cane and faced him directly. "I don't think you get it. I have a *brain injury*."

"Forget brains," he said. "I know about this."

I half expected him to grab me like some macho dude, and

I was ready to shove him off, but instead, he skimmed a finger over the back of my hand. I gripped my cane harder, stunned by the feathered tingling that ran along my skin. With a shock, I found his lips close to mine. I caught my breath.

"Remember me now?" he whispered.

I shook my head slightly.

"Not now?" he asked, and dovetailed his fingers lightly over mine.

My cane dropped away. My body, which had been a sluggish, uncooperative partner in my existence ever since I'd woken up in it, now electrified with sensitivity.

"Still no," I said.

He laughed softly. "Yeah, right." And then he kissed me.

I locked my knees. His pressure was tender and light. Different. A tiny desperate flag in the back of my mind warned me this was a mistake, but I ignored it. When I almost closed my eyes, he held back slightly, and it took me a sec to realize he was waiting for me to lean in, like this was a dance and I had a choice. I leaned in, touching a hand to his chest for balance. It turned out he knew exactly how to match his lips to my new ones. I tilted into him even more, riding instinct, and Tom's mouth moved easily with mine.

"Um," I mumbled. That was not supposed to be so good.

He held still, his chin half an inch away.

"Don't say you've forgotten me," he said. "You couldn't be that mean."

I lifted my gaze to his. My heart was still pounding with eager, visceral certainty, and I took a break from strict honesty.

"It's possible some small, unreasoning part of me remembers you," I said.

"That's what I'm talking about," he said, smiling.

He slid his arms loosely around me so my curved belly fit against him. My shirt met his. I pressed my tender lips together and glanced over his shoulder toward the barn, wary of onlookers. The warning flag in my mind kicked in again and produced a name—Linus—but before I could formulate a coherent thought, Tom dipped near to kiss me again. This time, he brought a teasing kind of heat, and I tapped my palms against his shoulders, uncertain whether I ought to hold him off or swallow him whole.

"Okay. Let's go to my place," he said. He scooped my cane off the ground, pulled me against his side in a supportive way, and turned us toward the road.

"What, now?"

"Have you got a better idea, genius?"

No matter how much I liked kissing Tom, I had just met him. The Linus flag prickled into a stab of guilt, too. I didn't know where I stood with Linus, but he still had the ability to make me miserable and confused, which had to count for something.

My mind still likes Linus. My body is all about Tom.

"Whatever you're thinking, I don't like it," Tom said.

"It's my first day back."

His eyebrow lifted. "How right you are." He gave my hand a little tug.

"Have we always had this—?" I didn't know what to call

192

it. We were somehow already back in each other's arms. My shirt felt clingy and hot.

"Much fun?" he said, smiling sideways. "No. It took you a while to catch on."

Before he could kiss me again, I extricated myself and took back my cane. Then I had to take off my sweatshirt because I was still too hot. I felt ridiculous.

"I would like to have some basic information about our relationship," I said.

"I'd say you just had a pretty good sample there, darlin'."

"I'm serious," I said. I brokered some real space between us. "I want to know how we met and where we started this baby."

He rubbed a hand along his jaw. "I could make up something here, couldn't I? And you wouldn't know the difference."

He was evil.

"Fine," I said, turning for the lane. "Don't tell me. I'm heading back."

He fell into step beside me and gently took my sweatshirt for me. "Tell me if this rings any bells. We met in eighth grade," he said. "I was a year older, but I got held back, and they put me in your class. We had math together."

"Why'd you get held back?" I asked.

He shrugged. "I didn't apply myself," he said. "You had this dark purple hoodie you always wore, and your fingernails were all black and chewed up. You were cool, in other words. We got put in this group project together about polynomials, and you kept calling me a 'maroon' just under your breath."

"The color? How nice for you."

"It was an insult, believe me. But it beat having you ignore me."

To our right, we had a view of the valley, and cloud shadows were moving slowly over the landscape, turning it dark in patches. Tom broke off a branch of laurel and balanced the stem on his palm.

"Don't tell me we started going out in eighth grade," I said.

"Gross. No," he said, smiling. "You asked how we met."

I laughed. "So then what?"

"Things changed fall of junior year," he said. "We had math together *again*, and you started up the same old routine. 'Get your stinking boots out of my face, Maroon,' you'd say all quiet. I'd be like, 'What? What did I do to you?' "

"Why was I so mean?" I said, pausing to face him.

"That's what I wondered. You weren't like that to anybody else," he said. "You were out of the hoodies by then. You walked proud, like you owned Texas, and that's when I developed my curse."

"What curse?"

He picked apart the flower. I noticed that his sideburns were slightly darker than the rest of his hair. Maybe he was blushing, too.

"Five seconds before you came through the door, any door, I would feel you coming," he said. "I'd look up, and there you'd be, every single time. You'd catch me staring like I'd been waiting for you the whole time."

"Oh, no," I said.

He brushed a hand back through his hair. "It gets worse,"

he said. "You could have laughed at me. Instead, you'd just shake your head, like *Really, Maroon? Again?* I didn't have to say a word. You knew exactly how bad I had it. It was humiliating. And worst of all? You quit teasing me."

"Poor Tom," I said, smiling.

"Exactly. You pitied me." He dropped the last shreds of the laurel to the road and stepped on them.

Pathetic as it was, I was glad he was telling me the whole story. "So what happened then?" I asked.

He glanced up to study me, all irony gone. "One night, I was riding home late from work when my motorcycle broke down. It was raining and cold. I couldn't leave my bike, so I was pushing it along the road. Then a truck slowed down in front of me, and it was you."

"Of course it was." For the first time, I felt like I was getting a glimpse of the real Althea, not just the daughter of Diego and Madeline. "Did I offer you a ride?"

"Yes, except I didn't want help from you," he said. "You got out and practically dragged my bike into your truck yourself. 'You should have called me,' you yelled. And I was like, 'What? You never would have come.' And you were like, 'How stupid can you be, Tom?' I had no idea what you were saying. I got in your truck, and my boots smeared black mud all over your floor. I expected you to yell at me about that, but no. And then I saw you were crying. I was like, crap. I didn't know what to do."

"What was wrong with me?" I asked.

"You really don't remember?"

I shook my head. "Tell me," I said.

"I asked you to pull over and tell me what was wrong," he said. "Turns out your collie, Gizmo, had been sick. Terminal. That night, you took him to the all-night vet to have him put down. His collar with the little name tag was right there on the dashboard, getting cold."

I could easily imagine a collar there, with the windshield wipers going and the ticking of the rain. "That is so sad," I said.

"Here's the thing," Tom added. "You went to the vet by yourself, without your parents. They had a party that night. Some fundraiser. They couldn't be bothered."

I stared at him. "That is not okay."

"I know," he said. "You told me about holding Gizmo for his final breaths, and then you started crying for real. I didn't know what to do. I didn't dare to put my arm around you, but you leaned into me a little, and then you just let go." He wedged the toe of his boot against the crushed laurel. "I'd never seen a girl cry like that," he said quietly. "It's strange, telling you this. We never talked about it."

"Is that when you became friends?"

He shot me a curious glance. "You mean *us*? We were never friends in the normal way, but after that, you weren't quite as mean to me. We started hanging out."

"Why was I still mean to you at all?"

"It was so obvious," he said. "We could never be even."

"Even, how?" I asked.

"We knew it was only a matter of time before you'd break my heart," he said.

He spoke simply, as if this was a given. I hardly knew what to think.

He smiled at my expression. "You asked for the truth."

"And when did all this begin?" I asked, and stroked a hand down my belly.

He glanced once more at me sideways and then aimed his gaze toward the valley. "You said you wanted to do it with someone you could trust before you went to college."

"We only did it once?"

"Ah, no," he said, and started walking again. His cheeks were definitely ruddy now.

"A couple times, then?" I asked, strolling beside him with my cane.

"Not exactly."

"How'd I get pregnant?" I asked.

"Classic faulty condom. As in, it never made it out of my pocket." He cleared his throat. "There you have it. The whole story."

Not quite. There was still the question of how I ended up on his motorcycle in the rain, but I got the feeling that would be best left for another day.

"What did you do after my accident?" I asked. "Did you start college?"

"No. I've been working for my dad, helping out at the ranch. I've been teaching a little karate, too. Dad's had some heart trouble. Lots of trips to the doctors. He's okay for now."

"Do you live nearby?" I asked.

"On the other side of Holdum. Not far." He watched me thoughtfully. "You really don't remember, do you?"

I shook my head. I felt a little guilty getting his whole story when I really wasn't Althea. "I need to tell you something," I said, pausing on the lane again. "It's going to be difficult to take in. I'm not really Althea anymore. During my surgery at Chimera, they implanted a dream seed into me from someone else. My mind really belongs to another girl, Rosie Sinclair. You can look her up. She was on *The Forge Show*."

"Your grandfather told me you might say something like this."

"He told you?"

"Yeah. When he warned me to stay away."

I was surprised, but also kind of relieved. "But you still told me all that about you and Althea."

"Well," Tom said slowly, "even if it's possible that you have a new mind, this is who you are now, right?"

"I guess," I said. I hadn't really expected that he would accept me as I am. I looked at him again, impressed. "I'm going to try to find my original body as soon as I can. She might need me."

"And then what?"

I hadn't thought that far. "I don't know."

I idly slid my hand down my belly, and just then, I felt another kick inside. It was like a gurgly stomach, but deliberate, and the nudge registered against the palm of my hand.

"Want to feel something?" I asked.

"Is the baby moving?"

I nodded. Tom stepped nearer. I guided his hand to the right place and held it there. I watched as he focused gravely, waiting, and the warmth of his palm penetrated the fabric of my shirt to my belly. A moment later, the rolling feeling came again, and Tom jumped.

"Hey!" he said, laughing. "That is totally wild."

I smiled. "I know."

"Little monster. Wow."

He returned his hand to my belly, more confident this time. I'd been examined and prodded by a million people in the last few weeks, but this was different. This was a personal touch shared by my baby's dad and our child and me, together for the first time. When the baby poked again, Tom's eyes filled with wonder.

"This little fighter has beat every odd," he said softly. "You know that, right?"

"Yes," I said.

"I can help you raise him or her."

Raise the baby. At one level, I had known that this infant would be born into the world and need diapers and food and parenting. I'd heard the heartbeat and held the sonogram photo. I'd started a list of names. Yet now it suddenly felt a lot more real. This was a person who would command relationships. He or she would bind me to other family. Permanently.

I reached blindly for my sweatshirt and put it on.

"Thea?" he said.

This was a *baby* I was having, not a temporary glitch in my life. A baby would completely derail my connection to Rosie and my old life.

"What am I doing?" I muttered.

My mind was racing. I shifted away and zipped up my sweatshirt. What options did I have? It was far too late for an abortion even if I wanted one, and I didn't. That meant childbirth. For real. After that, who would raise the kid? Me? Unthinkable.

I was sixteen! I'd had a life of my own and dreams and a future! Althea had lost her life, but I didn't have to lose mine, too, did I? I wanted to have the baby. Of course I did. But I *didn't* want to have it, too.

They would all hate me if I put my baby up for adoption.

"I'm not ready to be a mother," I whispered and instantly clapped my hand over my mouth. I glanced up at Tom, ashamed, and then I felt a surge of defiance. "I'm not!"

He looked startled. "Take it easy, Thea. I just said you don't have to do this alone. That's what I came to tell you."

"What do you mean?"

He put a gentle hand on my arm. "My proposal still stands," he said. "I get that things are complicated, but that doesn't change anything for me. Nothing could."

I stared while the meaning of his bizarre words sank in. I had to steady my grip on my cane. "You want to marry me," I said.

"That's the idea."

It would have been funny if it wasn't so horribly sad.

"I just told you I'm somebody else," I said quietly. "I don't even remember you. How can you possibly want to marry me? What do you think marriage *is*?"

His eyes flashed oddly as he released me.

"No. Don't answer that," I said, backing up a step. "I'm sorry, but this is all wrong. Wait. Did you propose to me before?"

He did. He must have. It was clear in his face.

"What did I say before?" I asked.

He slid his hands in his pockets and gave his crooked smile again. "Like I said. We always knew you'd break my heart."

— THEA —

THE RULE OF MIRRORS

I WALKED BACK ALONE to the house, taking my time. *The person he loves isn't me*, I told myself. *I didn't break his heart.* But that only complicated my sympathy for him. Plus we obviously had some chemistry. Big time. I'd been planning to focus on finding Rosie, but clearly I had the tangle of life as Althea to deal with, too.

What was I going to do about this baby?

Voices quickly hushed as I pushed open the kitchen door. Diego was wrapping plastic over a noodle casserole, and Madeline was scrubbing at a pot on the edge of the sink. Everyone else was gone. Though the rifle was out of sight, the air still bristled with tension.

"Where is everybody?" I asked.

Solana touched her nose to my knee, and I reflexively reached down to pet her head.

"Grampa's in his den working," Madeline said. "We sent everybody else home. We'll have a proper party later after you're settled in."

"Thanks," I said, relieved.

Diego slid the roll of plastic wrap into a drawer with a little click. "What did Tom have to say?" he asked.

I studied Diego coolly. "He says he'll be a good father," I said.

Diego's mouth set in a grim line "A good father," he echoed. "Over my dead body."

"Diego," Madeline said calmly.

"Is he gone?" Diego asked.

"Yes," I said. "You didn't have to hit him."

Diego left the casserole on the table and stalked over to the door. Solana followed. Diego put his fists on his hips, radiating fury. "Arrogant prick," he said. "Stay, Solana." He banged out the back door.

I turned to Madeline, who rinsed the pot in steaming water.

"Why does Dad hate him so much?" I asked. "Does he think Tom turned me away from you or something?"

"Let's not start, Althea."

"Why didn't you and Dad go with me to put Gizmo down?"

She turned and wiped her hair back with a damp hand. "Did you remember that, or did Tom tell you?"

"Tom told me."

"Of course," she said. "That was the night he first took advantage, when your guard was down."

He could have taken advantage, but he didn't, I thought. "That doesn't explain why you didn't go to the vet with me," I said.

"We were going to go to the vet the next morning together as a family, but you decided it couldn't wait," Madeline said. "Gizmo was perfectly comfortable. Your father and I had obligations we couldn't get out of that night. We trusted you to stay home, but you took Gizmo and went without us. Imagine how we felt when we came home and discovered what you'd done."

Her version was close enough to Tom's to make them both believable. I sank into a chair and set my cane aside.

"So I was disobedient," I said.

"No, you weren't normally. You had your rough spells like many kids, but you were a good kid. Gizmo's death was hard for you. It brought up some stuff."

"What stuff?"

She opened a bag of apples and started picking off the labels. "I'd rather leave it in the past."

"It's part of who I am. It might help for me to know."

She shook her head. "If there's one good thing about your brain injury, it's that you've been freed from your bad memories. Besides, there are too many things in your past for me to tell you about them all. How am I supposed to know which ones matter?"

"You could try for the major ones. Did you know Tom proposed to me last summer?" I asked.

Her voice dropped. "No."

"He did today, too. I turned him down."

She visibly relaxed. "Of course."

"People ought to know each other before they get married, I think." I slumped across the table and fingered a checked placemat. "He is cute, though," I added. "But is he really my type? That's the question."

"Funny. Very funny."

I felt a subtle shift happening in me. Even though we were talking about history I didn't know and some of it was strained, Madeline treated me like I really was her daughter. Like I belonged. It felt a little disloyal to my own mother, but I kind of liked it.

"How did you meet Dad?" I asked.

She began washing the apples. "I was in graduate school at UT Austin, and I wanted to talk to your grandfather about his helium research at NASA. He agreed to meet me, but he asked me to come here instead of Houston. He'd just had knee surgery so he couldn't travel. I wasn't going to say no. Your father was here looking after him, and that's when we met."

I took a critical look at her little figure and graceful hands. Madeline must have been pretty as a young graduate student. Smart, too, obviously.

"And?" I prodded her.

"Your father made us lemonade from scratch." She shook

her head slightly and smiled. "I'd never met a smarter, nicer guy."

I hadn't ever seen Madeline blush before.

"Aww," I said.

"It wasn't all clear sailing," she said. "I wasn't Latina, and it took a while for all of his family to come around. His ex-girlfriend was a handful, too, but that's long ago."

"Do you think Grampa set you up?"

She nodded. "He said he just had a feeling, when he heard my voice on the phone, that I was right for his son."

Sweet. It mattered that Diego's father had approved of her. Bumping down a generation, I wondered if Diego felt he de-served some say in who Althea dated. Maybe that was why he was outraged when Althea defied him by dating Tom. I tried to think how my own parents would react to me dating, and I shuddered.

Madeline turned off the water and put the apples in a wooden bowl. "I have to believe things work out the way they should," she said.

"Like with you and Dad?"

"And you being home with us again," she said, turning to me. "I know your father can be difficult, but it's only because he cares. He's noticed you've started calling him 'Dad.' That means a lot to him."

It was more of a courtesy than anything else. "It seems simplest," I say.

"Even so. It shows you're trying, and we appreciate that. I understand that you don't feel like Althea anymore. I know you have this other girl's memories." She spoke calmly, but her voice carried an undercurrent of emotion. "But I can't help hoping you'll return to yourself now that you're home. That's what moms do. We hope." She set the bowl of apples in the center of the table. Then she brushed her hands back through her soft white hair so that it stood out on both sides of her head. "I mean, just look at you," she said with a shaky smile. "I barely dared to dream, but now you're right here, in our own kitchen, and your baby's fine, too. It's just—" She broke off, waving a hand.

"Oh, Mom," I said.

I stood awkwardly from my chair, and she came over to hug me.

"You're such a child yourself," she said in a tight voice. "And now you're going to be a mother, too. I don't know if I can stand it."

I laughed over a lump in my throat and patted her back. "You'll stand it. You've stood worse."

"I guess that's true," she said, and kissed my cheek before she let me go.

〉〉〉〉〉〉〉〉〉

My jetlag kicked in, and I had to head upstairs. Althea's bedroom was easy to identify, decorated as it was in white and creamy blue, with a row of pristine, miniature dolls evenly spaced in a white case, and exactly enough books to fill three shelves. On her dresser was a little tree of earrings. Uneasy, I fingered a pair of dangly ones of hammered silver. To pick and choose items from Althea's life felt wrong, like I was sifting through a dead girl's tag sale.

A distant clank came from outside, and I lifted a gauzy curtain off a French door to find a small balcony with a view toward the stables. Beyond a stand of trees, the white-fenced paddock met the lane where Tom and I had walked.

Tom. The view. Solana. Madeline. The earrings. Everything here from the smallest stud to the deepest relationship was Althea's, and I'd stepped into all of it. It would be so easy, in a way, to vanish into her life. I had all these people to please here, and I already owed them so much. They weren't asking me to pretend I remembered Althea's old life. They just wanted me to move forward with them as their daughter and granddaughter and cousin and girlfriend. They just wanted to love me and my baby.

When I stepped into the hot water of the shower, the freshly stocked soap and shampoo suited me perfectly, and I guessed they were Althea's favorites. A little jar of face scrub smelled like apricots, and the creamy grit was soothing on my nose and cheeks. I was shaving my legs in the shower for the first time, flexing around my belly to slide the razor along my shin, when it hit me once and for all that this awkward, gangly body was mine. I was caring for it and living in it. Althea's body was the tool I now used to interact with the world, and her life was mine to make decisions with.

When I came out of the bathroom, I climbed heavily onto Althea's bed and sank into the mattress, exhausted. My pores were still damp, and my bathrobe felt bunchy and warm around me. My legs felt nice and smooth. I felt like I was home, but it felt wrong to feel that way.

I had too many interior contradictions: I wanted my baby, and I didn't want it. I felt like I was home, but I wasn't. I thought like Rosie, but I wasn't Rosie anymore. Any last, lingering, irrational idea that I'd ever be able to get back into Rosie's body vanished, which left me with the question: why did I want to find her?

For her sake. Because she needed to be found. Berg had the other Rosie captive, and I couldn't just forget and neglect her because I had new problems of my own. Besides, it went deeper than that. I owed it to myself to find Rosie. My nightmarish memories of lying helpless in the vault still haunted me, and no matter how safe I was in Althea's pretty room, I knew I wasn't safe inside.

>>>>>>>>>

The next morning when I awoke, Solana was sleeping on the rug beside my bed. She lifted her head as I got up.

"You're my buddy, aren't you, girl?" I said, and rubbed between her ears.

I pulled on some clothes, collected my cane, and took her out to do her business. The house was still when we came back in, but I heard a distant tapping to my right, and Solana headed in that direction, with her nails clicking on the wood floor between the carpets.

I followed, seeing how many steps I could take without using my cane for balance. Morning light spilled in everywhere, clean and clear. I passed a library that smelled of mahogany, an office, and a south-facing solarium with a proliferation of green plants. A weapons room showcased modern firearms alongside antique rifles, pistols, swords, tomahawks, and bows and arrows. The next room contained a collection of antique ship models all in large glass cases, like for a private museum.

The tapping came again, and I headed down a short hallway to a suite of rooms that felt newer. The ceilings slanted high, with open beams of golden wood. A mini kitchen led off from a sunken living room. I paused at the sight of a hospital bed in one of the bedrooms while a strange, eerie feeling crept through me. The bed was covered in plastic, as were a series of medical-looking machines that lined the corner. It smelled faintly antiseptic. A shelf held several empty vases and a willowy statuette of a girl with her arms extended and head thrown back.

This, I realized, was where Althea had lain in her coma. My host body had been in this place, for weeks, and now my feet had brought me back, like I belonged here. I felt a faint flicker of fear or premonition.

"Is that you, *mi corazoncita*?" Grampa called.

I backed out of the coma room. Then I followed his voice around a bend and found a small, cozy den with a big TV, an upright piano, and a large desk. I breathed more easily. Grampa's hat perched on a rack by a folded American flag.

"You're up early," he said.

"So are you."

A ship model was propped before him on the desk, and a hundred tiny timbers were spread out on graph paper. He wore special glasses with magnifying lenses built in so that he looked like a mad bug when he turned to me. "You found your old room?"

"Yes. How long was I there?" I asked.

"Three months. I thought you'd be there forever."

I came closer and leaned against the windowsill where I could watch him work.

"You talked to Tom," I said, thinking of the way Grampa had filled him in.

"Yes, I did. He kept calling. Seemed only right."

I liked that the old man had his own code of decency regardless of what Althea's father felt toward Tom. I nodded toward the ship pieces. "Do you make these?" I asked.

"I restore them," he said, holding up a tiny crow's nest. "What do you think?"

"Cool," I said.

He passed me the little piece, and then I watched as he clamped a different sliver of wood in a holder. He tightened the screw carefully and then began to shave the side with a delicate tool.

I set the crow's nest down softly and picked up a small round mirror. "How long have you been doing this?" I asked.

"Ten years now. I used to be an engineer for NASA."

I remembered Madeline had mentioned that. I held up the little mirror, gazing into the glass to inspect my face one small

211

circle at a time: an eyebrow, the swell of my cheekbone, my ear with the nick in the top.

"Do you miss your old face, then?" Grampa said.

"Sometimes. Do you want to see a picture of what I used to look like? I can get my phone."

"Maybe sometime," he said. He was still focused on the wood he was shaping, and his bright work light glinted in his glasses. "It's not particularly relevant."

His honesty surprised me.

"To you, or to me?" I asked, lowering the mirror.

"To anybody. It's how people reflect you back that matters."

I wasn't sure I understood him. "How can a person reflect me back?"

He kept his fingers lightly poised on his blade. "If I appreciate you for what you do or say, you feel it. You feel lovable. Understood. Deserving. Right? It's like a mirror." He gestured toward the circle of glass in my hand.

"I guess."

He sniffed. "A true reflection feels right."

"What am I reflecting to you right now?" I asked.

He straightened to look over at me, taking his time. His special glasses gave him four eyes and added an air of gravity to the inspection. "You appear to respect me," he said. "What's more, you're genuinely interested in my philosophical train of thought. It fits with how I think of myself. I'm clever. I have dignity. Too much, sometimes," he added, smiling.

I smiled back. "If you're my mirror, what are you reflecting to me?"

He rubbed his chin thoughtfully. "That's a little harder. As your doting grandfather, I'd normally reflect back how incredibly special you are, but I can't quite, can I?" he said. "You aren't my Althea, but I can't tell who you are yet, either."

He'd nailed the uneasiness between us, as far as I was concerned. I supposed that made him a true mirror.

"I'm Rosie," I said dryly. "Heard of her?"

"Your father told me. If that's who you are, she'll show through in time," he said.

His words reminded me of something Dr. Fallon had said when she was first guiding me to feel my facial muscles. "Dr. Fallon at Chimera said mirrors lie. She said some women are ruled by their mirrors. She meant glass, but I suppose it could apply to people, too."

"*Me gusta,*" he said musingly. "The rule of mirrors. So many possibilities. We seek until we find a true reflection of ourselves, like I had with your grandmother."

"I don't think that's quite what the doctor meant."

His laugh came gently, and he focused again on his work. "No, probably not. I never met her, but she doesn't strike me as a romantic."

I slid the mirror back on the desk.

It was true that my glass reflection didn't match who I was inside, and neither did my reflections from people. Romance aside, what Grampa said clicked with me. Everyone at Chimera had treated me like Althea, expecting me to be her, but that hadn't matched me. Now that I was here at the Flores home, the Althea reflection was even stronger, but it still didn't match me, and the effect was jarring. Maybe that was why I felt so unsettled. So lonely.

I needed to find the Rosie I'd left behind.

Wistful, I gazed past him out the other window to the valley. A second, smaller house was visible in a stand of trees, but no animals. I felt as far away from Doli as ever.

"Did you grow up here?" I asked.

"On the ranch? No. This was your grandmother Valeria's place. Been in the family for generations. It'll belong to your daughter someday, provided she wants it."

"She might be a boy."

"You're carrying high. She's a girl," he said. "You look exactly like Madeline did before you were born. I mean your figure, not your face."

"You think so?"

"Girl. No doubt about it."

I smiled.

Grampa kept at his work, and after a bit, he suggested I take a tour of the rest of the house. "Get to know your home," he said. "Explore while you can before your mother takes you off to doctors' appointments and P.T. See if anything is familiar. You never know."

"What I need is a computer," I said.

"There should be one in your room. Did you look in the desk? Our housekeeper might know where it is. She'll be in tomorrow."

I said I would take a look.

Out back, a swimming pool beckoned with bright blue water. Upstairs, half a dozen bedrooms were followed by a laundry room, a sewing room, and an exercise room with gleaming weights.

A narrow staircase led to the third floor, where I found six more bedrooms under the eaves, all with white paneling and tall, narrow windows. Two were filled with orderly bins, but the others were simply furnished, with polished floors and a rag rug next to each bed. A walk-in cedar closet, redolent and cool, was full of vintage overcoats and furs. A quaint little bathroom had a pull chain on an old-fashioned toilet and a claw-footed tub.

"Nice," I whispered.

I made up my mind. I might have to live in Althea's body, but I didn't have to live in her bedroom surrounded by her things. Until I could leave to find Rosie, I would start my new life up here.

>>>>>>>>

Madeline and Diego weren't thrilled about my choice to take an attic bedroom, but they didn't object. After my doctor appointments and a round with a physical therapist, Madeline helped me bring up some maternity clothes she'd ordered and a few things from Althea's room: a dozen books, her soaps and shampoos, the silver earrings, and her computer. My new room on the third floor felt deliciously fresh and simple. When I looked out my window, I had a view of the stables

215

and the western end of the valley. Below, I could see the balcony that jutted off Althea's French doors, and I realized I'd chosen the room directly above hers, like I was building on her roots. I liked that.

Bunching a couple of pillows against the headboard, I settled onto my new bed that evening. It took some jockeying to position the laptop against my knees and belly where it didn't jab too awkwardly, but then I cleared all of Althea's files into one folder and went to work. Finally.

Orson had told me of the Onar Clinic in Colorado, so I started with that and came up with a private research center. Hardly any info was available besides an address. I located it on a map and discovered it would take about twelve hours to drive there.

Twelve hours. Totally doable, assuming Rosie was still there.

I searched to see if there was anything new about her online, but there wasn't.

I checked my old email again out of habit and found, for the first time, that I could log in again. Maybe it helped to be back in the States. I had a zillion emails, but two were marked as read: one from Linus and one from Burnham. Both of their emails were months old, but I was still psyched. Then an eeriness set in. Only I knew my password. And Rosie. She must have read these messages before me, but when and how? Did it mean she'd escaped from Berg?

I had to be walking in her cyber footsteps. I checked my sent box, but there were no outgoing messages. I considered sending an email to myself on the chance she'd see it, but then

I realized an administrator like Berg could oversee my email, too. It wasn't safe. Rosie must have realized that, too.

I blinked at the screen, wondering if Linus had had any luck finding her. I hadn't talked to him since our one dismal conversation, weeks earlier, but maybe she'd called him since then. Things couldn't get much worse between us. I tried him again with the number from the email, feeling nervous.

"Linus here," he said.

I let out a pent-up breath. "Hi. It's Althea again."

"I remember. The liar."

My heart constricted. "I only lied a little bit so you'd talk to me. Everything I said that mattered was true."

"Rosie tells me you're not her friend, so the only question is, how did you know all that stuff about us?" Linus said.

"You've talked to Rosie?" I asked. I shoved my computer off my lap and tucked my feet under me. "Where is she? Is she okay?"

"Why is that any of your business?"

"Because she's *me*," I said. "*I'm* Rosie. They mined me out of her and planted me as a seed in another body. That's why I have the wrong voice, and that's how I know all that stuff about you and her. We have the same memories." I was afraid he'd hang up. "I just want to find her and help her. When did you talk to her? How is she?"

"She's almost as screwed up as you are. You get points for your seed theory. That's new."

"When did you talk to her?"

"Friday night, late. Or I guess early Saturday morning."

"*This past weekend?* Where is she?"

"She wouldn't say. She didn't trust me. Imagine that," he said.

I couldn't believe he'd talked to her only three days ago. She had to be free from Berg.

"What's her number?" I demanded.

"Not happening."

"Linus, she's *me*," I repeated. "I have to find her. I can help her."

"I don't think so. She wasn't particularly pleased to know you'd called me."

"You told her about me?" I was so excited. "What did she say?"

"I told you. She'd never heard of anybody named Althea."

Right. She wouldn't know about me. For all she knew, I didn't survive when I leapt out of our mind and left her behind. She had no clue I was seeded into anybody else. Come to think of it, she'd been furious when I was leaving, so she might still be mad at me. How strange it was to be imagining what the other version of me was thinking about this version of me. It was like a Ping-Pong match between the same player.

"Listen, I know this is hard to believe," I said. "But if I could just talk to Rosie, I know I could make her understand."

"Good luck with that. She's not answering her phone."

"Haven't you tried to find her?" I asked. "I know Berg had her at the Onar Clinic in Colorado. I have that address."

"Of course I've looked for her," he said. "She's in hiding. She said she was with friends, but when I tracked the address

218

connected to her phone number and paid a visit, they said they didn't know her. Then they said the phone I was tracking was stolen. I think they're lying, but for now, I've hit another wall. She doesn't want to be found, and they're keeping her secrets."

"I don't have any friends in Colorado," I said, puzzled. "Who were they?"

"A teenage girl and her older sister. They were getting ready for their mom's return from deployment overseas."

I gnawed the inside of my cheek. "How long do you think Rosie's been away from Berg?" I asked.

"She said a couple weeks. We didn't talk long. She was kind of scattered, honestly."

"Upset?"

"Yes. And different," he said. "I couldn't put my finger on it. You talk much more like the Rosie I knew, except your voice is wrong."

A little thrill hit me. "Then you believe me?"

"I don't know what to believe, but I agree we have to find her," he said. "Where do you think she'd go? Back to Doli?"

That seemed doubtful. I was pretty mad at my parents and she probably was, too. "When I tried to call home, my parents didn't believe I was me because of my new voice. They've blocked me."

"What's your last name?" he asked.

I hesitated only a second. "Flores. From Holdum, Texas. You aren't going to tell anybody about me, are you?"

"What do you think I am? The host of a TV show? Just kidding," he said. "I won't say anything."

I could hear typing on his end, and then a pensive humming.

"What?" I said.

"This Althea Flores I've found was in a motorcycle accident last fall. She was in a coma."

"That's right. For six months. I woke up at the Chimera Centre in Iceland. It's a private hospital and research center."

"This girl is kind of athletic and Hispanic looking. Big eyes, maybe blue. Are you saying that's you?"

"That's me," I said. "But my eyes are gray. I've gained some weight lately, too." Understatement.

"Who's this Tom Barton?" Linus said. "Your boyfriend?"

"*Althea's* boyfriend," I said.

A contemplative tapping came over the line, like Linus was beating something with a pencil. "Does he know about the real you?"

I picked at the hem of my shirt. "Not exactly. I've only met him once. Yesterday. He knows about my Rosie-ness in theory, but I can tell he doesn't get it."

"So he doesn't know about me yet then, either."

"No," I said. "Should he?"

More tapping noises from his end.

"Your voice is all Texas and you look completely different, but otherwise, you do sound a lot like her," he said. "Even this wildly unlikely story about being in another body is the sort of thing she'd come up with. This was always my problem."

"What do you mean?"

"There was nobody else like Rosie Sinclair," he said.

"Ever. She was, I don't know. Herself. Completely original. Completely, just, Rosie."

It was the nicest compliment I'd ever had, and the hardest, too, because it applied to a girl I could never be again. "You are the only one who's ever come close to understanding who I am," I said.

A silence stretched between us like a long, fragile thread.

"Even though it's impossible, I guess I want it all to be true," he said finally. "I miss her."

An ache tightened in my chest. "Me, too," I said.

What a bizarre thing to share with him. I stared absently toward the window.

"Do you think she'd come back to Forgetown?" he asked.

Leaning back against my pillow, I remembered Forge and the other people I'd known there, like Burnham and Janice. I couldn't imagine how I'd ever get them to believe I was Rosie. At least with Linus, I had some inside information from our private conversations.

"She'll come and find you," I said. "I don't know when or where, but she will."

"What makes you so sure?"

I glanced down at my hands. "She'll want to see you," I said.

It was what I'd want if I were her. I wondered if he understood this. He made a shifting noise with the phone on his end.

"She didn't sound like she wanted to see me," he said quietly. Then his voice became brisk again. "What should I call you? However you know Rosie, I can't deny that you do."

"I'm still Rosie, even though I've changed."

"What should I call the other one, then?" he asked. "Rosie Two? Or are you Rosie Ego and she's Rosie Id?"

I laughed, but it wasn't funny. He had a point. I couldn't keep claiming to be Rosie anymore, but I wasn't Althea, either. I needed a name to reflect that. *Althea* still sounded to me like Diego and Madeline's daughter from her pre-coma life. Tom called me *Thea,* and that worked a little better.

"You can call me 'Thea,' " I said.

"Thea." His Welsh accent gave the syllables an appealing lilt. "We should keep in touch, Thea. If I hear anything more from Rosie, I'll let you know. You do likewise."

He was wrapping it up. He was letting me go.

Perfectly understandable. I couldn't blame him. I'd just failed, once again, to convince him of the truth.

"All right," I said. "Sweet dreams."

"You, too."

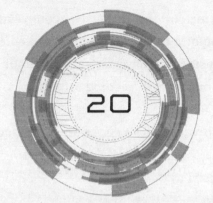

— ROSIE —

WAFFLES2067

HOURS LATER, OUTSIDE BILLINGS, Montana, Ian and I pull into a gas station. The miles have worn our tension down to a latent threat, like the line of sand mix that edges the road and invites a skid. Ian gets out to pump. I pull on my boots, check my pocket for the vials and syringes, and step out, too.

"You should stay in the car," Ian says.

"I have to pee. I'll be right back." I start walking toward the shop.

"Wait," he says. "Get me some cigarettes. Camels will do."

I'm about to remind him that I'm too young to buy tobacco, but he pulls out his wallet and hands me a fifty.

"Can I get some gum?" I ask, keeping it casual. "I'll share."

"Sure. Make it sugarless."

I pivot and start away again, feeling with each footstep that he's following me with his possessive, controlling gaze. I have one chance, maybe a five-minute window, to escape from him.

As I head inside, a bell jingles over the door. A small, dark woman in a brown sari is reading a fat hardcover behind the register.

"Can I help you?" she asks in an Indian accent, without looking up.

"Bathroom?" I ask.

"On the left."

I look down the aisle of chips to check for a back door out of the shop. I glance back at her book, noting the plastic wrap.

"Is there a library near here?" I ask. "Don't point."

She looks up for the first time, her face expressionless. I subtly jerk my head toward the car outside.

"My boyfriend doesn't like it when I read," I add.

Her gaze shifts outside for a moment and then back to me. "Take a right out of the lot and go two blocks. It's on the right. You can't miss it."

I slide the fifty across to her. "Delay him as long as you can, okay?"

She spread-eagles her book on the counter. "I shall call the police."

"No!" I say. "Please. Just delay him and don't tell him where I went."

I back a step away from her and take a last look at Ian, who is still filling the gas. Then I bolt out the back door.

I make it into the alley and cut behind a row of garbage dumpsters before I have to stop. My heart is ready to explode.

This is preposterous. I have zero stamina. Panting, I peek back to see if Ian is facing my direction, and when he isn't, I run across a gap to hide behind the next building. *Come on*, I urge myself, but I can only manage a fast walk along the alley that parallels the main road. Finally, three blocks down, I find a modest cement building with a flagpole and a couple of mailboxes out front. I hurry inside.

The library is an oasis of calm, with worn carpet and soft lighting, but I'm terrified that Ian will follow right behind me. I dive into the women's bathroom and think hard. Who do I have to call? My family? No. Linus? No. Burnham?

The thought of him tantalizes. Could I really? I have his email address. What are the chances he's online? If he's recovered enough and he's anything like the Burnham I knew at Forge, the chances are good.

I peek out of the bathroom door and see no sign of Ian. A nearby computer is unoccupied, so I slouch over and take a seat. The Internet is painfully slow, but I pull up an email chat, drop in Burnham's address, and hit call. I leave my visual feed off and plink down the volume so the rings are soft.

"Yeah?" he answers.

He sounds sleepy. It's three in the afternoon. He shouldn't be asleep.

I lean near to the computer and glance around the library, trying not to disturb other patrons. An old man looks at me briefly and then returns to his computer.

"It's me, Rosie Sinclair. Did I wake you?" I ask.

"Eat it, Horatio," he says.

"It's really me," I say, a little louder. "Can't you at least tell I'm a girl?"

"Rosie?" he says. "Holy crap. This is unreal. How are you?"

My heart soars. "I've got a problem. Can you help me?"

"Hold on a second," he says.

Rolling noises. I imagine him putting his glasses on. A thump. "What's up?" he asks.

And that's it. Immediately, effortlessly, Burnham's himself, as if he's been waiting for my call all this time, as if no accident ever happened, as if he doesn't blame me for a thing. I let out a laugh over a pain in my heart. Then in a few words, I explain where I am and how I have to shake a stalker. "I can't tell the police," I add. "It's complicated. If I can get to Atlanta, can I stay with you for a little while?"

I hear him typing for a minute.

"No problem. I'm sending a car for you," Burnham says. "Give me an hour to line it up. Can you stay put?"

"I was going to hitchhike," I say.

"That would be inconspicuous," he says dryly. "No one would ever recognize you."

"I'm glad your sarcasm's intact."

"It's a driver-free car," he says. "You'll need a code to get in it. Waffles2067, all one word. Can you remember that?"

"I've never been in a driver-free car," I say. "What do I have to do?"

"Just punch in the code and get in. It'll bring you here. We can finally talk," Burnham says, and he sounds happy about it.

We disconnect, and I hide in the bathroom again until a half hour has passed. Then I come out to check the window. Once I see Ian cruising by, but he doesn't stop. A bit later, the librarian asks if he can help me with anything, but I say no. Finally, a brown sedan pulls up in front of the flag, nose in. No one's driving. I go out, type the code onto the door panel, and get in. The dashboard has options for manual override, climate control, and rest stop, but the most conspicuous button says Start Trip, and it notes a location in Atlanta, Georgia. I've got nothing to lose. I push the button. A voice reminds me to fasten my seat belt, and after I do, the car starts moving.

>>>>>>>>

It's a long drive from Montana to Georgia. After an anxious hour of watching to see how the car performs, I settle in the back, where a seat is supplied with a little pillow, a blanket, and a bottle of water. A complimentary snack basket holds pretzels, beef jerky, peanuts, and cinnamon cookies. A charging dock is ready for any device a client might have. I have no devices. I literally own nothing but four stolen vials of sleep meds, several syringes, and the clothes I'm wearing, which, come to think of it, aren't mine. But I'm away from Ian now, and for the first time in ages, I'm practically giddy.

I spare one thought for how upset Ian must be. One. Then I'm done.

Every few hours, I hit rest stop, and the car finds the nearest place for a bathroom break. Since I don't have any money, I can't buy anything to eat, so I make my snacks last. States speed by. My chair reclines deeply, and I doze. I watch a couple of movies, then a couple more. At night, the car pulls up to a charging station and plugs itself in. The next day passes in the same manner, and somewhere in the second night, I leave winter behind and drive into spring. Late in the afternoon of the third day, the car arrives in Atlanta.

I sit up and run my hands through my hair. I don't need a mirror to tell me I look godawful. I've smelled better, too. Soon the car turns in at a driveway, and a man in a gatehouse lifts a hand in greeting as if he's expecting me. The wheels crunch over a gravel drive that winds through enormous oaks, heavy with Spanish moss. The car passes beside a pond and a pagoda, and then curves slowly toward a brick mansion with yellow shutters. A heavyset man rides a mower out front, and he, too, lifts a hand as I pass.

No kidding, you're rich, Burnham, I think.

Behind the mansion, the car pulls up before a carriage house with four garage doors. An apartment that spans the upper floor is easily ten times larger than the boxcar I grew up in. The car voice announces that we have arrived. Warm, honeysuckle sweetness greets me as I step out, and I'm filling my lungs when Burnham appears on the upper landing of the carriage house.

"You made it," he says, smiling down.

"Yes," I say.

And that's all that comes out, because Burnham looks unbelievably wonderful to me. He's thinner, and his fabulous long hair is gone, but he's nodding like he just scored a major win, and I love that he's so happy to see me.

228

"What should I do about the car?" I ask.

"Leave it. I'll send it back. *Get* on up here already," he says to me.

I grab the railing and mount two quick flights, and it's only then that I see Burnham's leg brace and the tight, unnatural curling of his left wrist and hand. I hesitate before I move in for a hug. It's only a little awkward.

"I'm so glad to see you," I say. "This is amazing."

"Pretty incredible," he says. "Let me see you."

When I draw back, he nudges his glasses and takes me in. I do the same to him. A red shirt like he always used to wear sets off his dark skin, and he's still wearing his St. Christopher medal around his neck. With his hair short, his face looks different, more square, and I like it. His baggy shorts sag in a relaxed way, and he's barefoot on the landing planks. Already I avoid staring at his wrist.

"You've been through it, huh?" he says.

"No worse than you."

"I want to hear all about it. Hungry?"

"I'm starving."

He brings me in. Before I can look around, a yip makes me turn to the kitchen where a small brown dog is standing on alert.

"That's my parents' dog," Burnham says. "They've gone up to DC to help my sister move into a new apartment, and they asked me to watch him for a couple days. Here, Waffles. Say hi to Rosie."

The dog sits instead and licks its tiny chops.

"He's not a very smart dog," Burnham says mournfully.

I have to laugh. "Do your parents know I'm here?" I ask.

"I didn't tell them yet, but I'm sure our guy at the gate has told them I had a girl delivered."

"Nice way to put it. Can you not tell your mother I'm here?" I ask.

"She's still one of your biggest fans," he says. "She'll be glad you're visiting."

I find it hard to believe she doesn't blame me even a little for the accident. "Even so."

He looks at me closely, and his eyebrows lift. "Not a problem," he says. "Do you like lasagna?"

"Sure."

He stops by a corner where a couple of computers are running and taps a few keys before he heads into the kitchen area. A smooth black stone sits on top of one computer, and a Ping-Pong ball rests on a paper clip, like the one back at Forge. I can't help taking the ball and giving it a toss. The place doesn't have a Ping-Pong table, though. No cameras, either, I notice.

A stone fireplace anchors one wall of the living room, and another wall is bright with large sliding-glass doors that lead to a deck. An elevator takes up another corner. I glimpse a couple of bedrooms and a workout room down the hall. Framed photos show three generations of his family, and he has tons of books and comics.

"I could like this place," I say, and absently give the ball another toss.

"Henrik sent me that," he says from behind the kitchen

counter. "I had the weirdest gaps in my vocabulary when I was first recovering, and for the life of me I couldn't remember 'Ping-Pong.' Do you want fresh Parmesan? I can call over to the house for it."

"No, I'm good," I say. "Whatever happened with your Forge School computer game?"

"I put it on hold."

"What have you been doing?" I ask.

"When I'm not in P.T.? School stuff and some data analysis for my parents," he says. "I've decided to become a doctor after all."

The oven beeps as he sets a temperature.

"Your parents must be psyched," I say. "What are you doing for high school?"

"I have this tutor. He's a bear. I'm going to take my GED early and apply to college next year." He waves his fingers at the oven. "This will take a few minutes to warm up," he says. "Do you want to clean up before we eat?"

"Do I smell that bad?"

He laughs. "No."

"I'm kidding. I'd love a shower."

He guides me to a guest bathroom, and I have never seen so many clean white towels in my whole life. The inside of the marble sink is ribbed like a giant shell, and the creamy paneling reminds me of those pictures in fancy architecture magazines. There's even a skylight over the Jacuzzi.

A pile of clean clothes has been set on a chair. I touch the soft pink of a shirt and look up at him.

"My sister left some stuff here," Burnham says. His voice is quiet in the cool, echoey space. "She won't mind if you use it."

He's just incredibly thoughtful. I hardly know what to say.

"This is an amazing place," I say.

He's looking up toward the skylight, not at me.

"Yeah, I'm lucky," he says, but his voice is oddly flat. "Take your time."

He softly closes the door, and a full-length mirror on the back of it gives me a sudden, unexpected view of myself. I'm skinny and dirty, in scuzzy boots and a sagging coat. My hair, I don't even know what shape it's in, and under my low, dark eyebrows, my eyes have a furtiveness that I've never seen in myself before. This dodgy girl in the mirror—frankly, she's scary.

Why Burnham should like a girl like me, I don't know. But he does. I can tell. And that makes me nervous. I hope coming here wasn't a mistake.

>>>>>>>>

After my shower, I brush out my wet, wavy hair and leave it to dry on my shoulders. The clothes Burnham set out include a new three-pack of undies and a black, spaghetti-strap camisole. No bra. The leggings are gray with George Washington University printed on the thigh. The pink shirt has a sweetheart neckline that dips a bit low on me, but it's soft and I like it, even though I haven't worn pink since I was five.

I take a stool at the counter while Burnham limps around on

the other side, cutting a loaf of French bread and setting out plates. He pulls a bubbling dish out of the oven and serves up two huge slices of lasagna. He's adept with his right hand, and he uses his stiffly curled left hand to brace things. Once a splash of red sauce lands on his dark skin, and he rinses it clean.

"What can I help with?" I ask.

"You could take these over to the couch," he says, nodding at the dishes.

We eat on his couch, facing the porch, and the lasagna is by far the best food I've ever had in my life.

I settle a foot under me and ask him about his recovery. He tells me about moving to different hospitals and rehab places. One of the best, it turns out, is right nearby in Atlanta. He had memory problems at first, and trouble speaking and finding the right words, but gradually that improved. His leg is improving, too. His wrist and hand, not so much. His family has been amazing, he says, and fierce about making him independent.

"What about you?" he asks. "Where've you been all this time?"

As I tell him about my months in the vault at Onar, I again feel my simmering rage at Berg. Burnham leans back, regarding me thoughtfully, and with a bit more prodding, I spill out the details of my escape, my time with Jenny and Portia, and my road trip with Ian. By the end, I'm so restless it's hard to stay on the couch. I set my empty plate on the coffee table and hug a pillow.

"What do you intend to do next? Go home?" Burnham asks.

I'm not sure I can tell him yet that I plan to go for Berg. "Maybe."

"You haven't called your parents yet, have you?"

I shake my head. "No. I don't trust them. They let Berg take me."

"Have you talked to Linus?"

"I did last Friday. It wasn't good." It was, in fact, a bitter, confusing dose of disappointment.

"How so?" Burnham says.

"He tried to apologize."

"And that's bad?"

"Why are we talking about Linus?" I ask.

Burnham slides his plate onto mine and sets both our forks neatly on top. When he glances up, his expression is inscrutable.

"Tell me something," he says. "I've watched the footage from the day we fell and the day afterward when you were in your so-called meltdown, so I know what you said to Linus about the dream mining. How much did Berg know about your suspicions before we fell from the ladder?"

"Are you wondering if he made me fall on purpose?"

"Yes."

Waffles climbs onto the couch next to Burnham, and he ruffles the dog's furry neck.

"I don't know," I say. "I don't see how he could have made us fall, or at least not directly." I take a deep breath. "I've never told anybody this, but I was having a déjà vu when we fell off the observatory ladder. It sort of predicted our fall as it was

234

happening. I had a similar experience once before, that time I half fainted inside the observatory."

"Do you think the déjà vu was connected to the mining?" he asks.

I nod. "Berg was mining *and* seeding me back then. In the observatory, I had a vivid image of the man who hanged himself there, a really vivid image of him down to his ankles and his black shoes. I think that image came from a dream seed, and I think being around the observatory became a kind of trigger, like it jostled my subconscious and made me dizzy."

"If you were having a déjà vu, and you knew we were going to fall, then what were we doing on that ladder?" Burnham asks.

"I didn't *know* we would fall," I say. "It wasn't a pattern that I understood yet. I'm still not completely sure. I was fine when I started up the ladder. Then, once the déjà vu started, I couldn't do anything about it."

Burnham keeps petting Waffles with his good hand while his eyes aim unhappily toward the windows.

"Just say what you're thinking," I tell him.

"I nearly died, Rosie."

"I know! I'm sorry," I say. "I never meant to hurt you."

He doesn't say he forgives me, which is what I want to hear. He doesn't say anything or do anything but pet his dog.

I can't sit still anymore. I shift off the couch and take our dishes to the kitchen counter. "I shouldn't have come here," I say. "You blame me for everything."

"Not everything."

"Thanks," I say with a pained laugh.

"I'd rather blame Berg than you." He shakes his head briefly. "Really it was my own fault. I knew we shouldn't go up that ladder. I saw the sign. I knew it wasn't safe, but I followed you anyway." His hand goes still on Waffles's back. "I never expected you'd actually come visit me. This is kind of a lot to handle, Rosie."

Regret seeps out of my heart with nowhere to go. "I'm sorry," I say. "I really am."

He looks up at me from his place on the couch. "Let's agree about something. Let's not blame anybody for what happened, and let's not be sorry for each other."

I clench the edge of the counter. "I blame Berg for ruining my life," I say. "I'm not giving that up."

"It's not going to help you any."

"It will, though. It'll help me get even."

I squeeze some soap on a scrubby and start washing the dishes. Burnham stands slowly and gives his left leg a little throw to get it moving. Then he brings over his glass. I wipe the counters while he puts away the extra lasagna.

"If you were going to get even with Berg, how would you do it?" Burnham asks, closing the refrigerator door.

"Why? Want to help?"

"Maybe."

I glance over at him. Burnham the do-gooder might have a nefarious side after all. "I need to learn more about Berg's research and find out how he's connected to the Chimera Centre,"

I say. "Ian told me there's another place for dreamers in California, and I want to know if that's connected to Berg, too."

"How many dreamers did you see under Forge?"

"Maybe fifty? Sixty? They filled an entire room down there. More than I could count."

"Then it had to be a serious project getting them out of there after you were expelled. They disappeared in a short time with nobody seeing," Burnham says.

This is a logistical problem I haven't considered before. "Good point," I say.

"Do you know where the dreamers come from originally?"

"St. Louis. Berg has them supplied from the Annex, according to Ian."

He nods. "Interesting." He glances toward his computer corner. "I might have an idea."

He takes a laptop and brings it to the couch. When he opens it up, I spot a piece of black tape covering the lens.

"We share the same paranoia," I say, pointing to the tape.

"I hate cameras. Come sit."

I settle in beside him, on his right. Burnham works the keyboard one-handed, with unerring speed. He pulls up a file with a bunch of numbers, and then a map of the United States with circles and dots spread all over it like bubbles. They look like files from his family's pharmaceutical company. "These are sales of a specific Fister drug by location," he said. "One sale is a dot. A thousand sales is one of these bigger circles. I can narrow down the time frames, and I can identify when a certain pharmacy has a peak of sales."

237

"That is scary precise information."

"Look here. This is Forgetown," he says, and focuses in on Kansas. He sets up an evolving cycle, showing sales of a drug over a period of decades. The circles fluctuate, but generally get bigger. He runs it through again. "The Forge School is a consistent customer of our sleep meds," he says. "They buy in batches eight times a year so the product is always fresh, but look here." He stops the map on an image when the circle is as large as my thumbnail. "Sometimes there are extra orders on top of the normal sales. The number of students doesn't change, so why the sudden increase?"

I puzzle over the map. "Maybe Berg needs extra meds for his dreamers," I say. "Or he could be buying the meds at the school and using them someplace else."

"Possibly. I have something else, too, but it's a little sick."

"Fine with me," I say.

He brings up another map of the United States. This one has several dozen pinpoints spread all over the country, from L.A. to Bangor, Maine, and from Ft. Lauderdale to Bellingham, Washington.

"These are Forge School alums. And these," he pauses to type, and a dozen of the pinpoint dots turn red. "These are suicides and accidental deaths of anyone who was ever on the show, whether they made first cuts or not."

"Like Emily Thorpe, the singer from our year," I say.

"Exactly."

I lean in, fascinated and sad, as if the misery behind the dots gives them gravitational pull. "I met her in the chapel basement, right before the cuts," I say. "She was in bad shape. She was in a car accident a few weeks later." There are twenty-one dots, and when I check the date range, they're all within the past five years. "This is awful," I say softly. "The trustees said the number of suicides was more like seven or eight, but this is way more." It doesn't take a genius to realize the numbers are much too high for one small school. I turn to Burnham. "Why don't people care more about this? Why aren't they looking into it?"

"I don't know," he says. "We all signed the waivers. Students and their families can't legally hold Forge accountable for anything. I'm not sure they even realize there's a pattern."

"But people should be warned. Students should know they're risking their lives when they go to Forge."

"Would it have stopped you?" he asks.

I think about how desperate I was to go to the school. I would have believed I could beat any odds. "Probably not," I say. "I didn't leave even after I knew wild things were happening at night."

He leans back. "There's a curious thing about statistics," he says. "People only believe them when it's convenient."

I pull my feet up on the couch and sit cross-legged. "I'm not sure what this proves. Why are you looking into all of this?"

"My parents wanted me to see if there was a correlation between the suicides and Fister drugs," he says. "So far, I can't find one, but I can't rule it out, either. We designed the twelve-hour med specifically for the Forge School. Maybe suicide is a long-term side effect. My parents insist it's not. They think there's a separate cause."

"Like the mining," I say.

"My parents are skeptical about the mining," he says. "But they do think there's an unknown separate cause."

I consider him with a new sense of appreciation. "You've been trying to prove me right, haven't you?"

"I was always curious about what was going on at Forge," he says. "At first, when I went there, I felt a kind of responsibility because Fister drugs were being used. I wanted to see for myself that everyone was fine at night, you know? So I stayed awake with the antidote a few times, and then one night, I saw Dr. Ash giving one of the other guys an IV. It looked like he was having a seizure. That didn't seem right. When you started looking for your ghosts with cameras everywhere at night, I realized you must have discovered something, too."

"That's when you gave me your note."

"Yes. I thought we could work together to figure out what was going on. But then we fell," Burnham says. He frowns for a moment. "Why do you think Berg got involved with the dream mining? Why would he risk it?"

"For money maybe."

He shakes his head and sets aside his computer. "He must have a better reason. Some personal reason. How much do you know about him?"

I consider what I know. "You once told me he went to medical school and law school. He has an ex-wife and two kids. Twins. They're about our age, and they live in New York. He also has a vacation place in Colorado where he pretends to keep me. And he likes to watercolor."

He laughs. "Like, paint?"

"Yes," I say, and I look absently toward the glass door. Evening has arrived without me noticing it, and a couple of small lamps have come on by the deck. "I talked to Berg a couple days ago. He said something disturbing, some question about me getting enough stimulation. He seemed to suggest that he let me go on purpose. He's still into mind games."

"It is strange that there's no news about you," Burnham says. "Do you think Jenny and her sister decided not to call the hotline?"

"Maybe Berg bought them off somehow," I said. "It's weird. I feel like he's just waiting for me to do something before he pounces out from nowhere and grabs me again."

"My sister Sammi said the contract you signed with Berg that made him your guardian wasn't legally binding. She thought it was just a gimmick for the show."

"Then why weren't my parents able to get me back from him?" I say. "Your sister's theory doesn't help."

"I'm sorry," he says.

"He's after me. I can feel it."

"Our security guy will tell me if anyone steps on our property," he says. "You're safe here."

For now, I think. I'm not sure I'm really safe anywhere. "I'd love to spy on Berg for a change."

Burnham takes off his glasses and rubs the lenses with a corner of his shirt. "Funny you should say that. I've tried to hack into the Forge computer system to dig around, but I can never get far. It runs on a closed network."

"But they're always collecting viewer data for the blip ranks," I say. "Can't you get in that way?"

"That's a separate system," he says. "I can't get to anything private, like Dean Berg's or Dr. Ash's files. The best I managed was to disarm the swipe locks of the doors once."

"What if you could get onto Berg's computer directly?" I ask.

"Then I'd be in, but I'm never going back to Forge." He rubs his eyes.

"Tired?" I ask.

"A little." He puts his glasses on again and aims his gaze toward the deck.

A red-tailed squirrel is poised on the picnic table, dissecting a nut so the shards of hard peel scatter around him. Burnham's place is so peaceful that I ought to be able to relax a little. But I can't. I'm wired all the time. Edgy.

I check around once again, reflexively looking for cameras. The corners of the walls and furniture are clear, and the white ceiling has no bumps or eyes along its seams.

"We're private," Burnham says.

"Do you ever get used to that?" I ask.

"No."

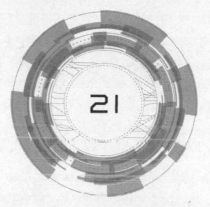

— THEA —

BEST DOG EVER

THE MORNING AFTER I talked to Linus, I searched the Internet again for any news of Rosie. There was none. She puzzled me. I was relieved that she'd escaped from Berg, but I couldn't guess where she was, and that bugged me because I felt that I should be able to reason out where she would go. She and I were growing apart now that we were both out of the vault, and as impatient as I was to find her, she obviously didn't feel the same. It was so tempting to try to reach her through our Forge email.

"Althea!" Madeline called from downstairs.

I closed my computer and rolled off my bed to stand in the doorway. "Yes?" I called down.

"You have some friends here to see you."

I made my way down to meet three girls I'd never seen before. They acted warm and concerned about me, but it was totally awkward. I mixed up their names. They wanted to take an ussie of the four of us. I said no. One of them got all teary-eyed, and I didn't know how to handle it. Madeline mercifully stepped in, and the girls left shortly after.

"No more of that," I said to Madeline, waving them off.

"They mean well," she said.

"Do they? I get the feeling they came to see the show."

Madeline didn't deny it. We headed back to the kitchen, where Solana dozed in a parallelogram of sunlight from the window.

"A couple of reporters have called asking for interviews," she said. "The press doesn't seem to know you're pregnant yet, but that won't last. I'll just keep telling them no, if that's what you want."

"Thanks."

My phone buzzed with another message from Tom. I glanced at it briefly and set it back on the table. Madeline filled me in about the appointments she'd lined up for me with a local neurologist and a nurse midwife. My physical therapist was coming to the house later in the afternoon. Madeline had made me haircut and manicure appointments, too, which was more than I'd bargained for. I gazed out to the pool where the morning light was reflecting on the blue water.

"What would you think about looking into summer classes at the community college?" Madeline asked. She stepped over to a tablet on the kitchen desk and began typing. A varicose vein showed below her knee. "Your baby will be a little older by then, and we can watch him or her for a few hours while you're at school. You could start with a basic psych class. See if it's what you're still interested in."

I hadn't even finished high school. "It's hard to think that far ahead," I said.

"It might help to have a focus," she said.

"Like I'm your focus?"

She stopped typing. "Excuse me?" she said.

I took a deep breath. "I don't need you managing my life for me."

"I'm only pointing out your options," she said.

This was bigger than that. I had a new name now. Being me wasn't about choosing between Althea and Rosie. It wasn't a war in my head. It was more of a melding truce, and I was going to have to stand up for who I was as Thea. "If we're going to consider my options, what would you think about me putting up the baby for adoption?" I asked.

Madeline's eyes narrowed, and her voice thinned to black ice. "Don't you dare."

"It might be the kindest thing to do," I said. "I'm not sure I'm cut out to be a mother just yet."

"We did not save you and your baby just so you could turn around and give up that baby for adoption. Out of the question."

"It doesn't hurt to talk about it," I said.

"Yes, it does," she said.

"Why?" I asked. "I thought Catholics supported adoption. Didn't you save me because you're Catholic?"

"Althea!"

"I just want to know," I said. It felt good to speak up. "You saved your daughter, but you never intended to save *me*, and now I want to know where I stand. What rights do I have? I'm not going to be friends with those girls who just left. We have nothing in common. What if I don't feel like going to community college? What if I don't want to be a mother? You can't just shoehorn me into Althea's life."

"What's all this about?" she asked. "We're not 'shoehorning' you anywhere. You've only been home two days."

"But I've been awake for weeks, and I'm telling you, I'm not Althea."

"You could still get your memory back."

"But I don't have it back now," I said. "Can't you see me as I am?"

Grampa came in, carrying a coffee mug. "Hello, ladies."

Madeline threw out her hand in my direction. "She wants to give up her baby for adoption."

"I didn't say that," I said. "I wanted to talk about it."

"No adoption. It's not going to happen," Grampa said.

"See? What did I tell you," Madeline said.

He set his mug in the sink and glanced over at her. "I thought you were going in to work today."

"Stuff came up," Madeline said. "I'm going tomorrow." She braced a hand on her hip and turned more fully toward me. Her white hair glowed in a gleam of sunlight. "We didn't keep you alive because I'm Catholic," she said. "I *am* religious, deeply, but I'm also a scientist. I don't blindly follow a set of rules. Our ability to reason is one of God's gifts, and it's our obligation to use our intellects."

"So then, why did you save me?" I asked. "I was all but dead anyway. Tom said I was suffering. He said I whimpered."

"And what does that tell you?" she said. "Does a dead thing cry?"

I stopped short. "I guess not."

"You had a fetus in you," Madeline said. "The sanctity of life is not a rigid ending point to an argument. It's a beginning. If you were already dead, mind and soul, then it didn't matter to you that we were keeping your body alive a few more months for the sake of your baby. And if, despite everything the doctors told us, some tiny, lost spark of you was still living inside you, then keeping your body alive might give that spark a chance to reignite, too."

I followed her logic, but at the same time, I couldn't get past the idea of Althea suffering and helpless. "Didn't it matter to you that I was in pain?" I asked.

She winced. "Of course it did. Watching you lie there, each day. It was torment. I'd have done anything to switch places with you." She set her lips tightly and shook her head. "If you want to kill someone slowly, give them a daughter in a coma."

Grampa moved over and put his hand on her shoulder. "It's all right," he said softly. "It's over."

Madeline looked at me like she didn't completely agree with him.

I felt bad, like I'd been disrespectful. I was still an outsider to what they'd suffered, even though I was intricately connected to it, too. "What if I hadn't woken up?" I asked. "What if, after the baby was born, I was still in a coma. Would you have kept me alive still?"

Madeline gazed past me, and her eyes lost focus for a moment. "I don't know."

"You don't know?" I asked, surprised. She seemed so full of conviction.

"I don't," she said. "We make each decision when we come to it and do the best that we can."

I supposed she was right. "That's what I'm trying to do, too."

"You aren't really thinking of giving up the baby, are you?" Grampa said.

I looked down at Solana, who yawned at me and beat her tail on the floor in oblivious contentment.

"No," I said. But that didn't mean I saw clearly how to live out my life with Althea's family.

Madeline's shoulders relaxed, but she shook her head as she looked at me, like she wasn't pleased with her first real glimpse of the stranger in her family.

〉〉〉〉〉〉〉〉

A couple of days later, after dinner, I took my first significant walk without my cane and went to the stables. It was a relief to have some time alone. Relatives had started dropping in to visit. They were nice, but between them and the housekeeping staff, the house was never quiet. Now twilight was falling, and I liked the slow wave of purple that eased up the valley. This time, the scent of the barn was milder, and I was able to wander in. The dark, solid woodwork gleamed beneath metal bits, coils of rope, and tack. Big animals shifted their feet in the shadows as I, the alien, ambled slowly past the stalls.

This isn't a bad place to be in limbo, is it? I asked my inner voice. To beckon her was instinct, but she wasn't there, and the back of my mind remained silent. That was another thing to ask Rosie when I ever saw her again: did she hear voices? Did she notice I was gone?

A horse raised its head to look at me with big black eyes, and I had no idea if he was mine. I didn't even know how to touch him. A flapping above drew my gaze, and cooing came from the loft.

"You used to play up there when you were little," Tom said.

I turned to see him walking into the barn, and my breath hitched. He looked different, and not just because of a recent shave and clean clothes. He seemed to be part of the calm of the barn, like he belonged here more than I did. The blue in his shirt was a good match for his eyes, and he watched me thoughtfully as he approached.

"I'm sorry I haven't replied to any of your messages," I said.

"So you got my texts? I came to see if your parents took your phone."

"They didn't."

"Good to know you avoided me all on your own," he said, smiling.

"I'm surprised my father let you come out here."

"He didn't. Your parents don't know I'm here," he said. "I'd rather keep it that way."

"How did you get past security?"

"I know a couple trails," he replied. "It's no big deal."

The alertness I'd felt around him before was back again, and I felt a new blush around the neckline of my shirt.

"Want to go up?" he asked, nodding his chin toward the ladder.

I took a look at the old wooden rungs. "No thanks. I've had bad luck with ladders before."

"So I hear," he said. "I did a little research on Rosie Sinclair. She acted pretty unglued at the end there before she was expelled. I'm not going to lie."

"She wasn't unglued. She just had nobody believing her," I said. "I thought you didn't believe I was her."

"I'm not sure what I believe, but I can tell she's important to you, so I looked her up. Nobody knows where she's gone," Tom said. "Do you?"

I thought of my phone call with Linus. "No," I said. "I don't know where she is. I wish I did. I'd like to help her if she needs it."

"Would she let you?"

I laughed, surprised by his astute question. "I don't know. That's a good point. She probably wouldn't know me at first."

"I'd like to see that meeting." He set a hand on the ladder. "You used to keep some stuff up in the loft. Want to see? I could bring it down for you."

"I guess. Sure."

He headed up the ladder, and the bird flew out with a rustle of wings. I heard some bumping, and a moment later, he came back down carrying a crate on his shoulder. He set it on a bench. Under a couple of gilded riding trophies, I saw a jumble of paper dolls and a crusty hand-held computer game. I sat slowly on the bench and pulled an old plastic halyard out of the crate, the sort kids made in crafts at camp.

He took the other end of the bench. "That's ugly," he said.

"Truly." I nodded toward the crate. "Althea won those trophies. I can't even ride a horse."

"So?"

"I don't know. I had a talk with Madeline the other day. She made a manicure appointment for me."

He laughed. "She should have known you wouldn't go for that."

"That's the thing," I said. "It feels like I don't have any control of my life here. My family wants me to be someone I'm not. They're nice and everything."

"But they don't know you."

I nodded toward the crate of memorabilia. "And here you are trying to prompt my memory. You can't resist, either."

"It's that obvious, huh?"

I leaned my head back against the wall and rested my hands on my big belly. "I don't blame you. You want Althea back, like everyone else does. But she's not coming. I'm a perpetual reminder and disappointment."

"I find you fascinating, actually," he said.

I glanced over at him, doubtful. He was flipping over a flimsy paper doll. He tried fitting the paper stand section in the notches.

"Do you have any sisters?" I asked.

"Nope. Only child." He set the paper doll aside and pulled out the ancient computer game. Frogger. He tapped the buttons experimentally.

"Do you live with your parents?" I asked.

"My dad. My parents got divorced when I was in seventh grade. My mom remarried and moved away."

"That had to be hard. Do you see her much?"

He shrugged. "No. It is what it is. I got the best of the deal, staying here with Dad. He wants to know when you're coming over, by the way. No rush."

"Good," I said. Because that wasn't happening any time soon.

I peeked down into the crate and lifted up a little pile of books: a couple of graphic novels, a volume of poetry, and a red school notebook tied with twine. *Private,* it said on the cover.

I held it up for Tom to see. "Did you know about this?"

He shook his head and held out a hand. "Let me see."

Some instinct made me hold it back, and I pressed it to my chest. "I don't think so."

His eyebrows arched in surprise, and he laughed. "I have more of a right to read that than you do."

"No you don't. You actually knew her. Since she kept it hidden from you, she had her reasons."

He stood up and came before me. "Let me have it. I mean it."

"No."

"Come on. I'm not going to fight you for it."

"Good," I said, rising to my feet. I had to steady my balance a second, but then I was fine.

"I know what," he said. "Let's leave it here. Or better yet, we'll burn it unread. That's what she'd want."

I looked at him, curious. "What are you afraid I'll find in here?"

I watched his gaze drop to the book in my hand, and then rise to my mouth.

"I just have a bad feeling about it," he said quietly.

He was lying. He was also standing unnecessarily close. I tried to back up, but my legs met the edge of the bench. His expression shifted subtly to some unspoken question.

"I've been thinking about something you said the other day," he said.

"What?"

"Actually, you didn't say it so much with words." He touched a hand to my arm and electricity lit up my nerves. He laughed softly, and his eyes went warm. "Kind of like that," he said.

I was acutely aware of how little space remained between my body and his, and the next thing I knew, my fingers wanted to go touching all over his clean blue shirt.

"I'm not sure how to say this. I have a boyfriend sort of. Or I did. It's kind of murky," I said.

"Linus left you," he said. "I watched the show."

"I talked to him just the other day, though," I said.

That stopped him. He glanced around the barn and then focused back on me, more intently than before. "I don't see him here."

"I know, but—"

"Just no," Tom said.

Then he kissed me.

I should not have melted, but I couldn't help it. I should have been able to step away, but instead I moved closer, right up against his shirt, which was just as soft as it looked. The journal slipped from my fingers, and I slid my hands up his back. His warmth spread into me, and I kept reaching for more until I was on my tiptoes. Gravity, I discovered, did not apply on planet Tom.

"This is really not right," I said, torn.

"Too much talking."

He moved in again, and I went along until I had to gasp for breath. I linked a finger through his belt loop and tried to clear my thoughts. I attempted to focus on his chin, but his chin was very close to his lips. I shut my eyes.

"Tom. We have to stop," I said.

He backed up an inch, but he didn't release me.

"There's a very nice loft up that ladder," he said. "I could help you get up. We'd be very careful."

I opened my eyes to look up at him. Logic warned me that going up that ladder with him would be a mistake, but the physical side of me was fully good to go. In a very serious manner, he brushed a strand of my hair back around my ear.

"You're not ready, are you?" he asked.

I shook my head.

He leaned in again for another kiss. "Okay," he said.

"Okay?" I said.

He nodded and stepped back. "Yes. We're good."

My knees were wobbly, and my skin felt hypersensitive. I was both relieved and disappointed. He ducked his head for a second and pushed his hair back from his eyes before he smiled at me again.

"I think you dropped this," he said, handing me Althea's journal. "I don't think you should read it, but it's up to you."

Right. I'd completely forgotten it. He could easily have taken it.

"Thanks," I said, brushing a bit of hay off the brown cover. I looked up at him again, and a mysterious light flickered in his eyes. I bit inward on my tender lips, then licked them.

He groaned and looked away. "Time for me to get on home."

Later that night, after I'd said good night to the family, I went upstairs to read Althea's journal. As I undid the twine, a photo of a collie slipped out onto my bedspread. I turned it over and read "Gizmo 2054–2065 Best Dog Ever." With a twinge of guilty curiosity, I opened the little book. Althea's journal was not a series of entries written over weeks or months. It was a single outpouring of tight, hard-pressed handwriting that gouged into the paper.

Gizmo's dead. I can't believe he's gone! He was my best friend, my one true friend always there when I needed him. Why does it hurt so much? He's okay now. He's out of pain now. Why am I so furious at EVERYTHING? My parents. Daniel again. Tom, and all he tried to do was be nice tonight. I hate that he's nice to me. He doesn't even <u>know</u> me. I wish I had Gizmo here with me! I would hold his sweet head and look into his trusting brown eyes. He had such hopeful eyebrows. His little eyebrows! He would understand me like he always does. This place will never be the same. Why'd you have to die? Why did I ever have to meet Daniel? How could he treat me like that? I still can't believe I trusted him when I should have known! I should have <u>known</u>! His filthy back seat. I can still hear him. He makes me feel disgusting. Oh, Gizmo. No. I'm stronger now. I don't have to feel this mess anymore. I didn't do anything wrong. Why am I crying over this again? I'm not thirteen anymore! I just wish Gizmo was here! <u>I miss my dog</u>.

R.I.P. Gizmo Flores
BEST DOG EVER
BEST FRIEND EVER

Her words buzzed straight to my heart. Poor Althea. Quietly, I closed her journal and picked up the photo of Gizmo again, holding it lightly. It was true that Gizmo's eyebrow bumps

256

made him look sympathetic. Whatever Daniel did to Althea when she was thirteen must have been deeply painful.

I felt so awful for her. What a life she'd had—some trauma at thirteen, then losing her dog, then pregnancy and a motorcycle accident at eighteen. Being rich hadn't saved her from trouble and loss. Then I remembered how Tom had said Althea walked proudly in high school. She had all those riding trophies, too, and her aim of being a psychiatrist. She'd felt deeply and suffered, but she'd been strong, too. I had the feeling she wouldn't want me to pity her.

The baby rolled inside me, poking a knee or elbow into my side. I slid heavily off my bed and slipped the journal into the bottom drawer of my dresser. A ping of headache made me cringe for a moment, and I opened my window for a crack of fresh air. The night had grown late, and the moon hung over the valley, clear and serene.

My phone buzzed on the dresser, and I saw I'd missed a row of texts from Tom. Nothing from Linus. For the first time, I called Tom back.

"How much do you know about what happened to Althea when she was younger?" I asked.

"Did she mention a guy?" Tom said.

"Yes. Daniel."

"When I saw her journal, that's what I was afraid of," Tom said. "She never talked about him much, just told me he raped her after a riding competition. She was pretty messed up about it. She almost quit competing because she was afraid to see him again."

257

"Do her parents know?" I asked.

"Yes. She saw a therapist for a while. That's really all I know. And the guy's family moved out of town. I always wondered if your dad had something to do with that."

"Did you know him?"

"No."

I could see a corner of the pool from my angle, and someone had left the lights on so the water glowed.

"Do you remember any of it?" Tom asked.

I shook my head. "No. The only thing I've come close to remembering, and it isn't even a memory, is a feeling I get when I'm with you."

I touched a finger to the window sash, waiting for a reply, while his silence pulled the thread of my nerves.

"I'm coming over," Tom said.

"That won't help," I said, and took a deep breath. "I think I need to leave for a while. I need to go see my own family. Rosie's family."

"Thea, this is your family now. Rosie's family isn't going to recognize you. You'll only confuse them."

"I still have to see them," I said. "I miss my mom. My sister, too." I tried to explain it. "I don't know why, but reading Althea's journal makes me realize how unfair this all is. I can't possibly take over her life and remake it into my own. She's not just some hand-me-down jeans."

"I know it can't be easy," he said. "But this is still where you belong. Thea would want you here. The old Thea, I mean. I'm sure of it."

"That's a crazy thing to say."

"She was a very generous person. She cared about people," he said, and stopped abruptly, like he didn't trust himself to go on.

This couldn't be easy for him, either.

I felt my pulse thudding oddly. "Maybe you should come with me," I said. "Do you want to take a road trip?"

I expected him to argue.

"How soon?" he asked.

I smiled with gratitude. "Tomorrow," I said.

"Then yes."

— ROSIE —

FLESH-EATING MAGGOTS

I'M BACK IN THE VAULT, and this time Berg himself is coming for me. He lurks as an evil presence in the darkness, just beyond my sight, but I know he's there, tinkering with something that causes a metallic, sharpening noise. When he steps into the light, I can't move or speak. *Hello Rosie,* he says. *You thought you could escape, but this is the only way to leave me.* He lifts a short, sharp knife and starts between my toes, slitting me up my skin, opening my leg so black worms and maggots spill out.

I scream and bolt up in bed. I clutch at my blanket and knock my hand wildly for the lamp. It crashes to the floor, and I leap out of bed toward the door. I yank it open, panting with fear. Only when I see light coming from a bathroom do I remember where I am. This is Burnham's place, not the vault.

I swallow hard, but my heart is racing and I can still feel the horror of Berg slicing up my leg. He could be here in this apartment. He could be waiting for me.

Burnham leans into the hallway. "Are you okay?" he asks.

I check my bare foot for a black seam of pain, but my leg is whole and unharmed. I search the shadows around us for movement. Violence feels ready to erupt around us.

"Did you have a nightmare?" Burnham asks. He's supporting himself with a grip on the doorframe. "Say something. You're scaring me."

"Am I still asleep?"

"No," Burnham says. "You're awake, Rosie. This is real." He snaps his fingers. "This is real."

I slide down the wall to the carpet and wrap my arms around my legs. Every bit of me is shaking. "It was horrible," I say. "Berg was slicing up my leg and letting out the black maggots." A shiver of them flashes over my sight again.

Burnham flips on another light. His chest is bare, and the waist of his pajama pants droops low. "Let me get my leg brace. I'll be right there," he says.

"Don't go!" I say.

"Two seconds," he says, and disappears into his room.

I'm afraid to look back over my shoulder. I'm afraid to be alone. I crawl rapidly down the carpet to Burnham's door, and I look in to see him on his bed, hunched over, attaching a brace above and below his knee, over his pajamas. He uses his one good hand and his teeth to pull the straps snug, and then looks across at me.

"What are you doing?" he asks.

"Making sure you're not getting eaten by maggots."

He swings his leg over. "I don't taste good enough."

And when he smiles, I finally trust that I'm awake. I'm safe. Berg can't be here.

Burnham looks way stronger than I expected. Shirtless, he has serious muscles in his torso and shoulders, even for his bad arm, and as he reaches for his glasses, I realize I'm staring. I shift back from the door and out into the hallway, which suddenly seems much safer than it did before.

He appears above me, one eyebrow raised. "That looks good on you," he says.

I glance down at myself and remember that, aside from my panties, I'm only wearing one of his tee shirts. I clutch at my neckline. "This is embarrassing."

He smiles and offers his good hand. "Come on. Get up. I'll make you a snack."

I take his hand and rise slowly to my feet. "I can't, like this."

His eyes travel over me again. "You're covered more than in a swimsuit."

Somehow, I don't find that at all reassuring, but I don't want to leave him to go back to my room. *Chicken.* As I release his hand, my fingertips are tingling. We've been hanging out for two days, watching *The Forge Show* and baking brownies when we're not trying to work out details about Berg, but Burnham has always had his shirt on up to this point. Tonight he seems different, and it's not just because I'm edgy from my nightmare.

I follow him into the kitchen where he turns on a row of lights. Outside, floodlights illuminate the back porch in one direction and the parking circle in the other. No one, certainly not Berg with a knife, can approach without being seen.

I slump onto a stool, and before long Burnham slides a mug of cocoa across to me.

"For starters," he says.

I take the mug gladly in my cold hands.

"Do you have nightmares often?" he asks.

"Yeah."

He opens the freezer and contemplates its contents, bracing his hand on the door. I barely notice his bent wrist anymore, but I notice the rest of him. He takes out a pizza box. He weighs it in his hand a couple times and then chucks it back in the freezer. If he were fully dressed and this were daylight, the whole routine would be blandly normal, but it isn't and he isn't, and I have to lower my face over my mug to stop looking at him. Even then, I can still picture him leaning back against the opposite counter with his arms crossed over his bare chest.

"Interesting," he says.

"What."

"I don't have to say a thing and you're blushing."

"I'm not."

He steps forward and leans on the counter that separates us. "I think it's an entirely new color. A kind of tomatoesque pink. Does it hurt?"

"Don't be a dork," I say.

"Let me see. Is it hot?" he asks, reaching for my hand.

263

I let him turn my fingers over in his before I realize my mistake. His touch is cool, but it only makes my skin burn hotter.

I pull away and grip my mug again. "It's just the heat from the cocoa."

"I see," he says slowly. He draws a finger through a drop of cocoa that spilled on the white counter.

I can tell he's looking at me, but I avoid his gaze. The ice-maker makes a rattling noise in the fridge.

"It's no accident that you came here," he says.

"I know," I say quickly. "You've been great. This has been perfect. I feel a ton better than I did when I arrived."

He straightens stiffly. "Don't do that."

"Don't do what?"

"Put your box around me. I'm not 'great.' It isn't 'perfect' here. Be real with me."

"What do you mean?" I ask. "I am real with you."

"Then wake up," he says gently.

I am awake, more awake than ever, and I'm sitting in his kitchen in a threadbare tee shirt. It barely covers my port. My legs have never felt so long and naked. I didn't consciously plan to be here, but somewhere along the way, I made the choices that brought me here.

He comes around the counter, slowly, so I could back away if I wanted to. I manage to get off the stool, but I'm still right there, in reach, when he stops in front of me. My lungs go tight, and I can't bring myself to meet his gaze. Or even look higher than his collarbone.

"I don't want to blow this," he says.

"Me, neither."

He sets his hand lightly on my waist so I feel his warmth through the cotton. I flash my eyes up for a second and find what I'm afraid of. He's tender and lonely, and funny and smart. I can't kiss him unless I mean it, and I can't mean it while I'm still all twisted and evil inside. But I owe him. I owe him so much.

"Don't you be dishonest with me," he says.

"I know," I whisper.

He doesn't move. I swear that heat particles are charging the shadow between us, but I don't know what to do.

"Do you trust me?" he asks.

I nod.

"Then let me try something," he says, and he touches his lips to mine.

I can't breathe. I can feel the rest of him just beyond this soft kiss. He's so warm and strong. If I move at all, I'll end up in his arms, but I can't be there. I'm not ready. I'm afraid.

Of me. Of everything.

My heart tumbles wildly around in my chest. I thought I knew how to kiss someone, but I don't know how to kiss Burnham. I falter back a half step. I can't look at him, but I hear him breathing.

His voice comes low. "Why?"

"I don't know," I say, and swallow hard.

He slides his hand away from my waist. With a spin, I'm on my way back down the hall to my room, where I lock the door with shaky fingers. Something's wrong with me. Broken. I don't know what it is. I feel this pull toward Burnham, but I can't stay here with him. Every instinct tells me to flee, and at the same time, I swear I'm being punished.

>>>>>>>>>

He's in the weight room with a trainer when I come out of my bedroom the next morning. I linger out on the porch until they're finished and I hear the trainer leave, and then I come back in to stand awkwardly by the couch. Burnham's shirt is damp with sweat, and his glasses catch a glare so I can't read his expression. He grabs a towel from the back of a chair and drapes it around his neck.

"I hope you slept well," he says, and aims into the kitchen.

I hardly slept at all. I kept the light on and huddled in my bed, feeling wretched.

"I'm sorry about last night," I say.

"Are you?" he says. He turns on the faucet to fill a glass with water.

"I think I should leave," I say.

He drinks long, his throat working, and lowers the glass to look at me. "Okay."

I didn't expect him to agree quite so fast. I take a couple of halting steps toward the kitchen, where I can see my cup of cold cocoa still on the counter.

"I might have to borrow some money," I say.

"I can order another car for you, or better yet, you can take mine."

"I can't take your car. Quit being so generous."

"What are you going to do? Hitchhike? Take my car, Rosie. I have three. You can bring it back someday when you're done with it. I'll give you some cash, too. How much do you think you'll need? Doesn't matter. I'll give you a wad."

I feel really, really horrible.

He scoops handfuls of ice out of the freezer and dumps them into a deep red bowl with a loud clatter. Then he turns on the faucet again so water rushes into the bowl. He turns off the water, carries the bowl to the table near the window, and dunks his bent wrist into the ice water.

"I'll pay you back for everything some day," I say. "I promise."

"I'll let you try," he says.

Worse and worse. I have to find some decent way to say goodbye to him.

"Remember the lady knight with the boobs?" I say.

His expression stays flat. "What about her?"

"I think you should still work on your game," I say. "Go ahead and be a doctor, but don't give up making your games, too. You were really good at it."

"Thanks for the inspirational pep talk." He wipes at his face with his towel. "How's your latest film going?"

I don't have one. I don't even have a camera. "Point taken."

He shifts his wrist in the bowl and winces briefly. He looks unhappy, and I know it's my fault.

"I'm really sorry, Burnham," I say.

He adjusts his glasses and gazes up at me again. "I don't get it, Rosie. We're so good together," he says. "Are you still jonesing for Linus? Is it that?"

"Of course not."

"So then, what? I'm too klutzy now for you?"

"Don't say that," I say.

"There's got to be some reason," he says. "I can't figure it out."

I shove my hands in my pockets and wish I could dig out of this awkwardness. I speak quietly, trying to put my thoughts together. "Something's different in me. Sort of scrambled. I'm afraid."

"Of what? Me?"

"No. I'd never be afraid of you," I say.

"Then what?"

"I don't know. I can't explain it." I keep feeling the vault in me. This weight. Fear. It's like my lungs still carry tiny, heavy particles of darkness from the vault, and they've attached themselves deep inside me. "Love is for happy people, not me."

"I'm sorry, but that's ridiculous," he says.

It stings. I shrug. "You asked for honesty. That's how I feel."

"No, the truth is, you care about me, too," he says. "You're just not willing to admit it."

His ice makes a clunking noise, and I fix my gaze on the bowl again.

"This is exhausting," I say.

Burnham laughs briefly. "Tell me about it."

I move a few steps closer until I'm in the sunlight of the window with him. "I need to figure out some stuff. I have to go back to Forgetown to see Berg."

"And Linus."

I hesitate, but that's true. "Yes, if he's there. But mostly, I need my revenge."

He shifts his wrist in the ice water again. "I see. You won't kiss me, but you'd risk your life to kill someone."

"I never said I'd kill him, per se."

Burnham looks at me, deadpan. Okay, he knows it's what I want to do.

I slide my hands in my pockets. "I'm not expecting you to help me."

"No. But it might make you happier," he says. He considers me a long moment. "I've been thinking about it. If I give you a peg, and if you can stick it in a port of Berg's personal computer, I can hack it remotely."

I move a step nearer to him. "That would be totally illegal."

"Do you care?"

"I don't care if it's illegal, but you're different."

He pulls his wrist out of the bowl and dries it with the towel. "That's where you're wrong, just like you're wrong about us," he says. "I want revenge, too."

— THEA —

THE BOXCAR

I CAME DOWN THE NEXT MORNING and found Diego, Madeline, and Grampa around the big kitchen table. Sunlight slanted in and bounced off the wooden floor. On the stove, a black iron skillet held a couple of fried eggs, and the place smelled like bacon. Madeline had her briefcase open on a neighboring chair, and Grampa was working a crossword puzzle from the paper.

"I'm going to take a little road trip with Tom," I said. "We should be gone three or four days, I expect."

Diego set his coffee mug down with a thud. "Unbelievable."

"It's important," I said. "I need to go see my other family back in Arizona. I need to do it now, before I have the baby. Before things get more complicated."

"Did you talk to them?" Madeline asked.

"No. They won't listen to me. I have to see them face to face," I said. "I'm aware that's a problem, but I still have to go."

"Enough," Diego said. "As long as you live under my roof, you'll do as I say, and I say you're not going."

"Then I guess I'm moving out," I said.

Madeline broke into a laugh. "Would you listen to yourself? You can't move out. Don't be ridiculous."

Grampa wasn't laughing. I looked at him. "You understand, don't you?"

He sat back and set his pen down on the crossword. "No, I don't. You belong here with us."

"I'm supposed to have eighteen million dollars," I said. "Where's that?"

"In a trust fund," Madeline said. "You don't get a cent unless your trustees agree."

"And who are my trustees?" I asked.

"Your mother, Grampa, and me," Diego said.

I should have guessed. "So the money isn't really mine?"

"It is for anything reasonable," Madeline said.

Which a road trip was not. I got it. This actually made things simpler. Fortunately, I hadn't gotten used to having money, so giving it up wouldn't be hard. I might have to lean on Tom financially for a while, but I could pay him back eventually. Once I got to Doli, if I stayed there, my parents would help. I could probably work at McLellens' Pot Bar and Sundries for awhile. I would figure it out.

"Okay, then," I said. "I'll let you know how I'm doing."

271

Diego set both his hands on the table. "Get that smirk off your face. I said you're not leaving."

"I heard you just fine," I said. "I'm still going. I don't need your money. Tom's giving me a ride, and if my real parents won't help me out, I'll ask him to support me just until I'm on my feet."

"*We're* your real parents," Madeline said. "I know you're confused, but you're still our daughter."

"Then treat me with the respect I deserve," I said.

Diego rose to his feet and glared at me with barely checked fury. "I'd like to say something, and I'd like you to listen to me good and hard," he said.

I twisted my fingers together. "Go ahead."

"Your mother and I, we've been through hell for you," he said. "You can't imagine what it's like. You won't know until you have that baby of your own and you agonize over every breath it takes. Quit acting like a selfish, self-destructive idiot."

"Diego," Madeline said.

He held up a hand. "Cut him loose, Althea," he said. "Don't waste yourself on some Podunk slob who can't even tie his own shoes." He stood stiff with pride and anger. "Don't *waste* your second chance."

"This isn't about Tom," I said.

"Isn't it?" Diego asked. "Do you think I'm blind? We know he's constantly calling and texting you. It's only a matter of time before he sneaks in past security." His expression hardened. "He already did, didn't he?"

I cleared my throat. "Yes. But that isn't what matters," I

said. "We can't keep pretending I'm just going to go on with Althea's life. I don't have her memories or her scars. I never knew Daniel or lost Gizmo. I never dreamed of being a psychiatrist. I have my own roots as Rosie Sinclair, and now's my chance to go home and face what that means."

Diego and Madeline stared at me.

"She's getting worse," Madeline said in a tight voice.

"No, I'm not," I said. "You're not listening. I'm just trying to be myself."

"By taking a *road trip?*" Diego asked, his voice contemptuous. He crossed his arms. "I'll tell you who you are. You're Althea Maria Flores, and you're not going anywhere."

"What are you going to do?" I asked. "Lock me up? Shoot me?"

Diego started yelling in earnest. Madeline wasn't much better. Grampa looked at me sadly, shaking his head, and of all of them, he was the one I was most sorry about. But I was done arguing and done trying to explain. I walked down the hall, picked up a bag I'd left by the stairs, and went out to the front porch, where Tom was just pulling up in his truck. I got in without a word and didn't look back.

>>>>>>>>

We drove west. A slew of country songs, some heartsick, some peppy, made a soundtrack for the passing hills. I shucked off my shoes, tilted my seat back, and pushed my feet up on the dashboard. The sky was a huge pewter plate above us, and the road was as straight as murder between acres of grit and sage bush. The holomap on the windshield was an old one, with a faulty glitch of a blank on my side, and the voice had a British accent that reminded me of Linus.

My first false contraction came, tightening the outer surface of my basketball belly in a slow wave of tension. It held for a long moment, focusing me inward. I ran a hand slowly down my shirt and stared absently out the windshield until it passed, releasing me. The baby stretched inside me as if to say *what on earth was that?* My midwife had told me about Braxton-Hicks contractions. They didn't mean labor, but they were a kind of practice. I was excited. Nervous, too. It was March 26th. I still had four weeks to go, but that was shorter all the time.

"I'll have to stop for coffee soon," Tom said.

"I can drive some," I said.

"Have you driven since the accident?" he asked.

"I wasn't there, remember?"

"Do you have your license in your old life?"

"No, but I've been driving since I was fourteen."

"How old are you in your old life?" he asked.

"Sixteen."

His eyebrows shot up and he glanced over briefly. "Are you serious?" he said. "That explains a few things."

"Like what?"

He waved a hand vaguely. "You're kind of nice. Sweet."

In my head, I wasn't sweet. "Wasn't Althea?"

"She was nice, but in a different way. She was more wound

274

up." He pulled his phone out of his pocket, glanced at it, and nudged it up on the dashboard. It had been making ding noises on and off all morning.

"Who's calling?" I asked.

"Bunch of journalists. Not Linus."

I hadn't talked to him in the last day or so. I wondered what he'd think of my road trip. "Let me drive," I said.

We changed it up. It felt good to be in charge. A vibration in the steering wheel registered in the bones of my fingers, and I smiled.

"This is a little freaky for me," he said. "I never expected to see you driving again."

"How'd my accident happen?"

"You were mad, that's for sure."

"At you?"

He laughed. "Of course. Your parents, too, I guess."

"Did we break up?" I asked.

"*We* didn't break up. *You* broke up with *me*," he said.

"Over the baby?" I asked.

"Yeah."

I settled in the right lane and hit cruise control. The road was long and straight before us, and I kept my gaze toward the distance ahead. "I'm listening," I said.

Tom told me about the day Madeline found Althea's pregnancy test in her bathroom. When she asked Althea about it, Althea said she intended to get an abortion. Madeline was flatly against it. Diego was against it, too, but he said the choice was Althea's.

"Your parents started fighting. You knew they'd be upset," he continued. "That's why you didn't want to tell them. You were leaving the next day for college. You were packing and everything. It was all pretty emotional."

A small, tight ache started behind my eyes, and I touched a hand to my eyebrows. "How about you? What did you think about the abortion?" I asked.

He shifted in the passenger seat. "I was mad that you hadn't told me you were pregnant. Then I said I'd support whatever you decided."

I glanced over briefly at his calm features and then back to the road. "Why do I get the feeling there's more to it?"

He took his time answering. "It wasn't enough just to support you," he said. "You asked me what I really wanted. I said it didn't matter what I wanted because it was your body, and you said it did matter because I was the father. You wouldn't let me just be neutral."

He fiddled with the button of his window, pushing it down and up a couple of times so the sucking wind alternated with silence.

"So what did you say?" I asked.

He spoke loudly. "I said we should get married, okay? I said, either way, whether you had the baby or not, we should go through it together." He jabbed the window down and up once more. "And you know what you said? You said I was a coward."

I glanced over again to see that his gaze was narrowed toward the horizon. Every line of his face was taut.

"But I wasn't a coward," he said. "That was the one time I stood up to you. And that's when you left me. That's when you took my bike and practically killed yourself."

The road churned beneath our wheels, and I held tight to the steering wheel. He was talking to me like I was Althea again, and I didn't know what to do for him, so I just kept driving.

He wiped a hand against his eye. "I should have told you," he said. "I wanted you to keep our baby. I'm sorry. I did." His voice cracked but he kept on. "I left you to make the decision alone. I thought that was the right thing, but you needed me. I should have told you how I really felt."

"It's okay," I said softly.

"No, it's not. You were so upset." His voice dropped low. "Can you forgive me?"

I glanced over, startled. He was wincing, with his eyes closed.

"Of course," I said. "Tom, Althea's accident wasn't your fault. She made her own decision to go riding that night. I'm sure she knew how you really felt."

"You haven't been listening," he said, and his voice went dead. "Of course she knew how I really felt. She wanted me to man up and say it, and I wouldn't. That's what I can't forget."

>>>>>>>>

Tom and I reached Doli at the end of the day, when the last sunlight was leaving the desert, and the sky was dimming to a grainy purple. We hadn't talked much more, but he seemed

277

calmer, like maybe talking to me had helped after all. Stars appeared past the bug splats on the windshield. South of town, the boxcars stretched out in a long, weathered line, hunkered down, waiting for another earthquake like the one that had stranded them there.

As we came down the ridge and hit the turn at McLellens' Pot Bar and Sundries, I rolled my window down to stare at the new construction and garish lights. Crickets chirped from the sage.

"Slow down," I said to Tom.

The McLellens had expanded. A lighted billboard promised ATV rentals, tourist info, clean bathrooms, and cold drinks. A cartoon drawing of a girl with dark curls was holding a video camera and riding an ATV. She looked vaguely like the original me. A big sign said BRING ROSIE HOME!

The next boxcar, previously a massage parlor of ill repute, was now a bar/gift shop called The Sandman's, and a dozen tourists were out on the deck nursing drinks in fancy, sweaty glasses. Tinny reggae music topped off the ambiance. I instinctively slouched down in my seat out of view, even though no one could recognize me.

"Don't stop," I said.

"I thought we were here," Tom said.

"No. Our place is at the other end. Go."

As Tom drove down the dirt road beside the row of railroad cars, I had a bad premonition that Larry had similarly capitalized on my fame. A drooping string of bare light bulbs ran from one boxcar to the next, illuminating glimpses of new, garish paint. Oil drums lined the road like guideposts, with pails of plastic flowers on top. The Doli boxcars had always been poor, but now they were cheap, too.

Yet when our boxcar came into view, it was the same rusty, unpainted metal as before. The same threadbare curtains hung in the windows, and a defiant old pot of real petunias sat on the top step. It felt like years since I'd been home, but it looked miraculously the same.

"Is this it? You sure?" Tom asked.

"I know my own home," I said.

"I think this has gone far enough Thea," he said quietly. "You don't want to bother these people."

"You probably ought to decide once and for all whether you believe me or not."

I opened my door and got out on stiff legs, straightening my shirt over my belly. The night was soft and smelled of dusty eucalyptus. A flock of thrushes landed in my chest. Behind me, Tom got out and slammed his door.

I glanced under the boxcar to where I used to store my bike and found Dubbs's bike in the same shadow. I climbed the familiar, sagging wooden steps to find a little sign had been posted next to the door, under the sconce light.

PLEASE RESPECT OUR PRIVACY.

THIS MEANS YOU.

THANK YOU.

THE SINCLAIR/HOGARTH FAMILY

I tugged at the door. It didn't open. "Ma?" I called. "Dubbs?"

"Thea, what are you doing?" Tom said. "They don't want visitors."

I tried to peer in the gap of the kitchen curtains, past the old screen. The window was up and the sink was empty. That was all I could see, but it tugged at me.

"Ma!" I called in the window. "It's me! Rosie! Let me in."

A scrambling came from inside.

"Rosie?" said a bright young voice.

A clicking came from inside, and then the door rolled open sidewise on its wheels. My sister Dubbs stood in the opening. Her face was alight with anticipation.

"Hi, Dubbs," I whispered.

Her face fell. "Who are you?" she asked suspiciously.

She was taller by almost an inch, with a new fullness to her cheeks. Her blond, touchably soft hair fluffed to her shoulders, and she wore a new striped sweater of purple and red. Before I could drink in any more, she started to close the door.

"Wait!" I said, blocking the door with my foot. "I need to talk to you about Rosie. I have news about her. Is your ma home?"

"Dad!" Dubbs called.

"What did I tell you?" Larry called from inside. "Never answer the door."

Dubbs was staring at my belly now. When her gaze lifted to mine again, her eyes narrowed. "You said you were Rosie."

"It's complicated," I said. "Rosie's changed. She has a new

body." I bent lower so my face was on a level with hers and smiled. "You wouldn't believe how happy I am to see you."

She ducked her head back on her neck and made a face as if I stank. Larry stepped behind her and set a heavy hand on the doorway. He was all stubby bulk and crew cut. He shot one look at my belly and another toward Tom, who stood behind me on the steps.

"Okay, that's enough," he said. "Move along. Can't you read?"

He smacked a hand on the sign. Dubbs withdrew behind him.

"I'm not a reporter," I said. "I'm a friend of Rosie's. She gave me a message for you."

"Did she now," he said. "Nobody's heard hide nor hair from her in months. What's the message?"

"Let me in and I'll explain," I said.

"She said she *was* Rosie," Dubbs said.

"Yeah, and I'm pregnant, too," Larry said. He regarded me skeptically and spat. "Move your foot or it'll get crushed." He began rolling the door shut.

"Wait! You read mysteries and you like to hunt," I said to Larry. "You had a pet parakeet that died a year ago."

Larry held the door at a gap and measured me. "What was its name?"

"You didn't give it a name," I said. "You just called it 'Bird.' I tell you: I know Rosie."

He picked at his neck. "What's your name?"

"Thea Flores, from Texas," I said. "We drove all day to talk to you."

"You called once before, didn't you? I don't forget a voice." Larry's gaze shifted from me to Tom again. "Who's this meathead?"

"He's my friend, Tom Barton," I said. "Can we please come in?"

Larry lifted his chin at me. "Are you mic-ed?"

"I'm not," I said. "Dubbs can pat me down. I don't have any cameras, either."

He gave me another long look and then backed up a step. "All right," he said. "But only you. The meathead stays outside. Leave him your phone."

I glanced back at Tom, who frowned in pure warning.

"I won't be long," I said, passing him my phone.

"This is nuts, Thea," Tom said.

"No, I'm good. Ten minutes."

I stepped inside, and Larry rolled the door closed behind me with a metal bang.

The stale orange couch, Ma's fabric softener, and the metal of the boxcar combined in a unique, homey smell. Above, the skylights were black, and wan lamplight pushed the dinginess to the corners. The red curtain still hung on its sagging wire, separating my and Dubbs's bunk beds from the living room, and the kitchen table had its same circular marks from wet glasses.

"I don't want to pat her down," Dubbs said.

282

Aside from growing taller, she looked sturdier, too, like she'd been eating better. I couldn't get enough of her beautiful little face and knowing eyes. I longed to see her break into her old smile.

"It's okay," Larry said. "She's doing the talking anyway, not us. Tell us. Where's Rosie? What's her message?"

My heart sank at the implication that he hadn't heard from her. "Rosie left Berg," I said. "She was able to escape the Onar Clinic where he was keeping her and get free."

"Onar, huh? Where is she now?" Larry asked. "Why hasn't she come home?"

"She's hiding," I said, inventing a theory. "She's afraid to come here in case Berg has you watched."

I glanced toward my parents' bedroom beyond the bookshelves, then toward the screen door that led out back, but there was no sign of Ma.

"Of course he has us watched," Larry said. "Some kid's been skulking around the place, and more cameras show up every other day. I shoot them as fast as I can, but there's always more. If you ask me, Berg's sick in the head. But he's also smart. Scary smart."

"Do you talk to him?"

"Can't get past his lawyers," he said. "Where's Rosie hiding? When did you talk to her?"

"I knew her at Onar," I said. "She wants you to know she isn't crazy."

"Of course she isn't," Larry said. "Or if she is, it's Forge that made her that way. I figure everything she told us was true. Rosie means big money to Berg, one way or another. That's why he's kept her."

It was great to know he believed in Rosie. "You're right," I said. "He was able to mine dreams out of Rosie and ship them to be seeded into other people. That's what he's been doing."

Larry started looking skeptical, so I plunged on.

"I saw this first hand," I said. "He's been working with a team in Iceland. They have a research clinic there, and they put Rosie's dreams into a coma patient there, trying to save her."

"Were you a dreamer, too?" Dubbs asked. "Did they mine your dreams, too?"

She was leaning against the back of the couch, and I turned to her.

"This is why I've come here," I said softly. "They put some of your sister into me."

Dubbs's little mouth opened. "But what did that do to Rosie? Is she okay?"

"Now, hold on," Larry interrupted. He shot me a warning look and gave a quick jerk of his head toward Dubbs. "Some of us have got enough nightmares as it is. I'm sure Rosie is just fine, wherever she is. You said she got free, right?"

My heart thudded painfully. "Right. She did."

"Then why doesn't she *call* us?" Dubbs said. "When is she coming *home*?"

I sank slowly to the armrest of the couch so my face was on a level with hers. "You miss her, don't you?" I asked.

She nodded. "She's my sister."

"You know she loves you, right? No matter what," I said.

Dubbs's big eyes were wary. "What did they put in you from her?" she asked. "Like, feelings? Dreams?"

"Some feelings," I said. "Some memories."

All of them, actually, I thought.

"Is that how you know about Bird?" Dubbs asked.

I nodded. "Yes. And I have memories about you, too, like all those times we walked on the tracks together and picked wildflowers to make crowns. Once we found a subway token all the way from New York. Remember? The one with the square hole?"

I touched my neck. I had threaded the token on a string of leather and I'd worn it as a necklace every day. She had to remember. Dubbs was standing very still, with her knuckles bent awkwardly against the couch. I could see her weighing my words, testing them against what she knew.

Then she shook her head.

"No," she said. "We didn't do that."

My heart ached. "I shared my cookie dough with you, right here on this couch," I said. "We did it the night you told me I should apply to the Forge School. It was all your idea. We watched the show on a tablet you borrowed from the school library, remember?" I could see it so clearly. I was still holding an ice pack against my face from when Larry had hit me.

Dubbs looked at my belly. "I didn't do that with you," she said.

"I mean, not with *me* as I am. With *Rosie*," I said quickly. "You shared the cookie dough with Rosie. I just have Rosie's memories, too. We had the same bunk bed, right over there. I gave you your glitter glue pens, remember?"

Dubbs backed up a step and reached for Larry's hand. "You're wrong," she said. "Something's wrong with you."

I caught my breath as the reality slammed me. Of course. From her perspective I was a pregnant stranger. With my big belly, darker skin, and higher voice, I looked nothing like the sister she'd loved, no matter what I said. "Rosie just wants you to know that she loves you," I said.

"I know that," Dubbs said. "She didn't have to send some freaky pregnant girl to tell me that."

A small, sharp twig snapped apart inside me. Back in the vault, I had staked my life on my love for Dubbs. It hadn't occurred to me that I would lose her love in the process. I glanced at Larry, whose frown was deep and hard.

"I thought for sure you'd understand," I said.

"You'd better go," Larry said. "Whatever they did to you, I get that it messed you up, but you have to go."

I rose unsteadily to my full height and looked around the boxcar again, scanning the books and the computer, the coffee table and the antlers. It all looked the same, but it wasn't. None of it was the same. It wasn't my home anymore. This wasn't my family. It would never be again. Loss poured through me, as wild and lonely as the moonlight on the wind.

The sound of footsteps came lightly up the back steps, and the screen door opened. Ma came in with a six-pack of beer and paused on the threshold, smiling.

"Who's this?" she asked.

"Dubbs let her in. She thinks she's Rosie," Larry said. "She was just going."

Ma looked startled. She batted away a moth that had come in with her. "That's a new one," she said. She looked me over carefully, and then nodded toward my belly. "When are you due?"

"Next month," I said, my throat suddenly dry. *Hug me,* I thought.

"That last month's the worst. Feels like it'll go on forever," Ma said. She walked to the table to set down the beer and wiped a hand on the back of her skirt. "We're kind of busy," she said. "Bath time for Dubbs. I'm sorry we can't be of help. They sell souvenir pictures of Rosie down at McLellens' if you're interested."

"Ma, it's me!" I said. "They put Rosie's memories in me. I'm your daughter! Won't you at least listen?"

She smiled sadly, took my arm, and steered me toward the door. "Come on, sweetheart," she said. "On your way. Do you have somebody to take you home?"

"She came with a guy. He's outside," Larry said.

"Wait, please!" I said. "Ma! Just let me explain! I grew up here. I remember Dad before he went MIA. We used to have tea parties under the table. You used to paint my toenails with watercolors, remember? Use your imagination now, please. Just try to believe me for one second."

Ma went pale. She released me. "Larry," she said calmly.

Larry crossed instantly to me and backed me toward the door. "Don't make it any worse."

I looked at my stricken mother, and my heart broke. I turned to Dubbs and tried to smile once more. I failed completely. "Just remember Rosie's message, okay? It's real, no matter what."

Dubbs hid her face against Ma, who hugged her tight.

Larry lugged the heavy door open for me.

"Watch your step now," he said, and guided me out.

24

— ROSIE —

A COZY BATHROOM

BEFORE I LEAVE BURNHAM, he buys me half a dozen recyclable phones. He also uses the Tor network to set up a private website where we can connect. This seems like overkill to me, but he says if our phones get tapped or our emails get hacked, it's good to have a backup. We agree on code word *Waffles67*. Then Burnham loans me a blue Honda Fit and stocks it with snacks and spare outfits from his sister, including a visor hat and sunglasses so I'm not so easily recognizable.

"Remember. You promised to pay me back," he says.

I don't know what to say. Leaving him is hard. We have an awkward hug, and I promise to call him once I'm in Forgetown. He's working on a way to get me past the cameras so I can get to Berg's computer in the dean's tower.

It's a long drive from Atlanta to Forgetown, seventeen hours by holomap and twice as long with bad luck. I'm not the best driver, and I can't risk getting pulled over, so I keep under the speed limit. I hit traffic around Nashville, and torrential rain in the Tennessee Valley. I spend my first night in the car getting wind-swiped at an abandoned drive-in. Nightmares haunt me, and I don't sleep soundly until day comes. I wake groggy around noon, and by the next evening, when I arrive outside St. Louis, I'm beat. The temptation to call Linus and maybe get an offer of a decent place to sleep is strong, but then again, I'm not even sure he lives there. He might be living back with Otis and Parker when he's not traveling for his job.

It's raining again when I pull off the highway and stop in a park, and the raindrops make a gentle drumming on the roof of the car. In the distance, I can see the Gateway Arch dark against the clouds, and I can't get over how big it is. Linus must see it every day that he's here. He and I haven't spoken since I was at Jenny and Portia's—a conversation that still troubles me—and I'm nervous about calling him now. The truth is, I'm not over Linus, but what that means exactly, I don't know.

I turn off my car. Then I take out one of my spare phones and dial Linus's number. When he picks up, I release my seat backward so I can stretch my legs, but I'm more tense than ever.

"Hey. It's me, Rosie," I say.

A shuffling comes from his end.

"Finally," Linus says. "You are one difficult person to track down."

"Not for Berg. You said your line wasn't bugged last time, but he called me right after I talked to you."

"I'm sorry," he says. "This line's encrypted, so he couldn't have heard what we said, but if he's tracing all my calls, he could have found your number that way. I'm really sorry."

I think back and wonder if checking my Forge email alerted Berg that I might call Linus. Hard to know. I decide to assume Berg can eavesdrop in, despite what Linus says.

"Are you in St. Louis?" I ask.

"I'm working in Stillwater, Minnesota," he says. "I can be in St. Louis tomorrow."

I gaze out again at the arch. "I'll be gone by then," I say.

"I can meet you in Forgetown, at Otis and Parker's place. Would that be better? I was planning to go there for the weekend."

This is what I want, I realize. It feels huge to admit it, like I'm letting a hammer break out of a block of ice. "Okay," I say. *Take that, Berg. I'm coming to town.*

Linus laughs. "Really? Good. I'm so glad. You sound a little tired. Are you okay?"

"I'm okay." I tuck my hair behind my ear. "Berg said something strange to me, like he let me out of the vault on purpose."

"Why would he do that?"

"I don't know, but there hasn't been any news about me," I say. "I don't think he wants anything contradicting his story that he's taking care of me."

"I know what you mean," Linus says. "I went to see Portia and Jenny. They wouldn't say anything about you. I think they were bought off. I think Berg doesn't want the public to know that you're missing."

So Linus tracked down Portia and Jenny. I wonder if he's trying to get me to confirm I was with them. What else does he know?

"Rosie?" he asks.

"I'm here."

"Have you talked to your parents?"

I get the sense he thinks I should. I don't want to. I frown as a drop on the windshield merges with another. "No."

"That girl Althea called me again," he says. "She wants to talk to you."

"I don't give a crap about that girl," I say, annoyed. "She's got nothing to do with me."

"Okay. I'm sorry," Linus says.

Confusion is churning in me, and I flip on the windshield wipers so they cut through the raindrops.

"I'm sorry," he says again. "It'll be better when we can talk in person."

"Will it?" I ask.

His voice is slow in coming. "What's wrong?"

I don't know. Except that it has to do with before. "You made me doubt myself, that last time we talked at Forge. You left for St. Louis like you didn't care, but then you came back to look for me. Why?"

"Because I did care about you, obviously," he says. "I watched you sign that contract with Berg, and I knew that wasn't good. It was my fault for making you admit what you thought to the cameras on the show. That's what got you in so much trouble."

"Then did you believe me about the mining or not? I still don't understand."

"I believed you enough to go down the clock tower pit and look for the vault of dreamers," he says. "Give me credit for that, at least."

I can't quite voice the next question, the obvious one: *do you believe me now?* That's the question that leads back to why he still hasn't done anything to expose Berg.

My throat feels achy. "How well did we ever really know each other?"

"I can only speak for myself," he says quietly. "I used to talk to you more honestly than I have ever talked to anybody else. I miss that. Don't you?"

I hold my phone tightly and nod out at the rain. He doesn't sound like a TV star tonight. He sounds real. "Yes," I say finally. "See you soon."

We say goodbye. Before Berg can call me, I drive to the nearest recycling bin and chuck my phone out the window.

>>>>>>>>

Late the next evening, near nightfall, I drive into Forgetown, Kansas, and unroll my window an inch. I've left the rain far behind, and the familiar smell of dry prairie blows into the Fit.

The towers and buildings of the Forge School loom darkly on the slope to the west. It's after hours. The students sleep. A light shines from a top window of the dean's tower, where Berg lives in his penthouse like an evil lord who controls all he surveys.

I turn away from campus, driving slowly along the shadowed streets of Forgetown. Even though it's Saturday, it's quiet. Most of the people who live here work at the school, and their schedules revolve around the daily timing of the show, which knows no weekends. I forgot to ask Linus for an address. In theory, I know where he stays because he pointed out the little gray house once when we were up in the lookout tower with Otis, but the angle is different from street level, and even though it's a small town, it takes me a few passes to find the right house.

I check for Ian's Jeep, just in case. It isn't there, and I don't see any other suspicious cars, either. Berg might have cameras aimed at Linus's house, but I'm hoping they won't pick up much in the dark. I park near the end of the block, take my jacket and a bag with a few of Sammi's clothes, and walk up the dark alley behind his place. An old golden retriever wags her tail and pants at me through a metal fence as I approach.

"Hey, girl," I say, keeping my voice low. I open the latch on the gate and go in, crouching down to pet her head and shoulders. "Good dog. Good Molly."

She sniffs my pocket where I have the vials and syringes.

"Nothing for you in there," I say.

I stay low, peering up at the house. I could call Linus, but I don't want to clue in Berg that Linus is getting a call from another new number. A bank of lit windows reveals a kitchen at the back of the house. I can't see anyone inside, so I wait, studying the place. This is Otis and Parker's home, where Linus started living when he was fourteen, after his time on the streets of St. Louis. He must have played catch with Molly in this very backyard. My stomach growls with hunger. Molly gets bored with me and wanders away.

In time, a light goes on upstairs, and Linus reaches up for a window shade. My stupid, hammering heart charges around like wild. He's right there. In the house. Right now. I see his dark hair, straight nose, and brown shirt. Then the shade comes down. I grin in the darkness, shocked by how powerful my reaction is. Clearly coming here was the right thing to do.

I scratch around in the grass for a pebble to throw. This gets Molly interested. She comes back to me and barks.

"Shh!" I say.

She barks again.

Above, the shade rolls back up, and the window opens.

"Molly!" Linus calls. "Keep it down out there!"

Molly wags her tail. She barks once more, proudly.

I push back my hood and lift a hand in a silent wave. Linus ducks to put his head out. He squints a moment, and then he smiles. I'm shredded. He lifts a finger to his lips. Then he goes back in, and the window closes. I stay where I am, with a hand on Molly's warm head. My heart lifts with anticipation. Soon the lights in the kitchen go off. Another minute later, he opens the back door and beckons us in.

Molly darts up the steps and wedges past his knees. I come a little more slowly into the dim kitchen, happy and shy, and a bit thrown by my reaction to him. Linus closes the door behind me with a soft click. Chili is simmering nearby, emitting a savory fragrance. Molly laps water noisily in the corner. I clutch my bag in both hands. For a moment, Linus silently looks at me. Then he shakes his head with a smile.

"Come with me. Be quiet," he says.

He leads me to a hallway and gestures for me to wait there while he goes back and turns on the lights in the kitchen again, like they were before I came in. The indignant voices of a political talk show yap from the front room, around the corner. The hallway has gray wallpaper and a smattering of family pictures in dusty frames.

"Did you let Molly in?" Otis calls from out of sight.

"Yes," Linus says loudly.

"How's the basement?" he calls.

"It's done. Give me ten minutes to take a shower and we'll eat," Linus says.

He gestures to me again, and I follow him softly up the stairs. At the top, he pulls me into a bathroom and pulls down the shade, the same one I saw from the outside. He leans past me and turns on the shower so the rushing noise fills the little space. As I get my first decent look at Linus, I find him covered with dust and webs, like he's been cleaning out a tomb. He's taller and his dark hair's short and his earrings are gone, but he's not the stiff, slick TV show host that I feared. He's still himself. I forgot how expressive his eyes and dark eyebrows could be, even when he's simply watching me back. Steam starts to fog the glass of the window and the mirror.

"Welcome," he says solemnly.

I burst out laughing and quickly cover my mouth with both hands.

He smiles in his grim, quirky way. "I cannot believe you're actually here. In my bathroom no less."

"Me, neither."

"Want to get naked?"

"Linus!"

"Worth a try."

It's a cozy bathroom, so when Linus stands with arms akimbo, one of his elbows is over the sink and the other bumps the shower curtain. Color rides high along his cheekbones, and his dark eyes gleam. He needs a shave. He looks wonderful, actually. He's looking me over, too, and I'm highly conscious of my pickings from Sammi's wardrobe: a gray jacket, a brown shirt, and skinny jeans.

He points to me. "Coat."

I shrug out of my jacket, and he hangs it on the back of the door. The drain makes a gurgling noise, and the shower keeps hissing into the tub.

"I have to get back down there. We'll have to talk later," he says, his voice low, and his gaze shifts to the shower. "You don't mind if I jump in, do you? Don't look. Or actually, look all you like."

I laugh again, but then I put down the toilet lid, sit on it, and gaze pointedly at the floor. Beige tile. He shucks off his sneakers. I hear him disrobe, and his dirty jeans and shirt hit the rug an inch from my shoe. Boxers in the jeans. The rungs screech as he adjusts the curtain, and I peek up to see if anything shows. It doesn't.

This is truly the last place I expected to find myself. Naturally, I want to giggle. Most uncool. I try to get a grip. Yes, he's Linus, and yes, he's in the shower, but I have to calm down. Tangy shampoo laces the moist air, and not seven minutes later, the water goes off. His hand reaches out for a towel, and I zero in on the floor again.

"How's that? Better?" he asks, stroking his jaw and looking for my approval.

He shaved in the shower. I didn't know guys could do that.

"Yes," I say.

Linus scoops up his clothes and passes me my coat. "Okay," he says. "Come quietly."

A brown towel hugs his hips, and drops glint on his skin. His bare feet leave wet tracks on the wooden floor as I follow him down the hall to a bedroom. He brings me in, closes the door, and points to his bed.

Am I really going to get on his bed? I am. I do. I sit on his blue quilt and try not to look, but I'm fully aware that he's jimmying into fresh jeans. Then I hear his zipper. I glance up as he towels his head savagely and then he chucks the towel in a laundry basket. He shoots me a smile, eyebrows up. Then he pulls a gray, long-sleeved shirt out of a drawer and pulls it over his head, covering his chest and lean belly.

I let out a breath.

"You look very sweet there," he says. "Stay put. Don't make a sound. Don't get off the bed." He dances his fingers downward. "The floor squeaks."

"I'm hungry," I say.

"I'm on it."

For a second, he hovers, considering me as if he's going to lean over for a kiss. The next moment, he rifles through his dirty jeans, digs out a phone, and slides it in his pocket.

"I won't be long," he says, and steps out of the room.

As he closes the door, I feel like a whirling tornado of energy has left the room. I silently set my shoes on the floor with my bag, pull my feet up, and try to get my heart to quit pounding.

I check around for cameras, just in case. Linus's bedroom is a small, corner room with an angled ceiling and two windows. On his desk, a box of Magic cards, in slipping stacks, rests beside a Swiss Army knife and a bucket full of pencils. Tinfoil gum wrappers litter the bedside table. Stacked wooden crates, filled with aging, fusty paperbacks, line one wall. A dartboard hangs on the back of the door, and extra holes pepper the wood. He has no photos of his parents. What I like most is a big Lego model of the Death Star that hangs from the ceiling. I suspect it was glued together, and I wonder if he did it alone or with Otis and Parker.

Distant clinks and voices come from below me, and my mouth salivates as I think of them eating. The last time I ate a proper meal was days ago, at Burnham's. I consider texting him to tell him I made it to Forgetown, but then I don't.

A faint static noise draws my attention to the bedside table; I'm surprised to find a walkie-ham, the twin of the one I had at Forge. It's connected to a small recording tablet. Impressed, I realize Linus has rigged a way to listen to the channels even when he isn't here. It takes me a bit to figure out how it works, but then I find two files marked *Emma* and *Woman 1*. Gently, I disconnect the tablet from the walkie-ham so I can't possibly send out an accidental signal. Then I turn the volume down, one notch above mute, and click the first file.

On comes a young female voice that I've never heard before.

"But you *promised*. You *said* you'd be here," she says.

"I know. I'm sorry. I feel terrible about it. Things just came up here, and I couldn't get away."

My skin shivers as I recognize Dean Berg.

"It was the one thing I asked you to show up for," she says. "*The one thing*. I even told my friends you were coming!"

"I tried to call you," Berg says.

"*After* the dance," she says. "I don't know why I bother anymore. Mom told me you wouldn't come. She warned me. I should have asked Darren like she said."

"Who's Darren?"

"Her latest. Don't you know *anything*?" she says.

I like this girl. *Give it to him*, I think.

"What can I do to make it up to you?" Berg asks. "Would you like a trip? I could take you to Paris. Brian, too, if you like. Let's make a memory."

"I already have enough memories of promises you don't

keep," she says. "You can stuff your Huntington's crap. I don't care about it anymore. I don't care at all."

"Don't say that, Emma."

"No," she says, and she sounds a little choked up despite her words. "Go ahead and rot. You won't find me crying at your funeral."

"I'll find an answer for you in time," Berg says. "I promise."

"Fifty-fifty, Dad," she says. "You don't even know if I have it."

"Please, get tested. I'm begging you."

She laughs. "Why? Because you care? You couldn't show up for *one night*." Her voice goes hard. "You know what? Don't call me again. You're worse than no father."

The recording ends abruptly, but her words leave a sizzle behind them. Emma has my complete sympathy. Berg sounds like a horrible father, and I'm glad she blasted him. Then I wonder what Huntington's is. I'm not familiar with it at all.

I puzzle over the device in my hand. I once overheard a rogue conversation between the dean and Dr. Fallon on my walkie-ham. The signal must sometimes, if rarely, cross over from Berg's phone to the walkie-ham frequency, and Linus must have been scanning for those crossovers. I try the next clip. This one is scratchy, but I recognize both voices.

"I suppose I could send some back," Dr. Huma Fallon says. "But why? You didn't lose a source, did you?"

"It's just a glitch," Dean Berg says. "We're letting the source recover, but in the meantime, we have another client who needs a supply."

301

"Which one, then? I'll talk to my staff."

"Sinclair Fifteen."

A faint crackle comes over the line. "Okay, what's going on, Sandy? What have you done?" Dr. Fallon asks.

"It's nothing," he says. "I simply want to help out this other client if I can. You do have the raw astrocytes, don't you? Not a cultured seed. I need the dream pure."

"It'll take me a minute to find out."

"I'll wait, then," he says.

"You owe me, Sandy. I'll call you back."

The recording stops, and there isn't another one.

I lean back, pensive. I wish I had a date for this one. Berg has been sending my dreams to Fallon all along, but is this call old, or does he need a dream returned now that I've escaped? I can't think why he would need one back.

It's frustrating. Plus I'm hungrier than ever.

I reach over to snag one of the gum wrappers off the bedside table, and I lick the lining for the film of sugar. As I reach for another, I bump a white plastic spoon that topples to the floor. Retrieving it, I find a bit of red yarn tied around the handle, like it's special. That's quirky. I run my thumb over the concave surface. I envy how the casual castoffs of Linus's life lie around here, undisturbed.

I miss having things of my own. I used to have a necklace with a New York City subway token that I wore all the time. Dubbs and I found the token on the train tracks near our boxcar, and it felt almost magical, a tiny portal to another time and place. I don't know what happened to it. Berg probably threw my token away, like he threw away the rest of my life. I run my fingers idly down my neck. Unbidden, that old, lonesome feeling I used to have, the one that yearns and can't be satisfied, twines its way into my hunger until I don't know where one begins and the other leaves off.

I blink slowly out at the stars, framed by Linus's window, until I don't even notice them anymore.

))))))))

When the mattress dips, I jolt awake. Linus is sitting at the edge of the bed. A small, shaded lamp glows on the bedside table, and outside the windows, full night has gathered near. In his hands, he holds a big bowl of chili with a bagel resting on the rim.

"I wasn't sure if you like cheddar and sour cream on your chili," he says quietly.

I sit up. I rub my eyes. My nerves jolt on again. The clump of grated cheese has melted on top of the brown chili, and I take my first bite with a taste of the sour cream, too. I half swoon.

"Who made this?" I ask.

"I did."

"It's amazing," I say, scooping up more. Then I take a thick bite of bagel. It's delicious, too. I go back to the chili. So good.

Linus reaches over to a computer on the desk and touches a button to make an indie playlist come on, just audible enough to cover our voices. Then he drops off his shoes and lounges on the bed, one elbow deep in the quilt. He brushes his bangs off his forehead. They fall back on.

"Tell me all about your famous life," I say. "Do they cut your hair for the show?"

"Every time we film a new segment. Makes for consistency. It's obnoxious," he says.

"I'm sure."

He smiles at me. "We were able to track down my Aunt Trudi. Contrary to our coverage of the reunion, she hadn't been looking for me," he says. "In fact, she didn't care one bit what had happened to me. We had to pay her ten thousand pounds to pose with me."

"Real nice," I say.

He shakes his head briefly. "I did like seeing Swansea again, though, and the whole thing reminded me how lucky I am to have Otis and Parker."

"How are they doing?"

"Good. They like when I visit. They put me right to work." His nods his chin toward me. "How about you? Where've you been?"

I'm not ready to talk about the vault. "Places. Denver. Atlanta."

"Really? With Burnham?"

"Yeah," I say, still eating. "He loaned me a car and everything. He was really helpful."

"How is he?"

I try to describe how Burnham is okay and how he's not.

Then I remember my awkward encounter with him in the night and run out of things to say.

"Interesting," Linus says.

"Yes."

"And then you decided to come here."

It's a leading sort of observation. I'm not sure it's smart to tell him about my mission to kill Berg yet, if ever, but I nod at the walkie-ham. "You've been listening in on Berg," I say.

"Did you hear the clip with his daughter?" Linus asks. "I think he could have Huntington's."

"What's that?"

"It's a disease where you start to lose your mind early, like in your thirties or forties," he says. "It keeps getting worse until you can't think right or control your body, and then you die. It's genetic. It's horrible. His kids have a fifty-fifty chance of inheriting it, too."

"He's looking for a cure," I say, thinking it over. "That's why he's involved with this dream mining research. He wants to save himself and his kids. It makes so much more sense now."

"I think you're right. That's why he's collaborating with the people at Chimera."

"That's the clinic in Iceland, right?" I read about it. I watch Linus carefully, curious to find out how much he knows.

His eyebrows lift slightly. "Okay," he says slowly. "I know you don't want to talk about this girl Althea, but she matters. She's been to Chimera. She woke up from a coma there, and she says she has your mind. I'm not saying I believe her entirely, but she's pretty convincing."

"Come on," I say.

"She knows everything about you up to the point you were in Berg's vault," Linus says, and he's serious. "She says that's where she left you."

A shiver creeps over my skin. I look out the window toward Forge. I can just make out a few lights through the budding trees. I wouldn't put anything past Berg, but if a second version of me is walking around on Earth, I'm not sure what to think.

"Is she like my mental twin, then?" I ask.

"It's hard to say. Her voice is different, but she sounds a lot like you. She says she thinks like you. She predicted you'd come here. To see me."

I frown at him, considering. He's blushing faintly.

"How often do you talk to her?" I ask.

"We've talked twice. Last time, a few days ago. Tuesday, I guess. She was in Texas. She has family there."

"Texas." I nod, like this makes sense. This makes no sense. Neither does Linus's blush. "I wonder if Berg knows about her," I say.

"I don't know if he does," Linus says.

"But you know something else," I say.

He glances uneasily at me and then sits up straighter on the bed. "I'm not sure how much this matters, but Berg asked to meet up with me once in St. Louis. He knows the producers of *Found Missing*, and he offered to drop by the studio and take me out to lunch. I didn't want to, but I thought I might learn something from him about where you were, so I went." He runs a hand back through his hair. "He spent the whole lunch reminiscing about your time as a student at Forge, Rosie. You were all he could talk about. It was bizarre."

"He had me asleep in the Onar Clinic all that time, but he wanted to talk to you about me?"

Linus nods. "I think he's obsessed with you. And that's not all. He wanted to hook me up and track my reactions to some footage of you. He offered to pay me a lot. I said no, of course."

"That is way too creepy," I say. "Why would he want to do that?"

"I don't know." He wedges a hand under of one of his feet. "I know you blame me for not doing more to shut Berg down, but I've still never had any good evidence for what he's done. The police have been all over him, and they've never found anything. He's incredibly sneaky and careful. What do you think he's up to?"

Berg is playing a deeper, bigger game than I've ever imagined. I recall the way Ian talked about another lab in California. I wonder if Althea has any information about that. Someone has to stop Berg. Soon.

Linus reaches for my dirty bowl, and as I shift my legs, the plastic spoon with the red yarn falls on the quilt. He picks it up and puts it in a drawer.

"You keep spoons?" I ask.

He looks at me sideways and smiles faintly. "You ate ice cream with that one," he says. "I didn't have anything else of yours, so I saved it."

"Seriously?" I think back. "Was it that afternoon in the quad? With the chocolate chunk coffee cinnamon swirl ice cream?"

"Your favorite. Yes. So?"

I smile at him, then laugh. "That's pretty pathetic."

"Thank you. I'm well aware."

I chuckle again, and then I stifle a yawn.

"When's the last time you had a proper night's sleep?" he asks.

The last two nights were on the road. Before that, nightmares at Burnham's. I guess my first night in Atlanta wasn't too bad. "Four nights ago?"

He shifts on the bed. "Time to fix that. Pass me a pillow."

"Are you going to sleep with me here?" I ask.

"No, I'm going to eat the pillow. Shift over."

I crowd toward the side with my back to the window, and though I tell myself that sharing a bed with Linus doesn't mean anything, my heart won't listen. He tugs the quilt a little, and I move so he can pull it free from underneath me. Then he settles onto the bed beside me, lying on his back, and he gently pulls the quilt over us both. It smells of cotton. He turns out the light and switches off the music. A faint hum of wind becomes audible outside the window.

"Is this okay?" he asks. "Warm enough?"

I nod.

"I've missed you," he says.

I don't move. I can hardly breathe. My eyes are adjusting, and he's just inches from me. His eyebrows are very black, and when he turns his face in my direction, the depths of his eyes are dimly visible. I didn't brush my teeth, and I hope my breath isn't too spicy. His isn't. He still smells clean from his shower.

"What are you looking at?" I whisper.

"Nothing," he says.

Inside my clothes, my skin turns on and my sleepiness vanishes. I wrap my arms around myself and shove my hands up my opposite sleeves.

"This is a good bed," I say.

"I know," he says softly.

He still hasn't touched me, not once. We used to kiss and make out on *The Forge Show* with a thousand cameras around us all the time. Now we're alone. The house is very still. I didn't hear Parker or Otis come up, but I can't hear the TV from downstairs, either.

"Let me have your hand," he says.

I rustle it out of my sleeve and feel him wrap my fingers in both of his warm hands.

"So little," he says.

It's a sweet thing to say, and I don't want to argue with him, but my hand is not small. It's just smaller than his.

"What's the matter?" he asks.

"What if I have to go to the bathroom in the middle of the night?" I ask.

"Wake me up. I'll make sure the coast is clear."

"Do Otis and Parker ever check on you?" I ask.

"Sometimes. Not often. I locked the door."

"Okay," I say.

"Anything else?"

I shake my head. But I keep watching him.

"What are you afraid of?" he whispers.

Nightmares. Ian. Berg. Linus himself. Myself with Linus. It's not a short list.

"What if I wake up back in the vault?" I ask.

"You won't," he says. "You'll be here."

But logic doesn't work. It *feels* like I could go back in the vault, like I'm teetering on the same vulnerability and helplessness. I'll never really feel safe. That's the problem. My breath catches, but I don't want to cry. This is so much harder than being close to Burnham, and he had no shirt on. Why is everything so mixed up?

"Rosie, shh," he says quietly. "It's okay."

I don't know what's wrong with me. I gulp in a breath. "Can you just hold me?"

"Of course," he says.

He knocks an arm awkwardly around my neck and then pulls me closer against his shirt. I readjust a couple of times until I land in a better place, with my cheek on his shoulder and my eyebrows near his jaw. He adjusts the quilt around us more carefully, and I curl my hand on his chest, right below my chin.

"Better?" he whispers.

"Yes. Thanks."

"Anytime."

As if I'll be here regularly. I could laugh, except it hurts. His chest rises and falls in a steady rhythm beneath my hand. The wind blows again outside. Linus is holding me closely, easily, with no pressure. But even still, I can't let down my guard. I feel like someone's been watching me even at the most intimate, personal moment of my life so far.

What did Berg say once? *They're always watching.*

He was wrong, though. It's worse than that. I've internalized the cameras. I'll never feel private again.

— THEA —

THE MIDWAY MOTEL

WE LEFT DOLI and drove far into the night.

"I overheard back there," Tom said quietly.

I tried to draw my feet up on the seat with me and curl into a ball so I could disappear, but my stupid belly got in the way. Of course it did. I wrenched the lever to make my seat tilt back again.

"It's going to be okay," he added.

"Can we just not talk right now?" I said.

"If that's what you want."

My family was lost to me. Completely gone. What else mattered? I didn't want to think at all. I wanted to mourn alone on a desert island and forget that Dubbs and Ma and Larry ever existed. I clicked my fingernail back against my window and traced the path of the crescent moon as we whizzed by.

Hours later, we pulled up to a motel in the middle of nowhere. I'd never stayed in a motel before. I didn't know we were old enough, but the cheerless clerk of the Midway Motel took one look at my belly and asked no questions. After Tom handed over his card, we trudged up to a beige room that smelled of air freshener. Two big beds were covered with brown, geometric spreads, and a painting of orange horses was nailed to the wall. It was perfectly dismal, just like me.

"I could go find some food," he said. "You should probably eat something for the baby's sake."

I wasn't hungry at all, but I knew he was right. While I took a shower, Tom went out to scavenge, and by the time I came out in my tee shirt and pajama shorts, he was back with some Indian food. We sprawled on the big beds to eat. When I took a paper plate and spooned some chicken tikka masala onto a little pile of rice, it was, unfortunately, the same color as the horse painting on the wall.

"At least try to eat," Tom said kindly.

"I shouldn't have gone to Doli," I said. "You were right. Are you going to be right about everything?"

"No. Just the important things. Go on. Eat."

I tried a bite. It was actually really good, so naturally I felt like crying.

"Listen," Tom said. "You're going to live a long time. Those people could still come around some day. They might not ever be your normal family, but they could still be something."

"They were never normal to begin with," I said.

"See, then? No problem," Tom said. "At least the people you love are still alive."

I moved a bit of rice between the tines of my plastic fork. He seemed to be saying that he knew Althea was dead. I waited to see if he would elaborate, but he didn't. In no time at all, he had helped himself to seconds and was eating steadily.

"Where are we? Where have you been driving us?" I asked.

"Back to Holdum," he said. "Where else?"

I had a sharp realization. I still had one other person in my family: Rosie. I had told Linus that I thought she would go find him, but it was just as likely she would try to find Berg. That was who she was mad at. Why hadn't I thought of that earlier? Berg was at Forge, and now that I knew Rosie hadn't gone home to Doli, I had to believe that Forge was her likely destination.

"I need to call Linus," I said, reaching for my phone.

"Don't bother him. It's the middle of the night," Tom said.

"I want to ask him if he's heard from Rosie. I think she might be going to Forgetown."

"Kansas? Is that where you want to go?" he asked. "They're not going to know you at the Forge School, either."

"I know, but that's the point," I said, my mind leaping. "I should take advantage of that. Everybody thinks I'm Althea, not Rosie." I started getting excited. "We can take a tour of the Forge School campus. I could spy around."

314

"What good would that do you?"

"I could find out about Berg and his research." I already knew exactly where I wanted to go. I had to get back down to the vault of dreamers. I wanted to see the place where everything went wrong, and I'd figure out the rest of it from there. "Definitely Forgetown," I said.

"Would that make you feel better?" he asked.

"Yes." It felt good to have direction again.

"Then we'll go," he said. "But don't bother Linus, and after that, let's go back to Holdum. Your parents still hate me, but they take the best care of you. That's where your future is."

He surprised me again. I took a long look at Tom, with his blond hair and even features. He was calmly cleaning up our take-out containers and napkins.

"What about your future?" I asked.

"What do you mean? I'm taking care of my dad, and you if you'll let me."

"But what about your dreams? What would you do if you could do anything?"

"Anything? I'd have my old Thea back," he said. "We'd get married and raise the kid together. Maybe have a couple more."

It was a sweet dream. Impossible, but sweet.

"What would you do for work?" I asked. "Take over your dad's cattle ranch?"

He straightened to look over at me and smiled slowly. "It's a sheep ranch, but yes. I plan to pay off Dad's loans and keep the ranch."

Nice, I thought.

"How about you?" he asked.

"If I could do anything?" I searched for the right idea. "If I could do it without hurting the baby, I'd get back in my old body. But that's impossible."

He waved a hand as if he commanded magic. "Okay. But suppose you did. Suppose you were back in your old body, and you could still do anything. What then?"

"I'd visit my family. Then I'd want to stop Berg from hurting anybody else."

"That's good. Berg stopped. Then what?"

I hardly knew. I smiled at him, feeling better. "My dream before was to make films," I said.

"You could still be a filmmaker."

I turned the idea over. He was right. I'd been so driven before, back when I started at Forge. What had happened to that girl? I watched Tom as he sorted through the items in his backpack. Maybe I was imagining it, but it felt like something had changed between us. He seemed more patient, but sad, too.

"Are you all right?" I asked.

"Yeah. Fine. I think I'll take a shower, too. Do you want the lights out?"

I had to brush my teeth still, but afterward, while he took a turn in the bathroom, I climbed into the bed near the windows. I put a spare pillow between my knees. When he came back out, I held very still, nervous that he might get into bed with me. The baby rolled languidly inside me. The lights went out, and then, with the rustle of fresh cotton, the covers of the other bed shifted. His bed squeaked as he got in.

"Good night," he said.

I eyed the crack of starlight between the curtains. "Good night," I replied.

The drain in the bathroom made a burbling noise, and I carefully smoothed my hair back from my forehead.

"I wish you had one of Thea's old memories," Tom said. His voice came quietly in the darkness. "Just one, about anything."

His wish lingered between us, tinging the night with loss. It hit me, finally, what had changed. If Tom accepted that I was really Rosie in Althea's body, then he was also accepting that his girlfriend was truly gone. As I lay listening, and finally sagged into the warmth of my pillow, I kept trying to think of something kind enough to say back to him, but I couldn't.

26

— ROSIE —

LIGHTNING

I WAKE TO A SOFT, padding noise on the other side of the door. Linus is still sleeping beside me, a weighty, warm presence in the bed, but I lean up enough to face the door and listen better. A faint creak comes from the hallway. I can't discern if it's human or dog. I try not to worry. Linus said he locked the door. I'm peering at the bottom of the door, the dark crack that offers no clue, and then, silently, the door inches open.

My heart takes off. I can't even whisper. I give Linus a nudge. He doesn't respond. The door opens another inch. I huddle back down, trying to hide behind Linus, hoping I'm invisible. The door opens further, noiselessly, until it's fully open, and standing in the hallway is the dark silhouette of a thin man. Ghostly moonlight shimmers around his shoulders and dark head. A shadowed forest shifts behind him. He's holding something toward me with both hands, something wet and dark. He doesn't move or speak because he doesn't need to. In a shift of the moonlight, it's suddenly clear that he's Ian, with his chest bloody and ripped open, holding his heart in both hands.

I slam awake.

I gasp with panic, staring at the door, which is solidly closed in the dark room. No Ian. No dripping heart.

"What is it?" Linus says quietly.

I can't speak. He was so real. He was right there. I shoot my eyes around the room. My skin's crawling off me.

"Rosie?" Linus says. He fumbles for the lamp, and I wince at the brightness.

"It's Ian," I say.

Linus is squinting at me with one eye. His hair is mussed, and his shirt is tangled around him. I run both hands back through my hair and take a deep breath, but it's no use. My imagination can't let go of Ian. I can still picture him on the other side of the door, confused now. He's wondering why I don't let him in. He's anxious that I'm in bed with Linus. His voice arrives straight to my brain: *You're the only one who can take care of my heart.* He's shifting through the door now, like a ghost who can pass through solid objects, hands and heart first.

"*Please,*" he whispers.

"I never wanted your heart," I say forcefully. "Stay back."

Linus snaps his fingers in front of my eyes. "Wake up."

Ian vanishes a second time, and I take a deep, ragged breath.

"You had a nightmare," Linus says.

That wasn't a nightmare. That was a visitation.

My gaze meets the Death Star. Then my empty chili bowl and my coat on the doorknob and Linus. His eyes are deep with concern.

"Who's Ian?" he asks.

I sag slightly. "I thought I told you. He's one of my keepers." In halting words, I try to explain the weirdness of Ian, and how he was taking me to some hunting cabin until I ditched him. "He's probably looking for me right now. He likes to stalk." I glance toward the windows, which don't have shades or curtains. The only buildings in view from the bed are up on the distant hill, at the school, so from the street level, Ian couldn't have an angle to see inside.

"He sounds dangerous," Linus says.

He keeps his voice low, and so do I.

"He is. But he also really cares for me. If he ever hurt me, he'd do it out of some misguided idea because he cares."

Linus rolls on the bed so he's facing me more directly. I shift to sit pretzel style, with my back to the headboard.

"Do you think he reported to Berg that he found you?" Linus asks.

"I don't know," I say. "He quit his job."

"People who work for Berg don't quit," Linus says.

"You worked for Berg. You quit."

He hesitates. "I wasn't on the inside, like the techies. Ian must have been deep inside Berg's confidence to be taking care of dreamers. Even now, he could be on a very long leash."

I hadn't considered that, and I don't like the possibility. "Ian doesn't seem like the sort of person Berg would trust. Then again, he was strangely proud of his job, like it made him a man."

"Did he think it was legit?"

"I think he did," I say. "He was aware that there are rewards for me, but he knew Berg was my legal guardian, so he didn't question his right to keep me there dreaming." I think back. "The whole thing's strange. I don't think Ian deliberately helped me escape, but he was definitely responsible because he messed with my meds."

"What do you think Berg would do with you if he found you again?" Linus asked.

"Mine me. I have no doubt. Then, I don't know. He might have to kill me."

"Has he ever said he'd kill you? Did he threaten you?"

I shake my head. "When I talked to him, he asked me if I'd had enough stimulation yet."

"What did he mean?"

I don't know. I don't know what to say. "Maybe he has me on a long leash, too."

"Rosie, this is bad. You can't spend your life hiding. You haven't committed any crime."

"Not yet," I say dryly. I pull my knees up to my chest.

Linus frowns at me. "You know, you could let me do an exclusive with you, once and for all. This might sound backwards, but if you tell the same story Berg's been telling, you know, that you've been in a private psyche ward somewhere recovering, Berg won't be able to hide you away again. You'll come off as really sane and healed, and you'll be out in the open."

"That's ass backwards, all right," I say. "What about the truth?"

"You have to think about the outcome. If you say one thing publicly, you can have a private life again," he says. "You can negotiate with Berg. Get him to give you what you want. Start your own film company. Be in control. We'd pay you, Rosie. Big time."

His company "we" throws me. Linus talks like I have a future ahead of me where money would matter, but I don't have a future, really. When I think of letting Berg get away with what he's done, a visceral loathing consumes me. I want him helpless and hurting. I want to pick through his brain the way he's picked through mine. I want him to know it, and die. That's all that matters.

"I'm sick of lies," I say.

"I'm just thinking about what's best for you," Linus says quietly.

"You're assuming Berg can't be beat," I say. "But *beating him* is what would be best for me."

Linus nods slowly. "Then we'll take him down."

I hug my knee, considering him. I'm not sure how much I want Linus to be involved. I'm not sure how much he can really help me, either.

He rubs his eye and blinks a few times and squints.

"Something in your eye?" I ask.

"No. It tingles sometimes," he says. "I can actually see a little better out of it in the dark lately. It's strange."

"Isn't that the eye you had injured, back when I met you? From the chef?"

"Yes."

"Is it tingling now?" I ask. "Look up."

I move nearer to peer inside his pupil, and he aims his gaze toward the ceiling. It looks normal to me, a clear, tight disk of black inside an iris ring of honey brown. I gently tug at his eyelid, checking in case a lash has fallen in. He looks in different directions, but everything seems fine to me.

"It's better now," he says. "Turn out the light."

I reach for the lamp switch and he flops back on the bed, belly up. He folds his hands behind his head so his elbows flare out like wings. My eyes adjust to the soft gray light diffusing in the window, leftover starlight and moonlight. It mutes all the colors so his gray shirt is the same hue as his cheeks.

He closes one eye, and then the other. I lean near again, trying to tell if his pupils have dilated the same amount, but it's too dark to be sure. Then I notice he's watching me closely, with a slight smile.

"Your eyes are fine," I say quickly.

"Don't move. You have a kind of halo."

I hold still, watching him, and then he lifts a hand to my hair. He tugs a strand, lightly straightening it out to its full length before he lets go and chooses another. A shiver lifts along my neck.

"I'm glad you decided to come," he says.

"I guess I wanted to see if anything we had was real."

"What do you think?"

I shrug. "It's only been a few hours."

His smile widens. I set my hand on his shirt, and his warmth seeps though the cotton to my fingers. I could try to hash out with him the reasons why we broke up, but that's not what I want to do.

"You used to think I was completely delusional," I say. "Why do you even like me?"

"I suppose it's the gap in your teeth."

"I mean it, Linus," I say. "What is it about me? Only me?"

He shifts slightly. He touches a finger to my chest, above my heart, an inch from my port. It makes me self-conscious. Then he peers back up, and I can feel him searching into me.

"It's this little hole you have here," he says.

He doesn't mean my port. I go still while the hollow, dark place inside me tests its edges. I've never told anybody about that lonely, reaching place. I study him, unsure.

"You have it, too?" I ask.

He nods, and then looks away. A painful, tiny crack opens inside me. I don't want him feeling as alone as I do. The window rattles once with a gust of wind. I slip my hand into his.

He glances up at me again, intently. "I'm only going to kiss you. That's all," he says. "Okay?"

He's still lying back on the pillow, all these gray-scale hues of skin and cotton, with black for his hair and the depths of his eyes. His lips are open a little in the middle. I can't quite imagine how he's going to move up to meet me, and then I realize he isn't moving. I'm the one moving. I'm touching my mouth to the curving lines of his, because that's how lightning happens, in the wrong direction, inescapably.

27

— THEA —

A TOUR OF FORGE

TREES DROPPED their spindly shadows on the hood of the truck as Tom and I drove up the familiar road of the Forge School. One state west, in Colorado, they still had snow, but here in Kansas, spring was early. The trees were fuzzy with buds, and the pasture was green with new grass. On my right, the observatory where I once fell with Burnham aimed its gray dome toward a blue sky, and the lookout tower cast its great lenses over the campus.

Tom and I had slept late at the motel and driven half the day to arrive at Forge by mid-afternoon. I'd checked in with Madeline enough to allay her fears that I was dead on the road somewhere and ask if I had any messages. I didn't. I didn't have any on my own phone, either, and by daylight, it was easier to resist calling Linus. What would I tell him, anyway?

I couldn't very well force myself into his life, even if I was visiting his proverbial back yard.

Now Tom and I pulled into the driveway behind the art building and parked before the giant wooden spools. One was still splattered with colorful paint. The other had been painted black and drilled with holes.

I'd had my first kiss by those spools, in the rain, in desperation. I had to wonder where Linus was at this moment.

"It all looks bigger than I guessed from TV," Tom said, as he locked the car. "Where are the cameras?"

"They're everywhere. Most of them are small buttons. They blend in."

"Like that?" he asked, pointing to one on a metal railing.

"Yes."

I almost told him not to point, which was taboo for students. Even though the cameras weren't broadcasting me, everywhere I turned I instinctively felt a prickling along my neck.

"Relax," Tom said, squeezing a hand into my shoulder. "No one's going to recognize you. They can't."

"I know. It's just weird to be back."

"We're simply taking a tour. No big deal."

I shot him a smile. "Right. Thanks."

We'd agreed to take a tour of the school and wing it from there. Tom knew that I hoped to learn more about Berg's research, but he'd pointed out that any real discovery was unlikely, given that I would have no chance to get off stage in broad daylight. I felt, distinctly, that he was indulging me.

I also sensed that he'd withdrawn from me at some level. I couldn't blame him. Each stop on our road trip was proving how little I resembled Althea. Then again, it was a relief for me to have someone from Althea's life finally get an up-close look at where I'd come from.

A dozen people were gathered on the steps of the student union, mostly parents and their teenager sons and daughters. In snug yellow pants and a black coat, a big white guy with pale curls stood out from the crowd. A tall, young black woman with hoop earrings idly met my eye, and then gave me a nod. Several others surreptitiously checked out my figure. I felt like my belly was huge. I wasn't recognizable as Rosie, but I was still conspicuous.

"You were here how long?" Tom asked quietly.

"Two months. A lifetime."

I could feel a level of eagerness in the way the others fidgeted. Visitors to the campus didn't merit any special attention, but they each stood a chance of being in the background of a Forge student's feed. After the tour, visitors could order memento clips of the background footage compiled from various feeds, for a price.

I didn't want anything to do with that, obviously.

My friend Janice came lightly down the steps of the student union and stopped before us, tucking her short hair back around her ear. I was stunned to realized she was our tour guide. She'd changed her hair from blonde to a burnished, golden-red color that made her eyes look almost purple, and she wore a white jacket with big black buttons over her black jeans and boots.

"Hi, everybody," she said with a friendly wave. "Welcome to Forge. I'm Janice. I'm a sophomore acting student, and I'll be your tour guide this afternoon. Before we begin, why don't each of you perspective students tell me your name and your art? Go ahead."

They started at the other end with the guy in the yellow pants, who turned out to be a singer. I scrambled to concoct what I was going to say, but when Janice came to me and Tom, she passed right on to the next young person. Startled, I glanced at Tom.

He leaned near to my ear. "I feel incredibly old and unartistic."

I smiled and nudged his elbow.

"Let's start with the drama department and work our way around the school, shall we?" Janice said. "If you have any questions, be sure to speak up."

"Weren't you friends with Burnham Fister and Rosie Sinclair?" someone asked.

I peeked around the others to see it was the tall black woman who had spoken.

"I was, yes," Janice said. She still smiled, but more tightly. "To be honest, though, I meant questions about the school. I'm not comfortable talking about my friends. If anyone wants to know more about Burnham or Rosie, or safety here at Forge, you can stop by the dean's office. They'll be able to answer your questions. Now, the music building, here on your right, was built fifteen years ago." She continued smoothly on with her tour info.

I was impressed with her aplomb.

"You knew her?" Tom asked me quietly as we moved with the crowd toward the auditorium.

"Yes," I said. "We're in the same year."

"What's her blip rank?" he asked me.

"You'll see on the board in the dining hall. Or you could check her profile on your phone."

Janice led us around the campus, winding over to the dorms and behind the dean's tower to the sculpture garden. Seeing her in the role of guide, both businesslike and anonymously friendly, made me itch to jolt her out of it, but I had to resist.

"How do you like Mr. DeCoster for a teacher?" I asked politely as we headed into the library. He'd been my favorite.

"He's brilliant," she said. "My Media Convergence class meets in the basement here."

"Could we take a peek?" Tom asked.

The others were interested, too, so Janice led us down the stairs. The Ping-Pong table and the couches by the fireplace were the same, and the boxes of Settlers of Catan and Dominion still occupied the coffee table. Burnham's computer had a Ping-Pong ball in a paperclip before it, just like the one I'd set there ages ago, after his accident. We didn't know then if he would recover. It was a horrible time.

I drifted near. Burnham wouldn't recognize me now if I tried to reach out to him, but I still felt guilty for my part in our accident. I would never be able to apologize to him. He didn't know I existed. I let my fingers hover over the small white ball. I missed my friend.

"Coming?" Janice asked from the doorway.

I glanced over to see that Tom and I were the last ones in the room.

"Yes. Sorry," I said.

After a stop in the main library upstairs, we returned to the quad, where Janice gave the history of the clock tower. I gazed up at the motto inscribed near the top: *Dream Hard. Work Harder. Shine.*

Lies, I thought. It should say *Dream Hard So We Can Mine the Best out of You.*

"Can we go inside?" I asked.

Janice hesitated. "We're running short of time."

"I'd like to go in, just for a second," I said. "For Rosie's sake."

Janice looked at me oddly. "Did you know her?"

"I feel like I did," I said.

She glanced around toward the others. A few were nodding. I wasn't on *The Forge Show* anymore, but Janice still was, and I could practically see her calculating. Her feed was live right now, and viewers who knew Janice and Rosie had been friends were watching her reaction. This could be worth a spike to her blip rank.

Her gaze went distant for a moment. "She used to look for ghosts," Janice said obscurely. Then she straightened and gestured to the tour group. "Go in if you'd like, but I'll wait out here."

She held the door for us, and I led the way into the tall, hushed space. High above, the mechanism of the clock made

331

its distinct ticking, and the chains with their cylindrical weights dropped down through the gloom. The narrow windows shot diagonal streaks of sunlight into the dim air, and dust moats drifted into the light like fairy dust. For me, this was the heart of the campus, a crux of nostalgia and danger. The others came in curiously, stepping softly as if respecting a sacred place. They touched their fingertips to the railing, one by one, and looked down into the pit as I had done the first time I'd been here with Linus.

I lingered with my back to the wall and let the quiet chill of the stones seep into me. Tom stood patiently nearby, saying nothing, and as the last visitor left, he stepped to the railing and peered down.

"I can't see the bottom," he said. His voice carried easily in the hollow space.

"No," I said. "It's thirty feet down."

Without warning, I felt a twinge of déjà vu, my first ever in my new body, and I breathed deep. The quirk of familiarity brought me super alive.

"Want to come look?" he said.

I saw myself step forward an instant before I did. I watched myself set my small hand on the black railing, knowing in advance how it would look around the metal. I felt a tug to lean over the railing, an impulse stronger than any déjà vu. I was certain to lose my balance and tumble head first into the black.

I held tight to the railing, leaning back as my heart pounded.

Take me out, I tried to say. But I didn't speak in real life. My voice couldn't escape.

Tom turned to me. "Are you all right?"

I foresaw myself capsizing down through a black rushing noise until I slammed into the floor and died.

"Thea? Let's go back out," Tom said.

A piercing headache spiked between my eyes. I gasped as Tom peeled my fingers off the railing. Blind with pain, I felt his arm come around me. He guided me out of the clock tower, and I blinked at the sunlight through a haze of needles.

The others were waiting in the rose garden, and Janice's spiel of information broke off sharply. "Is she all right?" Janice asked.

"We're just going to rest here a bit," Tom said. "You all go ahead."

I sank to a bench and leaned my head heavily into my hand.

"I can call the nurse," Janice said.

"No," I mumbled.

"It's okay. She gets a little nauseous sometimes," Tom said. "We're fine, really."

Dimly, I heard them discussing me, but I couldn't say anything more. My headache was crushing my brain into pulp. One instant it was so bad I thought I was imploding, and the next instant, just as suddenly, the pain vanished, like a vice breaking apart into atoms. Cautiously, I tilted my face back so the sunlight fell on my cheeks. Merciful tingles of pleasure danced down my skin like warm streams of water, and the world returned to focus.

"See? She's already better," Tom said.

"I guess," Janice said uneasily. She pointed to the nearest building. "There's a bathroom in the dean's tower if you need it."

"Thanks," Tom said. "We're all good. And thanks for the tour."

Janice gave us one last look, and then she continued with the others, veering off toward the studio art building.

"What was that about?" Tom said quietly. He sat beside me, and his eyes were lit with concern.

My baby kicked inside me, and I shifted slowly on the bench. "Just some weird spiking headache," I said. "It's gone completely."

"Can I get you something? I can take you to the hospital. Should we call your parents?"

I breathed again, deeply and calmly. "They'll only worry."

"Maybe they should. *I'm* worried."

"I'm really all right," I repeated. "See?" I straightened and produced a smile.

Tom shook his head. "Your eyes are strange."

"Really?"

"They're dilated."

I guessed things looked a bit brighter than usual. I rose to my feet, pleased to find that I was completely steady. I brushed my hair back around my ears. "This is my chance," I said, my voice low. "Wait for me here."

"You're not going anywhere."

"Actually, I'm going to the ladies' room, and you're not coming with me. I'm really okay," I said, and gave him a measured look. "Trust me."

He got it, finally, and quit arguing. I left him in the rose garden and went alone up the steps to the dean's tower. That headache was a killer, but it had given me the perfect excuse to go exactly where I wanted.

>>>>>>>>

The foyer's gold-leaf dome gleamed above as I entered the cool stillness of the dean's tower. To my right, the door to the dean's office was open wide, and I had a familiar glimpse of the thick carpet, white bookshelves, and lush curtains. Congenial voices and the clink of a teacart drifted out, reminding me of the time I'd been summoned to meet the board of trustees.

I crossed in the opposite direction, toward the elevator, and when it came, I pushed the B button and held it, hard. It yielded inward an extra click just as it had once before, and then the elevator began to drop. Instead of slowing at the next level down, it accelerated, falling deeper into the earth. With a thrill, I realized Dean Berg hadn't altered the secret button since I'd been here before.

Then I wondered why not.

When the elevator slowed to a stop, heaviness lurched in my gut, and then the doors opened on a quiet, dark landing. Cautiously, with one arm bracing the door, I leaned out, expecting a light to come on with a motion sensor. It didn't. I switched on my phone's light and cast the white beam before me. To one side stood a kitchenette counter with a dusty coffee machine.

Gone were the microwave and minifridge from before. Gone, too, was the table with the vase of flowers.

Before me, through the wall of glass where I had first seen the rows of dreamers, I found the dark of emptiness.

I stepped away from the elevator and let the doors swoosh softly closed behind me. The dark grew more intense, and my phone light seemed pitifully meager. My pulse picked up. I tried the door to the vault, and the handle gave unexpectedly beneath my fingers. Inside, the air was cooler, with a faint, sour tinge. The vinegar of my nightmares. I cast my light before me into a void, left to right. Deep in every direction, the room was bare. The overhead framework that had supported the tubes and wires for the sleep shells was gone. The floor was clear except for a couple of old, dried leaves. But it wasn't a simple empty space. Nightmares had breeded here. Silent screams had soaked into these walls. Berg didn't keep his sleepers here anymore, but I could feel their agony calling to me. I'd been one of his captives, too.

My heart began to thud painfully. I crossed to the far wall, to the door that led to the operating room where I'd been mined. The sense of déjà vu hovered near again, as if I was about to see the surgery tools and head cage from before, but when I scanned my light inside, the tables were gone along with every other sign of medical torture. The only thing left was a camera in the upper corner. That was all.

Where are you? I asked my inner voice.

If she was ever going to surface again, it should be here, where

Berg had tortured me. He'd asked me questions, clamping my mind on a pivot point where I was both awake and asleep. He'd found a way into me through pure fear. At the memory, sweat broke out along my skin. Somehow, searching for clues to Berg's research felt like a search for myself.

Can you hear me? I asked. *Are you there?*

Still nothing. And then I remembered. She had hidden then, too. She had burrowed deep to stay away from Berg. Of course she wouldn't surface here. This was a dead end.

I turned back to the landing by the elevator, and there I scanned my light around once more. Across from me, another door accessed the tunnel I remembered. It led to the bottom of the clock tower pit, and now that I thought about it, that tunnel extended past the pit, in a direction I'd never followed.

Where did it go? With a trickling of adrenaline, I made a decision: this was my chance to find out.

I tried calling Tom to tell him what I was doing, but my phone had no service this deep underground. I had to hope he would keep waiting for me and not call attention to my absence.

I pushed open the door to the tunnel and a skittering of leaves shifted along the floor. With my phone light aimed before me and my belly in the lead, I walked steadily along between the brick walls, sidestepping spider webs and the desiccated remains of a rodent. Soon I came to a glass-walled, octagonal chamber in the middle of the tunnel, and I knew I'd reached the bottom of the clock tower pit. I was curious to explore it, especially to look for the mechanism that opened the ceiling barrier that separated the glass enclosure from the pit above, but I didn't have time now.

Instead, I aimed down the tunnel in the direction I'd never explored before, hoping to find a new, hidden way in and out of Forge. The walls changed from brick to stone, and the floor became rougher, descending in a gradual slope that forced me to watch my step. Eventually, I came upon a side door on the left. Wooden, with an arched top, it was thick with undisturbed dust. I ruled it out. What I sought was an exit that had been recently used.

As the tunnel went on, the floor leveled out again. The dusty silence grew oppressive. I was about to give up and go back to the arched door when my light reached the end of the tunnel. Another wooden door shut me in, but the knob was free of dust, and the floor had more dried leaves. A thin sourness laced the air. A faint powdering of light came through the crevice under the door. I tried the knob and pushed hard, but the door didn't budge.

Frustrated, I turned and rested my back against the door, trying to guess how far I'd come. It was impossible. My back ached and my throat was dry. My phone still had no signal, and its battery was getting low. Not good.

A faint clanking noise came from the other side of the door. I pressed my ear to the wood and listened. A distant, mechanical, repetitive noise was punctuated by another clanking, and then a low mooing noise. A cow.

I laughed in surprise and suddenly recognized that sour

smell as a hint of manure. I'd arrived at a barn. There was no barn on the Forge campus, but I recalled at least one in Forgetown. I dug in my pocket for a nub of tissue and wedged it under the door, lodging it to the side near the hinges.

Then I turned around to start back. I trudged the flat length, then started up the slope. I passed the arched, dusty door and the octagonal glass room. I recognized a broken light fixture from before, and I finally opened the door to the landing for the elevator. I was almost out and eager to get back to the sunlight and fresh air. The vault, through the glass on my right, was as dark as before. I pushed the button to call the elevator and brushed myself off as I waited. A slight sound came from behind me.

"Lost?" Dean Berg said.

I spun around.

Berg. Here. He stepped through the door from the vault, and I stumbled back against the wall, unable to speak.

"One of my techies told me a visitor went missing," Dean Berg said.

"I was looking for the bathroom," I said hoarsely.

"It's back upstairs," he said.

The elevator doors slid open, and I scrambled inside.

Berg came more slowly. Every instinct in me recoiled from him, and I pressed back into the corner.

Slowly, deliberately, Berg pushed a button on the panel. Then he turned to look me over. His sandy blond hair was as tidy as ever, and he wore his classic jacket with the elbow patches. His pale eyebrows and ruddy cheeks made the picture of boyish good health, but I knew every expression of his, every manner, was a disguise for the blackest heart.

"You're expecting," he said, his voice lifting in surprise. "I'm Dean Berg. What's your name?"

The doors slid closed.

There was no point lying. "Althea Flores."

The elevator started up.

"I'm normally very good with names, but I can't quite place you," he said. "Have we met before?"

"No," I said.

"Very few people find their way down to the vault," he said. "Who told you about the elevator button?"

"Nobody. It just got stuck."

He smiled at me oddly. "Are you sure we haven't met?"

My heart lurched. It felt like he could see right past my Althea exterior to the depths of me inside.

"I'm sure," I said.

"I'd like to see your phone, please."

"It's dead," I said. "The battery's dead."

"That doesn't matter. Please." He held out his hand.

I slowly passed it over, and he smiled as the screen lit up.

"Not so very dead after all," he said.

He set his phone on top of mine, and the next moment, a barcode came up on the face of my phone. Dean Berg held his a couple of inches over it, so his camera lens lined up on the barcode, and a second later, he was thumbing through my phone.

"What did you do?" I asked. I couldn't see how he got past my password.

"I'm just checking your recent calls," he said, frowning. "Tom. Who's that?"

"My boyfriend. He's outside. Give me that."

"Mom. Dad. One unidentified. That's all your calls." He took a photo of my call list with his phone, and then glanced up at me. "You clear your history. Smart girl. And no photos. Very, very interesting. New phone?"

"Yes," I said. "Can I have it back now?"

He handed it to me as the elevator came to a stop. The doors slid open, and I hurried out.

"I'm glad we met, Althea Flores," he said. He stayed in the elevator, and his gaze rested on my belly again for a moment. He set a hand on the elevator doorway so the bumper jumped and retracted to stay open. "Before you leave, I have a little message for you to convey."

"What's that?"

"It's for whoever told you about the elevator and how to hold the button in."

"I didn't do anything special to the button," I insisted. "It just got stuck."

He smiled urbanely. "Tell your friend the button still works, but it's the only thing left. He'll never find any answers here. He should get on with his life."

Bewildered, I stared. Berg let go of the elevator doorway, and the doors closed him in with a soft hiss. A shiver lifted along my skin.

Tom entered the foyer from the main door. "Thea, where have you been?" he asked. He did a double take. "You're filthy."

"I got lost," I said.

I was more confused than ever. Could there be other dreamers who came back looking for the vault, like me?

Tom gently took my arm and guided me outside. The sunlight made me wince, and I glanced down at my clothes to see that Tom wasn't exaggerating. I had brushed myself off while waiting for the elevator, but dirty webs still clung to my sleeves and leggings. With a shudder, I wiped at them, and Tom brushed off my back.

"Are you going to tell me what happened?" he asked.

"Let me think. Can we just go?"

"Of course," he said, and we made our way to the car.

Berg's message kept replaying in my mind. Possibly, like me, other dreamers had been aware of the button and how it worked from their own trips down the elevator. Did they really come back looking for answers? I had this image of a horde of us zombie dreamers coming back here, driven by a restlessness we couldn't resolve.

Would Rosie come? I needed to find her more than ever.

Berg had taken a photo of the phone numbers I'd recently called: Tom's, Madeline's, Diego's, and the unidentified one that belonged to Linus. I nearly dropped my phone.

Berg was going to put it together. He hadn't recognized my name just now, but I was certain he was going to look up Althea Flores, and then he'd find out that I was connected to Rosie. Whatever advantage I'd had by being unrecognizable would be gone.

"I'm dead," I said.

— ROSIE —

VISITORS

"**LINUS! YOU UP?**" Otis yells from downstairs.

I wake in Linus's arms. It's daylight. He slams out of bed and leaps to the door. He opens it and leans out.

"What is it?" Linus calls.

From below: "You forgot to take the garbage out. Parker's upset. Come talk to him."

I reach around the rumpled bed for my shirt and pull it on. Underneath, I adjust my camisole straps.

"Give me one minute!" Linus yells down. He closes the door and spins around, all but naked in his underwear. Grinning, he swears under his breath. "Sorry," he whispers. He hitches up his jeans and pulls on boots. He scoops up his shirt from the floor, takes a whiff of it, whips it toward the laundry basket, and pulls a fresh one out of a drawer. He pulls it over his head, shrugs it into place, and runs a hand through his wild hair. "You okay for a minute?"

"Yes."

He's gone.

My lips feel sensitive when I touch them, and I'm not exactly embarrassed, but I'm fully conscious that we did a lot more than kiss last night. I pluck out my shirt to look at my port lump again, and though I hate it as much as ever, the rest of me feels pretty good.

I tiptoe off the bed and smooth out the quilt. On second thought, I change my old shirt for a clean one, one of Sammi's yellow, scoop-necked tees. I put on fresh undies and jeans. I rub the sleepies out of the corners of my eyes and run my fingers through my hair. Male voices talk downstairs, but I can't make out what they're saying. Then it's quiet. I'm looking for a hairbrush when the door opens again and Linus enters, carrying a giant mug of coffee.

"Hi," he says. He sets down the mug and tackles me back onto the bed.

"Hey!" I laugh.

He puts his finger on my lips. "Be very quiet or you'll get no coffee."

I squirm beneath him, and together we struggle to make no noise.

Otis and Parker finally leave for the day. I soon realize there's no point trying to get on the Forge campus until it's night. Besides, once I kill Berg, things could go very badly for me, so I decide to make the most of my day with Linus. I put off calling Burnham. Linus and I eat Cap'n Crunch cereal. We kiss some more. We talk. He asks about my ride in the driver-free car. I ask about the Lego Death Star. Linus teaches me to throw darts, but I'm no good because I throw too hard. We kiss some more.

It's hard for me to avoid talking about Berg because I'm nervous about the coming night, but the more I think of it, the more I decide it's better to keep Linus out of it. I don't want him involved as an accessory to murder, and I don't want him trying to convince me not to go through with it. He somehow has the mistaken impression that I'm going to get a good lawyer and emancipate myself from both Berg and my parents. Then my life is going to go back to normal. I don't correct him. He thinks we'll be able to date in the open, like regular people.

Late in the afternoon, he starts spaghetti sauce from scratch, cutting up tomatoes and onions. He wants it ready for when Otis and Parker come home around 6:30, and he wants me to eat with them. When he puts on a bib apron like back in his Forge kitchen days and ties the strings around his waist, it gets to me.

"What?" he says. "It keeps me clean."

"I know. You just look nice."

He smiles, shaking his head.

"Are you donating blood to Parker tonight? Is that why you're making spaghetti sauce? For your tradition?"

"No," he says. "I donated a couple of weeks ago. I promised spaghetti to Parker because I forgot to take out the garbage. Spaghetti's his favorite."

"You know, you could probably pay your rent with money now," I say.

He laughs. "I do in St. Louis."

"So you have an apartment there?"

"Yes. I'm only here on weekends when work allows," he says.

"You sound so grown up."

He makes a face at me.

I smile back. "Why are you still giving Parker your blood?"

"Otis still thinks it's good for him," Linus says. "We're family. How can I say no?"

Molly scrambles to her feet and gives a bark. The doorbell rings. Linus and I stare at each other. I glance out the back windows, afraid I'll see I don't know what, but the dusky yard is empty.

"Quick. Upstairs," Linus says, taking off his apron.

I light-foot it up as fast as I can.

Anyone who rings a doorbell can't be too dangerous, I tell myself. Still, I grab my bag and jacket in case I have to leave quickly, and I hide in Linus's room, crouched behind the desk, holding a dart for a weapon.

The footsteps of several people come up the stairs.

"Rosie?" Linus says, opening the door. "You in here? We have visitors."

I straighten slowly. Behind Linus, a jock-type guy comes in and smiles politely. He has blond, short hair and a homely, square face that belongs on an Army recruitment poster. He steps aside to let in a pregnant girl.

She's pretty, I think, taking in her dark hair, caramel skin, and hoop earrings. She's slender everywhere except for her belly, which bulges large under a clingy green shirt. I appreciate her red Converse sneakers. Her bag looks designer. Her face is arresting in a timeless, regal way, as if she's a lost princess, and she casts an uncertain glance around the room before she offers me a hesitant smile.

"Hey," she says. "I'm Thea. Althea Flores."

This girl is Thea? I'm stunned. I feel cheated. Nobody told me Thea was Latina or pregnant or older. Nobody warned me she was rich and pretty.

She's a threat if ever I met one.

29

— THEA —

MEETING ROSIE

SEEING MYSELF WAS A SHOCK. The girl in
Linus's bedroom had my body, but she was horribly thin beneath her yellow shirt, and her lank hair dragged around her
face. My face. Her eyes seemed darker and wilder than they'd
ever been when they were mine. She lowered the dart in her
hand, and I had the freaky sense that I'd escaped from a mirror,
only my image had become a living, untamed doppelganger.

The next instant, my mind flipped. I was still in Althea's
body. She was the real version of me. I was the imposter in the
wrong body.

"Who's this?" she asked, indicating Tom.

"Tom," I said. I jerked a hand in his direction. "This is Tom
Barton. From Texas. Tom, this is Rosie Sinclair."

"Hello," he said.

She gave him a cursory glance before she returned her cool gaze to me.

I didn't know where to start. I wasn't sure how much Linus had told her. He stood tensely in front of a desk, watching me like he expected me to start doing head-spinning tricks. I should have called first. I took a chance that he'd be home, but I hadn't expected that Rosie would be here, too.

"How far along are you?" she asked.

My voice sounded wrong originating from her. The low huskiness belonged between my ears, not coming at me.

"Eight months," I said. "I'm due in four weeks."

"Are you the dad?" she asked, glancing at Tom.

"Yes," he said. "It's nice to meet you," he added. "I've been hearing about you."

"Is that right?" Rosie asked. She rolled a dart in her fingers, studying me. "Why are you here?"

"I came to see Linus. I wanted to ask him if he'd heard from you," I said. "I guess he did."

"Did you know she was coming?" she asked him.

He shook his head. "No idea." He glanced at me. "I thought you were in Texas."

"We took a road trip," I said and turned to Rosie again. "I've been looking for you."

"Why?" she asked.

"Because I'm *you*," I said. It was freaking me out to talk to myself, especially when she was obviously suspicious of me. "I woke up in this body, but I started out in you. Berg had us in a vault of dreamers, and Dr. Ash came to mine us. Remember

349

how the white spheres were stealing Dubbs? Remember the golden strands of light?"

She tilted her head, frowning. "Go on."

"We had two voices, remember? We talked to ourselves."

"Lots of people talk to themselves," she said.

"But not like us," I said. "We were trapped together. You begged me to stay in the vault with you, but I couldn't. They were mining us away into nothing, remember? I took a chance. They were ripping Dubbs away, off the tracks, and I left with that dream of Dubbs. I had to."

She stood taller. "And look where it got you," she said.

I gasped. "Then you believe me."

She narrowed her eyes and took a step forward. "I have nothing to say to you, and I think you know why. Excuse me."

She stalked past me and out the door. I stared after her, stunned.

"Wait here," Linus said. "I'll talk to her." He left, too, and his footsteps went rapidly downstairs. His voice sounded below: "Rosie!"

I turned to Tom, who was openly fascinated.

"She hates me," I said.

"She's a trip," he said.

I choked out a laugh and hugged my arms around myself.

"She's different from how she was on *The Forge Show*," he said. "She's a little scary, to be honest."

"She's changed. It only makes sense."

"But she talks a lot like you, too," he went on. "It's not her voice, but, the whole thing's just bizarre."

"*Because we're the same person,*" I said.

I'd barely glanced at Linus's room when we'd walked in, but now I took in the angled ceiling, the windows, and the single, neatly made bed. Had she spent the night with him here? A lump tightened in my chest. *That should have been me.*

"What do you want to do?" Tom asked.

"Stay here, obviously. Figure this out."

Footsteps came slowly up the stairs again, and Linus leaned in the door. It was painful to be in the same room with him when he looked at me in such a measuring way.

"She's okay," he said. "She just needs a little time to herself."

"When did she get here?" I asked.

"Last night."

"I wish you'd called me," I said.

"We were busy," he said.

Was that color tinting his cheeks?

"I bet," I said.

He looked pointedly at my belly. "I notice you managed to omit that you were pregnant when we talked on the phone."

"Like it would matter to you?" I said.

"Thea," Tom said quietly.

I ignored him. "The truth is, I had a hard enough time getting you even to listen to me. I knew you wouldn't understand about this," I said to Linus.

"You're wrong," he said. "I understand pregnancy. What I still don't understand is how you know so much about me and Rosie."

"I told you," I said. "I *am* Rosie. I have the same mind as her.

351

Didn't I just prove it? *Rosie* knows me. And how can you be sleeping with her? She looks like a fragile wreck."

"*You're* the one who just upset her," Linus said.

"Thea, this isn't helping," Tom said.

"Leave me alone!" I snapped at him. "You weren't there, okay? You don't have anything to do with this!"

Tom stiffened. He eyed me coolly. "I'll be downstairs," he said, and headed out.

I pressed a hand to my forehead. I was a total jerk. No wonder nobody liked me.

"I'm sorry," I said.

Linus reached for a mug on the bedside table, and I knew in another second, he'd be going downstairs to get away from me, like everyone else.

"I mean it. I'm sorry," I said. "I'm not like this."

"No?"

I threw out a hand. "Will you try for just one second to imagine how frustrating this is for me? I don't want to be like this. This isn't my body. Nobody understands who I am."

A sharpness flickered in his eyes. "I tried," he said. "When we talked on the phone, I really believed you were Rosie. Even with the wrong voice, you convinced me. But you're nothing like her."

"Why? Because I lost my temper?"

He watched me intently. "Because it turns out you lied. You lied about the baby and who knows what else."

"You think *Rosie* never lies to you?" I asked. "I'd bet you anything she's acting all sweet and trusting, but she isn't. She doesn't know how to trust anybody anymore. That's who she is. That's what the vault does to you."

"Try speaking for yourself," Linus said.

"I am! I'm speaking for both of us. She was in the vault even longer than I was and I'm angry as anything."

"At Berg."

"At you!" I said, with all my heartache and fury boiling over. "All this time, you let him win!"

Linus stood tensely, frowning down at the mug in his hand. He shook his head, as if he had a thousand words pent up.

"Go on," I said, my voice low. "Tell me I'm wrong."

"I only have these kinds of conversations with Rosie," he said. "She's the only one who can make me feel this."

"This what?"

He looked up at me, his gaze hard. "Worthless," he said. "Excuse me."

He stepped out of the room.

I sank slowly to the edge of the bed and crushed my hands together. My anger evaporated. I had utterly and completely blown it. I was a crappy person. A *mean*, crappy person. So why did my heart feel slashed apart?

Another one of my false contractions came creeping over my belly, tightening everything inward. It wasn't painful, but it seemed like Althea's body was mocking me.

"Perfect," I muttered.

I was still tired from walking the long tunnel under Forge, and rattled from my meeting with Berg. All this time, I had wanted to find Rosie as if I owed her something or could help her somehow. What a joke. She wanted nothing to do with me, and I couldn't blame her. I didn't want anything to do with myself, either.

From the hall, light footsteps were approaching, and I glanced up as Rosie appeared in the doorway. She crossed her arms and leaned against the doorframe, studying me with obvious skepticism.

"That didn't take you long," she said. "You managed to alienate all three of us."

"It's my special skill."

She briefly pursed her lips. "Tom said you went to Forge today. Did you find out anything?"

"Actually, I did. I talked to Berg."

"Really? How?"

"He found me in the basement, by the vault of dreamers. I went down to investigate."

She leaned her head forward. "Are you serious? Tom didn't mention that."

"Because I didn't tell him I went down there."

Her eyebrows lifted in surprise. She came further in, and I could tell she was curious. "What did Berg say?"

"Nothing much, but he knows my name now," I said. "He's going to figure out I was at Chimera, and I'm guessing he'll know pretty soon that your dreams were seeded into me. That can't be good for either of us."

"How many of my memories do you have?"

"I have the same memories as you up to the point that I left the vault."

She looked at me thoughtfully. "Do you remember Ian?" she asked.

"He was one of our keepers in the vault," I said. "Dr. Ash mentioned his name. Creepy guy."

"He was disgusting," Rosie said. "I got him to lighten up on my meds by pretending to be his girlfriend. Then I snuck out one night and stole a car. I nearly froze to death, but I got free." She considered me another minute. "How long have you been in the States?"

"A week. We came home from Chimera last Monday." For a second, I considered telling her about Orson, our father, but this wasn't the time. I ought to tell her about seeing Dubbs and Ma and Larry, too.

"Does your new family know about you?" Rosie asked.

I nodded. "They're having a hard time accepting it. They keep hoping I'll wake up as Althea one of these days." I took a deep breath. "Listen, you might as well believe me. Why would I make this up?"

"I don't know. That's what I'm wondering," she said.

"Ask me anything," I said.

"Where did we go for vacation when I was ten?"

"The Grand Canyon. We took a road trip there. Larry got poison ivy and complained all the way back."

She smiled. "Where do I hide my journal?"

"You don't keep one, but Dubbs does," I said "She hides it under our bed. She sleeps on the top bunk so you have to pass it up to her each night."

She nodded. "What's her favorite stuffed animal?"

"Elmo. It's so old the black rubbed off its eyes, so you drew it on again with a Sharpie."

"This is deeply weird," Rosie said.

"I know," I said.

"How do you feel about Linus?" she asked.

My heart stopped. I glanced sideways, toward a Swiss Army knife on his desk. I made him feel worthless.

"Crap," Rosie said.

I couldn't help it. I had to know. "Did you sleep with him?" I asked.

She slid her hands down into her pockets. "No," she said. "I mean, yes, I *slept* with him, but we didn't have sex." She smiled, then made a goofy, embarrassed face. "How are you and Tom?"

"Awkward," I said. "He misses the real Althea, but he's such a decent guy that he's trying to take care of me."

A clanking noise came from the kitchen below, and I listened a moment for more.

"Tell me what you found out at Forge today," Rosie said.

"The vault itself was empty, but I followed the tunnel past the clock tower pit," I said. "It slopes down a long way and ends at a locked door. I heard mooing on the other side, which means—"

"The dairy barn," she said. "I was trying to think how Berg moved all the dreamers out so quickly. It fits. They could have loaded all the dreamers into ice cream trucks and driven them away. Nobody would have noticed. Does Tom know?"

I shook my head. "I was too freaked out by seeing Berg. I

didn't really want to talk. I just wanted to come here and see Linus in case he knew where you were."

"This is good," Rosie said. "Don't tell either of them. It's not their problem."

"What are you going to do?" I asked.

"I'm still working that out," she said.

"You wouldn't kill anybody."

She looked at me oddly. "I wouldn't admit it."

My heartbeat kicked in, and I wasn't certain what to say. I believed, deep down, that Rosie could want to kill Berg because part of me wanted to, too. But I wouldn't actually go through with it.

"You're too smart to mess up your life that much," I said doubtfully.

She gave a faint, feline smile. "Just promise me you won't tell anybody about the tunnel," she said. "Do that for me, and I'll keep your secrets, too."

"Okay," I said. "I promise."

— ROSIE —

BAGELS

WHEN WE GET DOWN to the kitchen, Linus has cleared away the cutting board and the mess. He brings over a bag of bagels. On the stove, a pot of marinara sauce is simmering, and the juicy smell is beyond amazing. The shades, pulled down to cover the windows, are backlit with gold from the evening sun. It feels like a totally ordinary kitchen, but this is arguably the strangest day of my life. I want to dismiss Thea's entire claim that she has my mind, but I'm also so shocked by her that I guess I *am* believing her. She has me second-guessing everything I say or do. It's like how I felt the first time with all the cameras at Forge, only a million times worse. When I lift my hand, I'm seeing the motion through my own eyes and wondering how it looks to her through her eyes at the same time.

Tom is in a chair at the table already, peeling an orange. Thea quietly apologizes to him about something, and though he seems a bit stiff, he says not to worry. He offers her a wedge of orange, which she accepts. She sits heavily in the chair beside him and lounges back in a relaxed, elegant way, as if she deserves to make herself comfortable.

I slouch.

"Coffee," Linus says, and puts a steaming metal pot beside the bagels. "We're out of milk. Help yourselves."

Thea and I pick raisin bagels from the bag and both smear cream cheese the same way, in dabs. I lick my fingers, knowing I shouldn't. She uses her napkin, which she rests on the top of her belly. What I don't understand is this poise of hers. If we have the same brain, I don't get why she's smarter and calmer than I am. Unless she only seems smarter and calmer. Could be she's as restless as I am inside.

She looks at Linus sometimes when he isn't looking at her, and I can't tell if she's wistful or chagrined. He hardly looks at her at all. He doesn't sit with us. Instead, he positions the fourth chair where Thea can put her feet up on it and tells her to do so. Then he goes back to brace his hand on the counter beside him.

I am not deceived. Some friction unites them. I don't want to care, but it eats at me because I don't understand it.

"Do you have déjà vus anymore, or any headaches?" Thea asks me.

I've never talked about the déjà vus in front of a stranger like Tom before, so the question makes me uneasy. "No. Do you?"

"I've been getting headaches," she says. "They're bad, but they don't last long. I also had a déjà vu in the clock tower today."

"She's supposed to report any headaches," Tom says. "They could mean a problem with her surgery."

"I'm not going back for any more tweaks," she says.

She fills us in about her recovery at the Chimera Centre, and she describes the lab she found there. I can see why she's not psyched to have any more surgeries.

"What if they had never put Rosie's seed in a new body?" Linus asks her.

Thea turns to him. "I'd be stuck in a petri dish, like all those other dream seeds," she says. "I doubt I'd even know I exist."

"What about Thea? What would have happened to her?" Linus asks.

"I don't know," she says. "Diego and Madeline were keeping me—I mean her—alive for the baby's sake."

Linus glances briefly toward Tom, and then back to Thea. He looks like he has more questions, but he doesn't ask them. Instead, he aims his eyes toward his feet.

"What's going on?" I ask.

Linus lifts his gaze toward Thea, as if she'll answer for them. She stares back at him, waiting likewise. I set down my bagel. This testy vibe of theirs bugs me. They had, what, two phone conversations together? I slept in his bed last night. I thought that counted for something.

"You might as well tell me," I say. "I can't read your mind."

"It's no big deal," Thea says. "Apparently, Linus thinks I'm nothing like you."

Linus crosses his arms. "That's not exactly true," he says.

"How are we different?" I ask.

"He likes the way you're trusting and sweet," Thea says, with her gaze still on Linus.

"I'm not," I say.

"I guess then we are similar," Thea says.

Tom lets out a low whistle.

Linus steps over to the stove. "You can stop anytime," he says quietly.

Steam escapes as he lifts the lid and gives his red sauce a stir.

"So, Thea," Tom says in a cheery, clear voice. "Did you tell Rosie about our trip to Doli?"

"What?" I ask.

Thea gives me a small smile. "I wanted to tell you I saw Dubbs yesterday," she says. "We went to visit Doli, Tom and I. Ma and Larry were there, too."

"Really? How were they all?" I ask.

"They were fine," she says. "They didn't recognize me, of course. They miss you. Dubbs looks good. I can't go home, but you could."

"Maybe someday," I say, and look toward the window. It's getting late. In a couple of hours, it will be dark out. All I want to do is get revenge on Berg. Nothing has changed that. I need to call Burnham and finalize my plans. It helps now that I know a secret way into Forge.

361

"You could also come with us to Holdum," Thea continues. "Althea's family would be glad to have you. The ranch is beautiful. I've been thinking about this, actually. You could take one of the bedrooms on the third floor near mine. We could sit out on the porch with the baby on sunny days and take turns pushing her swing."

Her fantasy is so unlikely that I don't even know where to begin. I lean back, studying her, and then I realize she's trying to give me alternatives to my revenge plans.

"Do you ever hear voices?" she asks.

"No."

"Me, neither. Do you ever miss it?"

Again, I feel awkward discussing this in front of others. "Sometimes," I say.

"What voices do you mean?" Tom asks.

Thea shifts her feet on the extra chair, and it squeaks against the floor. "I started hearing a voice in my head back when I was at Forge," she says. "It wasn't just a normal voice, like when you talk to yourself. It felt like another side of me with a will of her own." She glances at me. "Right? From deep inside?"

I nod. It's so strange to hear her explaining out loud what I have only known inside my mind.

"First she would just show up randomly and say something, but then we started having conversations," Thea continues. "Arguments, sometimes. After we were stuck in the vault, we talked even more."

"I think it started because Berg was mining us," I say. "It was a kind of response to that. A defense."

"A subconscious thing," Thea says.

"I suggested that before," Linus says. "Rosie Id and Rosie Ego."

"No, we were really more *us*," I say. "Two voices but the same individual. Subconscious or conscious didn't matter much by the end." I face Thea again. "You decided to leave," I say.

"Yes," she agrees. "It was better than waiting it out in the vault, sleeping our life away while they mined us down to nothing."

She sounds a little too superior to me.

"But leaving was suicide," I say, feeling my resentment kick in again.

Thea spreads her hands on the table. "Apparently not, since I'm still alive. I thought *staying* was suicide." She glances toward Tom as she goes on. "So we split. I took the conscious side of me and left."

"But *I* was conscious by then, too," I insist. "Just as conscious as you. You should have listened to me."

She looks surprised. "I *did* listen," Thea says. "But your main reason to stay was that you were afraid."

I stand up, ready to smash something: bagels, plates, anything. "I was not!"

"Calm down. It's not like I deliberately left you behind," Thea says. "I just did the best I could at the time. I was only trying to survive."

"Don't tell me to calm down!" I say. "I don't care what your excuse is. You *left* me in that hell. They kept mining me for months, Thea. *Months!* I'll never be the same!" I pull down the neckline of my shirt to show the port that still bulges under my skin.

Thea, Linus, and Tom go motionless. Tension sucks the air out of the room.

"I'm sorry," Thea says quietly. "I never wanted to hurt you. Us. I never meant to hurt us. I'm really sorry, Rosie."

I still want to destroy everything in sight. I want to scream it to her again in my head: *you left me!* Thea's chin trembles slightly. It hits me finally that she's upset, too, only she contains it better. I take a deep breath and release my shirt. Thea isn't the one to blame. She didn't mine me. She only tried to survive. She just needed to do it a different way, and she's paying, too.

The chill of my anger redirects where it belongs, toward Berg, and like a poisoned black arrow, it drives deeper into my heart.

I slouch back onto my chair, deflated, and jam my hands under my legs. "It's okay," I say finally.

"Don't be mad," she says.

It's hard to look at any of them. They're like a unit, all breathing and alive, teamed up against the monster on my side of the table. I focus on the coffee pot. "I'm not mad," I say.

I'm not anything.

>>>>>>>>>

Soon after, I excuse myself, pretending to need the bathroom. I collect my coat and bag from Linus's room, and then I tiptoe back down the stairs. The others are talking softly in the kitchen like mature, reasonable people. I let myself out the front door, pull my cap low over my face, and head for my car.

I drive out of town to a lot behind an abandoned antiques business and park where I can watch the wind moving over the prairie in long, slow ripples. In the wake of my anger, I'm strangely calm. Fatalistic. The stiff winter grass has yielded to new green, but the setting sun is painting it orange. Each blade is still perfect, making a sea of collective silk. The beauty brings a familiar pang of longing, and I wish I had my video camera. Without it, I have no choice but to live in the moment, so I do, memorizing it.

When I call Burnham to tell him I'm ready to go in, he says to give him a couple of hours to prepare, so I settle in. I crack my window. Gradually, the big sky deepens into darkness. Sirius, the Dog Star, shows up first, followed by the trio of Orion's belt, and then the other constellations, the ones I always wanted to learn the names of. Maybe I still will, but tonight their distant light seems aloof, uncaring.

I don't mind that the universe is uncaring. I can be uncaring, too. It's a lot easier that way.

31

— THEA —

THE TUNNEL

WHEN ROSIE DIDN'T RETURN from the bathroom, I knew that we had trouble. Linus and Tom searched the house. I instantly guessed that she would head for the tunnel, but I'd promised not to tell.

"She must have gone up to Forge," Linus said. He pulsed his hand into a fist. "Did she say anything to you about where she might go?"

"No," I said.

"Did she give you her phone number?" Tom asked.

"No. Do you have it?" I asked Linus.

"I don't have one for her," Linus said. "She called me last on a disposable phone."

"Are you serious?" I asked. "None of us can reach her?"

"Burnham might know how," Linus said.

"Burnham Fister?" I asked, surprised.

"She stayed with him a few days before she came here," Linus said.

She didn't mention it to me. I felt vaguely left out. Then again, we were different people now. She'd made that abundantly clear when she'd yelled at me.

"I'll see if I can reach him," Linus said.

He took off for Forge while Tom took me to the nearest hotel and got us a room. He was convinced I was worn down, and he was serious about nurturing me. I played along, and as I shucked off my shoes and climbed onto my bed, I was honestly grateful to sink into the softness. I was anxious about Rosie, but I couldn't do anything for her until I could shake Tom, and that was going to be hard.

"If she doesn't want to be found, she won't be found," Tom said.

"What did you think of her?"

Tom took off his boots one after the other. "No, thank you. I'm not getting in the middle of that."

"No, honestly. I want to know," I said. "Did you like her?"

"Honestly?" he said. "She seemed pretty dark and confused to me. It's hard for me to believe you were ever like that."

I knew it wasn't his intention, but I felt insulted.

"She was in the vault much longer than I was," I said. "I think she was mined a lot more."

"What does that feel like, exactly?" Tom asked.

"The mining itself? I was conscious for it one time, and it

was excruciating," I said. "Normally, you don't feel it, but afterward, you feel kind of frayed. Unglued. The headaches and déjà vus make you feel like you can't count on yourself."

He stood before the window with his arms akimbo. "I should take you home."

"I'm not leaving Forgetown until we know Rosie's all right," I said.

"I'm not sure that girl's ever going to be all right," he said. "At least call your parents and tell them about your headaches," he said.

"They'll only worry."

"Because they should," he said. "I'm worried, too. Something could be really wrong with you, Thea. I can tell you're exhausted. You need the right supervision."

"It's just that I'm pregnant," I said. "I'm fine."

"But your eyes are pinched. You're having a headache right now, aren't you?" he asked.

"No," I lied again. It wasn't a bad headache. Just a little, needling one at my temples.

He sat on the end of my bed. "Call your parents. If you don't want to, I can."

"They'll make me go home to Holdum."

"Maybe that's where you belong," he said.

Maybe nothing. He obviously thought so.

"I don't know why you don't get along with my parents," I said. "I swear you sound just like them."

Another Braxton-Hicks contraction tingled over my belly, drawing my muscles into a firm, rigid ball. I practiced breathing through the tension, and deeper inside, the baby rolled in response. As the contraction ended, I felt a tug on my toes, and then, wordlessly, Tom began to rub my foot. I wasn't sure I liked it at first, but he kept rubbing. Bliss traveled up my tired leg. My mind followed each sure stroke of his strong fingers under and around the arch of my foot. Then he tried the other foot. Tingles spread all along my nerves, even to my scalp. Gradually, my headache eased, and my limbs went limp.

All right. He proved his point. I was exhausted.

His blue eyes were grave. "Tomorrow we're going back home, no matter what."

"Okay," I said.

"I could have killed for some of that spaghetti sauce," he said.

"I know," I sighed. "Me, too."

"I'll go find us some dinner." He gave my feet a last squeeze and stood up.

It was nearly impossible for me, but as soon as he left our room, I dragged myself out of the bed, put my shoes back on, and left the hotel. I scanned the street for Tom, and then headed down to the dairy barn. My plan was simple. I'd look for Rosie in the tunnel. If she wasn't there, I'd come out again, no harm done. If I could find her, ten to one I could convince her to come back out. If I couldn't convince her, I'd call Linus and Tom for back up. An hour at the most I'd be down there. Two hours, tops.

>>>>>>>>

Only die-hard ice cream lovers were out that chilly evening, but they were the lingering types who took their cones from the small, brightly lit shop to the dairy barn out back. I ordered a cone of mint chip ice cream and wandered the well-worn path into the old, cavernous building. The smell of animal was almost too powerful for me to take. Rows of cows clanked in their stalls, chewing their cud, while suction cups attached to their udders milked them. Above, a rivulet of white milk trickled through a clear pipe and emptied into a vat in the next room.

Licking my ice cream, I moseyed toward a promising staircase and looked down. A wide, industrial-sized elevator chute dropped to the platform below. It would certainly be large enough to convey sleep shells or bodies up and down, assuming this was the way Berg had emptied the vault.

I glanced over my shoulder to see that the other customers had left, and I checked the corners for cameras. There were none, which fit my theory that someone wanted this area private. I walked down the stairs to the lower floor, and there, right before me, was a large wooden door, just like the one I'd seen from the other side when I was exploring the tunnel. A bit of tissue showed white underneath. Bingo.

I unlatched a heavy bolt, and the big knob turned easily from this direction. I wedged a scrap of wood into the opening so it couldn't close the entire way, and then, with the light on my cell phone to guide me, I headed into the tunnel, toward the dean's tower at Forge. The route was familiar by now and it didn't feel as long. I knew where the floor angle would tilt upward, and where to expect the side door. Once the floor leveled out, I came to the glass room at the bottom of the clock tower pit, and then the broken light fixture on the wall. Finally I reached the door to the elevator landing and the wall of windows that separated me from the vault of dreamers. I instinctively looked for Berg, but he wasn't there, and neither was Rosie.

I hesitated, remembering my promise to myself. This was far enough. I couldn't go searching further for Rosie. I might miss her in passing, and I'd certainly get caught, which wouldn't do her any good. I turned for the tunnel again when the elevator doors opened behind me.

Berg stepped out.

My heart hammered up my throat. "Where's Rosie?" I asked.

Instead of answering, he lunged forward and grabbed my arm. I screamed. He pinned me against the wall and wrenched my arm up behind me. I cringed, trying to protect my belly, but he caught my other wrist, too, and tied it in a tight binding behind my back. I struggled against him.

"You can't do this!" I said. "Let me go!"

Wordlessly, he hauled me back and lifted me bodily off the ground. I screamed again, shocked and writhing, but he carried me in a strong, painful grip.

"Let me go!" I yelled again.

But he was a silent, unresponsive machine. He backed into the vault of dreamers and slammed up against the light switches, which turned on. My fears jumped from mining to murder. He crossed to the operating room and set me down, holding me by my tied wrists. I could not believe how strong he was. He opened the door. I screamed again and tried to bite at him, but he twisted me around again and shoved me into the operating room. I fell against the wall and turned as he slammed the door.

Panting, I heard a key click in the lock. A key, not some swipe pass. Through the glass of the door, I saw him wipe a hand across his forehead. He looked at me grimly and then turned away.

I regained my balance in a wide stance. "You can't leave me here!" I yelled.

I spit out a strand of hair that caught in my lips.

I charged my shoulder against the door. It shuddered but didn't yield. On the other side of the glass, Berg strode across the vault and out of sight.

"My friends know where I am!" I yelled. "They'll come looking for me!"

The lights went out.

My heart slammed. I could see a faint glimmer of light from the direction of the doorway, and then that vanished, too. The blackness was complete. I screamed again, but only silence answered me.

I was scared. Beyond scared. I had to get out. I squinted in every direction, still seeing nothing but black. I put my back to the door and felt along with my tied hands for the handle. It turned, but didn't open. I braced my shoulder against the door and focused, twisting my wrists, straining and pulling against the binding. It was made of some smooth, narrow cloth that was cutting off my circulation. I used the door handle to wedge into one side of the binding, and I winced in pain as I extricated my right hand. I quickly untied my left hand, too, and shuddered with relief for that much freedom. I felt the length of the binding. A tie. It was Berg's tie.

I tapped my pockets. I still had my phone. I pulled it out swiftly and greedily tapped it on. No signal. Of course not. But it had light. I lowered the brightness to the lowest setting and checked my battery life: 45%.

He couldn't keep me here long. He wouldn't. I aimed the glow of my phone up toward the ceiling and discovered a camera in the corner. Hope flared in my heart.

"Hello?" I asked. "Is someone watching me?"

No answer came.

My belly compressed in a great, silent kneading. It was longer and deeper than any false contraction I'd had before, and I leaned over, bracing my hands on my knees. I willed myself to breathe through the pressure. *Unreal*, I thought. When the contraction eased away, I staggered back against the wall, my heart racing.

This could not be labor! It was too soon. I wasn't due for four more weeks. Even if I was in labor, it would take hours, and Berg could not possibly keep me here for long. That's what I told myself, but in fact, I was terrified. I couldn't have a baby down here alone in the dark! I wouldn't know what to do! I would die!

I lifted my phone again. It was down to 44%. At this rate, it would be dead in a couple of hours.

I looked up at the camera. "Berg!" I yelled. "I'm going to have my baby! Get me out of here!"

The camera did not reply. I was mad now. And stupid. I hadn't told any of my friends where I was going, so no one would know where to look for me. I checked around carefully for anything hard and heavy I could use to break the glass in the door, but I found nothing. I tried jamming the glass with my elbow and kicking it, but it wouldn't shatter.

Don't panic, I told myself. *Do not cry. Think.*

I had no idea when my next contraction would come. Maybe that first one was just brought on by stress. Maybe if I kept calm, I wouldn't have any more. My legs were still dry, which meant my water hadn't broken. I was okay.

Except I wasn't. I was alone in the dark in the operating room of the vault of dreamers, and nobody but Berg knew where I was. And I was maybe having my baby. I let out a desperate, gulping laugh and slid down the wall to the floor.

— ROSIE —

CAMPFIRE BOY

THE NIGHT IS HALF GONE before Burnham calls again.

"Okay," he says. "I think I can get us into Berg's computer if you can put in your peg. Do you need me to dismantle the swipe locks in the dean's tower?"

I think back to my last trip to the sixth floor. The staircase opened directly into the big room, and I think the elevator did, too. "No," I say.

"Are you sure about this, Rosie? Linus Pitts called and left me a message. He's looking for you."

"Did he say where he is?" I ask.

"No, but he sounded worried."

I chew on my lip, frowning. Then I shake my head. "It doesn't matter. I'm going in."

"Then call me right when you reach Berg's computer. You have the peg?"

I glance to see it beside my flashlight and other supplies.

"Yes," I say. "I'm heading there now. Give me about half an hour. I'll call you soon."

I don't tell him that I expect to get caught.

Returning to town, I drive slowly past Linus's house. Only one lamp is still on in the living room, and I can't see any action through the windows. I park farther down, near the water tower, and walk the last couple of blocks to the dairy barn. Up on the hill, at Forge, the penthouse apartment is a bright row of windows at the top of the dean's tower. The rest of the campus is dark and sleepy, illuminated only by streetlamps that make lace of the leafless trees. Deep in my jacket pocket, I carry the syringes I prepared, four of them, one from each vial I stole from Ian, each with its own white cap.

Outside the dairy barn, I pause, noting one car in the lot. I hear the sturdy clanking of the cows even before I enter, and then the penetrating scent of animal bodies fills my nostrils. At the far end of the barn, a farmer is dumping grain into a chute, and I duck low.

Stealthy, keeping an eye toward the farmer, I creep along the far wall past the noses and munching noises of a dozen cows. It's startling how huge the animals are with their heavy heads. The barn is a long L, with the cows in the long rectangle, and the milk pipes above. I'm searching for a door that matches Thea's description when I discover an open shaft elevator, large enough to accommodate cargo. Or sleep shells. Beside it is a narrow staircase. When the farmer moves out of sight, I dash for the stairs and sneak down.

Directly opposite the shaft elevator is a large wooden door, just as Thea described. It's unbolted, and a bit of wood props the door open a crack. I stop, puzzled. Someone has been here recently. They might still be inside. A shiver of fear runs over my skin, and instinct warns me this is a mistake.

But then my reckless heart warms to the idea. What's the worst that can happen? I've already survived the vault of dreamers. I'll kill before I let that happen to me again, and if I fail at killing, if I still end up being mined, I'll do what Thea did and escape that way. I flick on my flashlight and venture into the tunnel.

Clingy, ragged webs drape the walls and ceiling, and random leaves crinkle underfoot. This stretch of tunnel is old and decrepit compared to the tunnel I traveled when I was still a student. I cast my flashlight beam before me and hurry up the slope of the tunnel, never looking behind me. When I reach the dusty glass walls at the bottom of the clock tower pit, I breathe a small sigh of relief. Familiar territory. I hurry the last length of the tunnel, to the door that leads to the elevator under the dean's tower.

There, finally, I stop with my hand on the knob and wait, listening. Stillness expands around me, filling my ears like cotton. I turn off my light, and in the absolute darkness, I slowly open the door. Not even an exit light glows in the landing area. I turn on my flashlight again and scan the elevator, the counter area, the glass that separates me from the vault of dreamers. I know nothing is behind the glass. Thea told me so. Yet I feel images tugging at the corners of my mind: sleep shells glowing with their blue light, and children's pale, haunting faces under glass domes. This was where Gracie lay dreaming with her teddy bear. I'm a few paces from the room where I was first mined for my dreams, and the dark power of this hangs in the air, making it difficult to breathe.

A shimmer of nightmare draws me irresistibly to the vault's door, and I'm compelled to open it. I smell the vinegar, and something like tweed, as if Berg was just here. My beam trembles as I cast it around the empty room, and a shifting noise answers. Heart in mouth, I shine my light toward the sound, and a baby mouse runs wildly along the baseboard. It angles through the corner and vanishes into a crack. My light meets the door to the operating room. That's where it started. That's the place.

I'll die if I go in there, I think. *What's left of my brain will liquefy into black silage and run out my nose, and I'll be dead.*

I swallow thickly and back out of the vault. I press the button for the elevator.

"Come," I whisper.

When a scratching, rubbing noise, as faint as a whisper, comes from the vault behind me, I can't tell if it's the mouse or if I imagined it. My lungs contract with fear. The elevator doors open, and I step in gladly, wincing at the brightness. A rush of relief makes it easier to breathe. I push the button for the sixth floor, and my stomach dips as the elevator begins to rise. With a last reflexive shiver, I brush off my jacket and put my flashlight in my pocket. I can do this. I will win.

The doors slick open, and I step into the landing. I peer around the corner to a large, unlit room. This is where the techies work by day. Rows of desks and monitors gleam faintly in the darkness and descend toward the windows. I've been here once before, when I eavesdropped on Berg, but now the lowest corner, where Berg sat, is empty, and I tread softly in that direction.

I dial Burnham.

"I'm here," he says. "Show me."

It's pretty dark, and I have a shoddy disposable phone, but I turn the lens to the room so he can see what I'm seeing. I slide into the seat where I once saw Berg working, and I'm hit by misgivings. This computer doesn't look any different from the others in the room.

"He had special projection pucks when I saw him before," I say. "I can't believe I didn't remember until now."

"It's all right," Burnham says. "Put the peg into the computer before you start it up. We'll know in a second if it has what we want."

It's tricky to find a port in the dark, but I do and slip the peg in. "Okay," I say, and turn on the computer.

The screen seems dangerously bright. I quickly dim it down to the faintest setting. It's a blank green rectangle, with no text or icons. It doesn't even have a type box. My heart sinks.

"It's broken," I say.

"Just wait. Don't touch the keyboard or the screen," he says, and softly, I hear him typing in the background. A minute later, the screen comes alive with a watercolor scene of a dock at a lake. It's about the last thing I expected. Then I recall that Berg likes to paint.

"Burnham?" I say.

"Hold on."

I hear more clicking. The image shimmers, and with a reverse-dissolve effect, four icons appear around a silver circle, like the points of a compass.

"Good," Burnham says. "Pick a direction. Go ahead. You can touch the screen now."

"West," I say, and touch the left-hand icon.

Up comes a spreadsheet listing names, ages, blood types, and other medical information. Half the codes I don't understand, but I can see it's a ton of information.

"Are you getting this?" I whisper.

"I'm copying it now," Burnham says. "It'll take some time. You said you saw maybe sixty dreamers in the vault under the school?"

"Yes."

"There's a lot more people listed here," he says. "A way lot more."

"Should I wait or can I click back?" I ask.

The screen splits in half, with one half showing a shrunken version of the files he's copying and the other half showing the main icon compass again.

"Go ahead," he says.

I try the east icon, which takes me to an informal scratch pad of blue ink handwritten on a white board. Very retro. A bunch of equations with letters, numbers, and honeycomb symbols reminds me of science class. Burnham hums pensively.

"Can you tell what he's brainstorming?" I ask

"It's chemical compounds," Burnham says. "This looks more like he was explaining something to somebody. It's practically scribbles on a napkin. Let me check something." His typing goes again, and up comes a new series of equations in another box. "I don't know what this means," he says. "He's got the chemical compound for a common over-the-counter sleeping pill."

"Does your company sell it?" I ask.

"I'd have to look into it. We sell a ton of different meds," he says. "See what else is there."

I try the north icon.

At first, I think I've found a color wheel, the kind I've used to pick out a hue for a presentation project, but as I scroll over the wheel, different boxes expand upward toward me, and each box shows a different image that is predominantly the color in the wheel. A yellow dragon flies against an orange sky. A black castle melts into a gray sea. A roiling flash flood of blood and bones barrels through a slot canyon. I gasp.

"Do you see this?" I ask.

"Yes. Each file takes over 4G of memory," he says. "There must be thousands. I can't possibly copy them all."

"Are they dreams?" I ask. "Were they all mined?"

"I don't understand. These look like biological markers," he mutters. "Let me try something."

Another screen pops up to show a boy gazing into a camp-fire. He's a black kid with big glasses, wearing shorts that let his knees gleam in the firelight, and he looks familiar. A line of statistics flies past, and then still another screen appears in the corner. It's a headshot picture of Janice. I look back again at the boy by the fire, and my memory jolts. I've seen this image before. It was back in Dr. Ash's office in the Forge infirmary.

"Is that boy you?" I ask.

"Yes," Burnham says. "It's from when I was a kid at Camp Pewter, but it's in Janice's file. We knew each other there."

"Was it mined? Is it a dream?"

"I don't know," he says. "It's the sort of thing she might re-member, or she might have stashed the image in her subcon-scious. Berg has recorded it, in any case." He types a couple times. "I've never seen the format of these files before. There's no way to tell if it's a real memory or a dream or something she made up."

I skim over the color wheel again, looking at some of the other boxes. "This looks like a database of images, organized by color," I say.

"I think you're right," he says. "This is mind-blowing, Rosie. I'm trying to save a couple of these, but something's weird about the files. It's like they're dissolving. Give me a sec."

My screens do a quick fly around, and when they settle, a window in the lower right shows a room with rows of sleep shells, all glowing the soft blue I've come to know. I peer closely, thinking it's an old image of the dream vault under Forge, but the angle is from high up, and I realize the rows go on too far. This is a larger room, with more sleep shells. More dreamers. Dozens more. Over a hundred.

A chill skims my spine. "Burnham," I whisper.

"I see it," he says.

"Where are they? Are they real? Is this now?"

"I don't know where they are," he says. "I'm trying to sort for the most recent files in the system. What's this?"

A new image comes up, a close-up of a girl, me, lying asleep. It's shot in black and a soft, blue-tinted white. I'm resting in profile, so the line of my nose and lips and chin is distinct over the dimpled pillow. My dark hair makes a distinct curve along my forehead and ear, and moonlight falls on my cheek. The angle feels intimate, the effect both ghostly and loving. I'm surprised to discover that I could ever looked so lovely, and then a hand comes into the frame and lightly smooths a tendril of hair back from my temple.

The clip goes dark.

A shiver of dread runs through me. This isn't some old, photoshopped picture. Someone took that clip of me live.

"When was that taken?" I ask.

"You tell me."

I grip the desk. "Burnham!" I say. "That looked like last night! But there weren't any cameras in Linus's room. I swear there weren't!" I scramble for any explanation. "Could it be a dream?"

"No," Burnham says, his voice low. "That one's a regular .avi file. No question about it. Somebody filmed you in Linus's bed."

Not Linus. I refuse to believe he would film me. Especially not without asking. I can't get over how completely and utterly wrong this is.

"Hasn't this been a fun evening?" Burnham says dryly.

The computer flickers, and I think Burnham's doing something new, but then the icon screen vanishes, and instead, I find Berg's face looking at me.

My fear explodes.

Burham swears.

Berg leans nearer, peering with his eyes narrowed. He's found me.

— ROSIE —

THE BARGAIN

FOR ONE FROZEN SECOND, I can't even think. Then I turn off the computer and rip out the peg.

Berg knows exactly where I am. He's found me at his computer, in his tower. It's no less than I expected, but it's far more terrifying. And I've changed my mind. I don't want to challenge him at all. He's part of something much bigger than I ever guessed. I shove back from the computer and bolt up through the office toward the elevator. I've almost reached it when the door beside it bursts open and Berg runs out from the stairwell.

I lift my phone, aiming at him so Burnham can see him, for all the good that will do me.

"Stay back," I say.

"Put that down," Berg says, breathing hard. His white

sleeves are rolled to the elbow, and he holds his arms loose from his sides, ready. His piggy eyes gleam in his ruddy face.

I keep the phone up. "I have proof this time," I say. "We've stolen your files. You're through."

"As your friend is no doubt discovering about now, my files are not hackable," Berg says. "They deteriorate in ten minutes, but not before they infect whatever system copies them with a virus."

He moves with harsh, efficient speed and chops at my arm to make my phone fly out of my hand. Shocked, I scramble backward and grab a stapler. When did Berg get so strong and quick? I lift the stapler to protect myself. Berg crosses over to where my phone flew. He turns it off and slips it in his pocket. Then he pulls out a different one, his own.

"Guess where your friend Thea is," he says, tapping on his phone. He holds it up toward me, and the screen is mainly gray, with a small diamond of light. He steps closer so I can see that the diamond is the lit screen of a phone, and beside it, barely discernible, is Thea's face. She's lying on a floor, curled on her side with a cell phone before her, and she isn't moving.

My gut goes cold. "Where is she?" I ask.

Berg snaps off the phone. He tilts his head, smiling at me oddly. "Guess."

The vault. The tunnel. Somewhere locked. She could be anywhere dark and hard.

"You wouldn't hurt her," I say, backing away. "She hasn't done anything to you. She doesn't know anything."

He shakes his head and slips his phone in his pocket. "I

don't want to hurt anybody. Quite the opposite. I want to help. Who will take care of you when you start to decay?" he asks. "Who will take care of Thea?"

Nobody's decaying. I don't know what he's talking about.

"Where is she?" I repeat. "Tell me."

"She came looking for you," Berg says. "She came quite some time ago actually. She doesn't scare easily, but I think she's getting there."

"You can't keep her hostage," I say.

"You're right," he says. "That would be completely inhumane. And so we're going to bargain."

"Over what?" I ask.

"Your dreams, of course. What else?" he says. "Let's be clear on one point from the start. I very much want you alive and well. I've discovered the hard way that people need real life to feed their dreams. Too much time in the vault, even with the most careful monitoring, starves a mind down to nothing, and a steady stream of fear alone is poison."

"You're never getting my dreams again," I say. "I'll die first."

He takes another step forward, and I retreat again, shifting to put a desk between us.

"Don't say that. There's no one like you, Rosie," he says. "I'll admit some of the other Forge students are brilliant dreamers, too. They are. They're much, much better than the dreamers from the pre-morgue. But so far, no one else's dreams come close to yours. They aren't just vivid and potent. They're incredibly versatile, and I've yet to pinpoint why."

"Just my luck, I guess. Where's Thea?"

"No," he says, shaking his head. "It's never just luck."

He slowly rounds the desk, and I circle away from him.

"I thought at first it mattered that you knew what we were doing," he goes on. "I've tried recruiting dream donors and telling them point blank what we're doing, but their dreams were doggerel. Worries and lust, food and cars. Useless."

"I don't care," I say. "Tell me where she is."

"The ironic thing is, you must have walked right by her on your way here."

I'm confused. "The tunnel? The glass room under the clock tower? The vault? Tell me."

"You're getting closer. I've come to believe that fear is a key element," he says. "Or the overcoming of it. Hard to know which. There's still so much to learn." He takes another step toward me, lightly joggling the phone. "You know what I'm dying to do? I had no idea how important Thea was the first time I met her, but I've done some digging since then. Imagine my delight when I realized she's a product of the Chimera Centre. Dr. Fallon was holding out on me. Shameful." His eyes take on a strange glow. "How much of your mind is in Thea? Does she always believe she's you? Huma wasn't clear on that point, and my curiosity has been unbearable. Do you suppose she has the same dreams you do?"

"Thea isn't some 'product,'" I say. "She wasn't invented for you to play with."

He smiles slightly. "That doesn't mean I should overlook a gift horse," he says. "You must realize that you and your new friend constitute an amazing breakthrough. She's living proof that one mind can be seeded into another and become conscious there. Once we perfect the process, we'll have the key to immortality. Just think, a person could seed his brain into a young body, and when that body gets old, he could seed it into another young body, and so on. Imagine what people would pay to be immortal."

Is that what he wants, then? Is that his way around his illness?

"It'll never work," I say.

"People always say that when ideas are new," he says. "They're threatened by the prospect of change, even when it's good."

"I'm telling the FBI," I say. "They'll shut you down."

He leans a hand on the nearest desk. "The FBI isn't in the habit of believing minors who are just out of psychiatric facilities," he says. "Besides, you won't report anything. You're going to do exactly what I tell you."

"Why would I do that?"

"For Thea's sake and your family's," he says. "Now listen carefully. For the last five months, you have been at a private psychiatric hospital receiving the care you so desperately needed after your last breakdown. I need you to go public and corroborate my story."

It was just like Linus's idea.

"I won't," I say.

"Think carefully." He drums a couple of fingers on the desktop. "I'm sorry to say there's been an uptick in crime in Doli since you left. All kinds of random shootings have been happening back in your beloved boxcar neighborhood. It's perfectly possible that a little, innocent child could be gunned down just biking home from school."

"You wouldn't."

"On the other hand, it has occurred to me that these dreams might run in families," he says. "Dubbs could have the same rare kind of dreams that you do. But she's only your half sister, isn't she? She could be nothing like you. Hard to know for certain until I try."

The idea of him messing with Dubbs horrifies me. I clutch the stapler harder. "I'll never let you hurt her."

Berg smiles. "Fear's an interesting thing, isn't it?" he says. "We feel it more for our families than we do for ourselves. Now you and I are going to learn to trust each other. We're going to work out something fair to both of us."

Or I could kill him. That would solve a lot of my problems. I switch the stapler to my left hand.

"Here's how this works," he continues. "After you corroborate that you were in a psychiatric hospital, we'll say that you've recovered and you can resume your life. You'll be free. In public. I assume you'll want to meet up with Linus and other friends for a normal life, so you'll need someplace for school or work. Another boarding school isn't completely out of the question, but I suggest we skip ahead and set you up with a film production company of your own. It's even conceivable that I could void the contract you signed and let you go back to your parents, though I can't quite picture you in Doli. Can you?"

Unbelievable. He really expects me to keep silent about everything while he goes on stealing people's dreams.

"No," I say.

"No," he agrees. "The truth is, Rosie, I need you free and living your life for your own sake, and I need to mine you periodically, for mine. My research depends upon you, and I'm willing to pay what I must to ensure your cooperation."

"You think you'd mine me on a schedule?" I ask, backing up. I keep the stapler raised, hoping it will keep his gaze from my other hand, in my pocket, where I finger the syringes.

"No. The mining times won't be regular," he says. "They'll be random. They could happen anytime. That's better for the fear."

"You're sick."

"I'm determined, not sick," Berg says. "I'll be honest with you. Once the news of Dr. Fallon's success with Thea gets around, your dreams will fetch an exorbitant price, and there's no reason you shouldn't share in the profits. Thea's parents have already sent out feelers to see if her original seed is available for patches when she needs them."

I frown, startled. "They want more of my dreams? Do they even know I'm alive?"

"I think that's going to be a point in your favor." His expression turns darker. "And now we'd better get going. We don't want to keep Thea waiting."

"What do you mean?" In my pocket, I use my thumbnail to push off the cover of a syringe.

"I thought I told you," he says, his voice lifting. "I've been dying to get you two together on the same bench."

He lunges for me.

I whirl the stapler in a sweeping arc, and as he easily blocks my blow, I pivot and plunge the syringe into his shoulder. He roars and grabs me, but I'm able to shove in the depressor as we crash to the floor. Berg twists me beneath him and pins both my arms.

"What did you put in me?" he asks.

His face is a savage snarl above mine. I shove hard with my knee, but he's too heavy for me to lever aside. He takes both my wrists in one hand and reaches for the syringe.

"What is this?" he demands. He stares at it as if mystified and flips it over. "What did you give me?"

"Sleep meds," I say. "The same ones you use on me."

He slumps slightly, and I get one hand free. He grows heavier still, crushing my chest, but I shove violently to get an inch free.

"How much?" he asks.

"All there was," I say.

He presses a hand to my throat, cutting off my wind. "Where'd you get it?"

I twist my head and struggle to pull his hand away.

"Where?!" he shouts, and he releases my throat enough for me to gasp in a new breath.

"Get off me!" I say.

He tightens his grip on my throat again, and I seriously can't breathe. I thrash, bug-eyed and panicking, and I'm seeing stars when his grip slackens slightly. I pull at his fingers, desperate for breath, and inhale raggedly. Then I scramble and push furiously to get out from under the sagging weight of him.

Limp and unmoving, he watches me through hooded eyes.

Gasping precious air, I reach into my pocket for another syringe. I flip off the cap and lean nearer. He waves a weak hand to fend me off, but I clamp his arm down and hold the syringe poised above him.

"Where is Thea?" I ask. "Is she in the vault?"

He leers. "Find her yourself," he says thickly.

I jab the next syringe hard into the meat of his arm and plunge in the depressor. That's two doses, enough to mess him up for a good while if I'm not mistaken. Berg's eyes dilate with fear, like he knows this is bad. He's lying there like a toad, with a slick line of saliva drooling out of his mouth. He moves his lips, but no words come out, and I'm glad he's conscious. I'm glad he knows how helpless he is.

"How's it feel?" I ask. "You bastard."

I have two more syringes, come to think of it. I pull them out and weigh them in my fingers, contemplating. Berg shakes his head at them, his eyes wild. It would be easy enough to give him the rest of the sleep meds. The likelihood is high they'd kill him. Then I'd be certain he would never come after me again. It's tempting. Deeply. He deserves to suffer for what he's done.

His skin goes clammy and his eyelids droop, but then he regains his wild focus once more. He deliberately taps his own chest, right above his heart. Then he twitches a finger at me. "Nightmare," he whispers.

A shiver lifts the hairs on my arms. I can't tell if he's cursing me or accusing me. I reach for his shirt and pull it back to reveal the place he was tapping. He has a lump under his skin. A port, like mine. We're alike.

He's still watching me to see what I'll do.

I draw back slowly. This taunting, vengeful person can't be me. I don't want to be a sick monster like him. I put the caps back on my used syringes, and put them with the other two back in my pocket. Then I feel through his pockets for two phones, mine and his. He doesn't resist. He can't. He's a big body of slumbering flesh. May he rot.

34

— THEA —

A BEAM OF LIGHT

I HATED BERG. I really did, with everything in me. Wherever Rosie was, I hoped she was killing him. I hoped she was blowing his scurvy brains out.

I had been alone in the dark operating room for six hours, and I'd had enough. My contractions came randomly, but they came often enough to convince me my labor had started for real. Once, at the end of a contraction, I thought a bit of light came from the other room and Berg was returning, but then he didn't. Now and then, I thought I heard a mouse. I would nudge my phone for a glimpse of light, but its battery was practically dead, and I dreaded being in the total dark with no relief.

Another contraction rolled over me, and I focused inward and tried to breathe through the pain. With my knees and hands on my jacket beneath me, I tucked my head down and kept my eyes on the little glowing screen of my phone as if it could save me. The contraction eased just as the screen automatically dimmed to black, and I curled onto my side again, exhausted.

A thump came from the other room. I listened hard as footsteps came running. A glimmer flashed in the window, and a voice came like mercy through the muffling glass.

"Thea!" Rosie called. "Are you there?"

I staggered to my feet, bursting with relief. Her flashlight blinded into my eyes.

"Thank goodness!" Rosie said. "Are you all right?"

She rattled the door from her side. I lifted a hand against the glare. Her flashlight fell to the ground and cast an angle of iridescence up the window that separated us. She tried the door handle with both hands, and for an instant, our eyes met through the glass, directly opposite each other. For an eerie second, I saw Rosie's face glowing across from mine, exactly as if I were seeing my own reflection in a mirror. A keen wildness brightened her eyes. Then she dipped down for the flashlight.

"Stand back," she said, and tried slamming the flashlight against the glass. It didn't break. "I have to get something bigger," she said. "I'll be right back."

"Turn the lights on!" I yelled.

She vanished. A moment later, light illuminated the main vault, and I had a clear look at the room that had imprisoned me all this time: the bare white walls, the dusty tile floor. The camera in the upper corner was as still as a patient spider.

Rosie hurried back with a coffeemaker machine.

"Stand back," she said again.

I gathered my phone and jacket off the floor, backed into the corner, and covered my face. A bashing noise sent splinters scattering everywhere. I peeked up as she pummeled the machine against the window again, whacking the glass shards at the edge of the frame.

"Come on," she said. "I'll help you over."

I doubled my jacket over the lower edge of the window edge and gingerly gripped the sides, toppling over mostly backward to Rosie, who caught and shifted me through the opening.

"How long have you been down here?" she asked.

"Six hours. I'm in labor."

"Holy crap!" she said. "That bastard."

I put an arm around her shoulder to lean on her. "Did you see Berg?" I asked.

"Did I," Rosie said grimly. "I should have killed him while I had the chance."

"What did you do to him?" I asked.

"Not enough."

My muscles ached deeply, and every bone felt brittle and heavy.

"I have to know," I said. "Did you talk to him? Does he know about us?"

"Yes," she said. "He wants to get us together and compare our brains."

"I hate him," I said.

"What are you even doing down here?" Rosie asked.

"I came to stop you from going to see Berg," I said. "I was

worried you'd do something stupid. I've totally changed my mind."

"You, my friend, are an idiot."

Rosie kept her arm around me as we started down the tunnel. Each step caused a grinding wrench to my back. I couldn't go very fast, but I focused on the beam from her flashlight and put one foot in front of the other. We passed the glass room, and ages later, the side door. The floor sloped down, went on forever, and then leveled off again. Rosie kept encouraging me, but I barely heard her. I knew the door to the barn couldn't be much farther when another contraction hit me. I stopped to lean my head against the wall while my entire body clenched into a deliberate stone. I had to drop to one knee.

"You are not having your baby in this tunnel," Rosie said.

I ignored her, curling inward. *Breathe,* I thought, but instead a gasp caught in my throat, and I locked on it until my lungs wanted to explode. The pain was even more intense than before, ten big notches up, and when it finally stopped, I was a panting sweat ball of exhaustion.

"That was a bad one," I muttered.

"That *animal*," Rosie said. "Maybe I should go ahead and get some help."

"If you leave me, I'll kill you. I swear I will."

"Where are Linus and Tom?" she asked.

Linus and Tom. It took me a second to even remember who they were.

"I have no idea," I said.

"They must be looking for us," she said. "Didn't you tell them about this tunnel?"

"No. You said not to. Remember?"

"Unbelievable," she said.

I tilted my face to look up and found her scowling.

"Don't be angry," I said.

"I'm not mad at you," Rosie said. "I meant it's unbelievable that you kept your promise."

"You'd have done the same thing," I said.

Rosie looked at me oddly and let out a brief laugh. Then she offered a hand.

"We're going to get you out of here," she said. "Ready?"

I groaned as she hauled me to my feet. My legs were wobbly logs.

"Gently now," she said.

She drew my arm around her shoulders again, and I felt her support around my back. She steadied me against her. Together, step by step, we kept on. The flashlight beam jogged over the rough floor and walls.

"Another one's coming," I said, slowing.

"We've almost made it," she said. "I can see the door ahead. It's just a few more paces."

But I dropped down to my knee again and braced myself against the wall. I was beyond caring how dirty everything was. My stomach, my back, and every other inch of me went tight with pain. A gush of fluid broke down my leggings, and I moaned.

"Thea," Rosie said. "We've got to get you out of here."

I heard her only dimly. More than anything, I wanted to lie down right there and huddle up, just conserve my strength during my precious stretch of painlessness before the next contraction set in.

"No," Rosie said, tugging at me. "Up! We're not staying here!"

You're wrong, I thought. "Help me get my leggings off," I said.

I was afraid she'd argue, but she rolled down my waistband and guided my pants and underpants down my legs. She spread our two jackets beneath me. The next tightening began, and I leaned forward on my hands and knees. This contraction was harder and deeper than the last, a vice of pain that sucked in all the dark of the world and held onto it, laughing with evil joy.

"I'm getting help," Rosie said. She sounded frightened.

No. Stay with me, I thought, but the words couldn't get past my gritted teeth. I grabbed for her hand and kept her with me. The contraction suspended beyond what I could bear, and then it finally released me. I rolled carefully onto my side.

I caught a glimpse of her anxious face in the flashlight.

"Stay," I said.

She nodded. Her eyes were huge. "I will. Don't worry. I'm here."

I lay panting in the dark tunnel, calm as a stone. For this moment between contractions, my body relaxed completely. I let every last muscle sag downward into gravity, from my fingertips to my ankles. Even the muscles behind my ears gave up and went smooth. I breathed slowly and deeply, preparing, because I sensed that the next few contractions would count.

Without warning, a flashing, sunny image of a collie puppy surfaced before me. Gizmo. Gladness blossomed in me as the little dog turned his smiling snout my way and padded toward me on his oversized paws. A girl's young, tan hands, my own, sank into the silky fur of his neck. Behind the puppy, Grampa sat in a porch chair, smoking a fragrant pipe and holding a new leash.

"Like him?" Grampa said. "He's yours."

"For real?" The girl's clear voice was mine, and I was unmistakably Althea.

I knew he'd say yes. I knew the puppy was mine. I had a dog!

Then the next contraction came and slammed me back into the tunnel.

Moaning, I pushed back up onto my hands and knees and tucked my head, which felt like the only way to be. *Be ready,* I thought. *It won't be long.* My body said push, and there was no arguing. The impulse became a sustained urgency. I expected noise, flurry, fear. Instead, my baby was born quietly, sliding out into a beam of light. Rosie handed the newborn to me as I rolled back, exhausted and mind blown, and when Rosie brought the light around so we could see this new life, the baby winced and gave out a tiny cry.

35

— ROSIE —

BLOOD

"A GIRL," THEA WHISPERS. She sounds as exhausted and amazed as if she's taken a trip around the entire universe.

I don't know how she can be so calm when I'm on the edge of panic. This situation is way over my head. Thea has an actual, live baby snuggled against her chest. The tiny girl has still got the umbilical cord attached and a motley layer of waxy stuff on her skin, but she's out. She's breathing. I have no idea what to do next, but I am certain of one thing. We need help. Fast.

"Thea," I say gently. "I've got to get help. Just hold on and I'll be right back."

"Don't leave me," she says.

"I have to," I say. I know this tunnel can't be clean enough for Thea or the baby. There's more blood, too. Things are oozing and pulsing in ways that can't be right. "I'll be right back. I promise."

"Don't go!"

But I have to. I know I do. I leave her the flashlight, and I bolt out of the tunnel. I charge up the stairs of the dairy barn. Nobody's there but cows. When I try my phone, it has a real signal again, and I punch in 911.

"My friend's just had a baby," I say. "We're in the dairy barn in Forgetown. Down in the basement. We need help fast."

The dispatcher wants names and details. She asks if the baby's breathing. She asks about the afterbirth.

"What afterbirth?" I ask, alarmed. "I have no idea what that is."

"It's all right. Stay calm."

I am not calm. I scan around the barn as if medical supplies might appear before my eyes and magically tell me what to do with themselves, but I've got nothing, nothing at all. Thea still needs me. Empty-handed, I bolt back downstairs. I grab an old mop and bucket to prop the door open so the medics can find us, and then my reception cuts out as soon as I'm in the tunnel again.

"Rosie!" Thea calls, her voice husky and weak.

"It's okay. Help's coming," I say.

Thea's hunched and moaning. With feeble fingers, she pushes the baby toward me, and I take her, feeling helpless all over again. All I can do is nestle the baby against my shirt and tell Thea it will be all right, but I have zero guarantees. I'm listening for voices, hoping the medics will find us soon, when Thea reaches out a shaky hand and grips my arm. Her gaze is fierce, but at the same time, her focus is wrong, like she isn't seeing me.

"Thank Thea for me," Thea says. "Tell her to look after my baby."

A cool, light shiver passes over me. *"You're Thea,"* I say gently.

"Tell my parents and Grampa I love them," she adds. Her voice lifts higher and softer. Her Texas accent is clearer. "They did right by me."

My throat tightens. Who is this girl talking to me?

Her hand slips loose from my arm. Her eyes close. Her head tips limply back.

Pure panic rises up in me. "Thea!" I scream. "Rosie! Althea!" I grab her shoulder. I'm still holding her baby and don't know what to do for her. I can't tell who she is anymore. She's not responding.

I'm still screaming when the medics charge in. They bring light and supplies and a stretcher. Four medics surround Thea at once, and I watch in horrified awe as they work over her. Another medic takes the baby from me with gloved hands. I'm backed against the wall, clutching my hands into my shirt where the baby just was. I'm trying to see Thea between the medics, but I can't get a straight view. When Thea moans, I almost burst into tears at that sign of life.

"Is she going to be okay?" I ask. "Tell me!"

One of the medics looks over his shoulder at me. "Are you the one who called?"

I nod.

"Don't go anywhere. The police are going to have some questions for you."

"Just tell me she's going to be okay," I say.

"She's lost some blood, but she looks like she'll make it," he says. "Her heart's strong. She's young."

He doesn't know anything. He thinks Thea's a normal girl. He has no idea that she was in a coma, and I don't know where to begin explaining.

"Do you know when she was due?" he asks.

"She still had four weeks to go."

He nods and turns back to Thea.

We need to call her parents, I think. And Tom. Someone should call him, too. Thea still looks awful to me despite the medic's reassurance. They're hooking up blood.

Another team of medics jostles in, and it finally hits me the police could be next. I don't want to talk to them. I have no way to explain why Thea and I are in the tunnel, and I don't want them calling my guardian, either.

May he rot.

I pick up my jacket and Thea's from the ground. They're both bloodstained and filthy. My hands aren't much better. I take a step back, torn. I hate to leave without saying goodbye to Thea, but this might be my only chance to get away. Then again, someone should tell the medics about Thea's past. What if the birth sends her into another coma? Could that even happen?

I get another glimpse of Thea's insensible face, and then I grab one of the medics nearby. I leave blood prints on her white sleeve.

"You shouldn't be down here," she says, and then frowns. "Are you injured?"

"I'm her friend. I was helping her," I say. I thrust Thea's jacket into her hands. "She used to be in a coma a few weeks back. She's really fragile. She was talking really strangely before she passed out."

"Wait here," she says, and plunges into the group surrounding Thea.

I can't wait. I can't be caught down here. Already one of the other medics is looking at me like he recognizes me. I take a last, agonized look at Thea. Then I slip out of the tunnel and go up the stairs to the main floor. As soon as I get a phone signal, I call Linus.

"Thea's had her baby," I say. I push out the barn door into the fresh, cool air and veer away from the ambulances. "Call Tom and let him know. The medics are with her at the dairy barn. Tell Tom to call her parents and get them here as fast as he can."

"Is she all right?" Linus asks.

"I don't know," I say. "I'm afraid."

"Where are you?" he asks.

I'm already heading back to my car, the one Burnham loaned me. I feel like I've been in the tunnel for years, like this air on my face belongs to a new planet. The sky is the gray of pre-dawn. I need to run. I need to think.

"Rosie!" Linus yells.

I can't talk to anybody anymore. It's too much, all of it. I ought to be thrilled that I helped a baby be born, but I'm not happy. I've failed, somehow, and the truth is agonizing. Thea came looking to save me, and now she might be dying. Between Berg and Thea, I've lost something. Something huge.

I shove my phone in my pocket and run.

36

— ROSIE —

SUNRISE

BY THE TIME I REACH the dim street where I left my car, I'm breathless from running and my throat's aching from held-back tears. The water tower looms above in black silhouette while the first light of dawn touches the sky to the east. A shadow beside the car materializes into Linus, and I slow. If he says the wrong thing, if he tries to hug me, I'll start crying, and I don't want to do that. I dig for my car keys.

I struggle to make my voice calm. "How'd you find my car?" I ask. Like that matters.

"Georgia plates," he says.

Just as I expected, he goes to hug me. I lean back, gripping my dirty jacket to my chest, and he stops.

"What were you and Thea doing at the dairy barn?" he asks. "I went to Forge to look for you, and I couldn't find you anywhere. I tried to reach Burnham to see if he knew anything, but he wouldn't answer. Then Tom told me Thea was missing, too." He tilts his face. "You look awful. Are you okay?"

"I don't know if Thea's going to make it," I say tightly. "One of the medics said she would, but they didn't know yet about her history with the coma."

He swears softly. "Are you hurt?" he asks. "I can take you to the hospital. Let me drive."

I glance down at my dirty hands and yellow shirt. "I can't go there. I can't talk to the police. I did something horrible."

"It can't be that bad."

It is. It's that bad, or at least the police would think so. I was this close to killing Berg. I might actually have done it with the two doses I gave him. *Nightmare.* I find my key finally and try it in the car door, but I keep locking instead of unlocking it. I'm not like Berg. *I'm not.*

"Okay," Linus says decisively, and sets his hand over mine. "We need to go somewhere and talk. Don't say anything yet, though. I know this is Burnham's car, but someone could have bugged it since yesterday."

I almost laugh at his charade. *You're warning me about what's bugged?* I think.

I know all about the image of me sleeping last night, the image on Berg's computer. Linus told me his room was private, but the camera that filmed me was right up close. If Linus didn't take the footage himself, I don't know who did.

"Why are you looking at me like that? Let me have the keys," he says.

And I do. What does it matter? I'm fighting some unnamed despair that I can't yet figure out.

As we pass the dairy barn on our way out of town, I see that a couple of police cars have pulled up. So has a news truck. The ambulances are gone. I hunch down and don't straighten up again until we reach the open highway. I pluck a tissue out of a box and try to wipe some of the grime off my fingers.

"I'm going to need somewhere to hide," I say.

"Don't say any more yet. Please."

I spit on my palm and wipe some more. The gray prairie speeds by outside, and the silence lets me think.

Anger's safe. It protects me from needing to care for anybody. Revenge made me strong, but when I saw Berg's port, when I felt the ugly, desperate way we were the same, it ruined me. I couldn't kill him, even though he's the one who destroyed my life. Then, when Thea was suffering in labor, I couldn't help but care for her. I hated seeing her in pain, and once her baby was born, she was so little in my hands. So helpless. So powerful.

I'm weak now, and lost. I don't want to care for people. It hurts to trust them and feel for them. If they get hurt, it hurts me, too. I'd rather go back to when I was strong and I didn't care, but I can't. I crumple my tissue into my fist and bite inward on my lips.

Linus pulls the car onto a dirt road, and then he turns onto a track that's hardly more than a dent in the grass. The world simplifies down to a big, gray-pink sky over a long, dark horizon. We ride up a slope and down a curve until we reach another upswell of prairie, and there he finally parks, out of sight of the road.

As soon as I open my door, a soft, sweet wind surrounds me. I catch my hair back behind my ears, and for the first time in hours, I can take a deep, steady breath. The sun will be rising soon. Linus comes around the car, and we walk wordlessly through the grass to the top of the next knoll. A little moth rises out of my way in a flicker of pale wings.

"Okay, here's good," Linus says, slowing to a stop.

I know we need to talk. There's no way around it. If Berg can somehow listen in through Linus, even here, it wouldn't surprise me. I just can't say anything Berg doesn't know already, or couldn't guess.

When Linus turns to me, the breeze lifts the collar of his black jacket. A hint of stubble outlines his jaw. "First tell me why you think Thea might not make it."

"She lost a lot of blood," I say. "She was totally unresponsive to me by the time the medics came. One of them told me she'd probably be okay, but what if she goes into another coma?"

I don't tell him about the way she talked to me, like she wasn't herself anymore.

"That'd be bad," he says. "I'm sure you did all you could for her, though, right? We have to hope for the best. And her baby was okay?"

I nodded. "It's a girl."

"What were you doing in the barn?"

"We were in the tunnel when she gave birth," I say, and I can see I'm going to have to explain. "There's a tunnel from

411

the barn to the dean's tower. I found Thea in the vault under the school, in the operating room. Berg locked her in. She was there for hours in the dark with no way to get help, and she was in labor."

"She must have been terrified," Linus says. "Why would he do that to her?"

"He's sick. He wanted to keep her and compare her brain to mine," I say. Another idea hits me. Berg must have known I was coming to him. That was why he kept Thea so long. "He was waiting for me."

I look back toward the car, where I've left my jacket in the front seat. I still have two syringes hidden in my pocket. I still have Berg's phone there, too.

"You said you did something horrible," Linus says. "You didn't kill him, did you?"

I keep thinking about how Berg had a port, too. I could have put a third dose of sleep meds right in there. It would have been so easy, but it became completely impossible. I squeeze my fists together. "I don't think so," I say. "I'm not sure."

"Rosie," he says, his voice low. "What did you do?"

"He threatened my sister," I say. "I injected him with some sleep meds. A double dose. I don't think it was enough to kill him. I wanted him powerless. I wanted him to know what it felt like."

"Did you just leave him there?" Linus asks.

I nod. I lift my gaze to study Linus, trying to decide if his concern is for me or for Berg. "Don't you get tired of playing his game?" I ask.

Linus stares at me strangely and blinks against a breeze. "What do you mean?"

My heartbeat ticks up a notch. "Berg had a video clip of me sleeping in your room the other night," I say. "How did he get that?"

"From when you stayed over?" he asks. He seems honestly surprised. "Are you sure?"

"Positive. It showed you smoothing my hair off my forehead."

He tenses. "Rosie, I have no idea what that's about," he says. "Berg must have rigged it somehow. He has no shortage of footage."

"It wasn't rigged," I say. I try to think of any other logical explanation. "Is it possible he planted a camera in your bedroom? Could he have told Otis to do it?"

He shakes his head. "I've gone over my room a thousand times, millimeter by millimeter. I check it every single time I visit, sometimes twice a day just so I can be sure. It's private." His eyes change. "You think I'm lying?"

I do. I know what I saw.

Linus squints against the wind, and over our friction, I get an odd prickling. He once said that he could see better out of one eye in the dark. The sky is getting lighter now. I take a step nearer to Linus and peer up into his eyes.

"What are you doing?" he says, his voice defensive.

"Hold still. Look at me."

His eyes are a clear, caramel brown with dark lashes, and they look completely normal, aside from his anger. I think

413

back to the first day I met him. He was leaning against a giant wooden spool behind the art building. He had an icepack to his eye because the chef had hit him so hard his eyeball was filled with blood. Later, Linus went to the infirmary, and what did he tell me about his eye the next day, after his patch was off?

Dr. Ash did a little surgery to it.

"This isn't amusing, Rosie," he says.

"Could Dr. Ash have put a camera lens in your eye?" I ask.

His eyebrows lift in surprise. Then his gaze shifts away, and he closes one eye and then the other, testing his vision. "I hardly notice the difference anymore, except in the dark," he says. "I thought it was left over from my hyphema." He frowns. "They wouldn't do that. A camera?"

"Berg's capable of anything," I say. My mind's leaping. Back at Forge, Berg eavesdropped on our walkie-ham conversations. This is a million times worse. "He could spy on both of us through your eye. He could have done it the whole time we were at Forge. He could be spying on us right now."

Linus shakes his head. He backs up a step. "This is freaking me out," he says.

I let out a brief laugh. "Me, too."

"It isn't technically possible," Linus says. "He'd need some kind of transmitter on me. Wouldn't he? Do you think the camera's on all the time?"

"I don't know how it works," I say. "I'm just saying it could explain how Berg has an image of me in your bed. Did you wake up and look at me? Did you touch my hair?"

Linus nods, visibly trembling. "If this is true, he's been with me all this time, seeing everything I do."

"Exactly," I say, and jam my hands in my pockets.

He scowls at me. "You still think I'm lying to you! You think I knew!"

I don't know what to think. I never do with Linus.

"Great," he says. "Just brilliant." He runs a hand back through his hair. "I really hate that guy," he says, and then his eyes narrow. "Okay. We'll use this somehow. If I really have a camera in my eye, we'll use it against him. We'll feed him false information. We'll double-cross him somehow."

"He'd know. He knows everything," I say. I didn't plan past killing Berg. At some level, I figured I'd be arrested for his murder, but now, with Berg still alive, he'll always be coming after me. "It's hopeless, Linus. He can get to my family. I'll never be free of him."

"I think it's time to talk to the police yourself," he says. "I can go with you."

Not happening. I take another step back and turn into the wind so my hair will get blown out of my face again. This is as bad as before. Worse. I think of the data I saw on Berg's computer and the pictures of all those dreamers. Wanting a future causes all kinds of problems.

"I take it that's a no," he says.

I look up at Linus again, wishing I knew whether I could believe anything about him. "I have a lot to figure out. You included."

He steps near enough to shelter me from the breeze. "You should have told me you were going to see Berg. I would have gone with you."

I shake my head. "I wanted to kill him myself."

"But you couldn't," he says. "I could have told you you're not a killer, Rosie. Why did you ever think you were."

Because that's how I felt. It hurts. This whole thing hurts. And now here I am, caring about Linus, and he's just another one of Berg's tools. I can't look in his eyes without wondering if there's a spy behind them.

"Don't look at me like that," he says, and closes his eyes.

His face has never seemed so vulnerable, and I'm unbearably touched. I lean up to kiss him, and his lips are warm. His shadow of beard is unexpectedly soft, and he wraps his arms around me. The kiss deepens. Hope and misery lock into each other so that I can't tell them apart. When I have to come up for air, he keeps me tight against him, and I find I'm gripping him, too.

"You're leaving. I can tell. But I'm going with you," he says.

"No, you're not."

He kisses me again, trying to persuade me, until I have to break off. I steady myself against him. With my heart charging around, it's very hard to be rational, but I tuck my hair behind my ear again and try. He is watching me closely, and I'm sickened to think Berg might be observing me through Linus even now. Just thinking this puts Berg between us again. I want to cover Linus's left eye with the palm of my hand, but Berg could see that. Instead, I ease out of Linus's arms.

"Keys," I say.

His eyes grow dark. "Please, Rosie. This is a mistake. We can figure this out together."

"No," I say. "Not with Berg along."

I turn toward the east, where the sun has now topped the horizon. Then I look back down the slope toward the car. My family needs me. No matter what has happened, I'm still Dubbs's big sister, and it won't take too long to get home. If he hasn't already found me through Linus, Berg will be looking for me soon. I tap the pockets of Linus's coat for my keys, and then I dig them out. I squeeze my fingers around them so the metal bites.

"Let me give you a ride back to town," I say.

"Forget that," he says. "How will I reach you?"

I glance up to find him smiling in his old way, where his mouth curves but his eyes stay serious. Loneliness. I never realized before exactly what was behind his smile, but I get it now.

"I'll call when I can. I promise," I say. "Let me give you a ride back to town."

"No, I can walk back," he says.

"Seriously? It's far."

"That's the least of my problems."

I take a step backward, away from him, and a weird sort of thrill goes through me. I don't want to leave him, but now that I've decided to, I feel an urgency. It's a kind of power.

"You can't keep doing this to me," Linus says.

"I have to."

I turn and stride down the slope through the grass. I get in my car, close my door, and twist on the ignition. Linus is still standing on the top of the slope, a spare figure with a long shadow. With my heart aching, I memorize every line of him. Then I turn the car around and bump along the dirt road, back to the highway. For a moment there, I pause.

I blink out at the long, empty road and the early light on the wind-swept prairie. In a way, I have nothing now that my anger's gone, but I also feel like I've just started. Like I might have some hope. I gently rub the port lump in my chest and glance at my jacket, where I still have my syringes. Berg's phone, too. It could be useful.

I roll down my window to let in the sweet wind. Then I grip the wheel and accelerate, driving west hard.

ACKNOWLEDGMENTS

With warmest gratitude, I wish to thank the following people for their practical support and kind encouragement during the writing of this story: Katherine Jacobs, Kirby Kim, Claire Dorsett, Emily Feinberg, Brenna English-Loeb, Suzannah Bentley, Nancy O'Brien Wagner, William LoTurco, Lauren Dittmeier, Emily LoTurco, James Moen, Michael LoTurco, Cynthia Myers, Jennifer R. Hubbard, Robin Blomstran, Annie Greineder, Suzy Staubach, and Alvina W. O'Brien. As always, I'm grateful to my husband Joseph LoTurco for everything.

QUESTIONS FOR THE AUTHOR

CARAGH M. O'BRIEN

Spoiler alert: *The following Q&A covers major plot points of* The Rule of Mirrors *and would be best read after the novel.*

What was it like writing about a character whose mind ends up in two bodies?
I'd like to say I approached the project of *The Rule of Mirrors* with a clear plan, but though I knew Rosie's mind was splintering and she would wake up in two separate bodies, I had to discover how to write her story—their story—as I went along. At first, I explored how bizarre it was for Rosie to wake up in the unfamiliar body of Althea, the pregnant girl in a coma. After several weeks of writing Thea's story, I started writing the story of Rosie at the Onar Clinic, where she was struggling to wake up and manipulate Ian. I was immediately struck by how angry and vengeful Rosie had become, and that made me think a lot about how Rosie's and Thea's experiences caused them both to change. Dovetailing the two storylines together was ridiculously complicated. For instance, their original timelines were off by weeks, and keeping track of when the two girls said different things to Linus involved endless cross-checking. Yet I was fascinated by the two girls' voices and their relationship to each other. Writing

a double narrative was truly the only way to tell Rosie and Thea's story.

Which girl in *The Rule of Mirrors* do you think is most like the original Rosie in *The Vault of Dreamers*?
My editor, Kate Jacobs, and I have often talked this over. At a basic level, Rosie's personality from Book 1 leapt with her consciousness into Althea's body, while Rosie's body in the vault was left with the internal voice, the one that spoke in bold type. I keep hoping I've made it clear that Rosie and her internal, originally subconscious voice were both conscious by the last chapter of *Vault*, meaning Rosie had a dual but complete nature then, just before the split. This was her mind's way of adapting to and surviving the dream mining. Rosie's internal voice is as legitimately Rosie as her conscious voice is, in my opinion. Therefore, both girls in *The Rule of Mirrors* are true to the original Rosie, even though they're different. Beyond that, I think of Thea as the sweeter one, generally (she has her unsweet moments), and Rosie as the fierce, impulsive one.

Have you ever wondered what it would be like to meet a second version of yourself?
Yes, of course. *The Rule of Mirrors* made me think a lot about what makes us each unique, because once Rosie becomes two people, she's on different trajectories. She keeps changing away from who she was at the end of *The Vault of Dreamers*. In a way, that corresponds with the way we each change at the crossroads in our lives. For instance, I used to wonder what my life might have been like if I hadn't had children. I wonder what I would be like if I'd kept teaching instead of resigning to write. But our decisions compound, changing and preparing us for the next decisions. I don't think there was

a way to escape who I've become. Now, if I could somehow meet another version of myself, we would be very confused, I'm sure, but I believe we'd be nice to each other. We'd have a story to write.

What draws you to write about science fiction set in the near future?

I like playing with ideas of what's just around the corner for us. I can build freely off what I see around me now, as I do with reality TV shows and medical technology, but I don't have to worry that inaccuracies will distract my readers. I'm also very concerned with social justice, and I fear what climate change, inadequate health care, and inequitable schools will do to our most vulnerable. Writing fiction about the future helps me wrestle with my hopes and fears. Incidentally, one of my bookmarked sites is a calendar of the year 2067, when *The Rule of Mirrors* takes place, and I'm curious to see what the world will be like then.

How long did you work on *The Rule of Mirrors*?

I'm not a particularly fast writer to begin with, but writing *The Rule of Mirrors* took me even longer than usual, between a year and a half and two years altogether. In fact, there was a point in December 2014 when, despite constant work, I knew the novel simply was not coming together, and I pleaded with my editor to grant me more time. She spoke to the team at Roaring Brook and moved the release date half a year later, to February 2016, which isn't something a publisher does lightly. My relief was enormous. The book simply needed more exploration and more drafts. It took maybe twelve months altogether? Fourteen? Regardless, I am so pleased with the way the book turned out. I hope the novel seems effortless.

Some writers report that writing the second novel in a series is especially challenging. You've done that twice, with *Prized* from your earlier Birthmarked series and *The Rule of Mirrors* now. Was the fact of it being a second book part of why the book took longer?

It is true that *Prized* in the Birthmarked series also stumped me. Sequels involve the challenge of how to take familiar characters to another level without repeating the problems of the first book or simply adding more explosions. I also feel pressure to satisfy readers who enjoyed the first book, and a corresponding fear of disappointing them if I blow it. Yet I wouldn't say that second books are inherently more difficult to write. Rather, the order of where a novel falls in a series is just one more element to wrangle. For me, writing any book is a complicated, time-consuming, puzzling, humbling experience. It requires persistent faith in a process that I'm far from mastering.

What is it like for you to imagine a scene and bring it to life on paper?

It depends on what sort of scene it is. When two or three characters are present and talking, I usually let the dialogue evolve first. I hear the voices arguing or puzzling out a problem, and I get their words down as best as I can. Afterwards, I fill in the characters' small movements and descriptions, add the salt shaker or whatever to ground them in a tangible setting, and tighten it all for pacing or expand it for depth. Then I revise another ten times, or cut the scene entirely or move it, as needed. If I'm working on an action scene, like when Rosie's escaping from the vault and emerging to the snowy parking lot, I take the journey step by step with the character, seeing, smelling, feeling, tasting, and hearing it as she does. This means I'm discovering the action and the setting with my character, which is the best sort of daydreaming. Then, again, I revise ten times, and maybe move or cut the scene. It's very fluid.

When Thea is talking to her mother about why she kept Althea alive in a coma, she makes a point of saying that Madeline is Catholic and suggests that her religion guides her decisions. Would you say that your Catholic faith informs your writing?
To a degree, yes. I doubt I would have made Madeline Catholic if I didn't have a Catholic background myself, and once I knew she was Catholic, I would have felt dishonest if I'd avoided that conversation about the sanctity of life. There's a difference, of course, between what characters believe and what an author believes, but I can't remove myself entirely, nor would I want to. I go through cycles with my faith, and I suspect my questioning about religion, rather than a particular doctrine, is reflected in my art.

Have you ever spent any time on a ranch in Texas?
Ha! I would really like to lie here and say I grew up on a ranch, but I didn't. I've driven through Texas, attended book festivals there, and dined in the backyard of Texan friends, but I haven't been to a ranch. I rode horses at summer camp when I was a kid before I learned I was allergic, and I've visited horse barns as an adult. Everything else I learned long distance, through research. My novels tend to require lots of research.

Will *The Keep of Ages* be the last book in the series? If so, what's up for you next?
Yes. It's rather mind-boggling to think my time in Rosie's world is coming to an end. This series has been the sort of impossible

project Mr. DeCoster would demand of his students, and it has gone so much further than I originally expected. I'm deeply happy with how the third book has turned out and I'm excited that it will be released soon.

As for what's next? I keep getting ideas. I have this disgruntled character who's circling, daring me to engage, and her situation is absolutely perplexing to me. That seems like a good place to start.

WHEN ROSIE DISCOVERS THE TERRIFYING
IMPLICATIONS OF DREAM MINING, WILL SHE BE
ABLE TO SAVE EVERYONE BEFORE IT'S TOO LATE?

THE KEEP OF AGES

CARAGH M. O'BRIEN

BOOK 3: THE VAULT OF DREAMERS TRILOGY
FROM THE AUTHOR OF THE BIRTHMARKED TRILOGY

KEEP READING FOR AN EXCERPT.

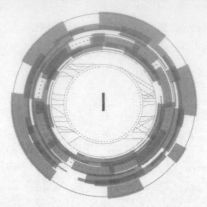

THE BOXCARS OF HOME

APART FROM A LONE cicada's keening, the desert evening is quiet. I lean my shoulder against a boulder and aim my binoculars toward the boxcars, where the empty laundry line cuts through the heat of our backyard like a white slash. Rolling my focus knob, I shift my circle view up the back steps to the screen door and then to each window, one by one. Nothing moves. I watch until the colors go drab, until the stillness corrodes my hope.

No one's home. After all I've survived to come back, my family isn't here to greet me. I'd laugh if I didn't ache so much, and if I weren't sick with worry. Ma and Larry haven't answered the phone since I started trying to reach them yesterday, but they normally never leave Doli. They have no other place to go. Their absence makes no sense.

Training my binoculars on the desert surrounding the box-cars, I pick carefully over each clump of creosote to see if Berg has anyone staked out to watch my home and wait for me. From this side of the old train, out of sight of the tourists, nobody bothers with fresh paint, and each boxcar home has faded to a rusty brown that's barely distinguishable from the desert.

A neighbor steps out the back of her boxcar and descends to a row of chicken-wire crates that huddle in the shade of a stunted oak. First she pours a measure of feed pellets in the top, and then she takes a rabbit out by the ears. It kicks its legs, indignant, but she holds it to a stump and dispatches it quickly with an ax.

The thunk reaches me a moment after the flash of the blade.

If I were smart, I'd go to the McLellens' place at the far end of the train and ask what they know about my family, but I can't yet. Hope and fear keep me here, peering at my home, waiting in case someone comes. Dubbs should be back from school. Larry should be drinking a beer on the couch. Ma should be frying onions. Those windows should be open like mercy to let in the air.

As the shadows turn and grow longer, I get too anxious to wait anymore. I have to see what's left, even if my family's bodies are baking inside that shimmering box of heat, bloating into a feast for flies.

No, I tell myself. *They're gone. They have to be gone, not dead. They can't be murdered.*

But my fear is real. I know how sick Berg can be. I lower

the binoculars so they hang from my neck, brace a hand on the boulder, and rise. Hitching up my jeans and crouching low, I pick my way between brush and rock, until I cross the dusty slope of the valley. I duck under our laundry line and when I open the screen door, it gives a dry squeak. We never lock our back door, but since it sticks, I give it a kick at the bottom, and for the first time in half a year, I'm home.

"Ma?" I ask into the hot, hollow stillness.

Late sunlight sifts through the skylights, intensifying the gloom in the corners. I take a cautious breath and step inside. The stifling heat has the familiar, egg-sandwich smell of home. Dipping my head out of the strap, I lift off the weight of my binoculars and set them on the shelf. The ceiling is lower than I remember, the room more cramped. Books and dishes are left in a typical mess, but nothing looks ransacked. In the kitchen nook, a paperback props open the door of the fridge, a sign it's unplugged, and now I know: this was a planned departure. The nearest lamp is unplugged, too. I can picture how Larry examined the electric meter while Ma went around disconnecting everything—hot water heater, toaster, clock—so not even the smallest appliance could draw any current and cost them while they're gone.

But where to?

And when did they go? Sweating, I shove up the kitchen window for a cross breeze, and then I look around hopefully for a note. My gaze scans over my little sister's school photo and a box of ammo on the coffee table. The pencil bucket stands spiky on the desk. No note. I try to tell myself that they didn't expect me, which is not the same as being forgotten, but still, it stings. As I trail my hand along the orange plaid couch, part of me clams over a lost pearl of grief. Where'd they go?

They wouldn't just leave for no reason. This is our home. They'd have to be driven or drawn away by something huge. Even then, they should have left me some message.

Despite my stepfather Larry's paranoia about surveillance in electronics, I'm sure my parents have a computer now. They've been coordinating the search for me and accepting donations online. Yet I can't find a computer or tablet anywhere. They could have taken it with them, but they haven't answered any emails lately, either. Things don't fit.

I try to think where my little sister, Dubbs, might have left me a message. Turning to the red curtain that gives some privacy to our bunk beds, I drag it aside along the wire, and I'm suddenly, keenly homesick, right here at home. Dust motes float in a beam of sunlight that lands on an upturned sandal. A gleam reflects off the little framed photo of my dad and me, him in his uniform and me in his hat, still on the wall where he hammered in the nail and hung it for me over a decade ago. My sister's bed, on top, is neatly made with her yellow patchwork quilt. Below, my red quilt has collected several drawings, a bird's nest, and a handmade, ceramic soap dish. I turn over the drawings, which have her name and age on the back, but no clues for me. Then I remember Dubbs's journal.

I drop to the floor, roll to my back, and push under my bed. Ignoring the dust bunnies, I inspect the pattern of metal wires for the little homemade booklet that she used to hide under the mattress. The booklet is gone, but in the same place, I find a folded piece of paper. *Yes*, I think. I pull the paper between the wires and stand to hold it in the sunlight. It's a lined sheet of notebook paper with the ripped parts still fringing one side, and it feels faintly brittle, like it was wet once and then dried. It says

To Rosie. From Dubbs.
See you

I turn the note over, looking for more, but though the paper is large enough for more writing, those are the only words. Frustrated, I check under the bed again. That's all she left. Was she interrupted? That seems unlikely, considering she had time to fold up her message and hide it under the bed. Absently, I brush the dust from my hair and shirt.

The phone rings. I jump and bolt past the curtain to the living room. My gaze flies to the doors. The front one is still closed. The back one is still empty. When the phone rings again, I grab it to my ear.

"Hello?"

A faint click is the only reply.

"Hello? Who is this?" I ask.

I spin around the room, searching for a camera lens on the lamp or the wall or the skylight. One could be anywhere. I instinctively back into the kitchen, taking the phone cradle with me on its long cord, and I peek through the window toward the road out front.

Still no voice comes from the phone, though I hold it hard to my ear. It doesn't disconnect, either, so someone's listening.

A Jeep is newly parked beside the tamarack tree, its windows rolled down, a gun rack clearly visible on the back window. A young man with a wispy mustache is smoking behind the wheel, and my lungs tighten with fear. Ian. My former captor from the Onar Clinic. He wasn't there when I entered the boxcar, but now he's watching it.

My heart thuds. "Is that you, Berg?" I ask into the phone.

The faint clicking comes again.

I slam the phone down in its cradle. Horror flashes along my skin. Out front, Ian opens his car door and flicks away his cigarette butt. He's lanky in a black tee-shirt, gray pants, and army boots. Beneath his pale hair, his expression is unsmiling, but I can tell he's jazzed. He loves tracking me down.

Before he can get any closer, I move swiftly toward the back door. Quickly, quietly, I step out and shut it. I wince into the setting sun, and then I sprint around the ragged fences and rabbit coops and grills behind the boxcars, heading for the McLellens'. A surprised voice calls out to me, but I don't answer. A crashing noise makes me look back as I run. Ian vaults over a pile of cement pavers. He's coming fast and aiming a gun.

A popping shot fires out behind me, and a spat knocks a water jug spinning by my right ear. I dodge left and run even faster.

"Peggy!" I scream.

My heart's pounding and my lungs are bursting from fear. I'm running so fast that everything's a blur except when I leap over a shovel or launch off a garden post or flip a folding chair behind me. My ears are primed for another gunshot. My scalp anticipates pain. I don't dare to look back again.

I scream for Peggy again, and now the McLellens' boxcar is in sight. It's ten yards ahead. Five. I'm almost there when I hear a much louder shot and jolt instinctively sideways before I realize the blast came from in front of me.

Peggy McLellen is standing on her back stoop, with her rifle raised. Her sundress rides up to show her sturdy knees and rugged boots.

"Get behind me," she says tersely.

I fly up the steps and stop in her shadow, panting. I look over her shoulder toward Ian, who has stopped back in the abutting yard. He hugs a bleeding hand to his chest, and his gun has fallen in the dirt.

"Explain yourself," Peggy says. "This next bullet's aimed somewhere more permanent."

"I've just come to collect Rosie," Ian says, panting. "I wasn't going to hurt her."

"She doesn't want to come," Peggy says. "That's what running away means."

"She doesn't know her own mind," Ian says. "She's sick in the head."

"*I'm* the sick one?" I say. "*You're* the one who works for Berg."

"Who sent you?" Peggy says.

"Her guardian, Sandy Berg," Ian says. "If you aid her, you're kidnapping, and that's a felony." He leans to reach toward his gun with his good hand.

"Leave it," Peggy says.

"I need my gun," Ian says.

"You need to get out of here or you'll get yourself mistaken for a gutless coyote and shot," Peggy says.

"It's just tranquilizers," Ian says. He lifts his voice. "I wasn't going to hurt you, Rosie. You know you're supposed to come."

"Where's Berg now?" I ask. The one good thing about him still being alive is that I can't get prosecuted for killing him.

Ian tilts his head and gives his bangs a little flip. "At Forge, like normal," he says. "But he'll come now that I've got you. It won't take him more than a few hours to get here. You can stay awake and talk with me in the motel 'til he arrives. Or sleep, if you'd rather. But it seems to me we've got things to discuss. You shouldn't have ditched me back in Montana."

"Where's my family?" I ask him.

"Looks like they ran, like cowards," Ian says.

Peggy takes another blasting shot toward Ian, who screams and ducks to the ground.

"Mind your manners," Peggy warns him.

Ian swears in a squeaky voice. "You don't have to shoot me! I haven't done anything!"

Peggy frowns. "Your folks are looking for you," she says to me, her voice low. "They got a tip. They left yesterday. Come on in and I'll tell you about it."

"What about him?" I ask.

Ian is crouched way down, with his hands over his ears. The right one's bloody. It also looks like he's peed himself.

Peggy gestures with her gun. "Stand up, idiot. Quit your crying. I'll only shoot you if you run."

He stands slowly, keeping his hands high, and he looks taller and more awkward than ever. Peggy walks behind him, picks up his tranquilizer gun, gives it a quick inspection, and tucks it in the belt of her dress. She gives him a nudge with the muzzle of her rifle.

"In you go," she says to him. She nods back up at me. "Rosie, take the hash browns off the stove and see if you can't find some duct tape."